the otherworldlies

Also by Jennifer Anne Kogler

Ruby Tuesday

the otherworldlies

jennifer anne kogler

To Carey,
Happy reading - Keep
on truckin - All the best,

Jennifer Anne Kogler

An Imprint of HarperCollins Publishers

August 29, 2009

Eos is an imprint of HarperCollins Publishers.

Library of Congress Cataloging-in-Publication Data is available.
ISBN 978-0-06-073959-1 (trade bdg.) — ISBN 978-0-06-
073960-7 (lib. bdg.)

Typography by Jennifer Heuer
3 4 5 6 7 8 9 10
❖

First Edition

To Jeremy and Jordan,
my very own Sam and Eddie

Contents

*"Expect everything, I always say,
and the unexpected never happens."*
—Norton Juster, *The Phantom Tollbooth*

1

the breakfast sunglasses

The bird swung lifelessly by a silken string from the corner of the wooden eave of the house. The McAllister
twins craned their necks upward to get a closer look.

"I think it hung itself," Sam said, unable to take his eyes
off the swallow. Moments before, Sam had spotted the
lifeless songbird hanging from Lee Phillips's shingled roof
and insisted his sister accompany him to investigate.

Fern's bird knowledge was no greater than that of most
twelve-year-olds, but she would have recognized a swallow anywhere. After all, the swallows were a big deal in
San Juan Capistrano. Each March, they would make the
six-thousand-mile journey from Goya, Argentina, to San
Juan Capistrano. San Juan was world famous for its week-
long celebration of the swallows' return, the *Fiesta de las
Golondrinas*, which included the Swallows Day Parade.

This particular swallow, though, was lost—the swallows weren't supposed to arrive in San Juan for months.

As Fern looked up at the dead swallow, a wave of panic swept over her. Taking a deep breath, she told herself that getting her brother worried wouldn't help. She filled her head with dewy morning air, fighting to regain her poise. She glanced at Sam; he hadn't noticed any change in her demeanor.

"It *is* a little spooky," Fern said, looking at the dead bird, "but birds don't do that kind of thing, Sam."

"How do you know that? Have you ever been a bird?" Sam asked.

"No, but neither have you."

"Exactly. So we can't be *sure* it didn't hang itself."

"Birds fly, chirp, lay eggs, and poop on people. They don't commit suicide."

"I think you've got a pretty narrow-minded view of birds. You're a bird bigot."

Fern smirked despite herself. "You're crazy, Sam, you know that?" she said, looking at the lifeless swallow through the dark tint of her sunglasses.

Sam pivoted away from his sister and returned his gaze to the bird. His mood darkened instantly.

"Think about it—if you migrated all the way from South America to California and then realized that your friends and family were gone, you'd be feeling pretty desperate."

Sam shaded his eyes from the sun so he could have a better look. Its puffed-out white chest made the swallow appear defiant in death.

"Look," Fern said, pointing at the half spiderweb that was loosely attached to a nearby branch. "It flew into that web and got part of the thread caught around its neck."

"A spiderweb isn't strong enough to hold a bird up," Sam said.

"Maybe it's a wire from the roof," Fern offered.

"We should say a few words," Sam said, eyeing his sister.

"A few words?" Fern questioned.

"You know, to commemorate its life or its journey or something."

"And people say I'm the weird one."

Sam halfheartedly scowled at his twin sister. "Yeah, well, I'm way better at hiding it." He smiled, picked up a stick, reached up, and tapped the bird with it. The swallow began to swing like a miniature piñata.

"Come on," Fern said, desperately wanting to take her eyes and mind off the small creature. "We'd better start walking or we're gonna be late." She hoped Sam couldn't tell how distracted she was. "I don't want to give Mrs. Stonyfield another reason to hate me."

"She doesn't hate you," Sam said. Fern rolled her eyes at him.

He paused.

"Fine, you're right, she kind of hates you." Sam laughed and ran across the Phillips' lawn, down La Limonar. Fern, happy to run from her worries for a few moments, chased after him.

The twins made their way to St. Gregory's Episcopal School, passing the house where their mother grew up, known as the Moynihan home. There, they were often told, their mother was instilled with the severe Catholic discipline of her deceased Moynihan parents, both Irish immigrants. Once past the old Victorian house, the twins made a sharp left and took their usual shortcut through Anderson's Grove. Fern, dressed in her brother's hand-me-down blue corduroy pants, slip-on Vans, collared polo shirt emblazoned with the school crest, and Breakfast Sunglasses, slowed to a walk. She was consumed by thoughts of the Voices.

That's what Fern called them—the Voices—probably because whenever she heard them, there were no bodies attached. They came to her out of the dry San Juan air, as if someone—and not always the same someone—was whispering in her ear through a funnel.

That very morning, Fern had heard them again, louder than ever. She had been lying in bed, waiting for her alarm to ring. Her spine had stiffened when she realized that, once again, *she* was the topic of conversation. This time, though, there were specific details. Maybe, she told herself as she tried to calm down, the dead bird was just a strange coincidence. As she and her brother continued toward St. Gregory's, Fern replayed exactly what she'd heard in her head.

"Vlad is in town." The male voice was so loud and so near,

Fern thought its owner must practically be next to her. She frantically scanned the room and realized she was utterly alone. The Voices were back.

"How can you be sure?" the second, more familiar voice questioned.

"Scores of birds have been dying unnaturally—flying into windows, plunging into pools, electrifying themselves on power lines."

"Maybe it's a coincidence," the second voice offered.

"It's no coincidence. Every single instance of birds acting irregularly has meant one thing: Vlad is close by. He's in San Juan and he's after the girl."

"You mean Fern McAllister?"

"Yes."

"You can't be certain of that! He'd have no way of knowing she's here or that she's an Unusual. Blimey, *we* don't even know if she's an Unusual!"

Had Fern been in a more advanced stage of transmutation, she might have been able to hear the whole conversation Mr. Joseph Bing and Mr. Alistair Kimble were having, nearly four miles away in the law offices of Kimble & Kimble. Fortunately for her sanity, she was like a radio with a broken antenna, receiving only patches of signals and broadcasts.

Fern had heard the Voices for the first time a few months ago, when she'd heard her name uttered by a man's voice. A woman responded, saying that she "didn't believe for a second that a girl could be allergic to the sun." Fern had no idea why she was being talked about, but her name wasn't mentioned again. It wasn't long before Fern figured out who was talking from the context of the conversation: Lee Phillips's dad was chatting with a woman who wasn't Lee's mother. Certain cues, such as when Mr. Phillips told the woman to "hurry and leave before my wife gets home," made Fern sure the two were doing something they weren't supposed to be doing.

Such information was hazardous for someone who was teased as much as Fern was. When Lee Phillips cornered Fern by the swings after class, Fern had nowhere to run. Lee towered over Fern, taunting her.

"You're disgusting." Lee hissed as Blythe Conrad stood behind her. Lee pointed at the sun blisters that had erupted on Fern's face.

"How does your mom even look at you without wanting to puke?" Blythe said, raising her voice. Fern said nothing, cornered by the fence on one side and Lee and Blythe on the other. A group of students moved around the girls, forming a loose half circle.

"I bet your mom wishes she could send you back," Blythe continued, feeding off the energy of the crowd around her.

"I bet that's why your *father* left," Lee continued. "He couldn't stand having an ugly daughter."

"At least my father isn't having an affair."

Fern let it fly without hesitation, though she was sorry

as soon as the words left her mouth. Lee, who had a nagging suspicion of this very fact, was in tears for the rest of the day. Fern had no explanation for how she knew about Lee's father, other than that she "just knew."

Although Fern's assessment turned out to be true (less than three weeks later, Mr. Phillips had, on the very same day, filed for a divorce from Mrs. Phillips and asked Sally White's mother to marry him), the revelation caused Lee to redouble her efforts to torment Fern. It also gave Fern a "spooky" reputation at St. Gregory's and landed her a weekly appointment in the school psychologist's office. There, Mrs. Larkey, a woman with thick red glasses and spiked black hair, would try to get to the bottom of Fern's "behavioral problems."

These ongoing sessions, during which Fern avoided such questions as, "Why don't you talk about your father?" and "Do you understand the difference between positive attention and negative attention?" and "Do you hate your twin brother, even a little?" usually lasted an hour. Then Mrs. Larkey would throw her hands up in the air, frustrated by their lack of progress, and send Fern back to class. Sam called these appointments "Interviews with the Freak Doctor."

If Fern told Sam about the Voices, she knew he would be the last person on Earth to narc on her, or even judge her, but she didn't want to burden him. Sam was fiercely protective of his sister, even if he secretly wished she didn't need so much protecting.

Today, as the twins rambled through rows of blossoming orange trees in Anderson's Grove, Sam an inch and a half taller than his sister, they didn't look like brother and sister at all. They also didn't look like best friends. Fern walked to school with a heavy heart, wondering who Vlad was and why he was looking for her; wondering where the dead swallow fit into things; unable to shake the feeling that somebody, somewhere was talking about her. Not that this last part was terribly unusual. Fern McAllister, though she hadn't realized it yet, was the kind of girl people talked about.

There's usually one in every family: the misfit, the black sheep, the oddball, the outsider, the nonconformist. Fern was weird. Not only that, Fern was also in an unfortunate period of her life for weirdness. Being weird in the regular world usually meant being tolerated and sometimes even applauded. Being weird in the seventh grade, however, meant being persecuted. Like all those who are truly weird, Fern was a rotten judge of her own weirdness. She could never tell what part of herself people were going to react to, so she could never have hidden it even if she had wanted to.

To everybody who knew her well, though, there was no doubt that Fern McAllister was very different from other children. When at age two Fern developed her first pair of baby teeth, both canines, both pointy, her doctor pronounced it "very odd." When at age six Fern claimed she could communicate with the family dog, Byron, her mother found it "exceedingly bizarre." By the time she was twelve, Fern had developed several other strange habits. She read the weather page of the newspaper every night and either agreed or disagreed with the forecast for the following day. She'd maintained a streak of two years and seventy-four days of correctly predicting the next day's weather. She filled a flowerpot with dirt from her mother's garden and stowed it under her bed because she claimed she couldn't sleep without it. She wore dark Ray-Bans while she ate her oatmeal in the morning, which she called her Breakfast Sunglasses, because she insisted that her eyes had to wake up "gradually."

All of these things were viewed by her two brothers as "kinda crazy," but they figured she'd outgrow them. Fern's mother, Mary Lou McAllister, refused to take such a laissez-faire approach. Worried about her daughter's social future, she tried to curb some of this odd behavior. As far as she knew, Mrs. McAllister had stopped Fern from communicating with the dog, Byron (although she had to admit that she would never be able to stop Byron from communicating with Fern—she did not, after all, speak Maltese). Still, many of Fern's idiosyncrasies remained. It was too exhausting for Fern's mother to try to extinguish them all.

In truth, by the time Fern was twelve, her behavioral plate was beginning to fill up with so many odd habits, strange comportments, and bizarre activities, there was very little room for the more standard side dishes of child-hood.

Her appearance certainly didn't help matters. Fern's closest relations were all blond and freckled in varying degrees. But Fern more closely resembled a real, live black sheep than she did either one of her brothers or her mother. Her long Sharpie-colored mane set her apart from her family. Many of the McAllister neighbors had taken to calling Sam and Fern the Salt and Pepper Twins. Even Fern's blue-tinted contact lenses couldn't dull the penetrating paleness of her eyes. She looked a lot like Snow White's suburbanite little sister.

Despite all this, being labeled an oddball hadn't become unbearable for Fern. She had Sam, and Eddie, her older brother, and, for the most part, found it easy to escape to her own world. Unlike Sam, Fern was one of those people who had a very short memory for sadness and distress, especially when it came to her own. After wearing the Wonder Woman cape from her Halloween costume to school the day after Halloween, Fern was teased mercilessly. "I'm just ahead of my time," she explained to Sam and her mother, refusing to let the naysayers bother her. "The cape keeps me warm and it doesn't have a zipper like my jacket, so my hair never gets caught." Fern saw her glass as always half full, even when it was filled with curdled milk.

Though it was true that Fern had displayed some of the hallmarks of a problematic childhood, in spite of everything, most people, including Fern, still thought her life remained within the boundaries of normal. Her family had successfully built a barrier that kept the great majority of Fern's oddities from the outside world.

Although the McAllisters didn't yet know it, the levee was about to break. After today, Fern McAllister would never pass for normal again.

While cutting through Anderson's Grove, Sam turned his attention to his sister. A breeze rustled the waxy leaves around them.

"What are you thinking about?"

"Nothing," Fern said, still afraid to tell Sam about the Voices.

"Are you thinking about the swallow?" Sam asked as he kicked up dirt beside her.

Fern hesitated. She knew Sam would not let up until he had an answer. "Maybe. I don't know," she said.

"Told you we should've said a few words." Sam whacked his sister gently in the arm.

"I guess you were right," Fern said, still preoccupied.

"When something creepy like that happens, it's better to try to make it fit into the normal scheme of things. I think that's why funerals were invented, to make death seem normal, even though it's totally not, you know?" Sam, who looked like a southern California beach bum in training, could be surprisingly philosophical. Fern realized that he was never like this with anyone else and treasured these moments. They were hers alone.

"Yeah," she said slowly. "I think we should cut the swallow down on the way home from school." She had no way of knowing that today, she wouldn't be walking home at all.

"Deal," Sam replied. "We're about out; you'd better take those things off," he added, nodding at her Breakfast Sunglasses.

Fern complied, crouching down and putting her head in her lap. She could almost make out the white stucco of St. Gregory's through the maze of tree trunks. Fern's sunglasses had caused quite a scene when she began wearing them into class each morning. If one of the cool girls had done it, like Blythe Conrad, it might have become a trend. But Fern wasn't the kind of girl who started trends; she was the kind who murdered them and made certain they'd never rise from the dead. When she'd strolled in wearing her Ray-Bans, she'd pretty much insured that no one would be wearing sunglasses to school for the next few years. Fern brushed off the whispers and stares. "If you want your own pair, I can ask my mom where they're from," Fern said to Matt McGraw, who couldn't take his eyes off her eyewear.

As always, it was Sam who recognized that the sunglasses were making his sister more of an outsider. Though at first he'd joked around with people that his sister wore sunglasses every morning to school because her future was so bright, the joke was tired to begin with and had gotten very old, very quickly. He suggested that they cut through

Anderson's Grove on the way to school, which would give Fern a chance to adjust without the sunglasses in private.

Fern let out a weak groan, covering her eyes.

"You okay?" Sam said, watching his sister wince in pain. Her eyes watered until tears ran down her face.

"In a second," Fern said, not deviating from their routine.

Three minutes later, Fern and Sam had walked up Bimini Lane and were sitting in the back of their core class. As Mrs. Stonyfield called roll, Fern imagined her Breakfast Sunglasses resting snugly in the tree in the northwest corner of the grove. The thought made her happy.

The beginning of the day passed slowly for the McAllister twins. Fern was having trouble letting go of the Voices. She felt as if she had a brick resting in the pit of her stomach. Sam could sense that all was not right with his sister. He searched for something he could do to help. Although Sam thought his watchfulness went largely unnoticed, he was wrong. Not only was Fern aware that Sam wanted her to be accepted, to fit in like he did, but his unstated concern made Fern love him all the more.

Today the students of St. Gregory's had come back from Presidents' Day weekend. Once recess began, the entire school was buzzing with renewed vigor.

"Look at your idiot sister," Lee Phillips said to Sam, casting a glance toward the elm tree in the corner of the soccer field. Fern sat perched on a low branch resting in the shade, her arms wrapped around her knees as she pulled them close to her face. The hem of Lee Phillips's pleated skirt was too high by an inch and a half at least, but the school's dress code never seemed to apply to girls like Lee.

"How could you two be related?" Lee Phillips scoffed.

"Someone should make her come down from there," Blythe Conrad said, shaking her head. "It's like she thinks she's special."

Blythe Conrad had not yet learned that some of the most special people have no idea of this very fact until someone or something calls it to their attention.

"Do you know if the water polo team won last night?" Sam asked, trying to change the subject. Lee's older brother played on the team and she attended every game.

"Does Fern act like this at home?" Blythe asked, unwilling to let the subject die.

"Give her a break," Sam said, knowing full well that Fern would get into more trouble if she were mingling instead of sitting up in the tree.

"We're serious, Sam," Lee said. "What's her deal?"

"What's her *deal*?" Sam repeated.

"She's just trying to get attention, and it's pathetic," Blythe said, inching closer to Sam and raising her eyebrows.

"She knows that everyone thinks she's weird. She could stop if she wanted—it's like she *chooses* to be a freak," Lee added.

"I don't know why you care so much," Sam said, pushing himself toward Lee. "She's not bothering you."

"I don't care so much," Lee said, stepping backward. "In fact, I don't care at all. I just thought, she's *your* sister and you might not want her holding you back anymore. Everyone likes you." Lee turned from Sam. Blythe followed her and they both walked away.

Sam watched as they strutted across the blacktop. His eyes then turned to his sister, who, from his vantage point, looked like a china doll someone had thrown far up in the elm and then forgotten about.

From Sam's perspective, Fern's outsider status had almost reached a breaking point this year. Her quirks had become defining. Even Sam's recent attempts to integrate his sister with some of his more laid-back friends had met with disastrous results. The harder Sam tried to defend his sister, the more hurtful his classmates' insults became. He found that the best thing he could do when girls like Lee and Blythe were out for blood was to ease away from the subject.

Once Sam had asked his sister why she climbed the old elm, and her answer was simple: "Sometimes I want to be where nobody else is."

"But doesn't it bother you that people stare at you?" Sam had asked.

"I'd rather have them staring at me from a distance than staring at me from up close. Besides, it's the best shady place in all of St. Gregory's." Fern, too, had begun to give up on the idea that she would ever fit in with her blond brother and the rest of his clan.

After recess was English, which used to be Fern's favorite subject before Mrs. Stonyfield got her hands on it. The class began discussing *The Giver*, a book they had completed the previous week.

"I'll assume everyone has read *The Giver*," Mrs. Stonyfield began, her voice as pinched as ever. "Although the mint condition of some of your books leads me to believe you haven't even bothered cracking the spine." Mrs. Stonyfield rose from her chair and leaned over her desk.

"Who can tell me what the major theme of the book is?"

The class fell silent, fearful that Mrs. Stonyfield might call on anyone still talking.

"Giving?" Matt McGraw said.

"Another wisecrack like that, Matthew, and I'll be *giving* you a detention," Mrs. Stonyfield said, disgusted.

"It's about being different," Gregory Skinner volunteered from the front row. "Whether or not it's better to allow differences and the bad consequences that go with them or to have no choice in anything and live happily in the dark."

"You're nearly there, Gregory," Mrs. Stonyfield declared, at her most complimentary with her most favored student. "Are there any positives to the world that Jonas lives in initially? Would you want to live there?"

"At least they weed out all the *freaks* there," Lee whispered to Blythe, her eyes wide as she smirked and pointed at Fern in the back of the class. The students around Lee snickered, glancing back at Fern. Fern felt her whole face turn beet red.

Fern tried to distract herself, hoping her anger would not show—getting angry would only satisfy Lee Phillips. She tuned Mrs. Stonyfield out and instead focused on *Lord of the Flies,* the next book on their reading list, which was tucked inside her copy of *The Giver.* As she surveyed the classroom from the back row, she was careful not to let any part of her smuggled book show.

Fern realized some time ago that if she paid attention to Mrs. Stonyfield about half the time, she could still do as well as she did when she listened to Mrs. Stonyfield's every word. She'd started *Lord of the Flies,* taking it in the shower with her that morning, and had been completely riveted from the very first page. She envisioned the boys first exploring the beach, alone, cold, and disoriented. Fern found the place she'd bookmarked and plunged on.

Ralph, she read, *turned neatly onto his feet, jumped down to the beach, knelt, and swept a double armful of sand into a pile against his chest.*

Fern imagined herself sweeping sand on her chest and legs, trying to bury herself—something she often did when she was at the beach. The water would be clear and bright, the sun almost unbearable. Imagination mingled with memory as the words on the page melded with her childhood. In Fern's mind, Ralph, Piggy, and his friends must have landed on a beach that looked a lot like Big Corona, which was about ten miles up the coast from San Juan. Big Corona was known for its wide swath of sand and the long gray rock jetties that guarded the entrance to Newport Harbor. Her mother took the entire family there on cloudy, cold days when Fern's fair complexion could handle it. In the morning, the sand was cool and damp and felt better than anything else against her skin. There was something about looking at the water that made Fern feel still and peaceful. The ocean roared, but everything in her head was crystal clear.

At dusk, Sam and Eddie would build a bonfire twice the size of Fern. Eddie would load five marshmallows on a straightened wire hanger and try to cook them all at once by sticking them in the bluest part of the flames. He would leave the rapidly blackening marshmallows in the fire until they were so singed, they cracked and oozed when he bit into them. Once it was time to leave, Mrs. McAllister would practically have to drag Fern across the sand and load her into the car. Fern never wanted to go home. Words failed her when she tried to explain it, but the beach felt like home too.

As Fern sat in the back of the classroom, it was easy to imagine the cragged cliffs on each side, fire pits, scattered palms, and ocean as far as the eye could see. Mrs. Stonyfield's voice grew faint as Fern's eyelids flickered shut. Slowly Fern felt a slight tingle run through her hands and feet. Her head grew ice-cube cold and her brain felt as if it were being jostled, bouncing from one side of her skull to the other. She felt like a feather being lifted into the sky, drifting back and forth on a black and gusty night. Her stomach surged and lodged in the back of her throat. The floating feeling frightened her. Fighting to regain command of her consciousness, Fern realized she couldn't open her eyes.

Unable to escape the darkness, she began to panic. Groaning, she tried to wiggle her body to find something, anything, real. A shadow had wrapped itself around her like a mesh vice. She no longer felt the rigid wooden desk chair beneath her. No . . . now she felt something entirely different against her body. Though she couldn't open her eyes to confirm it, she would have recognized the texture anywhere—Fern was now lying on a mound of warm sand. She could hear waves crashing around her. She let out a bloodcurdling scream.

Fern sensed that her eyes were open now, but all she could see was blackness. Part of her wanted to give up struggling, to curl up in the fetal position and wait for something to change. Instead she clenched her teeth and began pawing the sand, trying to dig her way to conscious-ness. Soon she felt the nudge of a human hand.

2

the sunburned man

Someone was poking three fingers into the middle of Fern's back. She tried opening her eyes. This time, though, her eyelids worked. The first thing she noticed were grains of sand. Fern hit the ground with her legs, determined to make her body respond. She was able to flip over so she was lying face up.

A man the color of an uncooked hot dog with a crusty long yellow beard leaned over her.

"Ya okay, girlie?" His formfitting white shirt was dirty and every inch of him was permanently sunburned. He had pink Bermuda shorts on and leaned against a long pole. On his left arm, he wore eight watches, three of them silver, four of them black. The watch closest to his actual wrist was shiny gold and different from the others—it looked like an antique that had been kept in mint condition for centuries. The top of the face had a small, gleaming crown. Fern traced the white pole down to the ground and immediately realized the man was leaning on a metal detector. Was she dead?

"Ya okay, girlie?" The man opened his mouth wide, revealing a conspicuous hole in the front of his smile. Although he was in very poor condition, the man seemed real enough. Quickly Fern ruled out the possibility that she had, in fact, passed on. There was no way St. Peter could look like such an unkempt slob.

"Ya got a pair a lungs on ya, dontcha?"

Fern wiped her eyes. She *must* gain control of herself.

"Yes," she said, brushing the sand off her uniform as she wobbled to her feet. She felt very shaky. Her whole body was numb except for her fiercely beating heart. She put her hands to her chest instinctively, hoping to contain it.

The dirty man looked up to the sky and then back down to Fern. He laughed and held his clumpy beard with one hand. He smelled like rotting seaweed.

"If it ain't my lucky day," he said, smiling. "Those eyes," he continued, peering longingly at her face. "Looks like someone took 'em out of Phoebe's head and put 'em in yours."

Fern held her hand out in front of her. If she slapped herself and couldn't feel it, she would know she was dreaming. As soon as her palm hit her face, she knew this was far from a dream. Her cheek stung from the force.

"Now then, there's no need ta be doin' something like that. This must be the first." The man inched closer to Fern. His mouth housed a random scattering of yellow teeth. "You'll learn in time."

"I fell asleep," she said as her mind started to work for her again. "I was trying to wake myself up."

"Ya didn't fall asleep, girlie. I's standing right here and I saw ya. Ya appeared from nowhere."

Fern stared into the man's eyes and a calmness descended over her. His clean blue eyes didn't seem to match his hole-ridden T-shirt and ruddy face.

She looked behind her as her survival instincts kicked in. She was on a small strip of sand between the rocks and cliffs. Fern recognized the place immediately: Pirate's Cove.

Pirate's Cove, partially hidden from the larger crowds and waves of the main beach, was her favorite part of Big Corona. The small beach was accessed from the same parking lot as Big Corona, but faced the bay to the north instead of the open ocean. Parts of the beach were quite rocky, and there were a few small caves bored into the side of the sandstone cliffs surrounding the cove. Each visit, the twins usually dedicated hours to climbing Rocky Point and exploring every inch of the caves. Today the cove was deserted.

"I's glad I seen it with my own two eyes," the man said as Fern began brushing the sand off her uniform. "A course, a course, you appear," the man said. "Today! The anniversary a da Titanomachy! I've been comin' here for a hundred years hopin' one a ya'd appear." Fern wanted to run as far as she could from this stranger, but he stood between her and the uphill path to the parking lot—the only outlet from Pirate's Cove. *Hundreds of years?* Fern began to step backward, away from the man, whom she'd decided was clearly a lunatic. For a moment, she contemplated launching herself into the bay and swimming to the main beach to safety.

"Don't be alarmed," the man said, his voice losing some of its strange drawl. "I want ta show you somethin'." He gave her a wry smile, then dropped his metal detector and scurried to the furthest cave. Fern stared at him warily, unsure what to do.

"I don't mean to hurt ya, girlie." His tomato red face contorted into a look of earnestness. "I mean ta help ya." His eyes bulged out of his head like a lizard's.

Fern, who'd happened to be paying attention when Deputy Fairbanks had come to Mrs. Stonyfield's class to warn the students about the danger of strangers, snapped back into stranger-danger panic mode. She stepped closer to the lapping tide, figuring she'd take her chances with the bay.

"I'll make a deal, then," the man said, touching his stringy hair with one hand. "I can tell yer afraid. The Den's open now, but ya should take a look for yerself. It's important to ya, I swears." He pointed to the cave closest to the path up to the parking lot.

"I've seen that cave before," Fern said, emboldened. She was sure she could outswim this man, should he lunge at her.

"Not like this, ya haven't."

"I really should go," Fern said, taking another step backward.

"Well, I'll be," he said, looking Fern up and down. "The first Unusual's a local girl. St. Gregory's. The rumors were true. I weren't sure, but thank my stars I've been preparin' based on what I heard."

At first, Fern's heart jumped. How did this man know this? But she then looked down at her uniform. The man had made an educated guess.

"What's yer name?" His watery eyes popped out of their sockets once more.

"I don't know." Fern said.

"Fine, fine. I don't got time for this now—we gotta make sure this stays under wraps," the man said. "What time did ya disappear?"

"What?" Fern said.

"What time did ya leave yer school?" The man displayed his gaping smile.

Fern had no idea what the man was getting at. The last time she'd looked at the clock on the classroom wall, it had been 11:15.

"Not very talkative, is ya? Well . . ." The man looked down at his left arm, scanning his seven watches. He twisted his wrist and the watches jangled together like metal bangle bracelets. Finally his eyes rested on the golden eighth watch.

"Let's see now," the man said, bringing his arm close to his craggy face. "It's eleven eighteen right as we speak. Now, supposin' you did 'appear' here, out a da blue, I'd say you should hang around before ya go telling people where ya are," he said.

"What?" Fern asked, finding the man less and less threatening the more he talked.

"Tell ya what. I'm gonna leave ya alone, and I suggest ya go into that there cave. Ya better allow enough time ta have walked here. No one's gonna believe that ya just appeared here from that thar school of yours. Trust me."

Of all the things for this man to be concerned with, why would he care if Fern got in trouble? Though she was still scared of him, Fern couldn't shake the odd sense of familiarity about him. Besides, he hadn't tried to hurt her or even close in on her.

The man picked up his metal detector, turned away from Fern, and began walking up the path to the parking lot. He was out of sight in no time.

The wind kicked up, bunching Fern's corduroys against her legs. The tide lapped a few feet away. None of the serene feelings the beach normally inspired passed over Fern today. She stared at the cave.

Fern told herself she would just take a peek into the cave on her way up to the parking lot. She had to, while she was here, or she would always wonder. Just a peek, to make sure nothing had changed.

Looking above her, Fern confirmed that there was no trace of the stranger. She wandered into the cave, which was only about seven feet deep and ten feet high. Fern scanned the jagged brown walls and sandy ground. Everything was still and silent. Fern kept turning around, afraid the sunburned man's plan all along was to ambush her in the cave. She was almost panting with anxiety now.

In the deepest corner of the cave, Fern noticed a hole about two feet wide. The hole had certainly not been there when Sam and Fern had explored the cave countless times before. She thought her eyes must be playing tricks on her, but a small amount of light was coming from this new opening. She crept closer.

Many visitors to the cave had tried their hand at carving their initials into the sandstone walls. Most attempts were unsuccessful or were destroyed by time and weather. But the small trace of light made it easier to see many of the carvings. She began feeling around the rim of this new discovery.

She jumped back when she saw it. There, etched deep into the stone wall directly above her, were two sets of initials:

MLM & PM

Mary Lou McAllister. Those were her mother's initials. PM? Could that be her father? It was probably a coincidence, but Fern was desperate to connect any dots she could.

Fern jerked her head around as her heart began to pound fiercely again. She was all alone in the cave. Almost as if by reflex, Fern was on her hands and knees, making her way through the new hole. The sand stuck to her knees and palms. She was through to the other side in seconds.

Fern gasped.

She'd entered another room of the cave. Deep cracks in the top of the stone let shards of sunlight through to the floor of the hollowed-out dome. The stone room was about the size of a jungle gym and the bottom of it was a perfect circle. The air was cool and damp. Fern was overjoyed at the thought of being able to tell Sam of this new discovery.

The walls were smooth, almost as if they were manmade. Fern scanned them first and then the floor. Her eyes focused on a line of faint writing in the very center of the room. She brushed the floor with her foot, clearing away sand, and the writing became clear.

Οὐδὲν ἄγαν

The carved handwriting was so perfect, even Mrs. Stonyfield would have given it high marks. Fern stared at the letters. Though she had no idea what they meant, she felt as if she'd seen them before, somewhere.

She walked toward the opposite wall. Directly in front

of her was a graffitilike image on the brown curved stone surface. She touched it with her hand. Though it looked as if it were drawn in chalk, it did not rub off. The picture was of a chamber similar to the one she was standing in. In the center was a white podium with an object resting on it. The perfectly black object looked like a sinister giant Easter egg. Its oval shape narrowed at the top.

Fern heard voices drifting into the cave. She turned around. Thankfully, the cave was still empty.

Her heart rattled in her chest. Fern's adrenaline stores were finally running out, and as she looked around her, she began to feel unhinged.

She was out of the cave and back into daylight in just under thirty seconds. The voices she had heard belonged to an elderly couple. They were at the cove's far end, letting the tide lap over their bare feet as they chatted.

Fern ran toward the path to the parking lot. Sand flew behind her and into her slip-ons. She knew she must look bizarre—the Episcopal school girl playing hooky in her full uniform, sprinting in the sand, her face caked with dirt and sweat. She looked over her shoulder, taking the stairs to the parking lot two at a time. Once there, she breathed a sigh of relief and slowed her pace, concentrating on what she needed to do next.

She zeroed in on the brown building at the far end of the parking lot—the public rest rooms she'd used on many occasions. She circled the building. The side closest to the parking lot had a pay phone. Fern grabbed the receiver, which was hot to the touch from the morning sun. She held it to her ear and put her index finger to the dial pad. Shaking, she laid the receiver back on the hook. Overhead a bird with massive wings circled like an oversized buzzard.

She took a deep breath, picked up the receiver again, hit 0, and then dialed her mother's phone number. The automated operator took over after her mother picked up on the first ring.

"You have an AT&T collect call. Caller, please state your name." Fern took a large gulp of ocean air. There was silence on both sides of the call.

"Caller, please state your name," the automated voice repeated.

"Fern McAllister," she said. She tried to keep her voice from trembling, but failed miserably.

3

the emergency conference

"**S**amuel, where is your sister?" Mrs. Stonyfield said, interrupting her discussion of *The Giver*.

"I don't know."

Sam had been wondering the same thing for almost a half hour. His stomach convulsed, as if it had been invaded by dozens of worms.

Although Sam had noticed his sister's absence from English class immediately, it took Mrs. Stonyfield a full twenty minutes before she was aware of the fact that her most challenging student's chair was empty. Sam, though terribly worried, had decided not to say anything for fear of getting Fern into trouble.

"Did anyone see Fern leave?" Mrs. Stonyfield inquired, growing more agitated by the second.

"Well, who is going to speak up?"

The class responded with a collective blank stare. Mrs. Stonyfield pursed her lips so they extended out like two soggy pieces of watermelon. Her mouth was always so overdrawn with lipstick that her students had been calling her Clownface for more than a decade.

"Are you trying to tell me not one of you saw her leave—that Fern just disappeared into thin air?"

"Maybe she went *poof*," Blythe Conrad cracked. The class erupted with laughter.

"Fern thinks she's magic," Lee Phillips said, as the chorus of laughter grew louder.

"This is not a laughing matter." Clownface's reading glasses were slipping down her face, giving the students an all-access pass to their teacher's menacing eyes.

Sam wished he knew why his sister had vanished—or where—but he had no clue. His anxiety grew with each passing moment. Soon the bell rang, causing an outbreak of movement.

"Wait! Just! One! Moment!"

Sam would have rushed out the door if it weren't for the fact that he could've sworn steam was actually coming out of Clownface's ears.

"No one is leaving this room until Fern returns." Mrs. Stonyfield paced from one end of the chalkboard to the other, never turning her attention away from her students. Her large posterior, which bounced back and forth with each step, made her pacing comical. Sam thought she looked like a hippo. Her voice was now shrill.

"Has she gone to the nurse complaining of a stomachache once again? I've never known any girl to have as many stomachaches as Fern McAllister in all of my years of teaching!"

It was against school policy for a teacher to discuss a student's health problems in front of her class, but Mrs. Stonyfield charged full speed ahead, her rump swaying like a pendulum.

"Or has her face turned into one huge blister again? Or is it that she *just knows* there will be a hailstorm at recess, so she went to get her protective hail gear? Why, maybe it's another one of her fainting spells, only this time she's trained herself to faint right out of her seat and out the door."

Mrs. Stonyfield's whole face was now the color of a stop sign.

"I knew that girl was going to be a problem the day she arrived with her sunglasses on, like she was walking the red carpet in Hollywood!"

The teacher stalked dramatically over to the telephone attached to the wall. She dialed the office.

"Yes, I need to speak to Headmaster Mooney. . . . Yes, we have a problem . . . Fern McAllister has disappeared. . . . If I had seen her *leave*, Ralph, I wouldn't have said she *disappeared*. . . . Yes. No, I understand. Well, if Mr. Bing finds her, I'd like to have some words with her as well," Mrs. Stonyfield said, hanging up the phone.

"Now," Mrs. Stonyfield said, turning around to direct

her comments to the class. "Headmaster Mooney is on his way here. He will be instructing all teachers to allow NO ONE to leave their classrooms," she said, looking grimly satisfied when several of her students let out gasps.

The entire school was in lockdown.

After considerable conferencing by Mrs. Stonyfield and Headmaster Mooney at the front of the classroom and increasing restlessness on the part of the students, information of Fern's whereabouts reached the school. Fern had called her mother from a pay phone by the outdoor showers at Big Corona. Mr. Bing, the custodian who had searched every hallway and bathroom and was now in the cafeteria, nearly shed tears of joy when he heard the news, but knew he could not do so without raising suspicion.

Fern McAllister was safe! Class was immediately dismissed. Sam stuffed his textbooks into his backpack and ran home by himself for the first time, anxious to find out what'd happened to his sister.

When Fern had placed the call to her mother, Mary Lou McAllister's reaction was loud and immediate.

"YOU'RE WHERE?"

Her mother's voice was so thunderous that the words were still rattling around in Fern's head an hour later. After retrieving Fern, making it from San Juan's Ortega Highway to Pacific Coast Highway in eight minutes (nearly a land-speed record), an irate but relieved Mrs. McAllister gave her daughter one chance to explain herself. Fern did her best, but without much to tell, she found it hard to convince even herself.

Her mother said simply, "I don't believe you," and nothing more for the remainder of the ride home. Of course, had Mary Lou McAllister realized that Fern was just as traumatized by the day's events as she herself was, she might have been a little easier on her only daughter. Instead Fern spent the entire afternoon and night grounded in her room. She wanted to ask her mother about the man and the initials, but with her mother still seething, she didn't dare. There was no way she'd get any answers now. Her thoughts turned from questions about the cave and the man to questions about her immediate fate at school.

Things as they stood were pretty grim for Fern. It wasn't long before her name was being mentioned in the same breath as "Emergency Conference." This all by itself was enough to ruin any student's day.

The Emergency Conference was a meeting between senior staff members and parents and usually meant serious trouble. Only two such conferences had been called in St. Gregory's history. The first one had taken place so long ago, the specifics had been long forgotten. The last one, nearly twelve years ago, had concerned Tucker Snude. St. Gregory's most legendary problem child, Tucker had unleashed three hundred crickets and an estimated forty rats into the school's chapel. This particular prank, viewed by Headmaster Mooney as an offense against God himself, resulted in one expulsion and two days of school closure for fumigation purposes. It was the last in a long line of Tucker Snude's escapades, several of which left teachers stranded on rooftops or afraid for their lives or both.

Rumors that a third Emergency Conference had been scheduled were making the rounds. So were exotic theories of how Fern had escaped detection and ditched school.

"I hear Headmaster Mooney and the Freak Doctor are meeting to figure out if Fern needs to be sent away," Lee Phillips said, loud enough for Sam to hear.

"Mrs. Larkey's in on it? Think Fern'll get expelled?" Frank Gambon asked.

"I'd love it if she did—serve her right. She's always doing the most ridiculous things to get attention," Lee responded.

"She can't possibly get away with it this time," Blythe Conrad added.

"I think she crawled out on her hands and knees; that's why we didn't notice," Gregory Skinner volunteered.

"I'm not even sure she was *in* class in the first place," Matt McGraw said, joining the spontaneous roundtable discussion.

One thing was certain: Fern was not in school that particular morning. Because Sam lived with two of the participants, he knew the conference was scheduled for today. But there was no way he was going to reveal this information—it would be cycled to the upper grades by the time they said the pledge in first period. Sam told anyone who asked that Fern was at home, sick. The speculation over Fern's future only intensified as the day wore on.

Meanwhile, at the McAllister household, tension was growing. Mrs. McAllister had joined Fern at home, taking a day off from the real estate firm she had founded a year ago. Fern had skipped breakfast, and by midmorning was up in her favorite tree, a giant jacaranda in the backyard, trying to distract herself by reading. She was plagued by questions of how she had vanished. Her mind replayed the sequence before the disappearance in a continuous loop. So Fern decided to start something she had read before— *Island of the Blue Dolphins*—mainly because she had not ruled out the possibility that her copy of *Lord of the Flies* was somehow cursed. After her terrifying vanishing act, she could leave nothing to chance.

She also knew she would have to wait until later if she wanted to do research on her disappearance. After all, there must be an explanation for what happened to her, right? If she began sherlocking around the Internet right now, her mother would surely catch her.

Mary Lou had come out to the backyard to talk to Fern. She caught sight of her daughter sitting up in the tree reading, just as she'd seen her doing countless times before. Mrs. McAllister could tell Fern had her sunglasses on, which she always wore if she was going to be outside for long. She held a book with her right hand and rested her left on Byron, the family dog, who slept next to her on the wide branch. Fern had somehow managed to coax the dog up the tree again. Mrs. McAllister shook her head, aware that many people would be startled at the sight of a girl in a tree, let alone a girl *and* a dog in a tree. In the McAllister backyard, it was commonplace.

Mary Lou wanted nothing more than to reach out to her daughter, to connect with her in some way, but she had no idea what to say.

"Fern?"

Fern lowered her book and looked over her sunglasses down at her mother. Her pale eyes brimmed with tears. Mrs. McAllister paused for a moment. Not knowing what else to do, Mrs. McAllister settled for tough love.

"Make sure you're not falling behind on your schoolwork," she admonished. "This is not a day off for you." She backed through the screen door with a heavy sigh, though she had not said anything she'd wanted to.

Banishing it from her mind, Mrs. McAllister was soon in the master bathroom battling with her hair, curly blond locks that rarely cooperated. She stared in the mirror, hoping to arrive at an answer or a course of action.

Choosing St. Gregory's for her children had primarily been a preventative measure to protect Fern. Nearly four years ago, Fern had come home from school in tears. When Mrs. McAllister asked what was wrong, Fern's response was simple.

"Do you believe me when I say I can talk to Byron?"

Mrs. McAllister had to think for a moment. "I definitely

think he understands you better than anyone else," she replied. That particular day at school, after some ruthless teasing about Fern's constant stomachaches by Curtis Bumble, who claimed that Fern was a zombie who was "rotting on the inside," Fern blurted out that Curtis Bumble's father liked to wear dresses and look at himself in the mirror when he was all alone in the Bumble house. When everyone in class asked her how she knew this, she responded that her dog, Byron, had found it out from the Bumbles' dog, a German long-haired pointer (who, apparently, was very loose-lipped about Bumble family secrets). Mrs. McAllister had told Fern that revenge was never a good idea and left it at that. But the larger issue—Fern's behavior—had Mrs. McAllister at a total loss.

As Fern grew older, her mother knew her odd personality traits would be less easily forgiven, less overlooked. Mary Lou's worst fear was that her daughter was in for a lifetime of teasing—or worse, rejection. Despite some serious reservations, she transferred her three children to St. Gregory's, her own alma mater, a few weeks later.

Mary Lou was sure that moving her daughter to the private Episcopalian school a few blocks away would help—that there Fern would get the attention and care she needed. There her odd way of dressing would be masked by school uniforms, and her strange habits would be appreciated. Or at the very least, thought Mary Lou, they would be tolerated.

* * *

Mrs. McAllister sighed loudly, even though she was the only one listening.

"Fern," she called, "are you almost ready?"

The McAllister females met in the kitchen, prepared for battle. Both sat focused at the table until the time came for them to make their way to the school. They were soon in the car, snaking toward St. Gregory's. Mary Lou drove past the upper campus, where seniors and juniors were filing out of the parking lot as they left for lunch. Fern tried to spot her older brother, Eddie, a junior football star, in the crowd. Her mother put the car in park and got out.

"I don't want you to answer a single question unless I tell you to."

"Okay," Fern said.

Today Mrs. McAllister was dressed in a pink St. John's knit with gold threading and had decided to control her flaxen hair in a bun. Several years ago, Mary Lou had worked for a nonprofit organization, Project Smile, which provided dental care for underprivileged children. Back then she'd rarely worn anything dressier than jeans and a T-shirt. Tired of struggling to provide for her children, she had gotten her real estate license and was now a San Juan Capistrano area housing specialist.

Mr. McAllister had been out of the picture for a long while now. *Out of the picture.* That was always the phrase Fern's mother used around other people. Fern didn't like it because it implied that family members, like dead flowers, could be snipped off with a pair of kitchen shears. She knew it was never that simple. Their father had left before the twins were born, and Eddie, totally closed off on the subject, never talked about him.

Single motherhood, though, had given Mary Lou McAllister an edge, a hardness that her children grudgingly admired. Behind her back, they called her "the Commander." The nickname had, over time, become mostly affectionate, though not entirely inappropriate.

Today, Fern thought as she followed her mother marching through the parking lot, the Commander was in control, taking no prisoners. Her mother did not slow down, nearly dragging Fern up the stairs to the second-story administration office. Mrs. McAllister was just over 5'8" and although she'd inherited her mother's hearty Irish frame, it wasn't her stature that intimidated. It was the look on her face, which made it seem as if she could breathe fire and ice at the same time, all while ironing the creases out of a silk blouse.

In unison, secretaries looked up from their attendance sheets and sick notes, taking time to stare at the McAllisters, who were making their way to the headmaster's office.

Inside, Headmaster Mooney and Mrs. Larkey were waiting for them, both seated behind his desk. Pleasantries were exchanged, though there was hardly anything pleasant about them. Headmaster Mooney, without fanfare, instructed Fern to tell them what, exactly, had happened the morning she disappeared. Fern looked at her mother, who nodded, signaling that it was all right for Fern to begin. Afraid to use extra words, Fern recounted her story.

She'd been reading *Lord of the Flies*, although she knew she shouldn't have been because the class was reading *The Giver*. She closed her eyes, and when she woke up, she was lying on the sand, by a fire pit, at Pirate's Cove. Fern decided not to press her luck with tales of the metal-detecting beach bum.

"You don't remember anything else?" Mrs. Larkey asked.

Fern stared at the Freak Doctor's spiked hair and thought she looked like an oversized sea anemone.

"No, that's all I remember."

"Has this ever happened before?" Mrs. Larkey questioned, eyeing Fern curiously.

"No," Fern said, searching her mother's expressionless face.

"Thank you, Fern," Headmaster Mooney said, stroking his gray mustache with one hand. "You may now wait outside until we call you."

Fern was instructed to sit in a wooden chair in the hall. She closed the smoky glass door behind her.

Inside, the conversation was just heating up.

"I'm sorry that we have to meet under such unpleasant circumstances, Mrs. McAllister," the headmaster began. "Mrs. Larkey and I feel that we need to have a frank discussion concerning Fern."

"I'm all ears," Mrs. McAllister said.

"There's no delicate way to say this: Fern has been exhibiting signs of Oppositional Defiant Disorder," Mrs. Larkey said. "She's developed a pattern of defiant behavior, disruptive conduct."

"You're saying she's O.D.D?" Mrs. McAllister almost looked amused.

Mrs. Larkey cleared her throat and pushed her glasses to the bridge of her nose and continued. "There are signs that this behavior is beginning to affect the other students."

"What Linda is trying to say," Headmaster Mooney jumped in, "is that we've taken a closer look at Fern's compatibility with St. Gregory's. As educators, we become cognizant of things that can easily escape a parent or guardian's attention. For instance, with Sam here—a twin brother who is successful and well liked—Fern may feel overshadowed. Not to mention Eddie, her older brother, a three-sport star. She could be acting out as a result. Have you ever thought about holding Fern back? It's not that she's not bright—"

Mrs. Larkey then interjected as they began their double team.

"Your daughter has special needs—needs that aren't being filled here at St. Gregory's. Now, there are a lot of options . . . ahem . . . a lot of schools deal exclusively—"

"What kind of disruption is Fern causing, if you don't mind me asking?" Mrs. McAllister's voice was as sweet and thick as California honey.

"Well, to begin, Fern is constantly going to the nurse's office complaining of stomachaches. We've also had complaints from both students and teachers about her. For instance, she's started climbing trees at lunch and recess. We've tried to stop her from doing this; it's dangerous and a severe disruption. But she always finds a way. Bing, the janitor, now keeps an eye on her because we don't want her getting hurt. You probably don't realize this, Mrs. McAllister, but with a case like Fern's, liability becomes a factor. We also must not forget the issue of her sensitivity to the sun."

"What about her sensitivity to the sun?" Mrs. McAllister said rather blandly, knowing full well that Fern's face had blistered due to sun exposure four times that fall alone.

Headmaster Mooney stared directly at Mrs. McAllister. He was surprised by how calm she was remaining. Tucker Snude's parents had not gone down so quietly.

"Well, her sensitivity is inconsistent. Some days Fern is fine; others, she has a terrible time with the sun and can hardly bear to go outside. Which indicates that Fern may be exacerbating the problem herself some—"

"Are you suggesting that my daughter is lying out in the sun deliberately, in the hopes of permanently scarring her own face with blisters?" A slight hardness had crept into Mrs. McAllister's voice.

"No, no, Mrs. McAllister, don't mistake my meaning. Let me simply say that in my thirty years as an educator and administrator at St. Gregory's, I've never seen any student with a problem similar to Fern's. It defies medical explanation!"

The Commander's eyes narrowed into an iron glare. The previous hint of hardness in her voice turned absolutely rigid. "I suggest, Headmaster Mooney, that you leave medical diagnoses to actual physicians. My daughter has enough trouble without those in a position to help offering nothing but criticism."

"That aside," said Mrs. Larkey, "there's the issue of Fern's disappearance."

"Yes?"

"Leaving during school hours without permission is grounds for expulsion."

"I'm so glad you brought that up," Mrs. McAllister said. "I have several questions regarding my daughter's 'disappearance,' as you so aptly called it." Mrs. McAllister leaned over the headmaster's desk and her eyes flashed, partnering up with her scowl. Instinctively, both Headmaster Mooney and Mrs. Larkey edged their chairs back two inches.

"Let me start with my first question: How exactly does a twelve-year-old girl end up miles away from school without her teachers, her classmates, or the St. Gregory's supervisors noticing?"

"Fern's escape without detection was unfortunate," Headmaster Mooney began, "but she deliberately evaded our security measures."

"How do you know she wasn't taken against her will?"

"You heard Fern's ridiculous story, just like we did, Mrs. McAllister," Headmaster Mooney said, pushing himself forward as his voice grew antagonistic. He peered down at Fern McAllister's folder, which he held in his palm authoritatively, wishing he could rid the earth of meddling parents once and for all. If they would leave the educating to him, everyone would be better off. The single parents, especially the mothers, were always the worst. "Can you honestly say you *believe* her?"

"Can you honestly say that a child might not make up a story after going through something traumatic?"

"What are you suggesting, Mrs. McAllister? That Fern was clandestinely taken out of class and then dropped off at Big Corona for a nice day at the beach?" Mrs. Larkey snorted as her glasses slid down her pointy nose.

"I'm suggesting that we don't have all the facts. I'm suggesting that sitting outside this office, we have a severely traumatized girl on our hands and we should concentrate on getting to the bottom of that trauma. Don't think for a second that I'm not aware that I have ample grounds for filing a case of criminal negligence. I know a number of mothers who might be very concerned to learn that student disappearances are treated so cavalierly at St. Gregory's." Mrs. McAllister paused. The serenity with which she first began the conversation reasserted itself. She took a lungful of headmaster office air and began again, calmly. "What I'm saying, I suppose, Headmaster Mooney, is that St. Gregory's seems to be very *lucky* that my daughter appears to be physically unharmed."

"Mrs. McAllister, please calm down." Headmaster Mooney smiled, his face rosy, his bald head showing slight beads of perspiration. Though Headmaster Mooney was known for his steadfast belief in his own instincts, his demeanor had changed in an instant, as if Mrs. McAllister had said a magic word. Or phrase. His voice was now full of feigned kindness. It was the same tone that had allowed him to rise to the rank of headmaster at a very young age, though he only used it when he felt he absolutely had to.

"I'm very calm," Mrs. McAllister responded.

"Your daughter will always have a place here at St. Gregory's. Eddie's a model student; Sam is too; we're just slightly concerned about Fern."

"Well, you're not nearly as concerned as I am, I assure you. Now, if you would be so kind as to instruct Mrs. Stonyfield to stop treating Fern like the class outcast, she might make some friends." Mary Lou McAllister got up, straightening her suit. "If you have any further problems with Fern, you know how to reach me."

"Of course, of course, Mrs. McAllister." Much to Mrs. McAllister's amusement, Headmaster Mooney rose out of his chair and bowed, if ever so slightly.

The headmaster knew he must resist the urge to tell Mrs. McAllister that when she had a PhD in education and a master's in child psychology, then, and only then, should she give him advice on youth education. But he cherished his position. Much as he hated to admit it, one aggrieved parent could ruin him. Especially one as cunning as Mrs. McAllister—turning the whole escapade into an issue of St. Gregory's security failure! It was perverse but brilliant.

"Mrs. McAllister?" Headmaster Mooney said.

"Yes," she said, stopping just short of the door.

"I do apologize if you interpreted any of this as a suggestion that Fern doesn't belong in the St. Gregory family. We just like to nip these types of problems in the bud," he said. "I know Mrs. Larkey agrees that Fern has one of the most active imaginations we've ever encountered."

"Of course, yes, I apologize," Mrs. Larkey added, following Headmaster Mooney's lead. "We value Fern, as we do all our students."

"I appreciate your apology," Mrs. McAllister said, letting Headmaster Mooney's backhanded compliment slide this once.

"Thank you for coming in, I think we're on the right—" Headmaster Mooney raised his fist in the air as if a pompom belonged in it. Mrs. McAllister slammed the door behind her, cutting the headmaster off in midsentence.

Fern was waiting for her mother as she exited the headmaster's office. Mrs. McAllister held her hand out for her daughter. Mary Lou's phony smile was still on her face as she nodded to the various secretaries. All eyes were on the well-dressed blond mother and her undersized dark-haired child as they traipsed through the office, down the stairs, and across the parking lot.

On the walk to the car, a wave of gratitude passed over Fern. She wanted to grab her mother around the waist and not let go. Although the door to the office was thick, Fern had been able to listen to the exchange between her mother and the headmaster as if there were no barrier at all. She'd heard every word.

"Thank you for defending me," Fern said.

Mrs. McAllister stopped dead in the parking lot. Her olive-shaped eyes were on fire.

"What's the matter with you?" Mrs. McAllister said, seething once again. She narrowed her eyes and looked at Fern with unmitigated anger. "Don't you dare thank me!" she continued. "You put me in a terrible position, Fern Phoebe McAllister. You deserve to be punished, but it will not be by that pompous excuse for a man!"

Fern spent the afternoon lying on her bed, reading *Island of the Blue Dolphins.* Mrs. McAllister had decided Fern would spend one week grounded in her room, without any television or computer privileges. At 6:30 sharp, Eddie summoned her to dinner. The three McAllister children devoured their mother's meat loaf eagerly. Eddie recounted an altercation that had interrupted football practice. Sam laughed at how Mrs. Stonyfield had caught Sally White clutching a drawing of a woman with Clownface written below it. Mrs. Stonyfield was too dense to realize the drawing was a portrait of her.

Mrs. McAllister was unusually quiet, finally dismissing

her children to go do their homework. On the way up the stairs, Sam and Eddie cornered their sister by the top of the banister.

"What happened today, huh?" Eddie said, his blue eyes glowing with excitement. "Was there a showdown between Mooney and Mom or what? Kinsey said she saw you and Mom storming out of the office."

"They were going to expel me. Mom convinced them not to . . . and got them to apologize," Fern said, almost embarrassed.

"Really?" Eddie said. "See, Sammy, you don't mess with the Commander, do you?" Eddie playfully hit his younger brother in the stomach with the back of his hand.

"When the Commander says jump . . . ," Sam started.

"We say, 'yes ma'am, how high?'" Eddie ended with a forehead salute. He grabbed the banister and hopped toward his room, saying, "Dodged a bullet there, sis! I swear, you're untouchable!" He closed the door to his room. Fern figured he was in a rush to call Kinsey Wood, his girlfriend of more than a year, as he did every night after dinner. Sam remained in the hallway.

"Fern?"

Fern looked at her twin brother. Maybe it was his blue eyes or the freckles sprinkled on his cheeks, but Fern couldn't help thinking that he was much younger than she was. She loved him, but she never felt that sameness, that twinness she thought she was supposed to. They were so different.

"Fern?" Sam asked again. He mouthed *Follow me* and headed toward their mother's office. Fern walked along the hallway, careful not to make too much noise.

Sam and Fern hadn't been able to talk alone until now. The Commander had made sure of that. She'd sequestered Fern in her room as soon as they arrived home from Pirate's Cove and had practically stood guard outside Fern's door. If Fern wasn't going to fess up and talk to her, Mrs. McAllister reasoned, then she wasn't going to talk to anyone else either. The Commander had spent the entire night before with her door open, half awake, listening for any sign that Sam might be trying to sneak into Fern's room. Fern was to be under bedroom arrest for six more days.

After spending a whole day unable to talk about the disappearance, Sam couldn't stand it any longer. He wanted to talk to Fern so badly, he was willing to risk it, even though his punishment, should he get caught, would probably include his spending a significant portion of his adolescence grounded with Fern. As he peered around the corner of the hallway and realized the Commander was still downstairs, probably watching the evening news, Sam figured he had at least a half hour before she would come upstairs to her room. He carefully crept around the corner of the hallway as Fern followed behind. They snuck into their mother's office, where they could talk and research with less chance of the Commander bursting in on them.

Once the twins were safely in the office, Sam plopped

down in the chair in front of the computer. Fern kneeled next to him, silently.

"Fern, what in the world's going on with you? What really happened?" Sam said, looking at his sister. He was whispering, but having had no opportunity to really *talk* to his sister since yesterday, he was excited and unable to keep his voice low.

"I don't know what happened, exactly. One second I was in class and then the next second I was on the beach."

"You really don't remember anything?" Sam said. "Like being taken to the beach or something?"

"Nothing."

"Unbelievable! Do you realize what this means?" He had no idea how to even process the information. He looked at his sister with wide, wild eyes. That's when he noticed the fear in Fern's. She had been remarkably composed throughout the whole ordeal up to this point, so it was easy for Sam to forget that she was probably terrified. He calmed himself down.

"What did it feel like?" Sam asked, trying to sound nonchalant.

"You mean disappearing?"

"And the reappearing."

"I don't know."

"Was it scary?"

"You know what it was like?" Fern said, trying to describe something that there were no words for. "The second drop in Splash Mountain. When your stomach feels like it flies out of your body and everything goes dark. You come out of it in a totally new place. Except, there was nothing to hold on to."

"So you really did just disappear."

"Yeah."

"Was it instantaneous?" Sam whispered.

"What do you mean?" Fern whispered back.

"When you disappeared," Sam said. "Did you go to the beach right away?"

"Yes," Fern said, anxious to confess to the only person who believed her. "Well, almost. Things went black for a few seconds. There was a strange person waiting there, Sam."

"On the beach?"

"Yeah. This sunburned man—he was the only other person at Pirate's Cove and he had this weird voice and a metal detector. He knew that I'd 'disappeared.' He said I disappeared because it was a celebration of the end of the Titanomachy. At least I think that's what he said, but I've never heard that word in my life."

"He sounds like he was talking gibberish."

"It wasn't gibberish."

"He was probably just some crazy guy. There are lots of those people at the beach."

"No, it was like he was waiting there for me. He seemed crazy but he wasn't. He knew I'd come from school, and he told me to go into the cave by the stairs. I found initials there that were the same as Mom's. M. L. M."

"Those could have been anybody's initials. The Commander would never deface anything."

"I know you're probably right." Fern said, feeling foolish for bringing it up. She continued, "There was also a second cave behind the cave near the entrance to the beach. The sunburned man was calling it the Den."

"What?"

"He pointed out this hole to me and after he left, I crawled through."

"That's impossible! We've been in that cave a million times before."

"It was there. I swear. There was a strange inscription on the floor, with strange lettering. It looked very old. And there was a drawing on the wall." Fern looked pleadingly at Sam, who looked confused. "I know all this sounds crazy, Sam, and that nobody is going to believe me, but you know me, I don't—"

"I believe you," Sam said. He looked at his sister with an earnest intensity. "I saw you disappear."

The twins looked at each other for a moment without saying anything.

"You did?"

"I almost talked myself out of it in the last day. Like I couldn't have seen it, but talking to you now, I know what I saw, Fern. You just vanished. Like a ghost."

"Maybe that's what I am."

"If you were a ghost," Sam said, "I wouldn't be able to do this." He grabbed her wrist and twisted his hands in opposite directions. "Indian burn!"

"Ouch!" Fern said.

"Shhhh," Sam said. "I just thought of something." He narrowed his eyes and began to focus on the computer screen in front of him. "There's a word for it. Like in *Star Trek* when Captain Kirk says, 'Beam me up, Scotty.' Only you can do it all by yourself." Sam began typing.

"Since when did you start watching *Star Trek*?"

"I don't know; the reruns are always on when I'm flipping through."

"You're such a closet nerd."

"Do you want to figure this out or not?"

"Sorry," Fern said, half smiling.

Sam clicked the mouse with fervor, scanning the rapidly changing windows. "Yes! Here it is. *Teleport*. I bet you teleported," Sam said, his whisper growing raspy with excitement.

He pointed to the screen. Sam had typed 'Beam me up, Scotty' into Google and had come up with thousands of websites. He'd navigated through a series of links and had come up with a page explaining the "Art of Teleportation." A man in the corner kept disappearing, than reappearing.

"'Although teleportation is not yet possible, it will be,'" Sam said, reading from the screen. "They've already done it with photons. It says here that researchers at Cal Tech did it in 1998."

"Photons?"

"I think they're like particles. See, it's exactly like *Star Trek*," he said, pointing to a sentence on the screen that mentioned Captain Kirk and Spock. "Only that was made up. And you're real!"

Sam looked at his sister with absolute wonderment.

"What's all this stuff about entanglement and destroying the object that you're teleporting?" Fern asked, quickly scanning a paragraph of text under the question "What do people mean when they say *teleport*?"

"Have you tried doing it again?" Sam said.

"Are you kidding? No way!" Fern said, shivering at the very thought of it.

"Why not?"

"What if next time I do it, I get destroyed, like it says in this article?"

"You're not going to get destroyed."

"How do you know?"

"Fern, don't you get it?" Sam said, impassioned. "You can do something nobody in the world has been able to do before. It's like you're a superhero."

"I'm not a superhero. I'm a freak."

"Superheroes *are* freaks. They're good freaks."

"Sam, there's no such thing as a good freak."

"Of course there is. *Star Trek* is full of good freaks. Superman's a good freak. Um," Sam said, trying to come up with other examples, "and Lance Armstrong—I hear his heart cycles blood twice as fast as a normal person. He's a good freak. Or Einstein—he was a good smart freak."

Fern let a halfhearted chuckle escape her mouth.

"Man," Sam continued, his face animated, "this whole thing is incredible!" He began to focus on the computer screen once more. "Now what was that word that the crazy man used?"

"Titanomachy," Fern said. "But I don't know how to spell it."

"Maybe he made it up, but we might as well check it out." Sam opened a new window on the computer screen and began typing.

"Here it is," he said, scanning. "Whoa. It's a word for the eleven-year war between the Titans and the Olympians."

"The Titans and the Olympians?"

"It's from mythology," Sam said, reading from the page.

Behind them, on the ledge of a window, a large bird with a bright red head and feathers the color of midnight rustled against the window. The twins turned around to look. The large bird turned its head. Fern could've sworn it was staring right at them. She began to grow hot under its gaze. It turned away from the window, expanding its wings until they loomed so large, the entire window was blocked with black feathers. The wings could have gathered up both twins with one movement. It stood absolutely still. After what seemed like ten minutes, the bird took off and disappeared into the night sky.

"What *was* that?" Fern said, looking aghast at her brother.

"I don't know."

"Feeeern!" Her mother was calling for her from downstairs. Sam instinctively jumped out of the chair and took a step back from his sister. He closed every open window on the computer and backed away from its glow.

"Fern, I'll be up in a minute to talk to you! I'd better not be hearing chatter up there!" Mrs. McAllister yelled.

"What am I going to tell the Commander?" Fern pleaded with her brother.

"I don't know if there's anything you can possibly say that will calm her down." Sam wore a tired half smile. "Stall her until we figure all this out. We won't tell anybody about any of it, okay?"

The two snuck out of the office and stood in the doorway.

"Okay," Fern whispered.

Sam turned toward his room with a slight frown, and waved good night. Fern waved back, retreating to her own room.

When Fern plopped down on her bed, she was sure she was more exhausted in that moment than she had been in her entire life.

A breeze drifted in through her open window. The bedroom walls were lined with maple-wood-framed photographs. All the photographs were of the same place—

Carlsbad Caverns National Park, which was Fern's favorite spot in the whole world. The family had traveled to New Mexico on a summer vacation and stayed there a few days. They'd toured many of the caves, walking downward into the earth. Fern couldn't quite describe it, but there, enclosed in stone, she'd felt serene and her head had tingled with pleasure. There was something about the still coolness, the masts of limestone, and the hanging prickly stalactites that seemed as if they could crumble at any moment.

Her brothers had left wishing they had come across a skeleton or two they could tell their friends about. Fern had left wishing she could live there.

Tonight Fern stared at the picture hanging over her bed. It was of the Crystal Spring Dome. The Crystal Spring Dome was remarkable because it was wet, which meant it was one of the only stalagmites still growing. She wondered if she were still changing or if she were like the famous and permanent stalactite, the Sword of Damocles. That particular formation had been named by park rangers in 1928 and had remained exactly as it was back then. Would she be like she was now forever? Or was she still capable of growth?

Knock, knock.

"Still awake?" Her mother's voice was unexpectedly soft and soothing. The truth was, Mrs. McAllister felt she might have been too harsh with Fern in the St. Gregory's parking lot.

Fern lay still. She could feel the bed sink from her mother's weight as she sat next to Fern. Her mother had changed into silk pajamas. In them, with her hair wild around her shoulders, she looked much too young to be a mother of a sixteen-year-old son. Mrs. McAllister grabbed *Lord of the Flies*.

"Ah, *Lord of the Flies*. The second best 'Lord of' book in all the land," Mrs. McAllister said, looking at her daughter sprawled out on the bed.

"What's the first best?" Fern said, raising her head up on one elbow.

"*The Lord of the Rings*, hands down."

"That's three books, isn't it?"

"Tolkien wrote it as one."

"I haven't read it yet," Fern said.

"You will."

Mrs. McAllister took Fern's copy of *Lord of the Flies* and flipped through it. "Why does this look like it's been through a hurricane?"

Fern had to admit that there was some significant water damage to the book. It kind of looked like a paper accordion.

"I've been taking it into the shower with me," she said simply.

"To read?"

"Yeah."

"Whatever gave you that idea?" Mrs. McAllister was shocked.

"It's dead time in the shower. I always want to find out what happens and I always have to go do something else, so it seemed like a shame to waste the time."

"Maybe you should have put it in a Ziploc first."

"Then I could only read the two pages on top," Fern said.

Mrs. McAllister paused to think for a moment. "Well, I guess we'll just have to start allowing more shelf space for all our books. This is twice the size it used to be." She waved the book in the air and the stiff pages crinkled.

"It'll look like we have more books that way." The two smiled at each other.

Mrs. McAllister inhaled. "Fern, sit up." She folded her hands in her lap, looked down at them, and continued. "I need you to tell me exactly what happened yesterday. I won't get upset, but I need to know."

"I told you what happened."

"Don't you know that what you say happened couldn't possibly have happened?" Mrs. McAllister looked at her daughter not with anger, but with sympathy.

"I don't remember. I felt the world spinning and I woke up on the beach."

"Why are you lying to me, Fern?"

Fern recognized the emotion that filled her mother's voice. It wasn't anger. It was disappointment.

"I don't understand this, Fern! This is unacceptable. What are you hiding?" Mrs. McAllister was growing frustrated. She couldn't seem to get through to Fern.

"I'm not hiding anything."

"You've never lied to me before, Fern. I can't understand why you're doing it now." Her voice was hard. If Fern didn't give in, would there be an end to her mother's resentment?

"I'm sorry," Fern said, beginning to speak as her mind worked on overdrive. She thought of the sunburned man's advice.

The first lie came rather easily. "I took the bus," Fern blurted out, louder than necessary. "I walked out of St. Gregory's and took the bus to the beach and I shouldn't have done it!" Fern was talking fast now, trying to get through it, so it would be over. Mrs. McAllister interpreted this eagerness as Fern unburdening her guilty conscience

"I'm sorry, Mom," Fern said, visibly upset. "I was sick of being teased. I guess . . . I guess I wanted a break, even for the day."

The Commander grabbed her daughter's arms and pulled Fern toward her, hugging her with reckless force. Fern felt like she might be squeezed into two equal halves. The hug was so fierce, it felt like an unspoken reproach.

"I shouldn't have left school," Fern said. Fern's words took the Commander back to her disciplinary stance. She pulled away from her daughter and delivered Fern a harsh look.

"No, you certainly shouldn't have!" The Commander's face was hard like granite. Fern realized she would receive no sympathy from her mother. "If you ever do something like this again, there will be severe consequences. I wouldn't try testing me."

Mrs. McAllister sensed that her daughter was on the verge of losing her composure once more. She placed her hands on Fern's shoulders. "Well, we're going to fix this, you hear me?"

"I promise I won't leave like that again," Fern said, knowing full well that if things kept going the way they were going, she was offering up a promise she couldn't keep.

"We'll talk more about this tomorrow. You're still very grounded, by the way," Mrs. McAllister said sternly, getting up from Fern's bed. She turned back to Fern as she reached the doorway. "You can always talk to me, Fern." As she left, she flicked off the lights.

Although Mary Lou McAllister was somewhat relieved, she still felt slightly uneasy. She'd known from the beginning that Fern was very different, perhaps even painfully so. Deep in the recesses of her mind, Mrs. McAllister knew it was unlikely that Fern had snuck out of St. Gregory's undetected and taken the bus to the beach. But like many people in her position, the Commander, when confronted with two realities, chose to believe the one that wouldn't keep her up at night. For this reason, Mrs. McAllister went to bed thinking she had a child whose odd conduct could still be explained within the normal parameters of adolescent behavior.

The moon came through the front upstairs window, bathing Fern's room in icy light. Though Mrs. McAllister hardly showed it, Fern knew she had made her mother feel better, which in turn had made Fern feel better. Even so, the heart of the matter gnawed at her: Mary Lou McAllister would rather have a daughter who had lied to everyone, including her own mother, and ditched school to take a bus to the beach, than a daughter who defied logical explanation. What if Fern couldn't control this teleporting thing, whatever it was? What if she disappeared again?

Fern hated herself right then. She hated the fact that she had no power over the things that made her stick out the most. She hated that she was getting worse. But she would try harder, she resolved as she lay in her bed. If it destroyed her, she would try to be more like Eddie, more like Sam. She thought of Sam and his excitement over her ability to "teleport." It was an easy thing to enjoy from a distance. When you were the one it was happening to, though, it was terrifying.

A slight rustle interrupted Fern's thoughts. She looked around her dark room. A white object fluttered in through the open window, landing at the foot of her bed. Her heart leaped as she wrestled with her comforter to get a closer look. It was a paper airplane, expertly folded. She opened it and held it up to the moonlight. A message was written on the inside of the white paper.

I know who you are. I want to help. Please meet me at Anderson's Grove at midnight tomorrow.

Fern was trembling as she crept close to her window. The jacaranda tree outside was motionless, as was the street below. San Juan Capistrano was, as usual, tranquil at this hour of the night. Fern's mind was anything but. The youngest McAllister closed her window and crawled into bed, almost paralyzed with fear. Her eyes wide open, she was almost afraid to blink. After two hours of restlessness, her stomach churning all the while, sleep finally overcame Fern.

4

the strangers in the living room

Mr. Wallace Summers had been living across the street from the McAllisters for a little over two months before he found a way to penetrate their living room. The next night he stood on the porch, anxious after knocking on the McAllister front door. Eddie answered, wearing pajama pants and a St. Gregory's football T-shirt. His hair was disheveled.

"Hey, Mr. Summers! What's up?" The McAllisters had just finished dinner and the twins were in the kitchen washing the dishes.

"Hi there, Eddie. I don't mean to impose, but my cable just went out."

"Oh man, are you watching the game?" Eddie, who was not permitted to watch television of any kind during dinner, had just turned on the night's Los Angeles Lakers game.

Sometimes Kinsey Wood would come over and watch whatever game was on with him, but tonight Eddie was flying solo. He and Mr. Summers had become friendly of late. They had recently struck up a conversation about Doug Flutie's historic extra-point dropkick against the Dolphins while Mr. Summers was on a walk and Eddie was mowing the McAllister front lawn. Since then, they had had similar discussions when they saw each other around the neighborhood. The eldest McAllister child was lonesome for anybody who was the least bit knowledgeable about sports.

"I know it's late and I'm probably intruding, but if I could watch the second half of the Lakers game here, I would really appreciate it," Mr. Summers said, speaking loudly, hoping the occupants of the kitchen could hear him. Fern detected something eerie in Mr. Summer's voice—something that made her feel as if there were a trail of fire ants climbing down her backbone.

"I'd love some company." Eddie invited him into the living room. He had a habit of saying yes to people even when he lacked the jurisdiction to do so.

Sam's face twisted into a glower. He didn't like Mr. Summers one bit. Any son would feel the same way after catching a man leering at his mother through her kitchen window, and Sam had spotted Mr. Summers doing this several times in the past few weeks with his gaze fixed on Mrs. McAllister, in her daisy-print apron, leaning over the sink and humming to herself while she rinsed dishes.

Now this stranger stood in their living room. It wasn't long before the rest of the family, still cleaning up the remains of dinner, had gathered in the doorway between the living room and the kitchen. Mrs. McAllister stepped forward.

"Eddie, are you going to introduce us to your guest?" Mrs. McAllister smiled widely. Fern could spot it immediately. Her mother was using her "manners" again—something she was always hounding Fern to acquire in the immediate future.

"How rude of me not to come in and introduce myself," Mr. Summers said, striding toward the trio of McAllisters gathered in the doorway. He was tall and thin, almost like a cardboard cutout of a real man. His dimples made him look much younger than he probably was. Still, he was handsome for someone older. Fern took into account his salt and pepper hair and pegged him as forty-eight—a few years older than her mother. Mary Lou was first in the greeting line. As Mr. Summers took Mrs. McAllister's hand, he bent his head and pressed his lips firmly against the back of it.

"Mrs. McAllister, I presume," Mr. Summers said. Fern thought he sounded like he was imitating Professor Plum from *Clue*. He continued, "I'm so sorry I've invited myself into your beautiful home. I'm afraid that much like your son, I'm a hopeless Lakers fan. And my cable has gone out. Wallace Summers, by the way,"

"Well, Wallace, you're welcome anytime," Mrs.

McAllister said, staring at Mr. Summers's soft brown eyes. "I'm Eddie's mother, Mary Lou. It's a pleasure to meet you." Fern was horrified. Her mother was blushing. It was the same color Sam had turned last week when she told him that she had overheard Sally White talking about "cute Sam McAllister."

Mr. Summers smiled back. The two stared at each other. Grown men, up to this point, had never played a significant roll in the McAllister household—Mrs. McAllister wanted it that way. But now that her children were older, it looked as if Mrs. McAllister was on the verge of breaking her own rules.

Fern looked at her twin brother. Sam's face moved like a revolving sprinkler head between his mother and the stranger in the living room. His eye caught Fern's. Sam put his index finger down his throat and made an audible gagging sound.

"Are you okay, son?" Mr. Summers had caught the end of Sam's display of disgust and failed to acknowledge that Sam was mocking him.

"I'm fine," Sam said. "But I'm not your son." His voice was full of contempt.

"Sam," Mrs. McAllister said, "where are your manners? It's a figure of speech. There's no need to take things so literally."

"Oh, it's not a problem, Mary Lou. I appreciate someone who says what they think." Mr. Summers extended his hand toward Sam like it was an olive branch. "Sam, I'm

Mr. Summers." Sam took the man's hand and shook it limply, refusing to look the neighbor in the eye. "Good to meet you," he said before moving on down the line.

"You must be Fern!" Mr. Summers bent over so he was closer to her eye level.

"You know my name?" she asked warily.

"Eddie mentioned it. Now what's this I hear about your record on predicting the weather? Is that true?"

Fern looked quizzical. She found it very unlikely that Eddie had told this man about her predictions on the weather.

"I'm pretty good at it," Fern said.

"Pretty good? I'd say correct forecasts over two years is better than *pretty good*."

"Yeah," Fern said, slightly embarrassed.

"You climb trees, too?"

"Yes," Fern said.

"Mrs. Atwood down the street works at St. Gregory's—she says all anyone's been talking about is your disappearance at school. Do we have a Houdini Jr. in our midst?"

"No," Fern said as her face turned hot.

"I remember playing hooky once or twice when I was your age." Mr. Summers smiled and his dimples made him seem perfectly innocuous. He looked up at Mrs. McAllister and winked. "Of course, I'm not encouraging such behavior."

Fern was now terribly self-conscious. Was she really that much of a topic of conversation? Sam stepped in between

Mr. Summers and Fern, rather awkwardly.

"Aren't you going to ask me any questions, Mr. Summers?" Sam asked with scorn. "Or is it only Fern that you're interested in?"

Mr. Summers took a step back. Fern thought she recognized a glint of anger in Mr. Summers's otherwise charming face.

Eddie, still on the couch, jumped up, yelped, and pumped his fist. "Holy . . . awesome!" Kobe Bryant had sunk a long three pointer just as the halftime buzzer sounded.

Mrs. McAllister caught Sam's eye and raised an eyebrow at him. She would deal with him later. The four of them were still crowded in the doorway.

"Please sit back down, Wallace," she said. "Sam, why don't you ask Mr. Summers if he would like something to drink?"

Sam didn't move an inch. He looked at Mr. Summers as if the two were about to duel.

"Sam? Did you hear me?" Mrs. McAllister said, losing patience by the second.

"Sorry. I thought you told me not to take things so literally."

Mrs. McAllister zeroed in on Sam and was about to send him to his room for the night when Wallace Summers stepped in.

"No, no, Mary Lou, don't trouble yourself," Mr. Summers said, sitting down. "I'll just watch with Eddie here and let myself out when the game's over."

Upstairs, minutes later, Sam was unable to shake his anger at Mr. Summers's intrusion. Fern, still grounded, had been sent up to her room after her brief encounter with Mr. Summers, and Sam snuck into her room, hoping to discuss the strange arrival. The two were now whispering back and forth.

"You really made Mom mad, Sam. I wouldn't be surprised if she grounds you or something. She hates it when you get mouthy."

"I didn't like all the questions he was asking you. What if he knows you can teleport?" Sam said, sliding their newly discovered word seamlessly into the conversation.

"I thought you said I shouldn't be worried about people finding out about me teleporting."

"You shouldn't worry," Sam said, folding his arms and sitting in Fern's rocking chair. "I just don't like him is all."

"You're mad because he has a crush on Mom," Fern said.

"I don't care if he wants to marry Mom. He seems nosy."

"Yeah, a little," Fern said, thinking of the chilly feeling she'd had when Mr. Summers arrived.

Suddenly, Fern doubled over in pain, clutching her sides. It was her stomach.

"Stomachache, again?" Sam said, unable to hide his alarm. She was having more and more of these lately—

usually right before something significant happened. Though Mrs. McAllister was convinced Fern had a case of irritable bowel syndrome, nothing helped.

Fern, near the point of doing anything to stop the pain, couldn't move her thoughts from the note she'd received last night. Earlier she'd resolved to keep its contents to herself. But she thought sharing it with Sam might ease the tension in her stomach.

"Look . . . ," Fern said, concentrating, trying to will the pain away. "Look . . . in my top desk drawer." Although slightly disappointed in herself, Fern could feel the pressure in her stomach relent.

Fern's desk, a rolltop she'd inherited from her mother, was cluttered with books and papers. Sam jumped up and retrieved a folded white piece of paper. He unfolded it gingerly, sat back down in the cushioned rocker, and began to read the note aloud.

"'I know who you are. I want to help. Please meet me at . . .'" Sam's voice trailed off. "Fern?"

"Uh-huh."

"Who wrote this?" Sam's eyes were as big as two pickle jar lids.

"I don't know." Fern's words came out slowly.

"When did you get it?"

"It came in through the window last night, after Mom left."

"I'm coming with you," Sam said, studying the note. He was determined—Fern could see that.

"Who says I'm going at all?" she asked. Though she was miffed at her inability to keep her own secrets, the shared burden was much easier to bear. If she did go, Sam would be with her every step of the way.

"Maybe it's Mr. Summers!" Fern said.

"We'd better find out who it is, that's for sure."

"I'm not sure I want to know."

"You have to go. This person says they can help you."

Sam's last sentence hung awkwardly between them in the dim light of Fern's bedroom. Sam, always the protector, was normally very careful to say nothing that indicated his confusion about Fern.

"You think I need help?" Fern could feel the lump in the back of her throat swelling. Her brother's view of her was no different from the rest of San Juan's. She was a misfit, through and through.

"You're different from the rest of us, Fern," Sam said, pleading.

"I know." Before she disappeared, none of this had mattered. Now, Fern thought, her difference was the only thing that mattered.

"We need to find out all the information we can. Who knows? Maybe I can learn to disappear, too."

"What if it's a hoax? What if it's a kidnapper—or someone out to get me?"

"If someone wanted to hurt you, instead of chucking a paper airplane through your bedroom window, they'd have come in themselves."

"You really think we should go?"

"Think about it, Fern. If we don't find out who this is, we'll worry about everything and everybody. Even Mr. Summers. We need to get to the bottom of this, whatever happens."

"Okay," Fern said.

"I'd better scram before Mom gets wise. I'll be back at eleven forty-five." Sam hopped off his sister's chair, still gripping the note. "I'm going to keep this for now, if you don't mind."

"What, are you going to dust it for prints or something?" Fern said, wondering what Sam could possibly do with the note.

"I don't want you losing it, that's all. It's our only clue to who you are."

Sam's last sentence stung Fern a little. Being a McAllister wasn't enough anymore.

Fern couldn't sleep—not that she expected to. Against her better judgment, she decided to pass the time by reading *Lord of the Flies*. (She was still a little nervous that somehow she might be transported back to Pirate's Cove, only this time at night.) Things were not looking good for Piggy, Ralph, and the boys. Jack, who had his eye on Ralph's position as chief, did not seem trustworthy.

A rustling caused Fern to look up from the book.

Pulling off the covers, she began to get out of bed, but she stepped on something that wasn't the floor. She stumbled and cried out. She was soon able to see what she had tripped over. Sam had managed to sneak into her room and had crouched beside her bed. He held his head in his hands and grimaced as he stood up.

"What are you doing? I'm not a human step stool!" Sam spoke in a fierce whisper, wondering if his mother had been awakened by Fern's yelping.

"You scared me half to death, Sam!" Fern whispered back. She took one look at her brother in the faint glow of her reading light and cupped her hand over her mouth to suppress her laughter. "What *are* you wearing?" Sam stood before her in camouflage pants, a black turtleneck, and a black leather hat with earflaps. He looked like Elmer Fudd on his way to a funeral.

"I'm going to hide while you meet with the note writer. I'll only come out if I need to, you know, go under cover."

Fern shook her head in disbelief, forgetting all about the potential danger that awaited her in the grove. Moments like these, when Sam tried his best to take on the role of the strong male protector of the household, cracked Fern up.

"Are you going to wave your earflaps at them if they make trouble?"

"Never mind," Sam said, annoyed at his sister for belittling his efforts.

The two siblings were silent for a few minutes, letting the situation sink in. Neither had any idea who or what was waiting for them in the grove. Sam hoped it was answers. Fern hoped she wasn't putting her brother in danger—she wouldn't be able to live with herself if something happened to him.

"The Commander came in and talked to me about my 'inappropriate' behavior with Mr. Summers," Sam said. "She came down pretty hard on me."

"You were acting a little psychotic," Fern said.

"I wasn't that bad," Sam said.

"Yeah? You looked like you were ready to bite his hand off."

"Whatever," Sam said, feeling a little guilty but trying not to show it. "Hey, is that what *you're* wearing?" Sam scrutinized his sister's outfit. She was wearing flannel pants with clouds all over them and an old Anaheim Angels shirt she'd inherited from Eddie.

"I'm going to put flip-flops on," she said. Sam walked to her bedroom window and lifted it open. Cool night air rushed into Fern's room. Her stomach contracted with pain, almost as if the air triggered it. She doubled over.

"You okay?" Sam said.

"Yeah. I'm just looking for my other flip-flop," Fern said, unwilling to give Sam another reason to worry about her.

Midnight was fast approaching.

"You're wearing both of your flip-flops, idiot."

Sam reached out the open window to the jacaranda branch just outside. He swung his skinny legs and feet over the windowsill and fell forward, so he was crouching on the branch with both his legs and arms wrapped around it. The branch let out a slow creak as it bent under Sam's added weight. Slithering along the branch till he got to the trunk, Sam looked precarious as he made his way down the jacaranda. He slipped down the tree and finally hit the grass with a soft *thud*.

Fern followed her brother, nimbly crawling from one branch to another. She had climbed up and down this jacaranda for much of her life—scrambling down its maze of branches and trunk was her preferred way of exiting the McAllister house. In the spring, when the tree was in bloom, she'd constantly be told she had bits of tree in her hair. No matter how hard she'd tried, she could never pick out all the lavender blue flowers. She was down in half the time it'd taken Sam.

The Salt and Pepper Twins faced the quiet street. Sam wished he'd thought to bring a flashlight with him. Fern longed for a sweatshirt. Silent, they made their way down to the grove under the flickering orange light of the suburban energy-saving street lamps. Walking quickly, they had reached the corner of Acacia Avenue and La Limonar when the crackling of breaking twigs stopped the twins dead in their tracks. On the left side of the sidewalk, by the McGraw house, a lone cypress tree swayed back and forth. Fern broke into a cold sweat, and even in the sputtering moonlight, she could tell Sam's face had paled.

The combination of movement and noise could have

been any number of things: a coyote, a cat, an escaped pet, a raccoon, even an opossum. But Fern and Sam both thought it was a sure sign of danger.

"Run," Sam said, in a voice so calm, it seemed less of a command and more of a plea.

"Wait," said a voice coming from the general vicinity of the cypress tree. It was almost as if the tree itself was speaking. The voice was female and young—the antithesis of dangerous. The cypress tree shook furiously. Soon a mess of arms and legs spilled out onto the sidewalk in front of Fern and Sam. A girl had fallen out of the cypress tree. Fern leaned over the body and could discern a fanned-out mane of black hair and a tall frame. The owner of the voice was lanky, wearing dark jeans and a ribbed blue tank top.

"Wait, wait!" said the tree person, who was out of breath and speaking into the sidewalk. As she got up and brushed various twigs, leaves, thorns, and dirt from her body, she looked up at the twins, standing in front of them for the first time. Her almond-shaped eyes blinked curiously at them; her dark pupils were massive. A thin brow and pointed chin gave her face a delicacy. She had the straightest and glossiest black hair that Fern had ever seen, resting just below her shoulders. Sam and Fern recognized the girl immediately.

"What are *you* doing here?" Sam stammered, still in shock that this familiar face had cascaded out of the tree.

"Nice to see you too, Sammy!" Her voice was chipper. Fern took in her red lips and round cheeks. All of her features seemed slightly exaggerated, but they came together to give her face sophistication rarely found in thirteen-year-olds. She turned to Fern.

"Fern, I'm Lindsey Lin, and it's a pleasure to meet you," she said, extending her tan arm toward Fern. Fern took Lindsey's hand for her second shake of the night.

"I know who you are," Fern said.

"I figured, but we'd never been formally introduced. I know Sam, here, because he's in my math class."

Anybody at St. Gregory's would have recognized Lindsey Lin. She was Associated Student Body President for the middle grades, boasted more friends than almost anyone, and was the MVP of the volleyball team three years running. Lindsey Lin wasn't just popular; she was a social force of nature. She was the kind of girl who could start the fashion of wearing underwear as a hat simply by doing it a few times.

She was also the person Fern and Sam would have guessed they were least likely to find at midnight getting closely acquainted with the inside of a tree on their street corner. Sam, unimpressed with the social icon in front of them, was all business.

"What are you doing here, Lindsey?"

"I was going to go meet you at the grove, but then I decided that we'd just be walking right back to your house, which seemed kind of pointless. I wanted to make sure you were actually going to come. The grove seemed so poetic, you know? But it wasn't practical and I knew

I couldn't knock on your door, so I picked the tree and waited. I've been here for fifteen minutes." Lindsey caught her breath. Fern had never heard anyone talk so fast.

"You sent the note?" Sam said. Fern detected the anger in his voice. Was this entire thing another prank perpetrated by one of the popular kids trying to get at Fern?

"Of course I sent the note," Lindsey said. "Why would I be here if I hadn't sent the note?"

"What did you mean by it?"

"I want to help," Lindsey said. "I heard Fern's disappearing story. My parents would kill me if they found out I was here, or I was messing with the 'balance' or whatever they call it, but I knew I just had to help. I just know you're all right—that you're one of us." Lindsey's beautiful smile radiated confidence in the dewy night. She put her hand on Fern's forearm gently. "I don't know how you got here, but you're not the bad kind at all. You couldn't be. Just look at you!" Lindsey then threw her arms up in the air, as if what she had just said followed normal conversational cues and logic.

"What is the bad kind? And why would your parents kill you?" Sam said.

"My parents are your stereotypical overly protective sorts. It's a school night," Lindsey said, waving Sam's question off. "Look, I don't have time to explain everything, but you have a dog, right?" Fern thought of Byron's soft ears and bad breath. The McAllister dog's specialties included lounging, licking and moping.

"Yeah," Fern said, wondering how Lindsey Lin knew anything at all about her family. "Byron."

"Good." Lindsey said, thinking aloud and talking to nobody in particular. She stepped toward Fern and grabbed both shoulders with her hands. Lindsey's breath was hot on Fern's face. Though nearly a head taller, she was staring right into Fern's eyes.

"You're wearing contacts, aren't you?"

"Yes," Fern said.

"What color are your eyes normally?"

"I don't know. You're the one who's looking *at* them."

"Are they gray?"

"People say they're gray or yellow," Fern said, wishing Lindsey Lin would release her. "The mean ones say they're the color of snot."

"I need to see your dog," Lindsey stated quickly, barely processing Fern's reply.

"You can't do that. You'll wake up the whole house." Sam said, annoyed. "Why did you say you could help? Why did you say you know who Fern is?" Sam's anger grew as he stared menacingly. The camouflage pants seemed to be going to his head. He wanted answers.

"Calm down, Sammy. I told you, I'm going to help, and I will help. But before I do that, I need to see your dog. If you've got a problem with that, I'll turn right around—"

"No, no. Come with us. We'll show you," Fern said, not wanting to alienate Lindsey Lin. Fern couldn't help staring at Lindsey as she and Sam retraced their steps back to the house.

"Jeez!" Sam exclaimed as he stopped completely.

"What is it?" Lindsey said.

"Look, another one," Sam said, pointing down to the small, still object in the middle of the sidewalk. It was a dead bird. A swallow, in fact.

Lindsey crouched down to get a better look.

"Whoa," she said. "You guys haven't seen a really large condor flying around here, have you?" Lindsey asked, as her face grew white.

"There was one at our window the other day, yeah," Sam said.

Lindsey's eyes grew larger. Her face then changed back to its normal expression. "Yeah, me too. It must be lost or something," she said. "That's sad about the little bird. Cycle of life, though. Ob-la-di, ob-la-da. The night's not getting any younger."

She turned away from Sam and began walking again, challenging the twins to keep up with her.

The twins decided that Lindsey would wait on the porch while Sam and Fern scaled the tree. Once inside, they would sneak downstairs and let Lindsey in. Fern and Sam were terrified of what might happen should the Commander awaken.

They reached the front door and opened it.

"What are you waiting for?" Sam whispered urgently. Lindsey stood frozen on the porch.

"I haven't been invited yet," Lindsey said, in her cool and casual manner.

"You need an invitation to come in the house when the door's already been opened for you?" Sam said in disbelief.

"It's cultural," Lindsey said, rolling her eyes.

"Come in, *now*," Sam demanded.

"Thank you, I will. Gladly," Lindsey said, smiling and snapping her head in agreement.

"Follow me," Sam said, with a tinge of resignation. Sam thought that they were as good as caught. Fern and Lindsey followed him into the living room, where he shut the door to the kitchen in order to muffle the noise.

"Now, what's this about?" Sam said.

"What Sam means, Lindsey, is what do you know about me?" Fern still couldn't believe the most popular girl in school—a girl Fern wouldn't have expected a slight nod of the head from as she passed by—was standing in front of her.

"Get your dog in here, will you?"

Sam, worn down, didn't argue. He exited the room and returned, dragging Byron by the collar. At just over seven pounds, Byron couldn't mount much resistance to Sam. He was, however, whimpering, ignoring Sam's whispered pleas to remain quiet. Eddie usually slept through everything from earthquakes to fire alarms, but Mrs. McAllister was sure to wake up if she heard Byron's high-pitched bark.

Fern looked at her brother and then at their guest.

Lindsey's face shone brightly, almost twice as brightly as Sam's. The McAllister dog was silent; his dark eyes were focused on Lindsey Lin. Byron, more than ten years old, had short floppy white ears and white curly locks. Although he was old, Byron was known throughout the neighborhood for picking fights with animals three times his size. Mrs. McAllister would always say Byron didn't recognize his own limits.

Lindsey grabbed Byron by the collar. She led him behind the couch and ducked down. Both McAllister twins lost sight of Lindsey and the dog. After three seconds, Lindsey popped up again. She still had Byron by the collar and led him out from behind the couch. Byron was whimpering with his head down to the floor.

"Fern, I want you to tell me what I just told Byron."

"What?" Fern said, very confused.

"Tell me what I just whispered into Byron's ear."

"How am I supposed to know? You were behind the couch"

"Why don't you ask Byron?" Lindsey said, still talking rapid-fire.

"How would he understand what you said anyway?"

"Because, I learned a few phrases before I came here tonight."

"From who?" Fern fired back.

"I did some research."

"Is this a joke?" Sam said, taking a confrontational step toward Lindsey.

"Ask him, Fern. Ask him and he'll tell you." Lindsey was focused, and she squinted at Fern as if she were looking at direct sunlight.

"How do you know about that?" Sam said, putting his finger right in Lindsey's face. "Why are you here?" Fern could see Sam's face turning red. If Lindsey hadn't been a girl, she was sure that Sam would've wrestled her to the ground and demanded answers with physical force.

"Calm down, Sam," Lindsey said with a coolness that made Fern want to trust her.

"How do you know about Fern and Byron?" Sam had never figured out Fern's relationship with Byron, but since Fern had been six years old, she could teach Byron to do all sorts of strange things: run in circles, use the toilet, dance to Madonna, or climb the jacaranda with her. The dog followed Fern everywhere.

"You told him that you think I'm a Rollen," Fern said quietly. Sam and Lindsey, who had both turned away from Fern, faced her. Lindsey Lin's steely pout gave way to a huge smile.

"What's that supposed to mean?" Sam questioned. "What's a Rollen?"

"Not only can he understand me," Lindsey said, still grinning, "but you can understand him. Just like I thought."

"What is a Rollen?" Sam demanded. "Why have you come here?"

"How long have you been able to do that, Fern?"

Lindsey said, ignoring Sam.

"I don't know. I can hear his voice in my head and he can hear mine."

"Fern," Sam said, grabbing his sister's arm, "don't give her any answers until she gives us some!"

"From what I know, fully developed canine communication doesn't kick in for another few years. You're a prodigy, though, so you must be one of them!"

"One of who? What are you talking about? Do you realize how crazy you sound?" Sam said with muffled anger.

"Look, don't mention that I came here. I don't think I'm wrong about you, but if I am . . . I could get in a lot of trouble," Lindsey said while reaching into her brown satchel. "Take these; then maybe you'll believe me."

"Believe what? You haven't *told* us anything."

"Believe that I want to help," she said, and looked thoughtfully at Sam and Fern. "This round bottle is for your skin—rub it all over—and the square one has eye-drops for the mornings."

Lindsey Lin handed Fern two white bottles. Each bottle was plain and fit in the palm of her hand. Both had W.A.A.V.E. printed on them in small ornate letters.

"Where'd you get these?" Fern asked, looking down at the bottles as if she held a magic potion in each hand.

"What is a Rollen?" Sam demanded as loudly as he dared. The door to the master bedroom creaked open. The three of them could hear the Commander prowling around upstairs. They froze instantly.

"Byron?" Mrs. McAllister called softly, hoping not to wake her children, whom she assumed were fast asleep. Byron went bounding up the stairs and into the arms of Mrs. McAllister. Lindsey, Sam, and Fern remained absolutely still, terrified that she might come down the stairs. They waited until their muscles cramped. After a few minutes, they heard the door to the master bedroom close.

"Use them; you won't be sorry." Lindsey Lin whispered at Fern. "You have a beautiful home," she said, grabbing the front door with one hand. She gave Sam and Fern one last glance, opened the door, slipped out, then closed it behind her. Sam, thoroughly dissatisfied, wanted to run after her and drag her back so he could force Lindsey to talk. But the Commander was awake, and any noise now might tip her off. Instead, the McAllister twins exchanged disbelieving, confused stares.

Fern and Sam were both exhausted from the night's activities. They ascended the stairs, Fern clutching her W.A.A.V.E. bottles, Sam sweating in his turtleneck and ear flaps, knowing they would figure out what to make of their midnight visitor in the morning. Things would be much clearer then. After all, they couldn't possibly get murkier.

Outside, Lindsey Lin, the second stranger to grace the McAllister living room in one evening, made her way home under a pale blue moon.

5

the haircut

Since Lindsey Lin's late night visit to the McAllister home, St. Gregory's had become a much less disagreeable place for Fern. Though Sam was fairly convinced that neither W.A.A.V.E. bottle was safe for Fern's personal use, it was hard to argue with the results: It had been ten days since Fern had walked to school with the aid of her Breakfast Sunglasses. The same amount of time had passed since Fern's tender snow-white skin had shown any effects of the scorching California sun. Fern might never be sure what was in the bottles Lindsey had handed over in the darkness of the McAllister living room, but she was convinced things would be better from now on.

Still, Fern's status as a loner remained unchanged: At lunch she sat by herself, behind the outdoor stage, across from the multipurpose room, with a brief visit from Sam.

Chapel was another of Fern's alone activities. Sam always invited her to sit next to him, but every time she did, his friends would stare at her to the point that she preferred sitting by herself.

For the middle and upper grades, chapel was required. Every Tuesday students would file into the triangular stucco building in their formal wear. For girls, that meant a gray skirt, a white oxford shirt, dress shoes, and a blue sweater with the St. Gregory's crest emblazoned on the right breast; for the boys that meant leather shoes, a navy school blazer, and slacks. On cold days, girls were allowed to wear pants. Fern usually chose to wear Eddie's baggy hand-me-downs.

A round stained-glass window that looked almost the size of a baseball infield dominated the front of the chapel. Each morning the sun would rise over the Capistrano hills and its rays would hit the chapel window. For a person sitting inside, the backdrop of bright light made the saints depicted in the colored glass glow neon bright.

Everyone at St. Gregory's called the steepled building a chapel, but one look disclosed that it was really much more. Ornately carved doors led to a cavernous aisle with padded, lacquered pews. Gold-threaded tapestries depicting some of the Bible's most celebrated stories hung on the walls. The silver organ pipes lined the tops of the cement walls. The pulpit and the area behind it were more than worthy of the sacred rites performed by Mother Corrigan.

On chapel mornings, Fern would linger in the bathroom, watching the clock until she had exactly one minute to cross campus and slip into the back row after everyone was seated but before Mother Corrigan began her sermon. It was Tuesday again and Fern found herself waiting in the girls' bathroom, counting down the seconds. She had nearly three minutes until it was safe to begin making her way across the quad to the chapel. The clock on the tile wall ticked and tocked at a slow pace.

When the door to the bathroom creaked open, Fern jumped and took shelter in the nearest metal stall. She waited, wondering who else would dare risk a detention by being late to chapel.

"Feeeeern," the voice said. "We know you're in here." Fern lifted her feet up and sat on the toilet seat. Although she didn't want to be right, she would know that voice anywhere. Lee Phillips had come looking for her.

"You may as well come out of that stall," a second voice said. Fern recognized this voice too. Lee Phillips rarely went anywhere without Blythe Conrad.

Fern spotted two pairs of black Mary Janes under her stall door. Soon every wall of the stall began to shake. Lee and Blythe were kicking the doors open, one by one.

Boom. Boom. Boom.

With four stalls to go before they reached Fern, Fern decided to preempt the girls. She popped out of her stall and leaned against the mirrored back wall of the bathroom.

"What do you want?" Fern questioned as she raised an eyebrow. The two girls smiled wickedly at each other and closed in on Fern.

Now they were an arm's length away from her. Both girls were nearly four inches taller than Fern, having already had their growth spurts. Their tan, slim legs were the envy of most of the girls at school.

"Oh, we don't want much," Lee said, flipping her strawberry blond hair behind her shoulders. Blythe reached into her book bag and pulled out a large pair of scissors.

"How come you always hide in here before chapel?" Blythe said, hissing, holding the scissors at her side. "You sneak in at the last minute and sit in the back row all by yourself. You think you're too good to sit with everybody else?"

"No," Fern said, a little puzzled and a lot worried. "I think nobody cares what I do."

Blythe and Lee inched closer.

"You think you're speeeecial," Lee purred, "don't you?"

"No, I don't," Fern exclaimed, backing up until she was flush against the wall. She glanced up at the clock. "If we don't leave now, we're all going to be late for chapel."

"Oh, I'm sure you don't have to worry about that. Why don't you just disappear there?" Blythe asked.

"I didn't disappear," Fern said.

"Of course you didn't disappear," Lee said.

"What do you want from me?"

"We're going to help you out by giving you a *special* haircut," Blythe said, putting her fingers into the scissors and waving them through the air with menace.

"Something freaky for freaky Fern, no?" Lee said, smiling devilishly.

Fern pushed off the wall and bolted between the girls.

Blythe lunged at Fern's hair, grabbing a fistful as she neared, yanking Fern backward. Fern grimaced, trying not to scream out loud. The skin on her scalp throbbed.

Lee gripped Fern's shoulders and slammed her against the side of the nearest stall. Pain shot up Fern's spine to her neck. She groaned and tried to twist free.

"Hold still," Lee demanded. "You don't want Blythe to accidentally cut something that shouldn't be cut, do you?" Blythe pressed the cold blades of the scissors against Fern's ear. Fern squirmed under Lee's iron grip. Several locks of her jet-black hair fell to the floor.

"The problem with you, Fern, is that you're a poser," Blythe said as she snipped away. Lee was leaning with all her force against Fern, making it impossible to move.

"You're going to get into real trouble," Lee continued, "if you keep pretending to be you're something you're not."

"I'm not pretending to be anything," Fern said.

"We are *so* on to you, Fern McAllister," Blythe said, raising her voice. "How does it feel to have nobody like you?"

They pressed up against Fern until she could hardly breathe.

"You are the only girl in school who doesn't have a single friend!" Lee taunted with a nasty glint in her eye.

"You're . . . ," Fern said, struggling to speak as Lee and Blythe crushed the air out of her. "You're both . . ."

"STOP THAT RIGHT NOW."

Both girls' blond heads whipped around. They released their iron grip on Fern, who slid down the wall into a heap.

Lindsey Lin stood in the entrance of the bathroom with her hands on her hips. She looked fierce. "What do you think you're doing?" she asked, her eyes focused and narrow.

"We're here helping Fern with a more stylish look," Lee said with syrupy sweetness.

"I mean, Lindsey, take a look at her. Actually, I can't stand to look at her, and that's the whole problem," Blythe added, talking quickly.

"It's like she shops at a thrift store for thrift stores."

"More like the trash in back of a thrift store," Blythe quipped.

"If people are looking at her hair, they might stop look- ing at her pleated parachute pants," Lee said, taking a swipe at Fern's oversized slacks.

"Somebody's already told Principal Mooney that you two aren't in chapel yet," Lindsey said without hesitation. "I'm sure he's got his search team after you."

"What? Did you rat on—" Blythe said, wide-eyed.

"Leave now and you might still make it," Lindsey

replied, unwilling to hear Blythe out.

Lee released her grip on Fern. She looked at Blythe. The pair stood in place.

"You have no idea who you're messing with," Lee said, pushing the swinging door open. "You may think of yourself as the class monitor, but this is personal."

"Well, how's this for personal," Lindsey said, with glassy eyes and a steel grimace. "If you don't leave the rest room right now, I'll make sure Mooney is on you every hour of every day. You won't be able to even write notes to each other without someone watching over you."

Blythe rolled her eyes and sighed loudly.

"Come on, Lee. Fern stunk up the place anyway," she said, holding her nose between her thumb and index finger and pushing on the exit door. Lindsey Lin may have been bluffing, but no one doubted the sway she had with St. Gregory's administrators.

Oh," Lindsey said as they brushed by her, "and Lee, why don't you empty your pockets for me. Blythe, leave the scissors, please."

"What?" Blythe glowered at Lindsey.

"Do it," Lindsey demanded.

"Fine," Lee said, turning her pockets inside out. Locks of Fern's hair fell out of the pockets and to the ground.

"Gross," Lee said. "Some of your nasty hair got into my pockets. I think I'm going to vomit."

Lindsey held out her hand.

Blythe blew air upward out of her mouth, causing her

bangs to float up from her forehead. She slapped the handle of the scissors into Lindsey's open hand.

"I'm sure these have lice on them now anyway," Blythe said, looking at Fern. The girls walked through the exit, and the door swung shut behind them.

Fern, in shock, gaped at Lindsey.

"Come on," Lindsey whispered, pulling Fern by the arm into a stall. "We don't have much time until the sweep." Lindsey lowered the lid to the toilet and climbed on top. She waved at Fern to join her.

The door to the rest room squeaked open once more. Lindsey put her index finger to her lips. The newcomer's footsteps echoed through the bathroom. Fern, flush against Lindsey as they both crouched on the toilet seat, remained statue still. She peered through the crack in the stall door. One of the campus supervisors, Ms. Mannitoli, was now standing in front of the pile of Fern's hair. She wore a bright pink visor and had frizzy yellow hair. Ms. Mannitoli was known as St. Gregory's most stringent enforcer. Legend had it, she once gave a student a year's worth of detention for spitting his gum out in a planter.

The campus supervisor bent her knees for a closer look at the pile of black hair. Fern tensed up as Ms. Mannitoli moved her focus to the stalls, scanning underneath the doors for any sign of life. Fern could see her squinting inquisitively at their stall. Ms. Mannitoli straightened and took a few steps in the girls' direction, then paused.

When Ms. Mannitoli walked down the row of stalls and

turned around, Fern had to stop herself from sighing out loud. Soon the campus supervisor was out the door and on her way to some other important, detail-oriented task.

Fern collapsed on to the beige tiled bathroom floor.

"How did you know Ms. Mannitoli was coming?"

"Mannitoli always comes in and does a sweep of the restroom after recess," Lindsey said, assuredly hopping down from the toilet. "She never looks in the stalls, though. Once she's through, you can stay in here for the rest of chapel and not worry about someone finding you out."

"You've hid here before?" Fern asked.

"A few times," Lindsey said, casually.

"What about missing chapel?"

"They don't take attendance in chapel. It would take too long."

"But how'd you know I was in here?"

"I saw Lee and Blythe come in today, and you always stay in here before chapel, so I put the two together."

"Oh," Fern said.

"Don't worry. It's not like the whole school knows you come in here to hide."

"Why did Lee have some of my hair hidden in her pocket?"

"I'm not sure. Those girls really have it in for you," Lindsey said.

"Don't you think that's really weird?"

"Maybe they're into Wicca and were going to put a hex on you or something—who knows?" Lindsey said, dismissively. She pawed Fern's hair to assess the damage.

Lee and Blythe had cut three random hunks off in the back—at least five inches worth. Fern now had patches of long hair and patches of short hair. A shorter piece had been cut off the front, giving her half a forehead of bangs. If Fern hadn't looked like a freak before, she was certainly closer to looking like one now.

"I don't understand *why* they're after me, though," Fern said, feeling the back of her head for the hair that was no longer there.

"They're jealous," Lindsey said, as if it were obvious.

"Jealous! Jealous of *what*?" Fern questioned.

"Sit on the floor," Lindsey said, taking the confiscated scissors from where she had tucked them into her skirt.

"Why?"

"Because I'm going to fix your hair."

"Do you know what you're doing?" Fern said, sinking to the floor just to the left of her chopped-off hair.

"Trust me," Lindsey said, kneeling over Fern and beginning to snip furiously.

"How do you know they're jealous?" Fern insisted as Lindsey worked away on her hair.

"Because you *are* special," Lindsey said matter-of-factly.

Fern wanted to believe Lindsey, but she was convinced Lee and Blythe's interest in her was a straight case of the school predators picking on the weakest of the herd. Fern's mind turned away from Lee and Blythe toward other things.

"Lindsey, do you know who Vlad is?"

Lindsey stopped snipping and leaned over Fern's shoulder so she could look her in the eye.

"How do you know that name?" Lindsey asked, astonished.

"I overheard a conversation," Fern said.

"Whose conversation?"

"I hear these voices sometimes. At first I thought they were voices in my head, but I think they're real people."

"Vlad is a very bad man. Evil, in fact."

"One of the voices said that he was looking for me," Fern said, anxious to get all the information she could from Lindsey. "So who is he? How do you know who he is?"

Lindsey looked puzzled. She got behind Fern once more.

"Fern, I can't talk about this with you right now."

"Why not? Why do you keep giving me all these half stories?"

"I'm going to help you in any way I can. You shouldn't worry about that man, though. Not yet anyway. I just can't talk about it right now. Please trust me." Lindsey's voice was distant and withdrawn. Fern turned her head to look back at Lindsey. Lindsey's most distinctive quality—her confidence—had all but drained from her voice and expression. Her face had turned pale and she looked deeply distressed.

Fern thought for a moment. There was a small part of her that thought friendship was not Lindsey's only motivation. After all, Lindsey already had plenty of friends. What did she want with Fern? The larger part of her was thrilled: thrilled to be bonding with a classmate, thrilled with the attention, thrilled to have an ally. Fern pushed the smaller part, her worry, to the back of her mind.

"Okay," Fern said.

The two did not speak as Lindsey worked with diligence on Fern's hair. Black locks fell on and around Fern. Finally, Lindsey spoke again.

"From now on, Fern, I want you to sit next to me in chapel."

"All right," Fern said.

"Is it all right if I come by every once in a while during lunch, like Sam does?" Lindsey asked.

"Sure," Fern said, unable to hide her surprise that Lindsey had even noticed Sam's lunchtime visits.

"Good," Lindsey said, standing up behind Fern. She patted Fern's shoulders, indicating she was all finished. "Go ahead and take a look."

Fern lifted herself up from the tiled floor. As soon as her head reached mirror level, she lurched backward. She hardly recognized herself.

Lindsey had layered Fern's hair very short in the back, almost up to her hairline. In the front, her hair was much longer, cutting a sharp angle on each side of her face as it tapered to the length of the back. The drastic angle—from short in the back to long in the front—made Fern's features pop out from her face. Her eyes now looked large and clover green. Her small pointed nose and red lips were focal points on her face.

"I look like a forest fairy," Fern said, unable to take her eyes off her new mirror image.

"Like an incredibly cool fairy," Lindsey said, admiring her own work. Fern, who sometimes passed for eight or nine, now looked much older than twelve, despite her small frame.

"Where'd you learn to cut hair like that?" Fern said, feeling the back of her head.

"You're my first," Lindsey said, smiling at Fern in the mirror.

"My mother may in fact kill me," Fern said, smiling back.

"If she doesn't kill me first."

Fern and Lindsey's smiles evolved seamlessly into laughter. Soon both girls were on the floor in a heap of giggles and hair. Several minutes passed before the bell broke up the girls' laughter. Chapel was officially dismissed. Fern and Lindsey crawled along the floor and cleaned up every visible scrap of hair.

Fern got up, feeling a slight tingle behind the skin of her forehead. This, she thought to herself, must be what it was like to make a friend—to have someone to talk to that wasn't related to you.

Fern was beaming when she pushed the door of the bathroom open, ready to take on the whole of St. Gregory's, knowing Lindsey Lin was right behind her.

6

the chapel mishap

To say Fern's haircut was big news at St. Gregory's would not be quite accurate.

It was a sensation.

After Fern showed up in class, her hair was all anyone was talking about. Fern looked so different, so changed, every pair of eyes was on her. Some of her classmates were convinced she now resembled an anime character, with her big eyes and small, perfectly round mouth. Others were convinced she was a younger, nymphet version of Catherine Zeta-Jones. Even Mrs. McAllister, who was a little bothered that Fern had cut her hair without any consultation, had to admit that her daughter had taken on a pixie quality that suited her.

When someone confirmed that Lindsey Lin had given Fern the cut while both girls were playing hooky from chapel, citing as evidence the scissors found in the girls' rest room, the whole story took on the aura of myth. By the end of the week, eleven of St. Gregory's socially elite had asked Lindsey Lin if she could give them a cut too. Lindsey refused, but always made sure to note that she gave Fern the cut because she was "cool but misunderstood." Fern's reputation was morphing. Though she was still a loner, she was becoming less of a punching bag.

In fact, the seventh grade was the kind of place where small adjustments could make a huge difference. The new association with Lindsey Lin had changed Fern's school life inside and out. When Fern was with Lindsey, she actually felt normal. Having a friend gave Fern a break from the questions about herself that tormented her.

Along with the lunch visits from Sam and Lindsey, Fern looked forward to chapel. Chapel now represented the locale where Fern sat next to the most popular girl in school. Lindsey would wait by the entrance as other students filed into the chapel, and then rejoin the line slightly in front of Fern, ensuring they would sit together.

Today Fern followed Lindsey Lin up the stone cut steps, as she had for the past three weeks.

Mother Corrigan stood at the chapel's entrance along with Headmaster Mooney, greeting the students with a warm smile. St. Gregory's Mother Corrigan never discriminated, always smiling brightly as each student passed by, bidding good day to all. Headmaster Mooney's role that morning, as it was every morning, was that of an enforcer. If a student failed to wear his or her formal dress on a chapel day, an after-school detention was administered on the spot. It was never much of a stretch to imagine that the headmaster delighted in this job.

"Lindsey, what are you doing?" Fern whispered over her friend's shoulder.

"Huh?"

"You're wearing running shoes!" They were forty feet away from the chapel, getting closer to the entrance by the second. Fern could see the shimmer coming from Headmaster Mooney's bald head.

"Darn it!" Lindsey said, looking down at her New Balance running shoes sticking out from underneath her pleated and cuffed dress pants. "This is my third time—I'm in for a Saturday school!" Lindsey rolled her eyes as she mentioned one of St. Gregory's most hated institutions. Saturday school involved spending five hours at St. Gregory's at the mercy of a junior or senior supervisor and Mr. Unger, head of the student recycling program, picking up trash on the school grounds and writing an essay on what kind of behavioral change was necessary to avoid receiving a Saturday school in the future. A student wasn't even allowed to do homework—that activity was not viewed as a sufficiently severe punishment. There were worse ways to spend a Saturday, but not many. "I wish there was something I could do to get out of this," Lindsey moaned as the girls kept walking.

When Fern and Lindsey arrived at the chapel entrance, Mother Corrigan, with her cropped haircut and wire-rimmed glasses, radiated the warmth and acceptance students had come to expect, but soon Headmaster Mooney was upon the two girls. Wasting no time, he scanned Fern's outfit: collared St. Gregory's shirt, trousers that had been Eddie's, and patent leather loafers that had been in the McAllister family for years. It certainly wasn't pretty, but it passed for formal. In combination with her new haircut, which had grown out a bit in the last three weeks, she looked absentmindedly stylish, even if it was all a huge coincidence.

Fern could see the headmaster's eyes lock on Lindsey's New Balances. He feasted on the impropriety of it all.

"Miss Lin, you must have lost your shoes," Headmaster Mooney said as if he were laying a trap for Lindsey.

"I'm pretty sure I'm wearing them," Lindsey said, giving Headmaster Mooney a coy smile.

"I mean that you must have lost your chapel-appropriate shoes," Headmaster Mooney said. "This is your third time this semester, is it not?"

"Actually, Headmaster Mooney," Fern said, almost beginning to stammer, "Lindsey lent me her shoes because she knew how mad my mom would be if I got a detention." She seized the chance to return the unspeakable kindness Lindsey had shown her. "She took pity on me—I'm the one who should get the detention."

"That's not true," Lindsey said. "These are my shoes."

Headmaster Mooney raised his hand, signaling his desire for the girls to stop talking. The line into the chapel had come to a dead halt, and other students craned their necks to figure out what the holdup was all about.

"Since neither of you is sure whose shoes are whose, you're both getting a Saturday school," he said, glowering at Fern and taking a pad and pencil out of his shirt pocket. "In fact, Miss McAllister, you'll receive *two* for lying. And since this is your third offense, Miss Lin, I'm writing you up for two as well."

Mother Corrigan cast her head down, slightly chagrined as the headmaster raised his voice at the girls. "You can spend the next couple of Saturdays reminding yourselves that making a mockery of chapel and lying to school officials will not be tolerated at St. Gregory's." The headmaster smiled with perverse pleasure at the two girls' plight. "Keep the line moving, please," he said to nobody in particular.

Faced with no choice but to follow Headmaster Mooney's instructions, Fern and Lindsey filed in to the chapel, which was bright with the light of morning.

"Why'd you do that, Fern?"

"Do what?"

"You just made the situation worse."

"I thought me getting a detention was better than you getting a Saturday school," Fern said.

"Yeah, well, I didn't ask you to do that. You made the whole thing a bigger deal than it should have been—now the whole school knows I forgot my shoes and thinks I'm a liar," Lindsey said, sitting down on the pew next to Fern while deliberately looking the other way. Lindsey was the one who had first drawn attention to the fact that she and Fern were friends. Was she embarrassed to be with Fern now?

Fern looked at Headmaster Mooney sauntering up the aisle. In Fern's mind, she'd acted valiantly by trying to save Lindsey from the pain of Saturday school. Yet Headmaster Mooney had twisted her act into something negative that turned Lindsey against her. Friendship was new to Fern and the idea that Headmaster Mooney had thrown a wrench into the mechanics of the whole thing made Fern terribly angry. As Fern sat in the chapel, St. Gregory's most spiritual place, she was sure she hated him.

On most Tuesdays, Mother Corrigan led the standing students in song, usually a psalm, and then began her sermon. Today, however, Headmaster Mooney marched up to the pulpit in order to address the entirety of the middle grades. Three hundred students watched him make his way up the wooden steps—steps that almost seemed to bow under the weight of the large man.

"Good morning to you all," Headmaster Mooney began, taking a sip of water from the glass on the lectern. His voice sounded deep and cavernous. He looked enormous. Perhaps Fern was used to the dainty presence of Mother Corrigan, but as the headmaster stood above her, overwhelming the pulpit with his large teeth and mustache, he reminded Fern of a beached walrus.

"I wanted to make a few remarks before I hand the podium over to Mother Corrigan," Headmaster Mooney said, clearing his throat. He directed his gaze in Fern and Lindsey's direction.

"Now, I've noticed a distinct increase in formal dress violations on chapel days. This trend is alarming. Many of you may wonder why St. Gregory's insists upon formal dress. Well, not only is it a tradition, it is also a means of displaying your reverence for this institution and God himself. I want to point out that certain members of the middle grades are defying the rules, and also lying after getting caught."

Headmaster Mooney's words echoed off the concrete walls. His gaze was so conspicuously locked on Fern and Lindsey that whole rows of students sitting in front of them turned around to figure out at whom the headmaster was directing his diatribe. Fern turned red from anger, not embarrassment. She stared right back at the headmaster, glaring, wishing to herself that something terrible would befall the headmaster at that very moment. *Maybe he'll fall off the pulpit and wind up flat on his face. Maybe something will drop down and hit him on the head. Maybe he'll blurt out something terrible, or his pants will fall down and everyone will point and laugh. Maybe he'll have an accident and not be able to make it to the bathroom in time.*

Fern closed her eyes, forgetting Lindsey's anger for the time being and concentrating on her own. As she imagined these scenarios, each seemed more delightful than the last.

"Not only are these students setting a terrible example for others, they also view themselves as, um . . . ." The headmaster's voice trailed off.

"They also view, uh, view them, or, um themselves," he continued, uncharacteristically stumbling over his words.

"They view . . . they view . . ."

A bated murmur gurgled throughout the chapel. Anticipation over Headmaster Mooney's next move heightened as his thick brown mustache contorted into strange positions on his face. The headmaster's discomfort was growing—that much was clear.

"Excuse me," Headmaster Mooney said, bolting down the stairs, his hands draped over the pleats of his pants. Fern couldn't see Mooney clearly from her position in the back of the chapel. The first four rows, however, could see him quite clearly. He sprinted to the side exit, marked EMERGENCY, now gripping the front of his pants. The entire chapel was buzzing with the excited chatter of an unfathomable event.

"Headmaster Mooney wet himself!" someone shouted.

The chapel chatter had turned into an official commotion. Wild laughter reverberated off the chapel walls. It did not take a PhD in psychology to figure out that there was no human behavior more contagious than church laughter.

Mother Corrigan, showing a good amount of agility, was

up at the pulpit and leaning into the microphone within seconds of Headmaster Mooney's unexpected departure.

"Quiet down, please." The ruckus began to subside. "Please. Thank you," Mother Corrigan said, as serenely as if she hadn't just witnessed the headmaster of St. Gregory's scramble out of the chapel with a large wet stain on the front of his pants.

"I'd like to begin with a short passage from Deuteronomy 31:8: 'He will not fail thee, neither forsake thee: fear not, neither be dismayed.'" Mother Corrigan looked up from her Bible and took her glasses off. "Now, that's all well and good," she continued, "but how do we incorporate faith into our everyday lives?"

Mother Corrigan had not missed a beat, but Fern promptly tuned her out, able to concentrate on little else but the headmaster's dramatic exit. She told herself there was no connection between her fantasy and what had just happened. Lindsey turned toward Fern, aghast. The two girls did not speak; Fern's eyes were wide with guilt.

Mother Corrigan spoke for fifteen minutes before ending her sermon with a series of hymns.

Fern filed out of the chapel lost in her thoughts. A few weeks ago, the unremitting sunlight beating down on her would have driven her to tears. But because of Lindsey's bottles, she felt no ill effects at all. Her mind wandered elsewhere: Could she have possibly affected Headmaster Mooney in that way? Was her imagination poisonous?

Fern was learning, in terms of her own life, that the most implausible answer was usually the right one.

Lindsey gripped Fern's wrist and pulled her out of line. Fern stumbled along behind as the two rounded the back of the chapel.

"Follow me," Lindsey said.

Fern trailed Lindsey up the steps and toward the library. Lindsey kept walking, turning around every so often to make sure that Fern was following behind her. She pushed through a pair of doors that led to the library. Fern ran to catch up.

The two girls were now standing in the Hall of Legends. Over a decade ago, an alum by the name of Davis Orbit had donated a sizable amount of money to St. Gregory's for a new library on the condition that the school would build a foyer dedicated to the "giants of Academia." It turned out that the donor had a very specific vision for the room. Columns lined the hallway and the marble floor was polished with great care. The gray stone walls were engraved with quotations in Greek characters with their English translations underneath. Three white marble busts stood on each side of the hallway, each resting on its own pedestal, all commissioned by the fanatical donor. Aristotle, Plato, Socrates, Pythagoras, Aristophanes, and Homer stared at Fern and Lindsey with their unflinching marble eyes.

"Why did you drag me in here?" Fern asked.

"I wanted to go somewhere private," Lindsey said resentfully. "The last thing I need is half the school watching us." Her voice echoed off the walls of the hall. "Now," she continued, "how did you do that?" Her voice sounded exactly as it had when she appeared in the bathroom that day. Only this time her wrath was directed at Fern.

"Do what?" Fern said, wondering how things had gotten so contentious so quickly. To Fern, the friendship gods seemed to be a pretty fickle bunch.

"You're a Poseidon and you know it. How else did you do that to Mooney?"

"What are you talking about? Poseidon?"

"Stop messing with me. Who taught you to do that, Fern? When did you find out you were a Poseidon? You're not really as clueless as you're acting." Lindsey grew enraged. "Do you realize how much trouble you could get in if someone from the Alliance finds out you did that in public?"

"What are you talking about? I didn't do *anything*." Fern narrowed her eyes and stood on the balls of her feet, tense. "Mooney wet his pants. I watched just like everybody else."

"You and I both know that Mooney did not wet his pants. That glass of water on the podium was full one second and then next second it was completely empty. You *moved* that water."

"It was the water in the glass?"

"Don't play dumb, Fern! Who taught you to do that?"

III

"Why are you acting so upset? What's a Poseidon? Why am I a Poseidon? Why don't you ever tell me what you know?"

"I want my bottles back," Lindsey demanded.

"What?" Fern was reeling.

"Don't say *what* to me like you don't know what I'm talking about."

"I don't have them with me," Fern said, knowing she couldn't very well give up what had made such a marked improvement in her life.

"I can't believe you tricked me!"

"I don't understand why you're getting so mad, Lindsey. We're friends!" Fern pleaded.

"You're not a friend. You've been getting help from someone on the other side. You're nothing but a dirty Blout, and you're going to regret it one day," Lindsey said. Without another word, Lindsey turned her back on Fern and marched away.

Now that she was all alone, Fern's resolve melted. "Wait! Lindsey, wait a second! I don't understand what's happening to me, you have to believe . . ."

Her voice trailed off when she realized Lindsey wasn't coming back. She stood in the Hall of Legends with the marble statues of great men as her only company. She fingered the small W.A.A.V.E. bottle of eyedrops in her front pocket, vowing never to give it up, all the while wondering what significance the words *Poseidon, Blout,* and *Alliance* had. Lindsey had hurled them like daggers.

What did she mean?

Exiting the hall, Fern ran down the stairs to the bank of classrooms and tried to spot her twin brother in the crowd. In the past, she had sometimes gone the whole school day without speaking to anybody. But at that moment, Fern McAllister was in desperate need of someone to talk to.

7

the view from splash mountain

"Sam!"

Sam McAllister was standing on the blacktop with painted P.E. numbers on it. He had never seen his twin sister in such a state: she was wild-eyed and out of breath. "What's wrong?" he asked.

"I need to talk to you," Fern wheezed, still panting.

"Can you believe Mooney took a whiz in chapel?" Sam, along with most of the seventh grade, was still buzzing from the spectacle Headmaster Mooney had made of himself.

"That's what I need to talk to you about," Fern said.

"Mooney?"

The warning bell rang four times. Students had exactly four minutes to get to class.

"I think I made him do it."

"You made him do what? Wet his pants?"

"He gave Lindsey and me a Saturday school."

"I saw; I was in line behind you."

"Well, after that, I was thinking about all the nasty things that could happen to Headmaster Mooney, and one of them was him running out of the chapel with wet pants. Then it happened!"

Fern gave Sam an imploring look. Everyone else would have dismissed it as a coincidence. But Sam knew her—nothing turned out to be a coincidence when it came to his twin sister.

"Did you say anything out loud?" Sam said, calmly.

"You mean like *abracadabra*?"

"No, more like *presto whizzo*." Sam laughed at his joke.

"This isn't funny, Sam. I didn't say anything. I just thought about it and it happened."

"That doesn't mean anything, Fern. I know the disappearance was weird, but this didn't happen just because you *thought* it. You're being overly sensitive."

"Lindsey confronted me after chapel. She was convinced that I had 'moved' the water from Mooney's water glass to his pants. She asked for her bottles back."

Sam paused, full of thought. His expression grew somber.

"I know you think Lindsey Lin is a real friend to you," Sam said, "and I'm glad she rescued you that day in the bathroom, but . . ."

"But what?"

"But . . . I feel like she wants something from you, Fern." Sam registered the anguish in his sister's expression.

"I know." Fern hung her head.

"Those bottles are probably some worthless over-the-counter concoction, and she's holding them over your head so you think you owe her something."

"She called me a Blout."

"A what?"

"She said I was a dirty Blout," Fern said, self-conscious about saying the word aloud. "And that I was a Poseidon." These names—names more mysterious than mean—had upset Fern more than the countless times she'd been called Freaky Fern.

"The girl's undercover crazy," Sam said, looking straight at his sister. "She really is."

"What do you think she meant?"

"I don't know, but if the worst thing someone can say about you is that you're a *Blout,* I think you're in pretty good shape."

As much as Fern had wanted to believe Sam, she couldn't. Fern was sure Lindsey meant those words as something terrible— that she believed Fern had betrayed her in some way. Sam saw that his sister hadn't been comforted at all by his words.

"We'll look it up when we get home," he offered.

"You McAllisters had best be getting to class," a voice said, coming from behind the twins.

Mr. Bing—St. Gregory's beloved janitor—had snuck up on them. Sam and Fern suddenly realized that the three of them were alone on the abandoned playground. The tardy bell had sounded two minutes ago. Large cumulus clouds swallowed the sun and made the landscape shades of gray. The wind kicked up, whipping through St. Gregory's open spaces. The empty swings swayed in the air current.

"Looks like you two are having a serious discussion, eh?" Joseph Bing was practically a folk hero at St. Gregory's. Everyone knew him. His plump face, white hair, and rosy cheeks made him hard to take seriously, even when he was terribly upset.

"Nah, Mr. Bing. We're just goofing around," Sam said.

"Well, goofing around could land you young 'uns in a lot of trouble, you know?" Though Mr. Bing never spoke of his Irish heritage, there was always a Celtic tinge to his voice. "Why don't I give the both of you a tardy pass, just in case Stonyfield's in one of her moods?"

"Thanks, Mr. Bing!" Fern said, grateful. Mr. Bing was always looking out for Fern, whether she was up a tree or off by herself in the far corner of the soccer fields. She considered him a friend.

"Not a problem, Fern. Everyone deserves a break now and again." Mr. Bing then took out a sheet of hall passes from a front pocket with MR. BING stitched on it, and filled them out for Sam and Fern.

"Good luck," he said before turning around. He was

whistling as he walked back toward the upper campus.

"Fern, meet me at the corner of the grove after school. We'll figure this all out, okay?" Sam offered.

"Sure," Fern said, already somewhat deflated.

The weather had gotten more ominous by the time the twins met in the far corner of Anderson's Grove. The leaves rustled in the wind as if someone was furiously shaking each tree's trunk. Fern wore Eddie's huge V-neck red St. Gregory's sweater, its arms longer than her own. Because of St. Gregory's grandfather rule, siblings of older students were allowed to wear St. Gregory's items from years ago, even if they were no longer standard issue. The sweater looked positively retro when compared to the hoodies that St. Gregory's now offered.

Fern squinted as dirt flew through the air. She saw the sky flash, electrified, and knew thunder couldn't be far behind. She'd brought an umbrella to school that day, having predicted that it would rain, but had forgotten it in chapel during the day's commotion.

"Can we go home already?" she said to Sam, practically screaming to be heard over the gusts of wind.

"Wait," Sam said while his blond hair blew into his face. He spit out some dirt that had landed in his mouth. "I want to try something." He crouched behind the tree closest to the sidewalk that skirted the grove. "See Dana Carvelle over there?" Sam pointed at a girl across the street, scurrying home with three of her friends.

"Yeah."

"See the water bottle she's holding?"

"Yeah."

"Make the water move to her head," Sam yelled, unconcerned that anyone would hear him over the howling wind. "Like you did with Mooney."

"I can't do that," Fern said, shaking her head at Sam and getting up. "That's ridiculous."

"I'm not saying you can, but we might as well test it. Just try." Sam rarely pleaded with his sister. "Then we'll know."

"Okay." Fern snaked around the trunk of the closest orange tree, keying in on Dana Carvelle. She had chubby white arms and was wearing a St. Gregory's polo. The freezing wind was causing her to shudder as she walked with two friends down La Limonar, slightly huddled. Fern closed her eyes. In Fern's mind, Dana watched as the water from her open bottle sprayed all over her hair and face. Dana was soaked, shrieking from the cold mixture of wind and water on her face. Her friends, puzzled, turned around to look at their soaked friend.

"Why in the world are you pouring water on yourself?" one of them asked. They all began laughing as Dana ran to catch up and threw one arm around each friend.

Fern opened her eyes.

The three girls walked in a row, Dana in the middle of her friends. Her hair and face were wet. Fern turned to Sam. She had never seen him look so astonished.

"Sam, why are you giving me that look? You're looking at me like I'm an alien!"

"You did it."

"What do you mean, I did it? I had my eyes closed; I couldn't see."

"Your eyes were open—I was watching you the whole time. You looked at Dana and sort of got this crazy far-off look, and then you did it. I couldn't see the water move, but it did."

The improbability of it all hit Fern like a punch to the stomach.

The sky opened up and the girls shrieked as they ran for cover. Rain pounded the grove. The sky flashed three times and the thunder rolled after it.

Without waiting for her brother, Fern turned and started running back home through the grove. The wind had picked up again, and with the water hammering every leaf, the grove seemed alive. The sky flashed and groaned.

Sam's blue eyes were expansive as he caught up to his sister. He pulled her aside and turned her. Their faces were dripping wet. "How are you doing this?"

"It just happens."

"But what do you do? I want to be able to do it."

"Don't you think if I knew, I would tell you?" Fern said. She felt as if the lightning was so close, it might strike them.

"We're twins, but you're so different from me, and maybe you want to stay that way, but I wish I was like you.

I wish you would tell me your secret."

"You think I'm hiding something?" Fern demanded.

"No—"

"You want to be a total weirdo like me, Sam?" Fern said, unable to keep her anger at bay. "You want to have to hide from the sun and have stomachaches you can't control and be laughed at by everyone? Freaky Sam doesn't have quite the same ring to it, does it?" The idea of Sam being jealous set her off. He had no idea what it was like to be different. Terribly, horribly different. Whatever she *was*, these things that she could do were slowly alienating everyone in her life.

Fern took off jogging down the muddy path that ran diagonally through Anderson's Grove. The sky burst into white flames and then dimmed within an instant. She could no longer hear her brother's cries through the rain, commanding her to wait for him. The wind whipped and thrashed around Fern. The lightning and rain left Fern feeling as if she were invincible. Her legs tensed, strong and energized. She made it back from the grove to her house in less than four minutes, a new record.

When she got home, Byron, loyal as ever, was waiting for her on the front porch. She nuzzled him as he licked her face. He was wet and shivering too, having been caught in the rain. She lifted Byron up onto the porch swing with her as the rain poured off the roof and all around them. She held him in her lap and began talking to the dog, leaving out nothing, including her confrontation with Sam. Fern knew that Byron, at the very least, would understand perfectly. She talked and Byron listened. Sam arrived on the porch, panting and soaked through, three minutes later.

"How'd you make it here so fast?" he questioned, wheezing with his hands on his knees. "You beat me by a lot."

Fern glared at Sam. She got up from the swing and placed Byron on the ground. Byron hit the grass running. Once he reached Sam, he growled and chewed angrily at his shoe. His ears flopped from side to side as he continued to work on the shoe.

"Why is Byron attacking me?" Sam said as Fern turned her back to him and walked toward the front door. "Fern?" Sam called after her. "Fern? What'd you say to him?"

The news that Wallace Summers would be arriving at the McAllister household at six p.m. on the dot made even Fern forget, for the moment, the day she'd had. Mary Lou McAllister had called a family meeting. Such meetings usually had predictable and mundane subject matters: a discussion about emptying the dishwasher more regularly, a decision on a bathroom schedule in the morning that would be fair for everybody, a conversation on what was and was not appropriate to say at the dinner table. Law and order were essential, in Mary Lou McAllister's mind, to a healthy and happy single-parent household. The Commander left nothing to chance, playing it safe by instilling four parents' worth of discipline in her children.

The afternoon sun had finally snaked its way into the living room through the large French doors that lined the back of the house. Steam rose off the wet wooden back-yard gate. A faint aroma of pot roast filtered in from the kitchen. Following Mrs. McAllister's announcement, all three younger McAllisters anxiously awaited the chance to put in their two cents.

"We barely even know the guy!" Sam said, rolling his eyes and crossing his arms. "What about inviting strangers into the house? Isn't there some rule against that?"

"He's not a stranger, Sam. He's a friend of mine, and if you don't do your best to make him a friend of yours, there will be severe repercussions."

"Why do we have to have dinner with him?" Sam repeated. "You can't just spring this on us five minutes before he's supposed to arrive. Shouldn't you have asked us beforehand?"

"That's—"

"Look," Eddie said, cutting his mother off while tossing a football to himself in one hand. "Our mother, Mary Lou McAllister, is a foxy lady." He broke into a huge goofy smile. "Mom doesn't want to hang out with you jackals all the time—she has needs," he continued, raising both eyebrows in quick succession.

"That's enough," Mrs. McAllister said fiercely.

"I'm kidding. All I'm trying to say is that I think Mr. Summers is a cool guy. I'm serious about that." Eddie turned to his brother and sister. "Give him a chance. Mom likes him."

All three children looked at their mother. Her expression had become more rigid. The McAllister children had seen the Commander tighten up like this before and, knowing what might happen if they did not back down, did so immediately.

"Maybe we just don't know him very well," Sam suggested.

"I'm sure it's nice for you to talk to someone your own age," Fern interjected. "Isn't he a pilot? You'll probably get free flights or something. We can finally go see the Taj Mahal like we've been wanting to."

Mrs. McAllister sighed.

"I know this is strange," she said, still looking in her lap. "I've been spending more and more time with Wallace. But I want you to get along with him. You three are the most important thing to me, you know that." Her voice was uncharacteristically flat.

Fern looked at her mother. She was wearing a red turtleneck and a suede skirt; her hair was perfectly coiffed, and her turquoise eyes sparkled. She had dressed up for the occasion, and she looked beautiful.

"We'll be on our best behavior, won't we fellas," Eddie said, winking at his younger sister and brother.

Before Fern and Sam had a chance to chime in, the doorbell rang, playing the beginning of *Für Elise*. Mrs. McAllister got up to answer it.

"Wallace, it's so nice to see you," she said. Eddie, Sam, and Fern stayed on the couch as their mother greeted Mr. Summers. He wore a green wool blazer and neatly pressed chinos. He would have looked handsome to Fern had she not harbored a deep mistrust of him.

"Eddie, Sam, Fern? You remember Mr. Summers, of course," Mrs. McAllister said, bringing him into the living room.

"It's nice to see you again, Mr. Summers," Sam said.

Mr. Summers crouched down as Byron ran toward him.

"Why, hello there!" Mr. Summers cooed. Byron jumped up and snapped his jaw, just missing Mr. Summers's nose. Byron was clearly trying to take a hunk out of his face, yipping all the while.

"Whoa there," Eddie said, grabbing Byron's collar and trying to settle him down. "Sorry about that, Mr. Summers. I don't know what's gotten into Byron lately," he said.

"Byron doesn't like strangers," Sam said, casting a disrespectful glance in Mr. Summers's direction.

"I'm a neighbor, Sam," Mr. Summers said, smiling good-naturedly.

"Most of our neighbors are strangers, Mr. Summers. But then again, most of our neighbors don't come over uninvited."

"I assure you, Sam, I was invited this time," Mr. Summers replied, trying to laugh Sam's rudeness off.

It was beginning to look like Mr. Summers and Sam were going to go the full fifteen rounds.

Mrs. McAllister, who had gone into the kitchen, returned with two glasses and a bottle of merlot.

"Wallace and I are going to have a drink in here before dinner. If you kids wouldn't mind setting the table and heating up the potatoes and green beans, I'd really appreciate it. Oh, I almost forgot—the roast is on a timer. When it dings, take it out, will you?" The Commander's voice was sweet and delicate.

"Everything smells just delicious, Mary Lou," Mr. Summers said, lightly touching Mrs. McAllister's elbow as the two sat next to each other on the couch. Fern couldn't believe her eyes and ears. It was like she was watching a cheesy dating show where her mother was the chief contestant. Sam, Fern, and Eddie gathered in the kitchen.

"This is going to be awful," Sam whispered as soon as the kitchen door swung closed. He could hear the faint laughter of his mother in the living room. "What if we go in there and they're making out or something?"

Fern was still reeling from the way Mr. Summers had touched "Mary Lou's" arm.

"Mr. Summers isn't going to be making out with anybody tonight," Eddie said, half laughing, half whispering.

"How can you be so sure?" Sam shot back.

"Because the Commander would never *ever* do something like that in front of all of us. Now just calm down, and before you know it, this'll all be over." He palmed

Fern's head and moved to the fridge to get out the beans and potatoes. The McAllister kids worked efficiently and silently to set the table and prepare the food—both things they had been accustomed to doing ever since the Commander had taken her high-powered real estate job.

Twenty minutes later, the McAllisters and Wallace Summers were sitting at the dining room table, shoveling pot roast, green beans, and mashed potatoes into their mouths. The dining room, the Spode, and the sterling silver hadn't been used since Christmas Eve, and it reminded Fern of drinking eggnog while Bing Crosby sang about chestnuts.

"So, Fern, I know Eddie here's a football star, but do you play any sports?"

"No, not really," Fern said. "St. Gregory's doesn't have a middle school gym, and I haven't been able to practice outside because of the sun."

"The sun?"

"Fern has sensitive skin, Wallace. But she's a really great runner," Mrs. McAllister said, jumping in.

"The girl may look undersized and scrawny, but she's got jets!" Eddie said, with every intention of embarrassing Fern. He, Fern, and Sam often raced from one end of the grove to the other, and Fern never lost. Fortunately, Eddie was the kind of older brother who never let a loss like that bother him. In fact, he celebrated it.

"And you, Sam?" Mr. Summers followed up.

Sam stabbed a couple of green beans with a fork. Everyone at the table stared at him. He was acting oblivious.

"Sam? Are you going to answer Mr. Summers's question?"

"Huh?" Sam said, looking up. "Oh, I'm sorry, I didn't realize that was a question."

"I forgot that you were a literalist, Sam," Mr. Summers said, unwilling to engage in hand-to-hand combat. "What sports do you play?"

"I play basketball and in the spring I do the triple jump and long jump."

"Ah, so you're going to follow in your brother's footsteps," Mr. Summers said, smiling at Sam.

"He wishes," Eddie said, nudging Sam with a friendly elbow.

"So, where are you originally from, Mr. Summers?" Fern asked, worried that Sam would be grounded for the rest of the school year if he kept needling Mr. Summers.

"Well, I'm from Maine originally, but I've been living the last few years in Tampa, Florida."

"Why'd you move?" Sam said, his voice lifeless.

"Nobody told me that Florida was an overbuilt swamp!" Mr. Summers said jovially. When he grinned, he looked very young—too young for her mother, Fern thought. "They have more bugs and snakes there than people."

"We have bugs and snakes here. Rattlers," Sam said.

"I also didn't like sweating as soon as I got out of the shower. The summers are brutal."

"Well, Wallace, you've come to the right place. Things

are so dry here we have brush fires year-round," Mrs. McAllister said in a voice Sam thought to be much sweeter than she usually used with any of her children.

"How do you like the pot roast, Mr. Summers?" Sam asked. Fern looked nervously at her brother. It was an odd question for him to ask.

"I've been too busy munching on these delicious green beans—I haven't tried it yet," he said. "But here goes nothing." Mr. Summers picked up the knife to the side of his plate. He stabbed the slab of meat and began cutting off a sizable hunk. He began sawing. And sawing. And sawing some more. He couldn't get his knife though the piece of meat. Sam picked up a bite he'd already sliced and put it in his mouth. He smacked his lips loudly.

"Having some trouble with the roast, Mr. Summers?" Sam asked, his mouth full of pot roast. "Mom used to have to cut mine up for me when I was a toddler. I'm sure she'd be perfectly willing to lend you a hand."

Wallace increased his effort to saw off a piece. His face had turned as pink as the center of the roast. Small beads of sweat rolled out from underneath his hair on to his forehead.

"Oh dear!" Mrs. McAllister said, getting up from her chair. "I'm afraid that you're using the defective knife! I honestly thought we put that in a drawer somewhere or in the trash. That thing wouldn't cut through a wet noodle—it's actually worse than a butter knife. I'm so sorry!" Mrs. McAllister got up from her chair and grabbed Mr.

Summers's knife. She was back from the kitchen with a replacement in the span of four seconds.

Fern tried not to acknowledge Sam. She knew, without a doubt, that Sam had set Mr. Summers's place at the table. He'd unearthed that dull knife on purpose. She wanted to kick Sam under the table.

"How do you like it here?" Fern said, trying not to look at her twin brother. Mr. Summers was now visibly flustered, but he carried on valiantly.

"San Juan's got so much history with the mission and the swallows and all." Mr. Summers easily cut through the pot roast with his new knife and devoured large slices. "Orange County is pretty homogenous—tract home after tract home—but I feel like Capistrano's an actual town."

"Have you been to the beach yet?" Eddie asked.

"No, not yet, but I want to."

"What about Disneyland?" Fern said, excited by the mere mention of "the Happiest Place on Earth." Although Fern had trouble going in the daytime, Mrs. McAllister had bought everyone an annual pass. They spent dozens of warm summer nights running from the teacups to the Indiana Jones Adventure.

"You know what? That's something that I've been meaning to do. In fact," Mr. Summers said, his face lighting up, "how would you all like to come to Disneyland with me? Show a novice the ropes?" He finished his question as if he were presenting the McAllister children with one of the finest things a man could offer, almost as if Mr.

Summers thought they would go to Disneyland with an older man and forget all the time they had spent without a father-figure. Fern wanted to gag loudly at the table. Sam had other ideas.

"I'm afraid we can't do that, Mr. Summers," he said matter-of-factly.

"Why is that?"

"Because a lot of the rides only have room for four, and so someone would be the odd person out all the time. That would be no fun." Sam said. Fern was astonished. Sam would not relent. Fern had no doubt that the Commander would be very severe with him after dinner.

"What about Splash Mountain? You can fit five in a log," Eddie said, trying to take the edge off Sam's remarks.

"I'm sure it's only four."

"No, it's five."

"Don't be an idiot, Eddie," Sam said, sounding much older than Eddie did.

"I'm sure of it, there are three seats. I think you can fit six, actually," Eddie said.

"It's four," Sam said. Eddie recognized the discussion as one wrought with unresolved conflict and went to work trying to smooth things over.

"Fern, you haven't weighed in on this important issue," Eddie said. "What's your opinion?"

He turned to his sister—only to find her chair empty.

"Hey, where did Fern run off to?" Eddie said.

Mrs. McAllister had noticed immediately. One second

she was staring at her daughter and the next moment she was staring at the back of her upholstered dining room chair.

"Oh dear, has Fern gone up to the bathroom?" Mrs. McAllister asked, her voice jumpy, directing her question at her two sons. Though Wallace Summers could not possibly have noticed, Sam and Eddie picked up on the harried tilt of their mother's voice. The Commander was panicked.

"Yes, she was grabbing her stomach," Sam said, recognizing what had happened and following his mother's lead.

"I didn't even see her leave, the sneaky thing," Mr. Summers said.

"Oh, she can be very sneaky. You know what, Wallace? Would you think me terribly rude if I cut our dinner short?" Mrs. McAllister smiled earnestly at Wallace Summers.

"Have I offended you, Mary Lou? Usually, I don't get kicked out until after dessert has been served and I've accidentally gotten whipped cream all over my face."

"Oh no, it's nothing like that. You see, Fern has stomach problems, and she's so self-conscious about them."

"Stomach problems?"

"Yes. Acid reflux, the purple pill—you know the drill. She's probably in a mess upstairs, and . . . well, I should go check on her."

"Of course, of course. I know how girls can be at that

age. I'll get out of your hair immediately." Mr. Summers tossed his napkin down on the table, taking his last bite of pot roast before standing up.

"Kids are under so much more pressure than they used to be," Mrs. McAllister said, shaking her head when she realized how much of an understatement that was in Fern's case.

"Mary Lou, I had a great time. I hope you'll invite me back often enough that Fern'll be comfortable around me someday."

"Yes," Mrs. McAllister said absently, completely dismissing Wallace Summers's romantic declaration. "I'll send Eddie over with some wrapped-up dessert," she finished. The Commander's eyes had glazed over and she rushed Mr. Summers out of the house. Sam and Eddie moved to the living room, exchanging knowing glances as they sat on the couch. When the Commander returned, her face was the color of a picket fence. She sat in the armchair and sighed deeply.

"Does either of you know where your sister is?" Mary Lou McAllister's voice was so calm and so collected under the circumstances that Sam began to wonder if his mother wasn't in on some sort of practical joke. He'd learn, eventually, that panic took many forms.

"Didn't you see her?" Sam said, unable to stay calm like his mother. "She was here, and then she got that look and then she was gone!"

"You're saying that Fern *actually* disappeared?"

Eddie asked with disbelief.

"What look are you talking about, Sam?" Mrs. McAllister said in an accusatory tone.

"I don't know. Sometimes Fern gets a look on her face, like she's a robot, and then strange things happen."

"How do we know she's not hiding under the table or something?" Eddie said, beginning to crouch under the table. "Fern's a rascal—I bet she just wanted Summers out of the house. Hey, Fern—come out, come out wherever you are!" Eddie said. Sam couldn't help but think that his older brother was painfully naïve.

"I think I know where she is," Sam said, almost weakly.

"Where?" Mrs. McAllister asked anxiously.

"Disneyland."

Fern had drifted off into her own thoughts at the mere mention of Disneyland. The McAllisters had been there over a hundred times and had watched at least a hundred fireworks shows over Main Street. There was something about its perfection that appealed to Fern. While sitting at the dinner table, she shut out the bickering between Sam and Eddie, closed her eyes for a brief moment, and imagined Critter Country, with its wooden structures culminating in the grassy hills of Splash Mountain. The twisted tree trunk flashed each time a log full of people rolled down the steep drop. The tree trunk itself had always fascinated Fern; its gnarled roots and twisted limbs almost made the top of the mountain look human. Sam's and

Eddie's voices drifted across the dinner table until Fern finally couldn't hear them any longer.

A familiar blackness took hold of her.

Floating alone in a space that appeared to have no beginning or end, Fern pawed the air, trying to find an edge she could hang on to. Then everything turned a shade lighter, and she could make out her own hands. The sound of rushing water thundered through her skull. She could feel her knees buckle beneath her.

She was on her back. Above Fern there was nothing but dusky sky. She shifted slightly, sat up, and leaned against something that felt like wet concrete. Fern looked to the right and what she saw was unmistakable: the majestic white peak of the Matterhorn across the way, at eye level. Fern could make out the bobsleds as they carried delighted passengers, rumbling around the wooden tracks of the snow-capped mountain. More immediately in the foreground, the place known as Tom Sawyer Island separated Fern from the red rock of Big Thunder Mountain. As high as she was, Big Thunder looked small and unintimidating. She shifted her weight on her legs, trying to peer over the ledge she was on.

Although she hadn't been sure before, all it took was one log passing through the white waters and into the foggy nest of thorns beneath her for Fern to realize that she was sitting on Splash Mountain, atop the hollowed-out tree trunk on the highest point of the mountain.

Her stomach sank. Panic coursed through her veins.

Fern grabbed the edge of the top of the trunk, shutting her eyes and hoping to wake up back in her dining room. The wind from the log whipped around her as she tried not to cry out in terror. The familiar landmarks of the Magic Kingdom—landmarks that had been larger than life to Fern for all of her life—now seemed small from Fern's bird's-eye view. She looked down the side of the trunk. She sat twenty feet above the rounded grassy top of the mountain. She couldn't jump down without risking sliding down the whole mountain or breaking her legs from the fall. Fern searched for a way down from the stump without drawing attention to herself.

Her efforts to remain inconspicuous were useless. Below her a crowd had gathered, all pointing up at the top of the mountain, shocked and awed by the tiny, pale-skinned, black-haired girl sitting on top of Splash Mountain, clutching the side of the trunk for dear life.

Word of the girl stranded atop Splash Mountain spread throughout the park. The ride itself was shut down almost immediately, as park officials roped off a large swath of the park to keep lookie-loos out of the way. Because of Fern's position nestled in the tree, she was easily visible from almost every part of the park.

Within minutes, Fern heard the distinct sound of a helicopter circling overhead. Sure enough, someone had tipped off a traffic chopper. Fern looked up, making out a helicopter with the Channel Seven *Eyewitness News* emblem painted on both sides. She closed her eyes, envisioning her dining room once again, trying to get back. She shut her eyes so tightly, they began to hurt.

After several minutes, she opened them again. Her first eyeful was the pastel flags flying above Sleeping Beauty Castle on the other side of Big Thunder. Tears began spilling down her face. Just as Fern McAllister was powerless to stop the mysterious force that brought her to the top of this barren mountain, she was equally powerless to reverse it.

Things were getting worse for Fern, not better. When she had disappeared to the beach, she'd been scared about being somewhere alone and not knowing how she'd gotten there. Now as Fern sat atop Splash Mountain, she couldn't imagine a worse place to have landed. Not only was she insanely high and in a very dangerous spot, the drumming of the chopper above reminded her that this was all on film. Her disappearing problem had become very public.

She put her hand across her face and wiped it dry. She would not cry; she would not give Blythe and Lee something to laugh about when they saw her on the news. Sniffing as the blades from the helicopter trumped all other sound, she sat up straight and leaned against the trunk of the concrete tree. It was cold on her back. The helicopter circled back around. She could spot the camera lens attached to its bottom. She was sure it was zooming in on her. The lump in the back of her throat began to swell. Her eyes brimmed with tears. She closed them and wiped her face again, taking a deep breath. She would not cry. She could not cry.

When she was ready, she opened her eyes again. This time, she actually *looked* out below her. The sun was setting to her right. It was a typical California sunset. The sky looked like someone had mixed together pink and orange paint—the colors swirled around one another. A few clouds picked up the orange light and shone so brightly, they looked like fluorescent flakes floating in the sky. Fern smiled to herself, realizing she probably had the best view in all of Orange County. The beauty made Fern forget her dire situation for the moment.

Fern was hesitant to turn away from the sunset and look the other way, but she figured she'd never have the chance again to take everything in from this vantage point. From as high up as Fern was, the rides looked nothing like themselves. The mountains—the Matterhorn, Big Thunder, and Space—looked similar to the way they looked from the ground. But from where Fern sat, the other attractions, like the Indiana Jones Adventure to the south, were nothing more than giant warehouses. She was gaining a whole new respect for the Magic Kingdom from her perch atop Splash Mountain. The magic, she discovered, was the illusion.

"DO NOT MOVE," a voice yelled from below. "WE ARE COMING FOR YOU. EVERYTHING'S GOING TO BE ALL RIGHT."

Fern inhaled again and realized something: She wasn't

scared. She had been terrified when she appeared at the beach and equally terrified when she appeared here. But she wasn't scared now. She would handle the disappearing because she had to. Perhaps the courage would leave her as quickly as it had come, but at that instant, Fern knew the Commander would've been proud.

Fern crawled to the edge of the small ledge and looked below. Three men in red suits with white helmets and harnesses were crawling toward her.

"CRAWL BACK FROM THE LEDGE!" the man nearest her shouted. He was ten feet away and quickly approaching. He had men on each side of him and below him, shadowing his progress.

When the man made it to the ledge, he climbed up and grabbed Fern as if her life depended on it. "It's going to be okay," he said. "I've got you," he whispered into her ear as he put a harness on her and roped her to his own. Applause erupted from the crowd lining the perimeter set up around Critter Country.

Two choppers circled above as Fern McAllister, safe in the arms of a rescuer, rappelled down Splash Mountain in the dusk.

Sam's guess made both Eddie's and the Commander's jaws drop.

"What?"

"I think she's at Disneyland," Sam said, terrified that he was right. "The last time this happened, she disappeared to the exact place she was thinking about. When we talked about Disneyland—that's when she got the look."

He walked over and turned on the television, flipping through the lower channels until he came to a live news screen with *Anaheim, California,* written in white letters across the bottom. A baritone voice reported on the scene, with the heavy sound of chopper blades heightening the drama of the live camera feed.

"Although park officials are refusing to comment on how the girl made it to the top of the mountain, you can see that a full-scale rescue operation is well under way."

Mrs. McAllister got out of her chair and walked to the television, kneeling so that her nose was near enough to nuzzle the screen. Four men in red jumpsuits with ropes were scaling the tree at the top of Splash Mountain. They looked like LEGO men as the chopper's camera zoomed in on Fern. She was clutching the very top of the tree trunk as the rescuers climbed closer and closer to her.

"Oh my God," Mrs. McAllister gasped, touching the screen. "My little girl! My little girl!"

Nobody said a word, waiting breathlessly as the men in the jumpsuits closed in on Fern. Within minutes, one of the men was clutching Fern in his arms and taking her down the mountain to safety. The newscaster cheered on the air. Mrs. McAllister gripped her forehead in one hand.

"Well, I think I speak for a lot of people when I say that I can't believe my own eyes. Thank goodness this terrible event has ended with such a fortunate result," the newscaster said after the dramatic rescue was over and everyone was back on the ground. "I wonder, though, what the parents of this poor girl were thinking when they let her wander off and into harm's way?"

"Turn it off," Mrs. McAllister said with large watery eyes. "I've seen enough." Eddie and Sam were paralyzed. "Turn it OFF."

Sam obeyed.

Mrs. McAllister stepped away and sat back down in the chair. Any emotion she might have shown was now gone from the Commander's face.

"Sam, Eddie, please go to your rooms. I'll let you know the instant I have news about your sister." Both boys hurried up the stairs. They could hear their mother pick up the phone and begin dialing.

"Hello? Alistair?" Sam had never heard his mother's voice so full of unmitigated anger. "Yes, we need to talk. It can't wait one second longer."

8

the man most likely to scare a child on a day other than halloween

Mr. Alistair Kimble rarely watched the news. He had a small television set nestled in a corner of his office that he only flipped on when the Angels were playing. Although he was known for his cool demeanor in the courtroom, he was now visibly shaken. In fact, few things panicked Alistair Kimble, but when Mary Lou McAllister called and demanded he turn on his television, Mr. Kimble was terrified.

"Bing! What are you doing here?"

A blue and red parrot sat perched on the back of one of the two red leather chairs that flanked Mr. Kimble's desk.

Alistair Kimble tried not to raise his voice. "How did you get in here?"

"Through the open window," the parrot croaked before he reassumed human form. Joseph Bing now stood behind the chair.

"Well, you really shouldn't transmorph unannounced like that. You're liable to give me a heart attack," Alistair Kimble said, shaking his head. "Take a seat."

"Your heart has survived a revolution and a civil war; I'm not too worried about a little transmorphing," Joseph Bing said, smiling as he momentarily forgot the grave news he brought with him.

"Well, what do you have to say for yourself?" Alistair Kimble said, losing patience with Mr. Bing, preoccupied by the phone call he had just received.

"Alistair, we have a situation on our hands." Joseph Bing's voice was troubled. He got up and turned on the television, still warm from when Kimble had it on earlier.

Each channel displayed the same image: a moving mass of rescue workers escorting a girl past Sleeping Beauty Castle and into the official buildings behind Main Street.

"I've seen this already—it's all they've been playing. Mrs. McAllister called me, enraged, a short while ago." Alistair Kimble's bushy beard, an inch-thick mixture of reds, browns, and heather grays, closely resembled a patchwork quilt. He always wore dark pinstripes and his chin darted out like the bow of a boat. Although over six feet five, he was as thin as a ghost. Fern and Sam often saw him lurking about town but were always unable to identify any express purpose for all the lurking. He'd be at the grocery store, but he wouldn't have a shopping cart or any groceries. They never saw him buying anything. He was just there.

Their experience with him was not unique: Mr. Kimble wasn't friendly to anyone. His pale yellow skin only added to his creep factor. His long chin, in combination with eyebrows that looked like arrowheads pointing to his forehead and narrow green eyes, made Fern conclude long ago that he was the person in town who should be voted Most Likely to Scare a Child on a Day Other Than Halloween.

"Mary Lou called you?"

"Yes. She's very concerned," Alistair said, turning the volume to a low level. "I'm somewhat surprised she didn't storm the office. Fortunately she had to pick the child up from the theme park first."

"It's worse than that, Alistair," Bing said, looking down in his lap. "The Assembly is reporting that two children tagged as possible Unusuals have disappeared in the last month. Both have been kidnapped."

"Two of the Unusual Eleven? How can you be sure?" Although Alistair remained relatively calm, his eyebrows popped up, conveying a look of general dismay.

"I've heard from two other districts," Mr. Joseph Bing said, buttoning the top button of his uniform. "Every district gives the same report. The abductions occurred from the homes with no trace, no disruption, no obvious motivation. In each place where the abductions occurred, there are reports of severely abnormal bird activity."

"We've had these kinds of scares before," Alistair Kimble replied. "They never amount to anything. It's simply paranoia on the part of the district heads."

"You know what everyone's been saying, Alistair," Mr. Bing contended, his eyes widening as he rested his hands on his rotund belly. "They're saying that Vlad is here in San Juan. I think he must be after Fern."

"So Vlad's plan includes kidnapping the Unusual Eleven one by one? That's ridiculous. *We* don't even know where they all are. Or who they are, or if they exist at all. It's merely wild speculation at this point."

"There's no reason to think that Vlad isn't taking the Unusuals very seriously."

"You really believe Fern is next? Come on, Joseph. We've covered our tracks too well." Alistair tried to reassure Bing. "We will carry on as we always have."

Joseph Bing directed his gaze toward the television, where the camera zoomed in on the top of Fern's head as she was shuttled inside. When he spoke, his voice was almost mournful.

"I'm afraid, old friend, under the circumstances that's going to be impossible."

Mrs. McAllister didn't have the strength or time to argue with Sam about his accompanying her to retrieve Fern. Although Sam was not often stubborn, when he chose to be, it was usually best not to argue. So the Commander made a snap decision: Sam would come with her to Disneyland,

and Eddie would stay behind to answer the phone calls from worried friends and relations, assuring anyone and everyone that the situation was under control without giving too much away. Mrs. McAllister knew she could trust Eddie with this task—her son oozed earnestness. Eddie was more than happy to help in any way he could.

Soon they were zipping north along Interstate 5. Sam noticed his mother's white-knuckle grip on the steering wheel and realized she was as anxious as he was.

"Sam," Mrs. McAllister said, glancing at her son, who sat in the passenger seat.

"Uh-huh?"

"Sam, I need you to do something for me." Mrs. McAllister looked straight ahead. They were fifteen miles away from Anaheim, home of Disneyland. The carpool lane was moving, but the rest of the freeway was suffering from the daily congestion of rush hour traffic.

"There are going to be all sorts of officials asking all sorts of questions when we get to Fern," Mrs. McAllister said.

"I know. I won't say anything," Sam said.

"I want you to say you were at Disneyland with Fern. You left the park and called me when you realized that Fern was missing." Mrs. McAllister was talking quickly.

"I did?" Sam asked.

"I know it's not the truth, Sam. But if we say Fern was at Disneyland by herself, that's just going to arouse more suspicion. We need to retrieve Fern and then get out of there as quickly as possible. The last thing we want is the police snooping around," Mrs. McAllister said, not taking her eyes off the road.

"Maybe they can help," Sam said, without conviction, confused by his mother's planned deception.

"After Fern's home safely, we'll figure out what to do next, okay?"

"Okay." Sam sighed, hoping he would lay eyes on his sister soon.

"Fern said she was going to the bathroom and that's the last you saw of her. I dropped you off after school, and you ran out of the park to call me when you couldn't find your sister," Mrs. McAllister said, merging out of the carpool lane as she made her way to the Disneyland Drive exit.

"What if Fern has already told them the truth?"

"Even if she has, they'll think she's lying," Mrs. McAllister responded.

"How do you know that?" Sam questioned.

"Because when Fern told me the truth, I thought she was lying. And I'm her mother."

Mary Lou McAllister may have initially convinced herself that her daughter had taken the bus to the beach, but it was now impossible to ignore Fern's disappearances: Mary Lou McAllister was now a believer.

She didn't bother parking in the lot, instead pulling her car right next to the entrance gates and turning on her hazard lights. A park official dressed in all khaki stood next to one of the turnstiles.

"I'm here to pick up my daughter," Mrs. McAllister said, gripping Sam's hand tightly before stopping in front of the man.

"The pick-up/drop-off point is just to the west, ma'am," the official said.

"I don't think you understand. My daughter is the girl on top of Splash Mountain," Mrs. McAllister implored.

"Excuse me?" The man took a step backward.

"My daughter is probably terribly shaken up, and I think the sooner she sees me, the better off we all are, don't you?"

The official reached behind his back and pulled out his walkie-talkie. He turned his back to the McAllisters and cupped his hand over his mouth as he talked into the device. Neither Sam nor Mrs. McAllister could make out to whom the official was talking or what he was saying.

"May I see some ID, please?" the official asked after ending his conversation.

Mrs. McAllister reached into a purse and pulled out her driver's license.

"Come with me," he said, handing Mrs. McAllister her ID back and opening a small gate next to the turnstile. Mrs. McAllister and Sam followed the man down a back alley of Main Street and into an unmarked door.

A fit man with wire-rimmed glasses was standing by the door, ready for them. The hallway was painted exclusively in yellow.

"Mrs. McAllister?" The man wore a large smile and extended his hand. "I'm Don Camille, director of operations here at the park."

"Hello," Mrs. McAllister said. Sam could tell that his mother was jumpy.

"I'm guessing you want to see your daughter?"

"Please, sir," Mrs. McAllister said.

"Right this way," he said. He led them down the corridor and to a large room with a plate-glass window. Several people were gathered outside, making no attempt to hide the fact that they were peering into the intense white room. Inside, Fern sat in a chair, with both elbows on a metal table. Her face was parallel with the table, almost as if she were hiding from the curious onlookers on the other side of the window.

Mrs. McAllister saw the top of her daughter's shiny mass of black hair and her petite hands covering her small ears—images she'd seen on her television not long ago—and nearly lost her composure. Without awaiting further instruction, Mrs. McAllister rushed through the door.

"Mom! Sam!" Fern's eyes were bloodshot and her face was tear-stained. Mrs. McAllister held her arms out. After two large bounds, Fern was in her mother's arms.

"I'm so glad you're okay," Mrs. McAllister whispered in her daughter's ear. "We're going to figure this out."

"Okay," Fern said. Her face regained some of its color.

"You stay here. I'm going to talk to the man outside," Mrs. McAllister said, squeezing her daughter tightly. Mrs.

McAllister left the room and Sam stood in front of his sister.

"Are you okay?"

"Sure," Fern replied, trying to hide the fact that she'd been crying. Sam watched his sister wiping the tears from her face.

"It happened again," Sam said, his voice full of compassion.

"Yeah," Fern said. Words were coming slowly as each twin tried to read the other's expression.

"You were on television," Sam said. "All the channels were showing you on the top of the mountain. You couldn't really make out your face, though."

"I could see the news choppers," Fern said, hesitating to mention out loud the vantage point from which she saw the helicopters. "So, I didn't look upset?" she asked. "I was trying not to look upset."

"Well, you did a good job. Actually, you just looked very small," Sam said.

"Could've been worse, I guess," Fern said.

"So . . . is this the Disneyland Jail?" Sam said, looking around at the white cell, trying to change the subject. The McAllister twins had often talked about what the Disneyland Jail must look like. Sometimes they figured the bars would be made of rubber or that Disney villains from the past would be painted on the walls as a stark reminder to potential theme park criminals. Though neither twin was mischievous nor brazen enough to land in the imagined jail, they had heard about its existence from multiple sources so that it began to take on a folkloric quality.

"I think it must be. When they first brought me in, they took me to a room where a nurse checked me out, and I think I passed some cells."

"Then I guess you beat me to it—you found a way into the Disneyland Jail," Sam said, giving a halfhearted smile to his sister. "Does this mean you're a criminal?"

Fern smiled. A little encouraged, Sam pressed on. "What were your cellmates like? Serving life sentences for jumping out of their boats on Pirates of the Caribbean?"

"I want all of this to stop," Fern said, her eyes brimming over once again. She was tired of being strong.

Sam tried to sound confident. "On the way over here, Mom said she'd figure everything out when we got home," he said, hoping to bolster his sister. "You know what that means, Fern, don't you? Anything the Commander says, goes."

"What if I can't stop doing this, Sam?" The composure Fern had found on top of Splash Mountain was gone. "I'm scared." Fresh tears fell silently down her face. Sam, having been by his sister's side for all her twelve years, was unable to look at her and lie, though he wanted to.

"Me too," he said, thinking of what else he could say. "I researched *Poseidon* on the Internet. Either Lindsey Lin was calling you a submarine nuclear missile or a god of the sea."

Fern looked up at Sam. She saw her mother through the

window. Within a few moments, Mrs. McAllister was back in the room, accompanied by Don Camille. She turned to her daughter.

"Come on, Fern, we're going home," she said, calm now that Fern was in her sight. "Mr. Camille has said he'll escort us out the back entrance."

As the McAllisters made their way home, there was an atmosphere of uncertainty in the car. Sam was the first to speak up.

"I don't understand, Mom. Didn't they want to ask Fern questions? Didn't they want to figure out what happened?"

Mrs. McAllister looked in the rearview mirror at her son. "Actually, Sam, they only wanted two things: to make sure I wasn't going to sue, and to make sure none of us would give any interviews," she said. At that moment, no one in the car had any desire to tackle the thorny topic of how, exactly, Fern had reached the top of Splash Mountain in the first place. They would later, when they were no longer in sight of the mountain itself.

"But why?" Sam said.

"Because a place like Disneyland doesn't want any bad press, especially when it comes to safety issues. Fern's climb is the exact kind of public relations nightmare that they want to avoid."

"So that's it?" Sam said in a low voice.

"Yes. We lucked out." Mrs. McAllister turned her attention to the passenger seat. "Fern? How are you feeling?"

"Fine," Fern said, looking straight ahead.

"Really?" her mother said in disbelief.

"Other than the fact that I keep disappearing and have no control over where I go or why I go, yeah, I'm fine," Fern said, turning away from her mother.

"Fern, I know nothing makes sense right now and that you're probably worried and afraid," Mrs. McAllister said. She didn't take her eyes off the road, and her face was illuminated by the low glare of commuter headlights. "I've already made an appointment with someone who's an expert in this kind of thing. I'm seeing him tomorrow."

"Is he a doctor?" Fern asked.

"Sort of," Mrs. McAllister said. Ironically enough, when Alistair Kimble had arrived on her doorstep twelve years ago, Mrs. McAllister could have easily mistaken him for a doctor. Now, though, there was no mistaking the significance of Alistair Kimble: He was the one and only link to Fern's past.

9

the undead sea scroll

A local news event sufficiently noteworthy to headline the front pages of both the *Los Angeles Times* and the *Orange County Register* was always large in scope and usually dealt with a disaster of some kind: wildfires blazing in Topanga Canyon, a huge earthquake in Northridge, the powerful gusting of the Santa Anas knocking down power lines, the Angels winning the World Series.

When Fern McAllister landed on the top of Splash Mountain, she also landed on the front of both local papers the next morning. The pictures of Fern were the stuff that photo editors dream of—a frightened little girl holding on for dear life above the surreal backdrop of the Magic Kingdom. What's more, the story had legs, making the national news on ABC, NBC, and CBS, as each network broadcast footage showing Fern's motionless body in the arms of a rescue worker as he rappelled down the face of Splash Mountain. They were calling it "The Climb of One Girl's Life."

Though Fern wasn't mentioned by name in any of the articles, the city of San Juan Capistrano was buzzing with the news. Fern thanked her lucky stars that she had disappeared on a Friday. Although she was to report to St. Gregory's at eight a.m. to serve the first of two Saturday schools, she knew there would be, at most, a handful of students there. Come Monday, St. Gregory's campus would be ablaze with talk of her latest disappearance.

Sam insisted that he would walk with Fern to school and would be waiting to pick her up at noon after she had served the first of her two sentences. As Fern and Sam walked through the grove, they hardly knew what to expect. Neither of the twins had much time to think before they spotted someone crouching at the outside border of the row of orange trees near the closest edge of the grove.

"Fern," Lindsey said as they approached, her eyes wide.

"Hey," Fern replied warily. Their last interaction had left Fern reeling from the sting of Lindsey's rejection.

"I'm sorry about chapel," Lindsey said. "I know you were just trying to help me out."

Yesterday Fern would have done almost anything to gain such an apology, but today Lindsey's admission angered her. Lindsey Lin had seen Fern on the news or in the paper, or had heard about her from one of the countless people who were talking about it. Now she was sorry. Fern McAllister may have been confused and scared by recent events, but she wasn't nearly desperate enough to trade on someone's morbid curiosity. Even if it was someone who, at one point, Fern had called a friend.

"Don't mention it," Fern said, walking away, knowing Sam would follow suit. Without speaking, she and Sam raced up La Limonar, hoping they might reach the gates of St. Gregory's before Lindsey had a chance to catch up.

"Fern, I'm sorry! It's going to be a long five hours if we can't even talk to each other." Lindsey was pleading, running behind the twins as they exited the grove.

"Don't you get it?" Sam said, whipping around to face Lindsey. "Fern doesn't want to talk to you right now." Sam glowered at her.

The twins hurried toward St. Gregory's. The campus was very quiet. The movement inside the iron gates was the wind whipping the cable for raising the flag against the flagpole.

"Do you know where you're supposed to report?"

"Room two hundred," Lindsey Lin shouted from behind them.

"I heard somewhere it's room two hundred, Sam," Fern said, ignoring Lindsey completely.

"Well, I'll be here waiting for you at noon. Don't get yourself into any more trouble, all right?" Sam spoke with a tone that was half mocking, but Fern sensed the genuine concern in his voice. She might not count Lindsey as a friend anymore, but she would always have Sam.

As soon as Sam left, Lindsey scooted to Fern's side.

"You're really going to ignore me for the entire day?" Lindsey questioned.

"Looks that way."

Fern pushed through the door to room 200. The classroom was completely empty. The walls were unmarked beige. There was no writing on the chalkboard. The back wall was lined with inspirational sayings like, "Do not let what you cannot do interfere with what you can do," and "Success comes to those who are too busy to be looking for it."

"Jeez," Lindsey said, scanning the wall. "I wonder what kind of new age teacher has this class."

Fern, acting as if Lindsey were not there at all, took a desk at the front of the classroom. Lindsey plopped down right next to her. Without speaking, Fern stood up and walked to the back of the classroom, choosing a desk in corner. Lindsey followed, selecting the desk next to Fern's.

Angered, Fern got up and chose a desk smack-dab in the middle of the room. She could hear Lindsey follow her.

"Just what do you think you're doing? Are you two years old or something?" Fern said.

"I can sit wherever I want," Lindsey insisted.

"Yeah, well, don't sit next to me."

"Please let me explain."

The door to the classroom squeaked open. A tall blonde with wavy locks down to the middle of her back smiled widely at the girls. Her deep blue eyes were remarkably bright for so early in the morning.

"Well, if it isn't Eddie's delinquent little sister."

Fern smiled at Kinsey Wood. Kinsey was junior class president and a star on the St. Gregory's tennis team. Though Fern was envious of Kinsey because Eddie now spent a significant amount of his time with her, Fern couldn't have disliked her if she tried. In truth, even the Commander was fond of Kinsey, whose impeccable manners she hoped might rub off on Fern.

"Hi, Kinsey," Fern said, her mood lifting.

Kinsey then broached the Splash Mountain debacle innocently, as if Fern had gotten the flu. "Eddie said you're doing much better after your scary day yesterday."

"Much better," Fern said. "So you're our Saturday school supervisor?"

"I'm afraid so," Kinsey said, flashing a smile at both Fern and Lindsey. "You girls really lucked out. Mr. Unger's not coming today. No picking up trash or recycling for you. In fact," she whispered, leaning forward, "we'll wait until the clock hits five past eight and if no one else shows up, I can let you go."

"Really?" Fern's eyes widened. Her hand had already begun to cramp up at the thought of writing an essay detailing what measures she would take to henceforth avoid Saturday school.

"It can be our little secret. I know you two won't tell. It was Eddie's idea, actually. Your big brother's always looking out for you, Fern."

"Kinsey, how can we thank you?" Lindsey chimed in.

"Thank Fern. And don't let *anyone* see you. If anyone does come by, I'm going to tell them I sent you both picking up trash around campus. You'll still have to write an essay, but you can give it to Eddie and he'll give it to me on Monday." She looked up at the clock. "Do we have a deal?"

"Yes!" Lindsey shouted, getting out of her desk.

"I'm sure I'll see you later, Fern," Kinsey said, putting her feet up as she sat down in the teacher's chair at the front of the classroom. She took a book out of her bag and began to read. "Tell Mrs. McAllister I said hi. Go enjoy the day!" Kinsey smiled at them and then concentrated on her book once more.

"Your brother's girlfriend is cool," Lindsey said, practically running to catch up with Fern.

"Yeah, well, she should have just let *me* go. She doesn't even know *you*."

"Fern," Lindsey pleaded.

"Fern *what*?"

"Look, I'll admit it—when I threw that note in your window, I was more curious than anything else. I'd overheard my parents talking about you," Lindsey said, casting her eyes toward Fern, "and I wanted to see for myself."

"Why were your parents talking about me?" Fern asked.

"My parents investigate people like you."

"People like *me*?" Fern said, quizzically.

"You know, people who might have special powers."

"Do they work for the government?" Fern asked, beginning to worry.

"Sort of," Lindsey responded.

"What do they want with me?"

"Nothing, really; they keep tabs on these kinds of things. It's research . . . like the census," Lindsey said. "Fern, I really am sorry for overreacting. I freaked out for no reason. I want to show you something."

"What is that?" Fern said as her resolve to hate Lindsey melted. She certainly was *trying* to get back on Fern's good side.

"It's at my house."

"There's no way I'm going to your house. Give me one reason I should trust you."

"I'm not out to get you or anything. I want to show you who you are," Lindsey said dramatically. "We can get Sam if you want."

After swinging by the McAllister house and convincing Sam to come (it didn't take much), the three made the ten-minute trek to Lindsey's house, near the San Juan Capistrano train depot.

"So what is it you're going to show us?" Sam said, still

feeling somewhat hostile toward Lindsey.

"You'll see."

Lindsey Lin lived in a bright white house with bright blue shutters on each side of every window. A picket fence bordered a well-manicured lawn. Flowerbeds at the front of the house showcased tulips in bloom. The perfect exterior of the house didn't surprise the McAllister twins.

Lindsey knocked on her own front door. "Whatever you do," Lindsey whispered to the twins, "don't let on that you know anything about anything."

"Well, hello!"

A woman in a yellow dress and sandals answered the door. She looked to be about thirty-five. Her resemblance to Lindsey was remarkable. It was as if someone had taken Lindsey's face, softened it up, and stretched it out.

"Hi. I brought some friends from school. May we come in?"

"Of course," Mrs. Lin said, motioning for the group to enter.

"This is Fern and Sam McAllister," Lindsey said, once they were safely inside.

"I'm May, Lindsey's mother. It's so nice to meet you both. Lindsey talks of you constantly."

Though it was clear that Mrs. Lin was extending a hearty welcome to both McAllisters, her gaze lingered on Fern for a moment, sizing her up.

"I really like your front yard," Sam said, trying to be polite.

"Why, thank you," Mrs. Lin replied, smiling at Sam.

"If it's all right, we're going to go up to the study and finish up our project," Lindsey said.

"That's just fine, dear," Mrs. Lin said sweetly. "Miiiiike!" she shouted. "Mike, come in here and meet Lindsey's friends."

Mr. Lin walked in through the doorway. He was tall, and his black hair cropped close to his scalp looked vaguely military. His face had some stubble and was slightly more weathered than his wife's.

"Mike, this is Sam and Fern McAllister." Though it was ever so slight, Fern saw Mr. Lin's eyes widen at the mention of her name. Mr. Lin stuck out his hand.

"It's a pleasure to meet you both," he said cordially. "Lindsey, I thought you were going to be at school all morning working on a project."

"We decided it would be easier to just do it here."

"Well, you two must stay for lunch," Mr. Lin said. "Mrs. Lin makes a very good barbecue chicken sandwich."

"Okay, thanks," Lindsey said, beginning to climb the stairs to the left of the entryway. Fern and Sam followed behind.

The Lin family study was spotless. A circular rug covered most of the dark wood floor. Bookshelves crammed with works of fiction and nonfiction spanned three walls of the room. A large desk with a computer filled one corner and a recliner sat in the other. Lindsey shut the door behind her.

"So," Sam said, sitting on the desk, "you told your parents you had a 'project' today? That's an interesting term for Saturday school."

Lindsey smirked at Sam and then went to work. She climbed on the recliner, reaching above her to the top bookshelf. Though it seemed out of her grasp, the book remained in her hands as she tumbled to the floor. It was a large hardbound copy of the novel *Moby Dick*.

"The secret to who I am is in *Moby Dick*?" Fern asked skeptically.

"Kind of," Lindsey said, lifting the cover of the book to reveal a carved-out rectangle in its center. She reached into the rectangle and pulled out one sheet of folded paper.

"Why in the world are you hiding one page from a book inside another book?" Sam said, getting up to take a closer look at the hollowed-out inside of *Moby Dick*.

"I had to hide this page because I stole it," Lindsey said, laying it flat on the ground.

"From where?"

"A book that belongs to my parents. It's called *The Undead Sea Scroll*. They publish an updated version every ten years or so. I hid it here because it's a special page that relates to you, Fern."

"This is crazy. *The Undead Sea Scroll*? You're just making all of this up," Sam said.

"Just hear me out. Fern, I think you're an Otherworldly."

"An other-*what*?"

"An Otherworldly. Listen. You know how there are different species of snakes or rabbits or whatever? You're a different species of human. One that has special powers."

"Special powers?"

"Yes. All Otherworldlies live a lot longer, are sensitive to the sun, and can predict or influence the weather—stuff like that. Some can talk to dogs. Culturally, they're not supposed to enter a house unless they've been invited."

"How do you know all that?" Sam said.

"Because I am one."

Sam and Fern froze, if only for a moment.

"What are you *saying*?" Sam exclaimed.

"Otherworldlies have existed for a long, long time, but because normal humans might persecute us, we keep it to ourselves. It's a little bit like a secret society—which is why I had to make sure that you were actually one before I spilled the beans."

"If you're an Otherworldly, then what's your special power?" Sam questioned dubiously.

"My whole family has the same talent: We can see events even when we're not there. I'm not developed enough to really use mine yet, though."

"Then how do you know you have it?" Sam said, wondering if maybe he hadn't developed his yet.

"I just know. The point is, Fern must be an Otherworldly—that's why she has these powers."

"Do all Otherworldlies have a special power?"

"Almost all do. It's usually a trait passed down from a person's parents."

"Wait a second. If Fern's an Otherworldly, why aren't I? Why isn't Eddie? If she's a different species, wouldn't it be like a cobra living with a family of rattlesnakes?"

"That's what I can't figure out. Either you just aren't exhibiting signs yet, Sam, or your mother knows something we don't."

Fern grabbed the sheet of paper Lindsey had laid out on the floor and began reading aloud.

"A Poseidon, so named after the Greek god of the sea, maintains an especially strong connection with the elements. His or her powers are at their strongest when surrounded by water. Powers may include but are not limited to water telekinesis and the manipulation of water's fundamental properties and the weather. Although Poseidons remain the rarest of all Otherworldly genotypes, their lifespan remains similar to that of other Otherworldlies, at nearly two and a half centuries. They share such Otherworldly attributes as an attachment to origin soil and a sensitivity to the sun. Poseidons are specifically susceptible to ulcers, esophageal hernias, and other stomach ailments."

Fern looked up, aghast. Sam looked equally shocked. "Lindsey, where did you get this?" Fern asked.

"I told you. It's a page from *The Undead Sea Scroll*."

"What does that even mean?"

"It's a book, which dates back to ancient times. It's like a compendium for all things Otherworldly."

"How do we know you didn't just make this on the computer?"

"Trust me, it's real. I would have taken the whole book, but my parents keep it under lock and key and would have noticed if the whole thing went missing. The book is dangerous if it falls into the wrong hands. Do you know how hard it was to break into my parents' office and get hold of their files? The penalty for showing an outsider is really severe."

"So that's why you called me a Poseidon?" Fern asked.

"Yes," Lindsey said, looking somewhat ashamed as she remembered her rage.

"Then why did you call me a Blout?"

Lindsey took a deep breath. "The thing with Otherworldlies is, there are two, um . . . tribes, kind of. There's the good kind, like me and my family. We're called Rollens. And there's the bad kind, called the Blouts. What you did with Headmaster Mooney and the water glass—well, normally a Poseidon has to be taught that kind of thing. I thought that someone was teaching you. That you were a Blout and you were just playing dumb."

"Why on Earth would I play dumb about all of this?"

"You're some kind of prodigy, Fern. That's why people are after you. I thought the Blouts had gotten to you."

"What about your parents? Why were they talking about me?"

"The investigate *really* special Otherworldlies. You're in that category because your powers have developed so early."

There was a knock on the door.

"Lindsey?" Mrs. Lin said through the door, almost on cue.

"Yes, Mom," Lindsey said, trying not to sound panicked as she wadded up the page from *The Undead Sea Scroll* into *Moby Dick* and snapped the cover shut. Not knowing what else to do, Lindsey sat on *Moby Dick* in order to conceal the book.

The door opened. "Lindsey, there's a girl named Kinsey Wood from St. Gregory's on the phone who needs to speak to you. She says it's urgent."

Mrs. Lin walked into the study and smiled graciously at Fern and Sam. She held the cordless phone out for Lindsey.

"Hello?" Lindsey said into the phone. Mrs. Lin waited expectantly.

"Oh, I see," Lindsey said. "No, I understand completely." The cordless phone beeped off.

"We need to go back to school," Lindsey said calmly. Fern's eyes bulged. What kind of trouble had they landed in this time? Had someone figured out that Kinsey had let them go illegally?

"Why?" Mrs. Lin questioned.

"Oh, it's nothing; we just left some important supplies and research there. We'll just work there."

"Well, that's a shame," Mrs. Lin said, her voice still sweet. "I was looking forward to having company for lunch," she said. "We'll just have to have Fern and Sam over again soon! I'll see you downstairs." Mrs. Lin walked out of the study and closed the door behind her.

"What was that about?" Sam demanded.

"Kinsey said Mooney showed up randomly and was asking all sorts of questions about where we were. She said that she said we were going to be back from picking up trash in a few minutes. So as long as we get there *soon*, we'll be fine."

"Why is Mooney at St. Gregory's on a Saturday?" Sam said.

"Probably because he wants to inflict the punishment he assigned us himself. He really hates you, Fern."

"Maybe he's a Blout," Sam said.

"That's giving him too much credit," Lindsey replied.

The threesome packed up their things and headed downstairs. Sam and Lindsey were waiting on the porch for Fern, who desperately needed to use the rest room before running back to school.

Mrs. Lin stood motionless in the living room.

"Fern?" Mrs. Lin said in her melodic voice. She walked close to Fern near the doorway. Fern looked at Mrs. Lin's almond eyes. They were brimming with compassion.

"Was it instantaneous?"

"What do you mean?"

"At Splash Mountain."

Fern was taken aback. How much did this woman know about her?

"Things turned black for a little first, but then I was there," Fern said, deciding to trust Mrs. Lin.

"I thought so." Mrs. Lin said, smiling at Fern. "I'm so glad Lindsey can call you a friend," she said earnestly. "I have a very good feeling about you, Fern McAllister."

"Thanks," Fern said, feeling slightly embarrassed.

"I *know* these years will be very hard for you. If you ever need help of any kind, please don't hesitate to ask. You may count on us for that."

"Okay," Fern said, somewhat dumbfounded. Mrs. Lin's kindness made Fern even more uneasy. What did she mean by "these years will be very hard"? Why had there been pity in Mrs. Lin's voice when she said it?

She walked out the front door of the Lin house.

"Race you to school," Fern said to her fellow Saturday school escapee.

Lindsey smiled at Fern. All that had transpired—the talk of Rollens, Blouts, Poseidons, Otherworldlies—disappeared in the brightness of Lindsey Lin's smile.

"You're so on," she replied. The two girls raced through the streets of San Juan, past the mission and the depot, as Sam trotted behind, keeping careful watch over his sister.

10

the sagebrush of hyperion

Though Fern had all of Sunday to recover, her hand still ached from the ten-page essay that Headmaster Mooney had insisted both she and Lindsey write. There was a vengeful tone in his voice as he chided the girls to write faster, pacing around the classroom and threatening to keep them even longer than was required. Kinsey Wood gave both girls sympathetic glances whenever she made eye contact with either of them.

As Sam and Fern walked to school on Monday, Fern felt a deep sense of dread. The first day back at St. Gregory's after her appearance on Splash Mountain was bound to be torturous. Fern, however, felt a little different. Her stomach had begun to hurt less. The knowledge that she was an Otherworldly, that she was part of a group, bolstered her spirits a little. She had a secret now—a secret that Blythe

Conrad or Lee Phillips couldn't touch.

Sam, on the other hand, had a less positive view of Saturday's revelation. Though he was happy there was *some* explanation for Fern's oddness, he felt a slight twinge of something else: jealousy. Why was Fern so different from him? He felt like they must not have all the information. Lindsey was hiding something. Though he and Fern had scoured the Internet for more information on Otherworldlies, they had come up with nothing.

Fern's and Sam's thoughts were interrupted by the sight of Lindsey Lin running down the street straight at them.

"Fern, I need to show you something!" Lindsey yelled, running behind the twins as they exited the grove.

"Well, hello to you too, Lindsey," Sam said sarcastically.

"We don't have time for greetings. Fern's in serious danger, Sam," Lindsey said, raising her voice. Lindsey's lanky body rose two inches above the top of Sam's blond head.

"Lindsey, this had better be good. The last thing Fern needs is to show up late to school," Sam said, trying to be the voice of reason.

"What is it you want us to see, exactly?"

"I was using my power—I've been doing that lately, just to, you know, see what's going on."

"Well, what is it?" Sam said, as both he and Fern followed Lindsey back into the heart of the grove. She led them to the farthest corner of the grove, in front of a knee-high silver shrub that grew at the base of one of the orange trees. Upon closer examination, Fern recognized that the shrub was singularly out of place amid the brown trunks and waxy green trees of the grove. The plant had wedge-shaped leaves, and Fern noticed that they had a blue hue. A few clusters of white flowers adorned some of the taller wedges. Lindsey kneeled down, slowly fingering the stalks of the shrub. She looked like she was gently awakening the plant out of a deep sleep.

"What are you doing?" Sam said, losing patience.

"It's a Sagebrush. I planted it here four years ago," Lindsey said, still rubbing the bush.

"So you like planting and petting shrubs," Sam said. "I really don't see what that has to do with your powers or Fern. Let's go, Fern, we're going to be late."

"It's not that kind of sagebrush," Lindsey said, excited and impervious to Sam's anger. "They call it a Sagebrush of Hyperion." Lindsey announced the name as if it was of utmost importance.

"Hyperion?" Fern asked, frowning.

"It means 'watching' or 'observing,'" Lindsey said. "It's like the term Poseidon. I'm a Hyperion, and I can use the Sagebrush."

"So what does it do, exactly?" Sam asked.

"Sagebrushes of Hyperion are plants that allow you to watch someone or something—to track someone even. They're sort of like a video camera, only much, much better. You have to know how to handle them—there's skill to it—but I know enough of the basics."

"Wait a second," Sam said, full of scorn. "I thought you said that you couldn't use your power yet."

"I can't use it fully. I know enough to get by. The Sagebrush must first be acquainted with the subject, whether it's a person or a place. You have to expose the plant to the source somehow."

"Why isn't it showing us anything?" Sam said skeptically.

Lindsey had regained her confidence. She stroked the bush once more. It began to sway violently.

Lindsey released the bush, backing away slowly. The Sagebrush, moving back and forth as if Lindsey were still rubbing it, crackled. A slow popping gave way to what sounded like a thousand sheets of paper being crumpled at once. The noise was overpowering. Sam and Fern stepped closer to each other, mesmerized. Within seconds, the top of the bush was alight with flames as blue as the Pacific.

"Whoa," Sam said.

Fern, Lindsey, and Sam crept closer to the Sagebrush of Hyperion as the blue flames died down and gave way to a round image. A circle the size of a trash can lid shone so brightly, it forced the threesome to shade their eyes. Fern could hear a voice, small and slight, coming from the bush. Then she heard another. Both voices were as faint as distant echoes.

"I took it from my parents and planted it here," Lindsey

said. "They have all sorts of these under lock and key. This one was labeled 'Mr. Alistair Kimble.' Normally what I find isn't that interesting. It's politics and stuff, like watching C-SPAN. But this morning I almost couldn't believe what I was seeing. So I ran to get you."

Staring into the light made Fern dizzy, but her lightheadedness soon gave way to a view of something more concrete: a room. The room came into focus as she began to see a woman take shape. The woman was so small, Fern felt as if she were staring into a telescope with borders of white light. But there was no mistaking what lay at the end of the scope. Surrounded by red leather furniture and maple shelves with dusty volumes, Mary Lou McAllister sat on one side of a large desk.

"Fern's in danger," a familiar voice boomed from the middle of the plant.

Her mother, Fern deduced, was sitting directly across from none other than Alistair Kimble, the Man Most Likely to Scare a Child on a Day Other Than Halloween. She couldn't see him, but she recognized his low monotone.

"What you're seeing is from Mr. Kimble's perspective. They're in his office," Lindsey whispered to Sam and Fern as if she were worried about being overheard.

"What in the world . . . ," Sam marveled.

The twins could do little else but stare at the image. They looked more like twins at that moment than they had before, with their faces aghast and jaws hanging open.

* * *

"What do you mean she's in *danger*?" Fern watched her mother shift in her seat and lean forward toward Alistair Kimble as she spoke.

"Her disappearances have drawn attention to her," Alistair Kimble said. Fern shuddered at the calm coldness of his voice.

"Why? What would anybody want with Fern?"

"Fern is different, Mary Lou. Surely you must have recognized that by now."

"We're all *different*, Alistair," Mrs. McAllister said. Fern had rarely seen her mother so earnest.

"Not like Fern, we're not. Fern's special—so special, in fact, that there will be people after her," Mr. Kimble said. Fern instinctively pulled her eyes from the glowing image, looking over her shoulder. Apart from Lindsey, Sam, and herself, the grove was empty.

"People? What kind of people? Why are you speaking in such vague terms?" Mrs. McAllister questioned.

"What makes Fern special, unlike most anybody else, isn't simply a difference in degree; it's a difference in kind," Mr. Kimble said. Fern noticed apprehension creep into his voice. "It's human nature, I'm afraid; someone will want to find her to exploit this difference—or worse, to extinguish it entirely."

"What exactly are you *saying*?" As the Commander panicked in front of her, Fern felt strangely detached from the conversation. It was almost as if she were watching herself watch her mother.

"I'm saying that this is no time to be indecisive. We must remove Fern to a place where she can be adequately protected."

"Over my dead body! You've told me nothing; you've answered none of my questions and instead have used these ridiculous scare tactics to bully me into seeing things your way. Now you want to take my daughter somewhere because of some perceived threat that no sane person would believe!" The Commander's face reddened as she got up from her chair.

"I came to you, Alistair, because we both knew and loved Phoebe." Fern's stomach began to feel raw inside as her mother continued. "You may have been responsible for bringing Fern to me, but she is my daughter, and if you won't help me—if you won't give me answers—I'll find someone who will." Mrs. McAllister pivoted on her inside foot and stormed toward the exit of the office on the top floor of Kimble & Kimble.

The large door had opened before Mrs. McAllister could open it herself. Mrs. McAllister gasped. In front of her stood Mr. Don Camille, director of operations at Disneyland.

"I'm afraid I can't let you do that, Mrs. McAllister," Camille said.

"Mr. Camille? What are *you* doing here?" Mrs. McAllister said, all the while trying desperately to keep herself from reeling backward. Don Camille, still in his wire-rimmed glasses, was now wearing a dark suit with dark shirt and tie beneath it. He looked like a strange mixture of banker and mortician. His graying sideburns and fine features only added to the effect.

"Mrs. McAllister, I'm sorry that I had to disguise who I was earlier. I had a lot of clean-up work to do at Disneyland to get Fern out of there safely. Needless to say, I've been waiting to meet you for a long, long time."

"I . . . I don't understand," Mrs. McAllister said, unsure of herself. Fern remained motionless as disbelief and confusion coursed through her body.

"My name is Kenneth Quagmire. I am chief of the V.A. and have been for the last seventy-five years," Chief Quagmire said.

"You couldn't be. . . . Seventy-five years? The V.A.? What are you talking about?" Mrs. McAllister's initial shock was quickly turning into rage. "Somebody tell me what's going on!"

"Mrs. McAllister, why don't you take a seat," Chief Quagmire said. Not waiting for her to react, Quagmire seized Mrs. McAllister's wrist. He stared directly into her eyes. They glazed over in an instant. Fern saw her mother's wrist go limp in his hand. Chief Quagmire led Mrs. McAllister, now almost zombielike, back to the red chair and helped her get seated once again.

Quagmire released her wrist. With a snap of the neck, Mrs. McAllister was growling once again.

"Where is my daughter?"

"You'll see her momentarily. Vigilante Bing informed

us a few minutes ago that he knows where your daughter is and will bring her here as soon as possible. Fern has been Vigilante Bing's ward for over a decade."

"No," Mrs. McAllister said, whitening. Fern whitened too, growing self-conscious in the span of a sentence. Was this why Bing had always been nice to her? He was *watching* her? "Bing? The janitor? Mr. Bing?"

"I must apologize for Mr. Kimble's insolence earlier. He couldn't provide you with any answers. He was simply following orders."

"Following whose orders?"

"Following my orders," Quagmire responded.

"Who are you?"

"As I said, I'm the chief of the Vampire Alliance."

"VAMPIRE!?!" Mrs. McAllister said, absolutely shocked.

"There's no way around it, Mary Lou. Your daughter is a vampire. And we need to bring her to our headquarters."

"Is this some sort of sick joke?"

Fern felt like she might lose her breakfast. She clutched her stomach, unable to breathe in as much air as she wanted to. Her mother's reaction only added to her nausea.

"I assure you, Mrs. McAllister, I never joke about such matters. Too many lives are at stake."

"I've heard just about enough of this. I'm leaving. Stay away from my daughter!"

"I suggest, Mrs. McAllister, for Fern's sake, that you at

the very least hear what we have to say." Fern examined the man who had casually torn her world apart; it was easier to focus on the man than on his staggering words. Even in the bright light of Mr. Kimble's office, it was impossible to detect a single wrinkle on Kenneth Quagmire's brow.

"I don't know who you think you are, making up these ridiculous lies. It's impossible," Mrs. McAllister said, dumbfounded.

"As impossible as your daughter's disappearance and then reappearance on the top of Splash Mountain, I suppose?" Chief Quagmire began, pacing the length of the room. "As impossible as her showing up on a beach with no possible way of getting there? As impossible as her sun sickness, her baby fangs, her ability to talk to the dog? As impossible as her knowing the weather before it happens? Or moving water with only her mind? It would seem to me, Mrs. McAllister, that your daughter specializes in the impossible."

The room stood still as terror began its creep into Mrs. McAllister's very being. Only a few miles away, surrounded by the solitude of hundreds of motionless orange trees, this same terror made its way into Fern McAllister's core. It was only seconds before the full import of Kenneth Quagmire's words sank in. Not only was it possible that she was a vampire, Fern thought, but it also connected the once unconnectable dots of her life.

11

the sad tale of phoebe merriam

"Fern?" Mr. Bing spoke softly, making his way back into Anderson's Grove as gingerly as if he were trespassing. After notifying Chief Quagmire of Fern's activities in the grove, he'd been given explicit instructions to retrieve all three of the children and bring them to Kimble & Kimble.

"Fern? Sam?" Bing raised his voice. He had no idea what condition the three might be in after what they'd overheard.

"Over here, Mr. Bing!" Lindsey said. Bing wandered to the easternmost part of the grove. Fern sat against a tree trunk, her head between her knees. Sam stared at the crown of his sister's head, his face the color of a ghost. Lindsey looked at Bing, wide-eyed, anticipating what might happen next. The Sagebrush of Hyperion was quiet now, almost ordinary-looking, except for the small blue flames crackling at the top. Bing made a beeline for Fern.

"Fern, are you okay?" Bing questioned, crouching near her. Fern didn't respond, still holding her head in her hands. "Fern? Did you hear what your mother and Mr. Kimble were talking about?"

"Not just that," Lindsey said, putting her face in between Mr. Bing and Fern, anxious to weigh in. "We saw it—in the Sagebrush!" Lindsey was proud that she'd been able to channel the conversation so effectively. It had been the most impressive display of her powers yet.

Fern remained motionless. Bing refocused on Fern.

"Fern, we're going to figure everything out, straightaway, you hear?" Fern kept her head bent in her lap. Bing whipped around and faced Lindsey.

"As for you," he said, scowling in a way that none of those present had seen before, "just what do you think you were doing?"

"What do you mean?" Lindsey shot back.

"Using your powers of Hyperion without supervision, without a license. You're lucky I don't report you, carrying on as if you've gone through your transmutation. There's responsibility that comes with it!"

"I don't see how I was hurting anyone. Somebody should be helping Fern stay out of danger!"

"Look at her now," he said, nodding his head in her direction. Fern was frozen in the same position. "Did you think about her reaction?" Lindsey's air of defiance vanished. "It's not right. This was no way for her to find out!" Mr. Bing, supposedly incapable of displaying anger, was seething. Fern finally looked up.

"A . . . a . . . a," Fern said, hesitating to form the next word. "A vampire?" She lifted her head from her knees and looked Mr. Bing directly in the face. "I'm a vampire? A *vampire?*"

"Yes, Fern. As am I."

"And Lindsey?" Fern asked.

"Yes," Mr. Bing said, with a bit of hesitation. "The Lins are actually quite famous in their own right, although they'd be ashamed if they knew their daughter was acting so recklessly," he finished, passing judgment in Lindsey's direction. Fern stared blankly at Lindsey.

"What about me?" Sam pleaded, not realizing the irony of *wanting* to be a vampire. "Am I one too?"

Joseph Bing was almost grimacing now. "Not exactly. Let's wait until we get to Kimble & Kimble before we get into this, all right?" Bing began to walk out of the grove.

Fern and Sam would not be put off. They wanted answers and they wanted them now. They hung back from Bing, talking in muted voices back and forth to Lindsey.

"Why did you tell me that I was an Otherworldly?" Fern growled at Lindsey, clearly wounded.

"Because you *are,*" Lindsey pleaded, realizing how upset Fern was. "The V-word freaks people out. I thought if I said that, it might scare you. They mean the same exact thing. *Otherworldly* is like the politically correct term."

To Fern they didn't mean the same thing—not at all. This *different* word made all the difference in the world.

"I'm sorry that I didn't tell you the whole truth."

"No wonder it's called *The UNdead Sea Scrolls*," Sam posited. "I should have put it together. Vampires. So is Fern undead?"

"No. Fern is very alive. Because vampires live much longer lives than regular humans, people started to refer to us as undead a long time ago," Lindsey said. "We've got certain 'undead' qualities, like lower core temperatures."

"But when you say *vampire*," Sam said, "you mean like Dracula and stuff? Like blood suckers and sleeping in coffins and the whole thing, right?" Sam was at once exhilarated and sick to his stomach. Fern just felt sick.

"Why didn't you just tell me all this when you figured it out?" Fern's tone was accusatory.

"I thought you might be a Blout, so I didn't know if I could trust you. Because Blouts are the bad kind of vampire," Lindsey said, looking to the left and right of her. "Rollens don't associate with them."

"Why are the Blouts so bad?"

"Blouts drink blood."

"What? Do you drink blood? Am I going to drink blood? Am I going to start having the urge?" Fern was panicked.

"I don't drink blood, and none of my family drinks blood. I'm sure you won't," Lindsey said. Her words were of little comfort to Fern.

"How do you know that?"

"I just do."

Mr. Bing, now ten feet ahead of the rest of his party, turned and fixed his gaze on Fern McAllister. He could see the panic in her eyes, the panic in Sam's eyes. He had been instructed to bring the children to Kimble & Kimble straightaway, but sympathy for the child who had been brought up knowing nothing tugged at him. He found a bench near the edge of the fenced-off part of Anderson's Grove. He motioned for the children to join him there. Lindsey, Sam, and Fern stood in front of him. He closed his eyes for a moment, took a deep breath, and began.

"You'll get a better explanation of this at some point, but let me try to clarify a few things for you. Many, many centuries ago, there was a divide among Otherworldlies. It had been common practice up until that point for Otherworldlies to take the blood of our human counterparts. The desire to do so was a chief characteristic of vampires and was viewed to be as natural as eating food or drinking water. Most vampires tried to do this inconspicuously, but the legend of vampires grew. What's more, there were certain advantages to this behavior: a strengthening of power, a longer lifespan, and the quenching of a desire that can't be put into words.

"It was the way things were done, children. Plain and simple. But it gave vampires a terrible name. An army of vampire hunters developed, and their main goal was to eradicate all Otherworldlies from the Earth."

"Like Van Helsing?" Sam asked, breaking up Bing's story.

"Van Helsing was a sham-artist who couldn't catch a cold in a hospital. But yes, that there's the general idea. At the turn of the fourteenth century, a group of people who became known as the Controllens began examining the Otherworldly life—a life of underground darkness, always on the run, perpetuated by literally feeding off those people much weaker than themselves. There was an enlightened resistance movement. The Controllen, or Rollen, philosophy began with one simple question: What if Otherworldlies didn't give in to this urge? What if they tried to live alongside Normals as equals? Was it possible? Could it be done? Should it be done? The period was one of upheaval, henceforth known as the Great Debate."

"So it's kind of like the Reformation, and the Rollens are like Martin Luther?" Sam had always paid very close attention in history class.

"You could say that."

"Could it be done? Did the Rollens succeed?"

"I don't think any of us would be sitting in this here grove if it didn't. The war has waged on, though, and each side thinks it's right. Rollens named those who still carried on the vampire tradition of sucking blood Blouts."

"The Rollens and the Blouts," Sam repeated out loud. "Sounds more like two kinds of fungus, if you ask me," he offered.

Fern had never given blood much thought before, but she now realized that its inescapable presence in her life would determine much of her future. Why was the red liquid so important? Sure, you needed it to live, but you needed a lot of things to live. Water did not plague her in this way. She was beginning to hate the stuff.

"Will I start wanting to suck people's blood as soon as I hit puberty?"

"Every vampire goes through a period called transmutation. We grow fangs, and yes, the desire to suck blood may be present."

"Yes, but how will I know if I'm a Blout?"

"Fern," Mr. Bing said earnestly, "no one is *born* a Blout. And no one is *born* a Rollen. In some, the desire for blood is stronger than in others, but it's a choice. We all must make a choice."

"How come you don't have any fangs?" Sam asked.

"In order to live up here without the threat of persecution, I had them removed, as almost all Rollens do. It's as simple as getting your wisdom teeth out." Bing looked at his watch. "All your questions about vampires are going to be answered, Sam, but we need to be going. We'll talk more there. Follow me, children." Before turning around, Mr. Bing fixed his gaze on Fern. She rose to her feet, looking almost stoic, her fiery pale eyes offset by the ebony frame of her hair.

Sam, Fern, and Lindsey followed Bing as he headed away from St. Gregory's toward the south side of Anderson's Grove. Sam walked behind his sister. She was walking in an odd manner, slow and deliberate. Sam imagined she'd walk exactly that way if she had to walk the plank. He was nearly paralyzed with unanswered questions.

Fern had just as many questions rolling around in her head.

"Vlad, the man who's looking for me—he's a Blout, isn't he?" Fern said with sadness in her voice.

"Yes," Lindsey said, shifting her gaze downward.

"Does he want to suck my blood?"

"Not all things revolve around that," Lindsey responded, awkwardly.

"You two must wipe clean your notions of vampires," Mr. Bing said, intentionally interrupting, still leading the children through the grove. "We're not at all like people think we are. It's much more complicated than that."

"Is there anything that *isn't* complicated?" Fern said, kicking the ground, frustrated.

The foursome had traveled out of the grove and down an alleyway. In front of them stood a chain-link fence and drainage ditch—the entrance to a network of storm drains that ran underneath most of the city. Without hesitation, Joseph Bing took a running start and hopped on the fence, grabbing the top pole. Using his arms as a fulcrum, he swung his legs deftly over the fence, flipping his feet high over his head and snapping them forward, then landing upright on the other side.

"Wow," Sam said. "Mr. Bing, you must be younger

than you look." Mr. Bing smiled widely, his cheeks spreading farther apart as he chuckled.

"It's been several years since I celebrated my two-hundredth birthday, I'll say that much. Now, give your sister a boost. Come on, then," Bing said.

Sam looked startled. The entrance to the drainage canal was dark and forbidding. "Um, are you expecting us to go in there?"

"It's perfectly safe—unless it rains, of course, and it's not going to rain for several weeks yet. Many of our fellow vampires use the sewers," Mr. Bing said, trying to bolster his young companions.

Our fellow vampires. I am a vampire, Fern said to herself. The thought made the knot in her stomach tighten. Fern ran her tongue along the cragged tops of her teeth. *No sign of fangs,* she thought, relieved.

"Why can't we use the sidewalk?" Sam asked, his imagination unable to let go of the dangers that lay ahead in the dark tunnel.

"St. Gregory's janitor and three truant students can't very well go wandering about town without raising some eyebrows. We must go this way." Bing's words echoed off the concrete walls of the canal.

"Aren't there bats down there?" Lindsey said.

"Certainly. Along with an errant Cyclops now and again, as well." Mr. Bing grinned tensely, unable to mask his stress. He yanked a flashlight out of his blue uniform. Lindsey hopped onto the fence, and Sam and Fern jumped up, joining her. They struggled to climb it together, the chain links wobbling beneath them. After a few minutes, the three were over the fence, though none scored a ten on the dismount as had the graceful Mr. Bing. With the damp ceiling above them and graffitied walls to the left and right, they descended into the unfathomable darkness.

Ms. Fannie Burrill had been working as Alistair Kimble's secretary for over two decades. Although she hadn't quite figured out her hirsute employer, she'd become accustomed to his quirks. He liked his coffee neither hot nor cold, but lukewarm. He never raised his window shades, preferring artificial light to the natural kind. In twenty-plus years, she could count on one hand the number of times he had laughed. He often worked late into the night, but sometimes he left at lunch and was gone for days, leaving behind detailed notes with instructions for what she was to do during his absences. And although he was the only lawyer in the entire state of California with an unlisted phone number, he had an abundance of strange friends with odd names calling him at all hours. Some days, it seemed as though the phone never stopped ringing.

So when Kenneth Quagmire walked into the upstairs office and introduced himself, she recognized the voice immediately. He was one of the worst offenders, calling around the clock without any regard for schedules or her sanity.

It had been a strange morning. First, a hysterical blond

woman demanding "to see Alistair Kimble at once" had confronted Fannie. Kenneth Quagmire appeared soon after. As she delivered bottles of water to the conference room, Fannie Burrill marveled at the newest arrivals: a man in a full janitor's uniform and three children. After depositing the children in the conference room, the man departed, claiming he had to get back to work.

"Is there anything else I can do for you or your guests, Mr. Kimble?" Fannie asked, blinking wildly and taking a long look at the unlikely group that surrounded the long mahogany table. This was surely the strangest child custody case Mr. Kimble had ever taken on.

"No, thank you, Fannie. We'll be in here for a little while, so if you wouldn't mind holding my calls and shutting the door behind you . . . ," Mr. Kimble said, smiling at his airhead secretary. Mr. Kimble preferred his secretaries to be somewhat dim; the smart ones always asked too many questions. Fannie left the room and watched as Mr. Kimble closed the blinds covering both of the glass-paneled walls. Alistair Kimble then took his seat and prepared himself for a long morning.

"Thank you all for coming," Kenneth Quagmire began, sitting to Alistair's left. Mrs. McAllister, glad to have her daughter back in plain view, held Fern's small hand in her own underneath the table. She looked at Kenneth Quagmire, who was full of dapper vanity. He reminded her of some of the wealthy fathers at St. Gregory's PTA meetings. Sam and Lindsey sat close by, not having spoken a word, per Bing's instructions, since they entered Kimble & Kimble.

"Does the chief vampire also work at Disneyland?" Sam whispered to Lindsey, unable to hold his tongue any longer as he looked at the man he had believed was director of operations at Disneyland.

"Of course not. Chief Kenneth Quagmire's one of the most powerful men in the world!" Lindsey whispered back emphatically, unable to take her eyes off the man sitting at the head of the table.

"Miss Lin, let's not get ahead of ourselves," Chief Quagmire said, letting the children know that Fern wasn't the only one with exceptional hearing. "Sam, I pretended to be Don Camille because I had to get Fern out of a bind. My name is Kenneth Quagmire, and I am chief of the Vampire Alliance."

"An alliance? How many vampires *are* there?" Sam asked without waiting a beat.

"Quite a few," Quagmire answered. "You must remember, as a people, we're very hard to kill." The chief laughed at his inside joke.

"So you are like the head Rollen?" Sam asked, unable to curb his curiosity.

Quagmire took in a large breath and waited a few moments before releasing it. He looked intently at Sam.

"The four of you," he said, looking at the McAllisters and Lindsey Lin, "are going to have a lot of technical questions about all this, but if you could save them for the end, I think it'll be a lot easier on everybody." His voice was strong and conveyed an authority that comforted Sam and Fern. Chief Quagmire continued.

"There are a few of us at this table whom the world would consider 'vampires.' Alistair Kimble you all know, of course. He's been head of the Grand Canyon District for decades now. I've already introduced myself. Lindsey Lin is the youngest of the Lin family, who are very important members of our community. Also, Joseph Bing, who brought you here and just left, you know as St. Gregory's custodian. He's been a custodian of a different sort as well, because of a special case. Now—"

"I think you should stop stalling," Fern said matter-of-factly. "I'm the reason we're all here, aren't I? I'm the 'special case,' right? I'm tired of being lied to. So if someone would just start explaining all of this to Sam and me and my mom . . ."

Though Mrs. McAllister gave her daughter's hand a tight squeeze under the table, the look of shock in her mother's eyes made Fern want to race out of the room. The only thing keeping her there was the hope of learning more. Although Fern didn't know what exactly she was expecting from this conversation with Mr. Kimble and Chief Quagmire, one thing was clear: There weren't going to be any easy answers. Only hard ones.

"You're absolutely right, Fern," Chief Quagmire began. "You are the reason we're here. There's no way around it. We need to discuss who, exactly, you are and what we plan to do about it. I think we should start with the sad tale of Phoebe Merriam." Chief Quagmire finished by taking a sip of his water and turning his head toward Alistair Kimble.

"Give her the letter, Alistair," Chief Quagmire said.

Alistair Kimble looked very pained.

"There's no sense in waiting," Chief Quagmire added, looking irritated.

Alistair Kimble placed his index finger on his cheek and rested it there. He then cleared his throat and began to speak.

"Shortly before she died, Phoebe wrote her last wishes down in a letter and gave it to me," Alistair Kimble said, exhaling as he spoke. "The letter should be yours to keep, Fern."

"I'm not sure *this* is a good idea!" Mrs. McAllister exclaimed.

Ignoring Mary Lou, Mr. Kimble pulled a crinkled and dirty paper out of his coat and laid it on the desk in front of Fern. Fern seized the letter, which was handwritten in blotted blue ink. Everyone was watching her now, especially her mother. Her eyes fixed on it.

Alistair,
If you're reading this, then I haven't made it.
There is a woman, a lifelong friend, named Mary Lou McAllister. Take Fern to her. I know it's not customary to leave Otherworldlies with

Normals, but I want her out of harm's way.
Mary Lou will raise Fern and love her as her
own. I beg of you, respect my wishes.

Yours,
Phoebe

Fern hadn't even looked up before Alistair began to speak again.

"Your mother," he said, glancing at Mrs. McAllister, "your birth mother, rather—Phoebe Merriam—lived in a town called Barstow off the interstate on the way to Las Vegas. You were born there," Alistair continued, as dryly as if he were reading the synopsis to a movie he was thinking about renting. "By bringing you to Mary Lou, we honored her wish." Sam and Lindsey blanched.

"Is that what the letter says?" Sam demanded.

"Yeah, is that true, Fern?" Lindsey echoed.

Every eye in the room shot toward Fern and Mrs. McAllister. This latest revelation made Fern dizzy. She wanted to go somewhere, to leave all of it behind her.

"I'm . . . I'm . . . ," Fern started. Her mother's grip had tightened like a noose around her hand.

"I'm adopted?" Fern said, finally getting the words out.

Mrs. McAllister turned in her chair and faced her daughter. There was pain and confusion in Fern's face. This was not how she had wanted Fern to find out! There was no plan, no thought. Yet she was powerless to change the facts. This was one battle the Commander didn't begin to know how to fight.

"I love you, Fern, more than anything," she said. "We all do."

Mrs. McAllister's eyes shot down to her hand that, a moment ago, had been interlocked with Fern's. She opened it.

It was now empty.

Fern was gone. She looked at Fern's empty chair. "No!" she shouted.

"Wow," Lindsey said under her breath.

"Unbelievable," Chief Quagmire said, curious but calm.

"She's teleported," Alistair Kimble said. "We shouldn't have made such a grave departure from protocol, Kenneth."

"You and your protocol, Alistair. Sometimes I find it hard to believe you have a beating heart underneath that three-piece suit of yours. Do you think we should have waited until she started disappearing right and left? I'm afraid we're there, Alistair," Chief Quagmire said. "She had to find out sooner or later."

"What have you people done?" Mrs. McAllister demanded. Kenneth Quagmire got up almost immediately and walked behind Mrs. McAllister. Putting his hands on her shoulders, he started to speak.

"You *will* calm down, Mrs. McAllister. We still have a

few things to discuss and we *will* find Fern."

"Fern's adopted?" Sam asked.

"Yes," Chief Quagmire said, looking at Sam briefly before turning back to Mrs. McAllister. "You must hear me out for one minute. We will find her momentarily. Now, what makes Fern particularly unusual," Chief Quagmire continued, "is that she is the first Otherworldly on record to be raised by Normals." Chief Quagmire scanned the table. "Ordinarily, it is our policy to put orphans with Otherworldly families, without exception."

Sam looked at his mother, whose expressionless face blinked now and then, but otherwise seemed dead. Chief Quagmire must have put his mother in a trance.

"Sam and Mary Lou, you are two of only a handful of Normals who know about us Otherworldlies. We're putting trust in both of you by telling you all this. We've lived alongside Normals without major incident for centuries. I'd hate for that balance to be disrupted," Chief Quagmire said, looking only at Sam.

"We have to find Fern!" Sam said. "She's got to be really upset." Chief Quagmire looked at him and within the instant, Sam fell silent, with a dull look in his eyes.

"Vampires have evolved, much like humans, into a sophisticated species. We are much different from what you may think of when you think of a vampire. Which is why, today, there is a movement to abandon the term *vampire* altogether. It's too laden with terrible baggage. We are peaceful, for the most part," Quagmire continued, reaching to his neck and loosening his dark green tie. "But just as there are humans of questionable moral fiber, there are also Otherworldlies with similar qualities."

Mr. Kimble had not spoken a word and was stewing in his seat.

"Fern's ability to teleport—the reason she's been disappearing," Chief Quagmire said, "sets her apart from almost every vampire in existence. It's an ability that we've never seen before. These corrupt vampires, Blouts, as they are commonly known," he continued, clearing his throat, "may want to eliminate Fern because she's different. They'll view her as a threat.

"Her appearance at Disneyland on TV," he continued, running his fingers through his glossy black hair, "has made her a prime target."

With that, Chief Kenneth Quagmire released Mrs. McAllister from his gaze. Her head snapped back and the color returned to her face. She looked around, skeptically eyeing Quagmire as he returned to his chair. Lindsey's mouth opened; she tried to speak, but couldn't.

Mrs. McAllister bolted toward the door. Sam's face returned to normal as he quickly followed. They pushed the conference door open.

"Where are you going?" Mr. Kimble said.

"We're going to find Fern," Mrs. McAllister said.

"I'll bet you one thing," Sam said, narrowing his eyes at the two men. "She's certainly not gonna wander back here."

Lindsey Lin jumped up and stood next to Sam.

"I'm sorry that things have worked out this way, but you've got to remember that we're on your side," Chief Quagmire said.

"I'll be the judge of that," Mrs. McAllister said, stepping in front of Sam and Lindsey. "And I'm afraid the verdict's still out." Mrs. McAllister didn't stop the door from slamming shut behind her.

Mr. Kimble and Chief Quagmire sat motionless in the conference room.

"They'll find her, Alistair," Chief Quagmire said.

"Before Vlad does?" Mr. Kimble said, holding back some of his fear.

"Vlad doesn't know who Fern is for sure. We have time."

"I'm going to get in contact with Bing and determine if he can't figure out where she teleported to," Mr. Kimble said.

"Well, I've got to get back to headquarters. Please keep me posted," Chief Quagmire said, abruptly rising from his seat.

Without fanfare, without a red carpet, a motorcade, or so much as a good-bye, Kenneth Quagmire, the highest-ranking member of the Rollen Assembly, the man in charge of the Vampire Alliance, walked out of the offices of Kimble & Kimble.

Slim shards of sunlight slipped through the blinds, marking the hardwood floor with a gratelike pattern.

"Mr. Kimble?"

Alistair Kimble, previously deep in thought, looked up from his desk. Fannie Burrill stood in front of him.

"Yes, Fannie? What is it?"

"Was that the girl from Disneyland? The one on the news?" she asked timidly. "In the conference room before?"

"You know that's confidential. A very sensitive case, in fact," Mr. Kimble said.

"She's a cute little thing," Fannie said, rather timidly. "She looked very pale though. Is she going to be okay?"

"I don't know," Kimble said, in an uncharacteristically candid moment.

12

the day the water flew out of the pool

"When he looked at me, I couldn't do or say any-thing," Sam said. Recounting the incident gave him a slight chill. "It was like I was watching a movie of myself."

"I felt the same way," Mrs. McAllister said, still amazed.

Lindsey ran into the living room, breathless.

"That's because," she said, breathing heavily, "Chief Quagmire's one of the most powerful Hermes around."

"What?" Sam asked.

"He's a Hermes."

"Another one of your stupid names."

"It's not *my* stupid name. It's got history and it's the

way everything is categorized. Everything has a name, Sam. You've just never heard these before, so you think they're strange. Anyway, a Hermes is a very rare and powerful type of vampire. From what my parents say, Chief Quagmire's a whiz at mind control and a bunch of other things." Lindsey sank on the couch. Mrs. McAllister, Lindsey, and Sam had reassembled in the McAllister living room, having searched San Juan for the last three hours.

"Did you find anything at the grove, Lindsey?" Mrs. McAllister said, changing the subject.

"I checked every inch of it," Lindsey said. "She's definitely not there."

"I looped past Swallow's Inn and through the mission. She's not there," Sam offered. "And Byron's not here either; I bet they're together. Those two are always together."

"I've been yelling her name through the whole neighborhood," Lindsey added.

"Maybe she doesn't want to be found," Sam said, almost to himself.

"Did you check the TV?" Lindsey said.

"Yes," Mrs. McAllister responded. "No sign of her there, thank God." Mrs. McAllister's face was lined with worry.

"I'm sure she's around here somewhere," Lindsey said. "I think she teleported on purpose this time."

"I know you're against them, but maybe it's time you

got Fern a cell phone," Sam said to the Commander. "If she's going to keep disappearing like this, it might come in handy."

"That is not a helpful comment right now."

The three sat on the leather couches, staring at each other. The house phone rang, cutting through the tension in the room. Mrs. McAllister got up and went into the kitchen to answer it.

After a minute or two, she returned.

"That was Mrs. Larkey," Mrs. McAllister said.

"The Freak Doctor?" Lindsey blurted out.

"That's what you call her? Well, she wanted to let me know that Fern hadn't come to school. Because kids had seen her outside of school, Mrs. Larkey wanted to make sure Fern was all right," the Commander said.

"Yeah, we were almost inside the gate when Lindsey pulled us back to the grove," Sam said.

"Wait," Lindsey said. "She called *just* to ask if Fern was really absent? Isn't that strange?"

"It did seem odd," the Commander answered.

"What if Larkey has something to do with the Blouts looking for Fern?" Sam said, concerned. "What did you tell her?"

"I told Mrs. Larkey that Fern was sick."

"Mrs. Larkey's new to St. Gregory's, right? Didn't they hire her this year?" Lindsey questioned.

"Yes," Sam answered.

The front door opened. Eddie raced into the living

room, out of breath. Though Mrs. McAllister did not tell Eddie everything, she did inform him that Fern was missing as soon as he came home from school. Eddie vowed to cover every inch of San Juan looking for Fern until he found her.

"Guys!"

"What is it, Eddie?" the Commander said, rising from the couch in one movement.

"Mr. Summers's house!" Eddie said, pointing across the street. "It's on fire!"

Most houses in the neighborhood had switched to Spanish tile roofs because the wooden shingles of several older houses had gone up in a blaze fanned by the Santa Ana winds the previous summer. Mr. Wallace Summers, though, was probably unaware of this when he moved in.

The gathering broke up as everyone sprinted to the front yard. Sure enough, red flames danced along the wood-shingled roof of the house. Hot glowing ash floated in the air, landing on roofs up and down the streets. If one ember ignited a dry piece of wood, the whole neighborhood would erupt in flames.

Lindsey, Eddie, Sam, and Mrs. McAllister convened across the street from the blaze as a steady stream of dark smoke curled up to the sky. The street was still; apparently no one else was home to see the blaze.

"Someone go in and call nine-one-one," the Commander ordered.

"I'll do it," Eddie said, running back toward the

house. The flames grew taller as the fire swallowed more shingles whole.

Sam was the first to see the water splash onto the rooftop.

"Look!" Sam said, pointing at the sky. A perfect arc of water about a foot wide flowed above them and landed on the burning roof, dousing the flames. It was as if they were standing underneath a rainbow of water flowing through the sky. Spray from the arc sprinkled down on the McAllisters and Lindsey. Sam followed the stream of water from the rooftop with his eyes. It disappeared behind the fence in the McAllisters' backyard, which Sam reasoned was an odd location for a fire truck.

The flames dancing on Wallace Summers's rooftop dwindled as the steady stream of water drenched the shingles. Sam ran to the fence, hopping up and onto the upper support beam of the wooden planks.

"The water's flying out of the pool!" Sam exclaimed.

The cascading stream above Mrs. McAllister mesmerized her. It could have very well come from a hose, a powerful hose with an extremely wide nozzle, back behind the fence. She rushed over to Sam to see for herself.

"Oh . . . my . . . Lord." Her pumps sank into the muddy planter just beyond the fence.

She turned back around. A few neighbors had come out of their houses and had wandered into the middle of the street. Lindsey was now across the road with Mr. Summers's garden hose in her clutches. The stream of water had disappeared; the doused rooftop sizzled and smoked, but the fire had been extinguished.

"The water pressure was really good," Lindsey yelled, holding out the hose after Doris Grady asked how she had managed to put out the fire. Mrs. McAllister took a deep breath and crossed the street.

"Good thinking, Lindsey—turning the hose on the roof like that before things got out of control." Mary Lou winked.

Sam marveled for a minute at the Commander, who was in full form. He was confident that she would handle the situation. In the distance, he could hear the frantic whirring of sirens. The fire department would arrive soon, but Sam had other things on his mind. Slipping back into the house, he ran to the backyard. Water lapped in the pool, which was now half empty.

Sam began a careful inspection of every tree, leaf by leaf, that lined the fence next to the Gradys' yard. When he got to the oak in the southeast corner of the lot, he stopped.

There they were: the red rubber bottoms of Fern's slip-on Vans. He could make out Fern's school uniform among the leaves. Fern had climbed high up before, but never this high. Sam estimated her height at around thirty feet. He caught sight of Byron's shaggy white tail right beside his sister. Fern had managed to coax the dog up with her once again.

"Fern, I know you're up there," he yelled.

He received no response.

"I knew it had to be you—that you must be in a tree— or how else would you have been able to see both the fire and the water?"

"Why don't you just leave me alone?" Fern said, her voice drifting down to Sam.

"Fern, please come down! I want to talk to you," Sam said, pleading with his twin sister.

"Go away!" Fern yelled.

"I know you're the one that saved Mr. Summers's house. You moved the water, just like you did with Dana Carvelle. Only it was a lot more water this time," Sam said, turning around toward the half-empty pool, amazed at just how much water his sister had used. He turned back around and squinted at the tree. The breeze rustled the leaves.

"Fern?" He could no longer make out his sister. "Fern, where'd you go?" Byron whimpered, having been left all alone, thirty feet up in an oak tree. Fern McAllister had disappeared for the second time that day.

When Fern had teleported from the offices of Kimble & Kimble to the oak tree in the backyard, she had developed a slight headache. When she reappeared this time, her head ached so much she thought it might split right down the middle. Part of her figured this would be a fitting end to what was turning out to be a pretty miserable week.

She was in the fetal position, practically eating dirt. The

last thing she remembered thinking to herself as she hid in the oak tree was *I want to be anywhere but here.* Anywhere but here, it turned out, was in a far-flung corner of Anderson's Grove. She needed to get her ability to teleport under control, and she needed to do it quickly.

In the distance, she could hear the faint cry of Lindsey Lin calling her name. Coughing as she rose to her feet, Fern sensed someone standing behind her.

"I have been waiting," said a voice so low it sounded like the deep rumbling of an earthquake.

Fern almost jumped out of her skin. She stumbled into the trunk of a nearby tree. A few oranges dropped to the ground around her from the impact she'd had on the trunk. She looked down, only to be greeted by several dead birds gathered under the tree.

"No!" she shrieked, unable to contain her terror, backing away from the oranges and birds.

She turned around and caught sight of a man, over seven feet tall, towering above her. A dark goatee, neatly trimmed, framed his thin red lips. Shiny locks of black hair fell to his shoulders. His eyes were the color of wet clay and his fingernails were long and clear. He wore a black bow tie and dress shirt, red suspenders, and a coat with black coattails. A gold pin in the shape of a star shone from his lapel. Fern rubbed her eyes to make sure her rough landing hadn't caused her to hallucinate. The lanky man extended his left hand. On his wrist he wore a golden watch, polished and shiny. Fern recognized the watch immediately, though she made no motion to shake the man's hand.

"I am Vlad. Pleased to meet you," he said. His eyes looked like dark gray clouds with no delineation between pupil and iris. The deep chill in his voice made Fern's knees buckle.

"Do not be afraid, Fern. I am not going to hurt you." The man smiled, revealing gleaming white teeth flanked by a pair of magnificent fangs. He was very formal in tone and his speech had a thickness to it. Fern couldn't place what kind of accent he had; it was unlike any she had heard before.

"That *watch*," Fern muttered, thinking aloud.

"You recognize it?" Vlad peered at Fern. Fern's first instinct was to run and get as far away from this man as possible. However, he was twice her size, and she was sure if he wanted to hurt her, there was little she could do to stop it.

"I've seen it before," Fern said, unsure how much to reveal. The man felt oddly familiar to her, though. "You're a vampire?"

"Yes," Vlad replied, almost gently. This was the first vampire Fern had met with actual fangs.

"Why are you here?" Fern asked. The dark man's head was nearly at the level of the top of the blossoming trees.

"I have been searching for you for a long time, Fern." Vlad's voice was low like a voice that narrated a movie. "When you arrived at Pirate's Cove, I knew you were the girl I had been looking for all these years," he said.

"So that *was* you?" Fern said.

"Me borrowing someone else's body, yes. I was making my annual visit to the cove. Of course, I tend to raise a lot of suspicion looking the way I do, so I had to change while I was exploring the cove."

"You sound so different now," Fern said.

"Unfortunately, if I borrow a body, I also inherit the voice. So I was forced to talk to you in that ridiculous manner." Vlad gave Fern a good-natured smile.

"You can morph into other people?" Fern felt nervous energy course through her at the thought that the beach bum was actually Vlad—that she had talked to him without knowing it.

"For a short time, yes. I suppose you could describe it that way."

"But you're wearing the same watch now," Fern said. "You changed into all his other clothes."

"You are very observant for one so young." Vlad smiled at Fern the way a proud father would. "Well, I always make sure I take my watch off and put it back on after I've morphed. It was a gift from my father. It has great sentimental value."

Fern couldn't avert her eyes from Vlad, or the real Vlad. Although there was something about him that inspired mistrust, his fangs, although sharp, didn't seem threatening. He looked like he belonged in a Charlotte Brontë novel.

Fern's hands were trembling. She didn't know if Vlad intended to harm her or not. He hadn't harmed her the first time they met, Fern reasoned. He might have some answers for her.

"Why does everyone think you're looking for me? Are you looking for me?"

"I knew your mother," Vlad said intensely.

"My mother?"

"Your true mother. Phoebe Merriam."

Fern was speechless.

"Fern," Vlad said, "there are certain things you must know."

"Who are you?"

"That is unimportant—it is who *you* are that I am concerned with."

"Well, who am I, then?"

"This," Vlad said, opening up his coat and taking something from his breast pocket, "is the best clue I have to who you are."

He held a piece of paper out in front of Fern. It was a simple drawing of a rock within a cave. The rock was black, like obsidian, and appeared to be about the size of an ostrich egg. The cave was shaded with brown pencil. It was an exact replica of the drawing she had seen in the disappearing chamber at Pirate's Cove.

"What you are looking at is the Omphalos Oracle," Vlad said, pointing to the center of the sketch, right at the rock. "Also known as Rhea's Rock." Vlad placed the paper in Fern's hand. She took it. "The true extent of its powers have never been tested, but it is believed to be the most powerful oracle in all the world." His words and tone were dramatic.

"What's that got to do with me?"

"The stone tells the future, Fern. What it has predicted has always come to pass." Vlad paused. "The last known prophecy predicted by the stone, according to most estimations, is about someone much like you," he said, his eyes flickering.

"Me?"

"You are unlike any other vampire that has come before you."

"It says all that on this?" Fern questioned, holding the drawing up to Vlad.

"It takes some interpreting."

"I don't understand," Fern said, confused and scared.

"Thousands of years ago, Rhea's Rock predicted a day in the future when the heavens would meet the earth. On that day, according to the prophecy, any vampire born was to have a special significance—a significance that could not possibly be measured."

"When the heavens meet the earth?" Fern said, lost.

"A little over twelve years ago, there were dozens of severe electrical storms, all occurring at the exact same time, spanning every part of the globe. The heavens met the earth on that day, you see?" Vlad said, patiently. "Vampire births are extraordinarily rare. But eleven vampires were born during the storms and they all seemed to have characteristics predicted by the Rock. All were easy births, and all the infants were born with a caul. People began to believe that the prophecy had been fulfilled. These children were thought of as somehow special, though no one was sure how. They were called the Unusual Eleven. Of course, there are still many people who feel that this was not a true fulfillment of the prophecy—that the so-called Unusual Eleven are no more unusual than any vampire. Some refer to it as the Unusual Hoax."

"And you think I'm one of these children? I'm an Unusual?"

"You have been disappearing, have you not?"

"Well, yes."

"Every one of the Unusual Eleven, it is said, will have the ability to 'move without moving.' Teleporting, you see? No vampire that has come before you can do such a thing. No human being, for that matter. The Unusual Eleven will to have the ability to lead thousands, and to calm any beast, including the hecatonchires."

"The heca-what?"

"Hecatonchires. It is a rather fearsome creature. Very rare. I hope you never have the misfortune of running into one."

There was silence between them.

"Do you not realize, young Fern?" Vlad almost seemed anxious.

"Realize what?"

"You will grow to be one of the most powerful vampires the world has ever seen! Everyone will seek to influence you."

Fern blinked hard. The weight of Vlad's words was almost more than she could bear. She stumbled backward and sat on the dirt beneath her.

"Why . . . why are you telling me all this?"

"Because your life is changing, and you cannot continue to live with these Normals. You do not belong among these people anymore, Fern."

"This is my home," Fern said, almost as if she were asking a question.

"Those Rollens—Alistair Kimble, Kenneth Quagmire, Joseph Bing. They are not trying to protect you. They only want to promote stability—to preserve the pathetic little lives they have carved out for themselves. They file off their fangs as soon as they go through transmutation. They hide who they are, desperate to appear more like Normals. Mark my words, they will betray you to protect themselves and preserve their precious assimilation!" Vlad's voice hardened as he lowered his head and narrowed his eyes.

"And the McAllisters? Do you honestly think they are going to love you and care for you now that they know the truth about you? Normals have never understood our kind. They are incapable of seeing us as anything more than beasts. It will not be long before even your own mother looks at you as she would a monster!" Vlad sneered once more, flashing his white fangs. "You cannot love something that terrifies you!"

"That isn't true!" Fern exclaimed.

"I have not come to upset you," Vlad said, much calmer now. "But there is a reason you teleported here, Fern, in front of me. Deep within you, you know where you belong. You must be tired of having no one you can trust to tell you the truth. I know this will not be painless, but you are a Blout just as your mother was a Blout."

"A Blout?" Fern got up, her heart pounding. "My *mother*?" According to everything Fern had heard, Blouts were terrible creatures. Was that why Lindsey had assumed she was one? Blouts were also very dangerous. How dangerous was Vlad? Why hadn't he tried to hurt her yet? She was poised to start running.

"There is nothing to be done now, Fern," Vlad said. "I will give you time—time to think and choose. At some point you will realize that you are nothing but a burden to your family, even if they decide not to throw you out into the cold after they realize the full extent of your differences."

Vlad made it seem as if Fern had been clinging to her past life by the brittle tips of her fingernails. "I don't believe you about any of this!" His bleak portrait of her future pushed her beyond reason. She was near tears now. "I don't want to choose anything."

"I am afraid you must, dear child," Vlad said. He placed his large hand on Fern's head. Fern's head tingled.

"Sometimes we have no choice but to make a choice. This has been your fate since birth. You can neither deny nor escape it!" Vlad's eyes misted over and turned into shimmering opaque pools.

The terrors that haunt regular children—boogie monsters, kidnappers, bullies—they were far in the distance now. Here, in Anderson's Grove, a monster with sharp fangs was real and so much more terrifying than the worst thing Fern's imagination could invent. Worse still, a part of her wondered if this man was the only one giving her the truth.

Lindsey Lin's voice was growing nearer. Fern sensed that she was in the grove.

"I will be back in one month's time," Vlad said. With a flash of light, Vlad was gone. A large California condor stood in his place, squawking loudly and expanding its large black wings before flying away. It was the same bird that had appeared at the window the previous week. Fern shuddered. Vlad had been watching her. She folded the drawing of Rhea's Rock and stuck it in the waistband of her pleated skirt.

Vlad soared high above San Juan Capistrano, hundreds of feet above its red tile roofs and chestnut hills. He glided through the air, pleased, knowing he had planted the seed of doubt in Fern's McAllister's mind and hoping he'd not pushed her too hard too soon. Now he knew the only thing to do was to wait.

13

the disappearance directory

Fern wasn't entirely forthcoming about her activities after she'd disappeared from the offices of Kimble & Kimble. Over takeout enchiladas, she described Vlad, and her family obsessed over every detail. When she explained that he'd left by turning into a great big bird and flying away, Sam gasped and shouted, "The bird at the window!"

Eddie, having not been present at the Kimble & Kimble roundtable, had to be filled in on all things vampire related. He took all the news in stride, telling Fern that she was "even cooler" than he thought she was and vowing to "beat up" Vlad or "shoot him out of the sky" should he ever approach Fern again. Anyone who knew Eddie could tell that he meant every word. Mrs. McAllister made Eddie vow he would not tell a soul—including Kinsey. Eddie, of course, promised. Though he told Kinsey most everything, this was a pledge he intended to honor.

What Fern did not describe at the dinner table, however, were certain details of her conversation with Vlad. She told them about Vlad's proclamation that Fern would grow into a powerful vampire and mentioned the prophecy in vague terms. Though she also spoke of the fact that Vlad thought she was part of the Unusual Eleven, she didn't tell them he was the same person as the vagabond on the beach. She also left out his predictions of her alienation from everything she loved and his assertion that she, like her mother, was a Blout. Why she left these facts out was no great mystery: Her family would of course deny such accusations, but that wouldn't put her mind at ease. They'd only overcompensate and make her feel worse. How they acted over the next few days would tell her more. One pitying or disgusted look from her mother or Sam or Eddie might confirm Vlad's prediction. After learning the secret of her adoption, Fern felt a distance from her family like never before. She wondered if it would ever be fully bridged. But why *did* she feel the need to keep some things from her family? Was she seriously considering Vlad's proposition? Was it possible she felt closer to the monsterlike Vlad because he understood who she was? She banished all these thoughts from her mind.

As the meal was winding down, there was a knock on the door. Mrs. McAllister rose to answer. The door opened and then shut. Mrs. McAllister had gone out to the front porch to speak with the unseen visitor. The McAllister siblings looked at one another. Without saying a word, Fern, Sam, and Eddie got up from the table and snuck toward the door. They leaned against it and listened in.

"I don't understand why I can't thank the kids in person," Mr. Summers said. "I hear they're responsible for saving my house."

"They're not home, Wallace."

"I saw them in there," he insisted.

"How did you see them, Wallace? Have you been in my shrubs looking through windows?" Mrs. McAllister's voice grew angry.

"You haven't been returning any of my phone calls, Mary Lou. I thought that things were going along great. All of a sudden, your tone changed after you had me over for dinner."

"It's been very busy around here."

"I don't understand why you won't be honest with me."

"You want me to be honest with you?"

"Of course," Mr. Summers said earnestly.

"I'm very glad your house wasn't more severely damaged. But I would like you to leave immediately," the Commander said. "I can't handle this right now. I need to focus on my children. Please understand. I'll call if things calm down."

"If?"

"Good night, Wallace."

The conversation ended as abruptly as if the Commander had bellowed "Dismissed."

Sam, Fern, and Eddie stampeded back to the dining room table in time to be seated as they had been when Mrs. McAllister left them. She sat back down and put her cloth napkin back in her lap, continuing to eat as if nothing happened.

"Who was that?" Sam said, forcing the issue.

"Mr. Summers. He came by to thank all of us for our help today."

"That was nice of him," Eddie said.

"Yes," the Commander said. She got up from her chair. "Eddie, could you make sure all the windows are closed and locked before you go upstairs to call Kinsey?"

"Sure," Eddie said.

After the plates were cleared and her children had retired to their rooms for the evening, Mary Lou McAllister moved to her office. She knew that she should go talk to Fern and set the record straight about Phoebe. But not knowing precisely how to approach Fern, she reasoned it could wait a little longer. It was important that she say exactly the right thing to Fern. The business with Mr. Summers had put her on edge. Maybe Mr. Summers was actually interested in *her*, but she was beginning to think that Sam might have been right all along about his obsessive interest in Fern. Could he possibly be involved in this whole vampire mess?

Flipping through her Rolodex, she picked up the phone and called Alistair Kimble. At first she had trouble convincing his dingbat secretary that her call was of the greatest urgency. She was soon connected to him. Mrs. McAllister explained the events of the day. When she finished, Alistair Kimble jumped in.

"Fern is unhurt?"

"Yes, she's okay,"Mrs. McAllister replied, sensing an unfamiliar edge in Mr. Kimble's voice. "Who is Vlad, Alistair?" she demanded. "Why is this man stalking my child and sneaking up on her in abandoned orange groves?"

"We have all that under control."

"You have *nothing* under control!"

"Anger will do little to help Fern, Mrs. McAllister."

"I want you to listen very carefully to me, Alistair. Either you start giving me some answers—and I mean actual *information*—or I will take Fern and my family and run so far and so fast, you'll never hear from us again."

"That would be a very foolish decision."

"People don't usually get very far by underestimating me."

"I assure you, that is not my intention."

"If you have no interest in answering my questions, in full, then I'm afraid we have nothing more to talk about. Good-bye—"

"Wait . . . please, Mrs. McAllister, wait one moment,"

Mr. Kimble said. He was acutely aware that Chief Quagmire had given him explicit instructions to do whatever it took to get Mrs. McAllister on board with their latest plan. As much as he didn't want to furnish a Normal with any actual information, he would have to, if that's what Mrs. McAllister required. "What is it you want to know?" Mr. Kimble asked.

"Who is Vlad and what is he hoping to accomplish?"

"He is a revolutionary and the unofficial head of the Blouts. Vlad has been under the impression for many years that he's Dracula's messenger."

"Dracula's messenger?"

"In the fifteenth century, Blouts came into prominence under the brutal reign of Vlad Tepes. You probably know him as Count Dracula. Most Otherworldly historians credit Count Dracula as the founder of the Blout movement. Dracula was so notorious, however, that even Normals knew about him—but what Normals know about him only scratches the surface. His legend grew. Count Dracula wanted vampires to emerge from the shadows as the master race. Assimilation was not a viable option—the entire Blout belief system was founded upon this principle. Dracula's brutality against Normals was the beginning of a larger plan.

"The man Fern met in Anderson's Grove also calls himself Vlad, though that's not his real name. He began referring to himself as that during the Blout resurgence and the name stuck. It's impossible to say if he actually thinks he *is* Dracula's messenger or if his name is the marketing ploy of a madman. But it's worked to a large degree. Lately, he's gained a substantial following. His army calls itself the Legion of the Hundred-Handers."

"Excuse me? The Legion of the Hundred-Handers? It sounds like you're making all this up."

"I wish I were, Mary Lou. The Hundred-Handers get their name from a fearsome mythological beast called the hecatonchire, or 'hundred-handed.' Have you heard of it?"

"No."

"These creatures have one hundred hands, as you might have guessed, and were arguably the most powerful beasts in ancient Greece. The Legion of Hundred-Handers hopes to inspire the same kind of fear the hecatonchires do. There are fifty or so 'official' members of the Legion. Their loyalty to Vlad is unswerving and they are known for using the most brutal tactics to terrorize anybody who stands in their path. A group like the Hundred-Handers survives by feeding off other people's fear."

"Are you and the Blouts at war then?"

"No, not really. Both Blouts and Rollens still depend upon keeping a low profile. Can you imagine what might happen among the Normals if our existence was common knowledge? Neither group has enough of a population to survive the kind of persecution that would inevitably occur. Our need for secrecy acts as a mutual deterrent that keeps both Blouts and Rollens from overtly escalating any conflict."

Mary Lou McAllister processed all the new information. After a minute of silence, she spoke. "I appreciate the fact that you're finally being forthright with me, Alistair, but you still haven't explained why Vlad is after my daughter."

"I was about to get to that. Vlad feels that it's his duty to finish what Dracula started."

"What exactly is that?"

"World dominance and the subjugation of all those who disagree with him. Those who call themselves Rollens grew out of a resistance movement to the Blouts' views. Rollens, and specifically the Vampire Alliance, believe that Normals and vampires can coexist peacefully."

"Why is he so powerful?"

"He's a naturally gifted Otherworldly. His ability to morph into other forms sets him apart from most of our kind. He also has the appearance of a very powerful man. Many people speculate that his watch, nicknamed 'the Keeper,' holds tremendous power. Some believe that it was once owned by Dracula himself and that its wearer inherits the power of those who possessed it before. Vlad does an excellent job of portraying himself as all-powerful."

"And Vlad thinks Fern can help him, then?" Mrs. McAllister let fear slip into her voice.

"Yes."

"But she's a little girl."

"To be perfectly frank, if the prophecy is true, Fern will

be one of the only people able to stop Vlad. Because of this, we—Chief Quagmire, Bing, and myself—have always assumed that should he find Fern, he would try to kill her—as he would any Unusual he encountered."

Mrs. McAllister, not known as a gasper, huffed into the phone as if she were choking. Alistair Kimble continued.

"But he was right there in front of her and he did not kill her. He must want something else. Are you certain Fern told you everything?"

"Yes, I'm sure."

"Mary Lou, we can't risk your daughter's safety any longer. You must allow us to bring her to headquarters. She'll be safe there until we figure out what Vlad is planning."

Although Alistair Kimble endorsed the idea of Fern going to headquarters, the plan was not his. Less than ten minutes before, he'd received a phone call from Kenneth Quagmire introducing the idea. Kimble's job was to convince Fern's mother to let Fern go. Though Kimble had struggled to keep Mary Lou on the phone, the hardest part of his task was still ahead.

"Absolutely not," Mrs. McAllister said, keeping a steady tone despite her panic. "We can hire security for the house and inform law enforcement in the area and have them patrol."

"This is not a problem that can be dealt with using the measures you're accustomed to, Mary Lou. There is no security detail in the world that could stop Vlad. Surely you must understand that?"

"What can you offer her that I can't?" Mrs. McAllister insisted.

"Protection in a secure place that no Blout has ever succeeded in infiltrating. It's a stopgap until we know more."

"I must be allowed to go with her," Mrs. McAllister said.

"I'm afraid we cannot permit that. We have a background check that takes months before a person's even allowed in the front gate. It will be a struggle to convince the committee to allow Fern there, but a Normal? They'll never reveal the location for that."

"Unacceptable," Mrs. McAllister blurted out. "If Fern's so precious to you and your cause, you'll do anything to protect her, right? That includes allowing me to accompany her."

"The harsh reality of the matter, Mary Lou, is that the Alliance will go to great lengths to protect her, but they will not compromise headquarters to do it."

"You are heartless!" Mrs. McAllister barked. Alistair Kimble let the word roll off him—in his long lifetime, he had been called much worse.

"I'm willing to do everything I can to protect Fern. But I'm not in a position to make the rules. The Alliance is a democracy."

There was a pause as both Mary Lou and Alistair considered their positions. Alistair spoke up.

"What if Fern carries my mobile phone with her at all times? We'll hide her away for the week. You'll be able to call her anytime you want," Mr. Kimble said, reasoning that although Fern would be hundreds of feet underground and outside of cell phone reception, Mrs. McAllister could *call* her anytime she wanted. She just wouldn't be able to reach her. "Allow our people to try to locate Vlad, gather intel, and after the week is over, we'll reevaluate."

"I can't let you just take her!" Mrs. McAllister said, beginning to sound like a broken record. Alistair Kimble sensed slight doubt in her voice and pressed on.

"Do you really want the blood of your only daughter on your hands, knowing you could've protected her? Is that what Phoebe would have wanted?"

The two paused at the mention of their long-dead mutual friend.

"I don't know what Phoebe would have wanted," Mrs. McAllister said, her voice full of sad resignation. "I'm not sure now I ever really knew her, Alistair, considering the fact that she kept all this from me all those years."

"Being a vampire does not change who a person is, Mary Lou."

Overcome, Mrs. McAllister placed the receiver on the desk. She held her head in her hands, shaking from the inside out. She resolved not to break down. She must think about this rationally.

Though it would nearly break her heart, the Commander decided to make a tactical decision. After taking a single deep breath, Mary Lou reached for the phone once again.

"When can you come and pick her up?"

Alistair Kimble had known Mary Lou McAllister for three decades. Still, he had never heard her voice so full of steely resolve.

"It'll take me several hours to get the clearance and transport together."

"When will you be here?"

"Noon tomorrow."

"Fine."

Mary Lou McAllister hung up the phone shortly thereafter and told herself she would talk to Fern after she took a shower.

Fern didn't sleep much that night. She lay in her bed, tossing and turning. Feeling antsy, she got up out of bed and wandered out of her room. She half expected to find Vlad's condor perched on the windowsill. As she made her way down the dark hallway, she noticed the sound of her mother's printer whirring away. It was unlike the Commander, who kept strict hours, to be working so late, so she tiptoed to the end of the hallway.

Sam sat behind the Commander's desk, his face bathed in the dim blue light of the computer screen. Mrs. McAllister had vacated the room after her phone call an hour or so earlier, hoping to take a long shower and formulate how she would break the latest news to Fern.

"What are you doing?" Fern whispered across the desk at Sam.

"Something for school tomorrow," Sam said. He was acting very jumpy. "I'll be done in a few minutes," he insisted.

"Okay," Fern said. She didn't want to press Sam, but she was confused.

"I'll come to your room as soon as I'm done, Fern," Sam said, annoyed that Fern was lingering by the doorway. "You better head back there, though, before Mom hears us."

Fern moped dejectedly down the hallway and back into her room. What was Sam doing that he couldn't show her? Though she had tried to banish the thought from her head, Vlad's predictions of her isolation troubled her. She returned to her bed, her body taut with worry. Was everything going to change now?

It was an hour before Sam was finished with his project. Creeping down the hall, avoiding the spots in the floor that squeaked, he slipped into Fern's room. But now, Fern had lost the urge to talk. She just wanted to be left alone, to fall asleep and be released from the thoughts that endlessly plagued her.

When she heard Sam open the door, she shut her eyes and pretended to be asleep. Fern could sense that Sam was standing above her, watching her. He placed something gently next to her head on her pillow. Fern remained still. The door didn't open again. Before long, she heard Sam's heavy breaths coming from the foot of her bed. She raised herself up. Sure enough, curled up at the foot of her bed, Sam was fast asleep, snoring.

Fern picked up the object Sam had left on her pillow. She held it up in the light from the open window. It was a palm-sized book, loosely bound with twine. The cover had the title *The Disappearance Directory* stenciled in with a Sharpie. Inside, Sam had written a message in his distinct handwriting.

Instructions: When you've disappeared to somewhere you don't want to be, look at one of these pictures and get yourself home! Practice makes perfect. The last picture is sort of a joke. —From Sam

Fern flipped through the book. Sam had printed pictures and pasted them in the book. There was a picture of Fern's bed, the jacaranda tree, the grove, a fuzzy Internet picture of Pirate's Cove, and the McAllister living room.

The last picture made Fern struggle to keep her laughter inside and not awaken her slumbering brother. Sam had taken a picture of the McAllister toilet, unflushed. Her twin brother had been known to clog the toilet from time to time, causing Eddie to call him the John Jammer. She shook her head with a sly smile. Fern had placed the drawing Vlad had given her, of Rhea's Rock, inside her copy of *Island of the Blue Dolphins*, now resting on her nightstand.

Almost instinctively, she fished it out and slipped it into *The Disappearance Directory*.

Fern looked appreciatively at her brother. She got a blanket from her closet and covered him. Sam still accepted her, Fern thought. He still wanted to be friends, to be close to Fern. Would he feel that way if he knew she was a Blout? Fern shut her eyes. Sam's kindness was just enough to make her forget her other more troubling thoughts. It was only minutes until she fell asleep. Sam snored loudly below her. Fern clutched *The Disappearance Directory* until morning came.

14

the backyard experiment

Sam knew he should let his sister sleep, but his excitement prevailed. He shook her awake, standing over her as she opened her eyes. There was still an hour before they had to depart for school. Enough time, Sam thought, to experiment with *The Disappearance Directory*.

"Fern, wake up!"

The middle McAllister child's blond hair sprouted like a weed. His face was marked with red zigzags from the rug. Fern rubbed her eyes with her fists. She'd never been a morning person. However, things had gotten much better since she'd received her W.A.A.V.E. products from Lindsey Lin. Reaching for her nightstand, she grabbed the bottle of eyedrops. Her Breakfast Sunglasses, now rarely worn, were gathering dust next to her alarm clock. Two drops in each eye, some lotion on her face, and she was ready to go.

Both Sam and Fern changed into their school uniforms and raced outside. The backyard was filled with the immaculate light of sunup. The pool had been painstakingly re-filled with the hose, and the jacarandas, oak, and elms were tranquil. Fern hadn't let *The Disappearance Directory* out of arm's reach since Sam had placed it on her pillow. She clutched it now as the birds chirped wildly behind her.

"Let's start small," Sam said, as the twins stood on the grass in the middle of the yard. "Why don't you try to go from here to your room?"

"Okay," Fern said, opening the *Directory*. "Should I just stare at the picture?"

Sam started laughing. "I don't know," he answered. "I'm not an expert or anything. You're the one who's done it before." Fern shrugged her shoulders at her brother, slightly embarrassed. She looked at the picture of her bed and desk. Her bed was unmade and a few of her white polo shirts from school lay strewn about. If the Commander had seen the picture, she would have called the state of Fern's room a disgrace. Fern refocused on the picture. She had to concentrate. She zeroed in on the bed, closed her eyes, and thought hard.

She reopened them and Sam stood directly in front of her.

"No luck, huh?" Sam asked.

"I don't know why it happens when it does happen," Fern said, frustrated.

"Well, what are you thinking about right before it happens?"

"I don't know."

"When you were reading *Lord of the Flies*, you don't remember thinking anything? What about when we were having dinner with Mr. Summers? Nothing?"

"I don't know, all right?" Fern grimaced. "I'm sorry, Sam," she said. "I'm just in a bad mood."

"If we get you on track with this teleporting stuff, then if you are ever in danger, you can just teleport your way out of it," he said. "We've got to figure it out eventually."

"Wait! I know," Fern said, as a thought struck her. "Usually, right before I teleport, I think to myself that I would rather be some other place. Either because of a happy memory or because of something unpleasant."

"Do it, then," Sam said.

Fern looked at the picture of her room. She thought of how much she wanted to lie down in bed, to rest, to not be standing in the middle of the backyard worried about whether or not she had it in her to teleport.

Nausea hit first.

Fern's knees buckled and she felt the ground crumble beneath her feet. The blackness took hold. What felt like a minute to Fern was actually less than a second.

Soon she was able to open her eyes. Dimness transformed into sight. Fern jumped up with her fists in the air. She was in her room. Her messy, beloved room. Fern ran out of the room and to the window in the hallway. She spotted Sam below in the backyard, looking up at the second floor of the McAllister house. Fern cranked open the window and stuck her head out.

"You did it!" Sam said, cupping his hands around his mouth like a megaphone. Fern smiled down at her brother. The feeling was better than almost anything. "Hurry back down here! Let's try somewhere else . . . somewhere farther!"

Fern bolted down the stairs and was in the backyard within the minute.

"What about the *Directory*?" Sam said.

"What do you mean?" Fern said, rejoining her brother in the middle of the lawn.

"When you teleported, the *Directory* went with you?"

"Yeah," Fern said, looking down and realizing for the first time she was still clutching the *Directory*.

"That means you can take things with you!" Sam tussled his own blond hair. "I wonder if you could take me with you?"

"Maybe," Fern said. She opened the *Directory*.

"Let's see if we can both go all the way to Pirate's Cove!" Sam said excitedly. "We can finally check and see if the hole's still open—and copy down the writing this time!"

Fern grabbed Sam's shoulder, flipping through the *Directory* with her other hand. She came to the out-of-focus picture of Pirate's Cove. Studying the picture carefully, she focused on the curvy shoreline and brown cragged cliffs. Sam put his arm around Fern's shoulder and held on tightly.

I wish I was somewhere else. I wish I was anywhere but here.

The process seemed so simple and lacked any mystery now. She thought the words and then she was somewhere else. It was a perverted version of Dorothy and her ruby slippers, only without the slippers.

Her stomach wrenched as she flew out of the darkness and fell face forward onto a mound of sand. Brushing herself off, she turned around. Fern was back at Pirate's Cove, but Sam wasn't with her. She'd landed at the western end of the beach. The beach was cold and damp. Fog rolled in off the Pacific, cloaking everything in pale gray. At a quarter to seven in the morning, the sandy beach was so empty it was spooky.

Fern's head was beginning to throb. This was almost the exact spot where she'd met a disguised Vlad with his metal detector. Not wanting to be alone and at Pirate's Cove any longer than she had to, she ran to the cave where the hole had been before. The back of the cave was dark at this hour of the morning. She felt around the back of it. She pressed her face up against the wall. Finally, she spotted the initials:

MLM + PM

She pressed her hands below them.

The hole was gone. Hard rock stood in its place.

Fern no longer wanted to be anywhere near Pirate's Cove. She ran back onto the beach. Shivering, she opened *The Disappearance Directory* and found the jacaranda tree. A small inferno burned in her stomach. Fern made an effort not to double over. Just in time, she felt the blankness come over her.

Her arrival in the jacaranda tree was much more graceful than it had been on the beach. Though Fern wasn't sure how to control the smoothness of the arrivals and departures, she was overjoyed at the prospect of controlling when and where she disappeared. She climbed out of the jacaranda, her head still throbbing and her stomach still on fire. She ran around the house to the backyard. Byron was waiting for her; he nipped at her heels. Sam smiled but looked disappointed.

"I'm sorry I couldn't take you along," Fern said.

"That's all right," Sam said. "Was it still there? Did you see the hole?"

"It was gone," Fern said.

The twins turned around as Mrs. McAllister opened the sliding door that led to the patio in the backyard. "What are you two doing out here so early?" the Commander questioned.

Mrs. McAllister had fallen asleep just after her shower, telling herself she would lie down for a few moments before going to talk to Fern. Her exhaustion soon took hold and she fell into a restless sleep, still in her slippers.

"We're practicing," Sam said. "I think we've got Fern's disappearing under control!"

"Maybe not under control," Fern said, not wanting to overstate the tenuous grasp she had on her teleporting skills, "but I went to my room and back and the beach and back."

"Really?" Mrs. McAllister said, looking at her daughter.

Fern couldn't put her finger on it, but her mother's gaze made Fern uncomfortable. Her mother was looking at her as if she missed Fern, even though Fern was standing right in front of her. She wondered whether what Vlad had said about her mother was already coming true.

"Don't worry, Mom," Sam said, picking up on the strange look in his mother's eyes. "We're about to take off for school. We won't be late."

"You're not going to school today," the Commander said.

"Really?" Sam said, gleefully.

"Yes," Mrs. McAllister said, looking away from her daughter.

"All right!" Sam said, excited by the prospect.

"Why aren't we?" Fern asked, defensively.

"You *want* to go to school?" Mrs. McAllister replied.

"Well, I don't want to *not* go to school," Fern said.

"I don't understand," Mrs. McAllister said.

"Are we not going to school because I embarrass you?" Fern asked. Fern, who rarely confronted anyone about anything, had taken her mother completely off guard.

"That's ridiculous, Fern." The Commander was not prepared for this scenario. She knew she had four hours until Alistair Kimble arrived and had planned on waiting to tell Fern until it felt like the right time. She had to adjust, and quickly.

"There's something I need to talk to you both about. Please come sit down in the living room."

Mrs. McAllister marched back into the house, leaving the sliding glass door open so her children could follow. Fern thought the atmosphere very similar to one of the many family meetings that her mother had called. But the haphazard nature of this one was disconcerting.

Sam and Fern sat down and their mother began.

"I had a talk with Alistair Kimble last night," Mrs. McAllister said. She wasn't looking at either of them. "I'm not trying to alarm either of you, but Alistair thinks the man who visited you, Fern, is very dangerous and may come back to hurt you."

"Why wouldn't he have just hurt Fern right then?" Sam questioned.

"Mr. Kimble didn't know the answer to that question."

But Fern did. Vlad didn't want to hurt Fern; he wanted her to join his ranks. Her stomach lurched inside her.

"Mr. Kimble wants to make sure you're protected, Fern, until they can figure out what Vlad wants with you." Mrs. McAllister looked at Fern, trying to detect any fear that Fern might be feeling. Fern flinched.

"Protection?" Fern asked. "That's why I can't go back to school?"

"Is Fern going to get a bodyguard?" Sam asked.

"I talked it over with Mr. Kimble, and we both think that you need to be taken somewhere that is absolutely safe—somewhere Vlad can't get to you." The Commander's resolve was tested when she looked into her daughter's eyes. She was doing this, she repeated silently, to save her daughter.

"Unfortunately, Normals aren't allowed where you're going. It's just for the week, to make sure that we know what Vlad is up to before we let you go back to school and continue on as usual."

"You're sending me away?" Fern said. Why were they so worried about Vlad when he hadn't hurt her the first time? Were they worried that she would follow him?

"You mustn't look at it like that. I want you to be safe, above all. This isn't going to be easy for me either, worrying about you all the time while you're away."

"Where am I going?"

"He wouldn't say, but you'll have a cell phone with you and you can call me or I can call you any time. Mr. Kimble assured me of that."

"I don't want to go," Fern said, crossing her arms. "That's the last thing in the world I want to do!"

"Well, I'm not giving you the choice," the Commander said, angered that she was being challenged on a decision that was difficult in the first place. "You're not safe here with this madman on the loose."

"What if it's Mr. Kimble that's the madman?" Sam interjected.

"I've known Alistair Kimble for over thirty years. He's the one who brought Fern here in the first place." The Commander's voice hardened. She thought she might break down. "He'll be here to pick you up at noon."

Fern thought about trying to make herself disappear, right then and there. Instead, she chose the more traditional adolescent response: She got up from the couch, marched up the stairs to her room, and slammed the door, pouting.

Mrs. McAllister frowned as Fern climbed up the stairs.

"You really think she needs to go to that place?" Sam said, trying to reason with his mother.

"Yes, Sam, I really do. Fern's nothing like us. We're out of our league here. If we want to keep her safe, we're going to have to work with her kind, at least for the time being."

Fern grimaced as she heard her mother's words through the door. *Fern's nothing like us.* She wished she hadn't been able to hear them. Grabbing a pillow, she put it around her ears. Maybe she didn't belong here. Maybe things would be like this from now on. One unhappy thought followed another, and miserable tears tumbled down her face. Byron sat next to her on the bed. He began licking her face. Fern smiled weakly at him through her tears. Byron, it seemed, was the only one that hadn't started acting differently because of her powers.

Fern, no longer worried that *Lord of the Flies* was cursed, set upon taking her mind off her upcoming exile. She had almost finished the book last night in the shower. Things had taken a terrible turn for the boys on the island—all of them had taken on the qualities of savages, and some of them had died. *And in the middle of them,* Fern read, *with filthy body, matted hair, and unwiped nose, Ralph wept for the end of innocence, the darkness of man's heart, and the fall through the air of the true, wise friend called Piggy.*

Fern read the last few lines and shut the book. She shuddered, filled with unease. Even Ralph, the supposed hero of the book, had fallen prey to savagery. Though she tried to put the story from her mind, she couldn't help but think about whether there was something similar inside her—a darkness that she couldn't contain. The heart of a Blout. Maybe her tears were for the very same reason.

Soon Sam came into her room and stayed with her and Byron, but Fern grew more sullen as the day wore on. He tried, in vain, to convince her that this was all for the best. It wasn't long until noon arrived. None of the McAllisters figured the lawyer would be late. He wasn't. Just as the grandfather clock in the living room struck twelve, the doorbell rang. Alistair Kimble was at the door in a navy mock turtleneck and dark khaki slacks. His thick calico beard looked alive and his blue sports coat was without a single crease.

"Hello, Mary Lou," Alistair said, holding a dark leather

briefcase in his left hand. Sam and Fern rushed to the front window to look at what might be parked in the driveway.

There had been a lot of speculation as to what kind of car Mr. Alistair Kimble drove. Because he worked such odd hours, very few people had ever seen him behind the wheel. The McAllister twins marveled at what stood parked in their stone driveway.

A white truck, with RALPH'S GROCERY STORES emblazoned on both sides next to pictures of large heirloom tomatoes and even larger juicy steaks, engulfed the entire driveway. After counting all eighteen wheels on the strange vehicle, Fern recognized Mr. Bing in the driver's seat. Everyone, it seemed, was playing hooky today. He was dressed in a red flannel shirt and looked much more casual than usual.

Before long, Mr. Kimble was in the living room sitting on the couch with Mrs. McAllister. Fern and Sam turned away from the window, and both sat on the sill with their legs dangling.

"Fern, I told your mother that I wanted a minute to discuss this with everybody."

"Go ahead and discuss it then," Fern said while rolling her eyes, on edge.

"As your mother has informed you, you will be placed in my protective custody for the next week until we discern what, exactly, Vlad is planning."

"Where are you going to take me?"

"Headquarters. It's a compound also known by the name New Tartarus."

"Where is that?"

"I cannot provide you with that information."

"What does that mean?"

"Fern, I don't even know where you're going," Mrs. McAllister said. "But you'll find out and you'll call me and check in every day. Mr. Kimble's going to give you his cell phone."

"I'm not going," Fern said, growing defiant.

"You must!" Mrs. McAllister said.

"I'm not going," repeated Fern, "unless Sam comes with me."

Sam perked up.

"I'm sorry, Fern, but we cannot accommodate that request," Alistair Kimble remarked flatly.

"Well, then, I'll just have to take my chances with Vlad trying to kill me."

"Don't talk like that," Mrs. McAllister snapped.

Fern's eyes flashed. "Vlad told me a few things that you might find interesting, but I guess there's no need to tell you now," she said.

"You haven't told me everything, Fern?" Mrs. McAllister scowled. Fern was acting so out of character. Mr. Kimble stroked his beard and remained the calmest one in the room.

"You never asked," Fern shot back.

"We may just be able to work something out," he said, getting up from the couch. "If you'll excuse me for one moment while I make a phone call." He walked into the kitchen and let the door shut behind him.

The McAllisters stared at one another. Mrs. McAllister searched for something to say. Fern had never talked back before. Her daughter was changing before her very eyes.

"Fern, I know you don't want to go, but believe me when I say I'm the last person who would send you somewhere if I didn't think it was absolutely necessary," she said.

Alistair Kimble walked back in the room.

"I've made the arrangements. They'll allow it this once, but I reserve the right to send Sam home at any time."

Sam was astonished. Almost every part of him wanted to tag along with Fern and make sure she was all right, but there was a small fraction of him that was deeply afraid. He suppressed his fear.

"Do I need to pack anything?" he asked. Fern perked up too, realizing she hadn't thought about what she would need for the week.

"No. You will be well looked after. Pajamas, toothbrushes—we have all that," Mr. Kimble said formally, before pulling his sleeve up to look at his watch. "We'd better get on the road, as they're expecting us."

Fern felt queasy. Had Fern known that Sam's stomach was experiencing the same kind of panic, she might have taken some comfort in it. Both twins put on their brave faces.

"Wait just one second," the Commander said, unwilling to accept this new change of plan. "I never agreed to letting you take both children. If you can make arrangements for Sam, why can't you make them for me?"

"Bringing along Sam is already testing the patience of most of the Assembly, Mrs. McAllister. What's more, he's a child!"

"Mom, it'll be fine. It's better this way. I'll give Fern some company. Someone has to be here to tell Eddie what's going on when he gets home from school."

Mrs. McAllister's agitation subsided slightly, but she was still angry. "Alistair, I don't think there is a single step in this process that you haven't bungled somehow. I'll let Sam and Fern go, but only because I don't feel I have a choice. Take them with the knowledge that if anything should happen to them, I'm holding you responsible," she said as her jaw jutted out, completing the look of unremitting wrath that had overtaken her face.

In his days as a district head, Alistair Kimble had battled five Hundred-Handers at one time, and still he preferred their slimy vileness to the fearsome glare of Mary Lou McAllister. As Mr. Kimble walked out of the McAllister house, with their Maltese nipping at his heels, he hoped he would not be back under such unpleasant circumstances.

15

the atlas ride

The back doors of the truck swung open.

"Good mornin'," Joseph Bing said, stepping down from the bed of the truck. In the past, he might have appeared slightly grandfatherly in his janitor's garb, but now the image was complete. Mr. Kimble wasted no time climbing into the back of the huge Mack truck only partially parked in the McAllister driveway (the rest hung out into the street). After saying good-bye to their mother on the porch, Sam and Fern ran toward Bing. They climbed the two stairs into the truck bed, full of anticipation.

Fern gasped.

The inside of that Ralph's Grocery truck was the single most marvelous thing she'd ever laid eyes on. Fern's fear and anxiousness dissipated in the cold air of the truck. Antique mirrors adorned walls with velvet lining. Oriental rugs lined the floors. Brown leather recliners faced out from both walls, each chair with its own dark maple table and flat-screen monitor. Blue tear-drop glass light fixtures hung from the ceiling and several bookcases gave the room a library feel. Sam followed Fern, gasping himself at the swanky furnishings matched with state-of-the-art technology.

"I'm glad you're coming along with us today," Bing said jubilantly. "I'd best be getting up to the driver's seat, but enjoy your first ride on the Atlas!" He then disappeared behind a curtain at the end of the room. As Bing drew back the curtain, Fern noticed that this narrow room gave way to another compartment on a platform a few steps above the one they were in.

"If you two get seated, we can be on our way," Mr. Kimble said, businesslike, pointing to the leather recliners.

Sam looked at Mr. Kimble, puzzled. "Are we on the *Air Force One* of eighteen-wheelers?" he asked.

"Planes can be too easily traced," Mr. Kimble said. "So we must use ground transportation."

"Sir?"

A creature had come through the curtain and down the steps, and was now standing in front of the group. Patches of mud-colored hair grew from its compact body. Where there was an absence of hair there was rough skin the color and texture of tree bark. The beast was Fern's height, but must have weighed three times as much. He had ears like small bugles, shoulders the size of sandbags, large flat feet, and toenails the color of newly cut grass. He was wearing a pair of battered OshKosh B'Gosh overalls. In the center of the creature's face, one large black eye blinked as it scanned the room.

"Sir?" the creature asked again. His voice, high and thin, reminded Fern of Sam's when he plugged his nose. The voice was strange enough on its own, but coming from the mouth of this squat beast, it seemed stranger still.

"Sir, I just wanted to make sure that it was permissible to begin our route."

"Of course, Telemus, please proceed."

The creature, hindered by his large feet, waddled back up the stairs and closed the curtain behind him.

"What in the—," Fern began, overcoming her initial speechlessness.

"Shhh," Mr. Kimble said, putting his index finger to his mouth. After pausing for a moment, he began.

"Telemus is a Cyclops. They are known for being extremely sensitive, so please refrain from making any comments. The last thing we need is a cranky Cyclops on board." Fern and Sam were expecting Mr. Kimble to laugh, but he did not.

"Telemus is young, so he's extraordinarily susceptible to bouts of moodiness," Mr. Kimble continued in a low voice. "They take fifty years or so to grow to full size."

"How full is that?" Sam asked.

"Most are over eight feet tall."

"What kind of animal is it related to?"

"Cyclopes are not animals at all. They are loosely related to the giant family, to be precise. By the time they're fully grown, they're not very useful in a setting like this because of their height."

"How old is Telemus?" Fern asked.

"Telemus is about your age, I believe."

"Why haven't I *ever* seen one of those before?" Sam said, still in disbelief. "Where *are* we?"

"Cyclopes have existed for centuries. However, they've been hunted so viciously in recent times, few remain. Those that do remain live underground and in hiding."

"Why have they been hunted?"

"Because human beings make a practice of destroying what they cannot explain. Cyclopes are a reminder of a past left behind long ago."

"What does Telemus do?" Fern asked.

"He runs all of the equipment here on the Atlas," Mr. Kimble said. He looked tired from answering questions, but then perked up a bit after a long look at Fern and Sam. "I can show you the control room, if you like," he said, trying to act gracious, but not knowing how.

Sam and Fern nodded in agreement. Mr. Kimble got out of his seat and pulled the curtain back. Bright light streamed out of the opening. Sam and Fern followed Mr. Kimble, stepping up into the smaller room.

Sam and Fern could have sworn they were back outside the Atlas. Bushes were growing out of planters jutting from every inch of wall, crawling up the walls in an evenly spaced pattern. White flowers adorned most plants. The abundance of sunlight made the room hot and steamy. There must have been over twenty bushes, and each was ignited with a blue flame surrounding an image. Every image was different, but each was shaped in a circle. Fern realized exactly what she was observing: Sagebrushes of Hyperion!

She looked up. A glass panel, tinted green, bubbled out like a huge skylight, letting in the California sun. No wonder it felt as if she were outside. Telemus the Cyclops sat in the middle of the space in a swivel chair with two feet of maneuvering room on each side. Telemus's eye roved across each bush. It looked as if he was taking them all in at once. He turned his chair from one side to the other, keeping his amazing eye attuned to everything.

"We call this the mobile greenhouse," Alistair Kimble said. Fern thought he made a pretty lousy tour guide and had about as much passion as Mrs. Stonyfield did when she talked about why she had become a teacher. But he did seem to be trying. "It allows us to monitor events while we travel. We also get clearer images with real sunlight. It's our most effective surveillance system."

"Does, um, Telemus monitor everything all the time?" Sam asked, having to stop himself from saying "the monster" in place of the Cyclops's actual name.

"Things are not always as they seem. Telemus does with one eye what we would need twenty eyes for. He's exceptional at processing a lot of information at once," Mr. Kimble said. "Cyclopes have a real talent for that. Of course, there is a few seconds' delay."

"So these are all Sagebrushes?"

"Yes, they are. I understand you both got an education on their powers from Miss Lin," Mr. Kimble said, displeased.

"What is he keeping track of?"

"Anything and everything. Activity in all the districts, what's going on at headquarters, the rival movement, abuse of powers. We switch what we monitor from time to time, which means we must cultivate new bushes depending on the intelligence we get from our network, whether it be from vigilantes or district heads."

"Don't people mind that you're spying on them?"

"It's for their own protection," Mr. Kimble said dismissively. "Cyclopes can also smell a Blout coming a mile away, which we find tremendously helpful."

"That's because they stink, sir," Telemus said without taking his eye off the bushy walls, still swiveling back and forth.

Fern looked down, hoping no one witnessed the process of her cheeks turning red. Her veins flowed with nervous energy. She inched away from Telemus so he couldn't smell the Blout in her.

"We should return to our seats," Mr. Kimble said. "Mr. Bing informed me before we left that it may be a bit bumpy."

Sam and Fern each took a leather recliner. As soon as Fern sat down, she realized how tired she was. She struggled to keep her eyes open.

"Pssst, Fern." Sam was leaning over Fern's table, speaking in a low voice. "Turn on your monitor."

Fern looked to her left and pushed the toggle switch on the bottom of the black screen. It flashed on, displaying Joseph Bing, flannel shirt and all, in the driver's seat. Mr. Kimble waved at Fern and Sam from their screens.

"Now hit alternate view," Sam said, leaning over again. The pictured changed to the view from the passenger side window. Sam and Fern remained captivated by the video feed as they passed the nuclear power plants at San Onofre. At this hour, the Pacific was gray and the sand looked damp. It wasn't long before a train passed by, half-empty, gliding along the tracks between the interstate and the ocean.

"I see you've figured out how to work the view box," Mr. Kimble said. He'd meant to disconnect the feed before the children boarded, but in the confusion, forgot. Normally he would have worried that they'd be able to discern the secret location of New Tartarus. But Kimble knew Kenneth Quagmire would see to it that they remembered nothing from their trip. "We don't have any windows in the back," Mr. Kimble explained. "Telemus installed the cameras himself."

"Are we headed south? On the five?" Fern asked.

"Yes," Mr. Kimble said. "New Tartarus is the unofficial Vampire Alliance headquarters. It also contains several other facets of the V.A."

They were just south of Camp Pendleton Marine Base and the racetrack at Del Mar. Before long, they could see the San Diego skyline in the distance. The truck was soon bending along Mission Bay in San Diego.

The screen fuzzed over and then went blank. The truck began to sway. Fern could tell they were gathering speed. She put her recliner upright and gripped the armrests.

The screen blinked back on. They were zooming along beside San Diego Bay, heading straight for Coronado Island. The Coronado Bay Bridge looked like a giant blue snake teetering on white stilts above them. The truck didn't slow down, barreling ahead, getting closer and closer to the water's edge. With a sharp turn, they were off road, bouncing through the gravel alongside the street. Fern looked over at Sam, who had closed his eyes and turned almost completely white.

"We're headed straight for the water!" Fern said, watching the screen. Mr. Kimble calmly closed his eyes and leaned back, staying absolutely still.

"THREE SECONDS TO IMPACT!" Telemus bellowed from the other compartment.

A forceful slap hit the front of the truck. The noise was deafening. The sound of the truck crashing into the azure water of San Diego Bay obscured Fern's piercing scream. The water thundered all around them. The truck rolled back and forth and Fern felt upside down for a moment.

The lights and monitors flicked off completely.

Fern felt as if she were on a roller coaster with only loops and no lights. She wanted desperately to teleport somewhere, like back to her bed, but knew she would never forgive herself if she left Sam here alone to fend for himself.

The rumble of the motor stopped abruptly.

The cabin was now still, silent, and dark. Seconds passed. Fern tried to find her brother in the darkness. She wished that the Commander hadn't allowed her to come on this death trip. She wanted to be anywhere but inside the grocery truck. She wanted to scream out to Sam that she was sorry for making him come along. All this was her fault. Vlad wasn't half as scary as sitting in the dark, listening to the truck creak beneath them as if it had fallen into a black hole. There was no escape. They were doomed.

"Bing," Mr. Kimble finally shouted through the darkness, "you're out of practice." He sounded disgusted. "That was the absolute worst approach I've seen in a long time. You almost missed the tunnel."

"Took a few seconds to get the rust off, for sure, Alistair," Mr. Bing's voice answered back, full of the humor that Mr. Kimble's lacked.

"I apologize for not warning you children," Mr. Kimble said, now addressing the cabin. "But I think one's better off if one doesn't expect it."

Fern couldn't believe that everything in the truck had remained in place.

"Where . . . ," Sam said, out of breath. "Where are we?"

"We are most likely under the Hotel Del Coronado by now," Mr. Kimble said.

"We're *under* Coronado Island?!" Fern said.

"Yes," Mr. Kimble said, knowing that the children would not be permitted to remember any of this.

"Where is New Tartarus?" Sam asked. "Under Coronado?"

"It starts at North Island and continues from there."

"The naval base?"

"There's no safer place for an underground complex than underneath a military base, I assure you," Mr. Kimble said.

"FIVE SECONDS TO ARRIVAL!" Telemus said, his high-pitched voice filling the cabin.

"Hold on this time!" Mr. Bing's voice boomed over the rattle of the compartment.

The truck lurched forward as Sam's and Fern's seat belts tightened around their torsos. The truck then jerked backward as the tangle of the twins' bodies slammed back against their seats. The lights blinked on.

"Whoa," Sam said, brushing himself off as he got up and tried to get reoriented.

Mr. Kimble, still sitting, rose and calmly walked to the back doors of the van. He opened them. Bright light flooded into the truck. Anxious to be on solid ground, Sam and Fern followed the light. Fern hopped out first.

They were in a concrete room. The Atlas, dripping water but still in remarkably good shape, was parked in the center of the room. Despite the abrupt stop, not one of the eighteen rubber wheels had left a skid mark—just a damp trail. Gray concrete engulfed them. Fern estimated the ceilings at fifteen feet. Large oak doors stood on both sides of the room. Over one, there was a sign that read BAY TUNNEL in large brass letters. Over the other, there was a sign that read NEW TARTARUS in the same brass lettering.

Joseph Bing stepped out of the driver's seat and knocked on the New Tartarus door. A small grate slid open. One midnight eye, complete with a gray lid and thick dark lashes, stared out at the new arrivals. Telemus waddled to the grate, which stood at exactly his height— about four feet, five inches.

"Greetings, Telemar," he said. "It is I, Telemus. I have in my possession District Head Alistair Kimble, Vigilante Bing, and two visitors who request the right to be granted entrance." His voice bounced off the concrete walls and filled the room.

"Greetings, Telemus. Tell Mr. Alistair Kimble to come forward," said the creature behind the door, whose voice sounded much like Telemus's.

Mr. Kimble put his eyes flush against the grate.

"What's going on?" Sam whispered to Bing, who was standing next to him.

"Telemar is sniffing him, specifically his eyes, to make sure he's not a shape-shifting Blout. They're always doing anything they can to infiltrate headquarters," Bing said. "Here, they call him the Nose. He's got the best sense of smell in all of New Tartarus."

Fern thought of Vlad's first appearance at Pirate's Cove.

"Why are they talking like that?"

"Cyclopes are very particular creatures; they pride themselves on professionalism and formality. You'll never see a Cyclops break protocol. A lot of people call Mr. Kimble a two-eyed Cyclops behind his back because he's the same way," Bing whispered to the children.

Mr. Kimble stepped back and summoned Bing to the grate. Telemus escorted him. Then it was Fern's and Sam's turn. Fern held her breath, scared senseless. They stood frozen as Telemar sucked in mouthfuls of air. They could both feel his hot breath as he exhaled.

Telemar slid the grate closed. The two oak doors opened out in front of him. Fern had escaped detection, once again. Maybe she wasn't a Blout, at least not yet.

Mr. Kimble and Bing immediately walked through. Fluorescent light swamped the open door. Sam and Fern exchanged nervous glances and walked forward. Once everyone was inside, Telemus and Telemar closed the doors behind them. The *thud* reverberated loudly off the concrete. Telemar climbed back on his stool and resumed his watch.

The drabness of the place was uniform. The ceiling was high and the walls were unadorned gray. Fern, who had been expecting Oz beyond the oak doors, wondered how many cement mixing trucks it must have taken to create this fortress. Long rows of buzzing lights hung from overhead. The room looked like a warehouse; Fern imagined Costco would look much like this if it were emptied out. There were six pairs of white windowless sliding doors with red scrolling letters above each set. Two dozen people were scattered around the doors. Everyone was middle-aged and professional, some with briefcases, wearing skirts or neutral-colored ties. Fern imagined that these tired, pale people looked much like the people who took the subway during rush hour in New York City. The scrolling signs announced what Fern figured was a destination and a departure. The one closest to her read W.A.A.V.E. HEADQUARTERS—4 MINUTES.

When a gray-haired woman with glasses and a striped suit noticed Sam and Fern, she couldn't take her eyes off them. She tilted her head at Fern and pushed her glasses up the bridge of her nose.

"Alistair?" she questioned, taking a few steps toward the new arrivals. "Alistair, is that you?"

Mr. Kimble stepped toward the woman.

"Millie," he said without any excitement. "Good afternoon."

"Well, well. Alistair Kimble, before my very eyes."

"How is Outreach treating you, Millie?"

"Oh, you know, more of the same, doing the best I can, and all that." Millie's voice was high-pitched and fast.

Every time she spoke, it was similar to the moment before someone breaks into song during a Broadway musical. "It's been a few years since you've been to NT, hasn't it? When was the last time—it must have been the VC four years ago? Right about the time you stopped talking to me. Are you still the DH of the GCD?"

Millie, it seemed, was overly fond of abbreviations and acronyms, which frustrated many less-than-knowledgeable eavesdroppers, Fern included.

"My work keeps me aboveground for the most part," Mr. Kimble said.

"You know, all my friends warned me about you. They told me I should never get involved with someone like you, who's always putting the job before everything else. But you could have called, at the very least—just to say good-bye."

Mr. Kimble appeared to be in pain.

"I'm sorry you feel that way," he said, standing more stiffly than before. Mr. Kimble followed Millie's eyes to Fern and Sam, one freckled and blond, the other pale and dark. His salt to her pepper.

"Well, how did you go and pull a thing like that off? I've never seen a child here before. Are these yours, Alistair? Did you find a woman crazy enough to marry you?" More and more people were turning away from their doors and looking toward Mr. Kimble and Millie. Mr. Kimble took two steps back.

"They are not mine," Mr. Kimble said, offering up very

259

few answers. Bing stood nervously by, fidgeting with his collar.

"Oh my word! They're alleged Unusuals! Don't tell me you've become mixed up in all the hoopla," Millie said, her voice so loud it was bouncing from one concrete wall to the next. Her glasses magnified her eyes and made them appear as large as poker chips. "I'd heard there was an Unusual in the western United States, but two—well, that must be it! There's no way Chief Quagmire and his cronies would let them in otherwise."

"I don't think it's wise to jump to conclusions," Mr. Kimble said in his most patronizing voice.

"Vlad and the Legion have everyone running around scared, but I had no idea the paranoia had struck this deep. You know there's no such thing as the Unusual Eleven, don't you? Hah! Small children at New Tartarus . . . what next!"

Fern glared at Sam. She may have been on the small side, but Sam certainly wasn't. A voice seven times more melodious than Millie's shrill one came onto a public address system, though there were no speakers in sight.

"Tram to Outreach Command Center approaching portal two. Please allow passengers to exit before entering. Thank you."

"That's me," Millie said, turning away and lining up in front of the closest pair of doors. Fern marveled at the idea that Mr. Kimble, who was so formal and cold, could have possibly been somebody's boyfriend. Vampires had relationships too, she supposed.

The doors to the tram dinged and slid open, giving way to a brightly lit interior. The seats inside were gleaming white, as were the vertical poles. The outside of the tram was white with a single red stripe running alongside. Two windows on each side of the tram provided the only other break from the glaring whiteness of the transport.

"Why is everything so white?" Sam asked.

"A few years ago, the Assembly went to great lengths to brighten up New Tartarus," Bing said. "There were claims that the darkness was making the Rollens who worked here 'depressed.' I think we've strayed a bit too far from our gothic roots, personally," he added.

Normally Fern would have laughed—but normally she wasn't standing in the middle of a concrete room with twenty pairs of eyes focused on her.

"Tram to W.A.A.V.E. Laboratories approaching portal six. Please allow passengers to exit before entering. Thank you."

Although a few passengers got off the tram, no one boarded the latest arrival. Fern's heart expanded in her chest as she watched a man approach their group. The man had a large mop of curly hair and a thick mustache that coiled around his lips and climbed all the way down to his chin. He knelt in front of Sam.

"You're one of them, aren't you?" There was a badge hanging from his lapel with a picture of him on it. Underneath it read HARRY ROGERS, DEBUNKER BUNKER, CHIEF

DISPELLER. Harry Rogers held his arms out in front of him before wrapping them around Sam and bringing him close to his chest. Sam squirmed in the arms of the affectionate stranger. His hot breath made Sam's neck feel as if it were on fire. After a few tense seconds, the man released him, looking almost tearful.

"I'm sorry," he said, "I just can't believe you're here . . . it's amazing."

Harry Rogers voice trailed off as he struggled to his feet and locked his eyes on Sam with a look of sheer admiration. Mr. Kimble wasted no time stepping in front of Harry Rogers and blocking his view of Sam.

"Tram to Alliance Offices approaching portal four. Please allow passengers to exit before entering. Thank you."

There was a loose circle of people around them now.

"We must be going," Alistair said, pulling Sam and Fern with each hand. They stepped through the sliding doors and left the man standing amid a gathering throng of other people. They all stared at Sam and Fern, whispering to themselves. Fern looked away, all the while hating the fact that she and Sam were a spectacle.

"People from the bunker are prone to theatrics," Mr. Kimble said, expressing his annoyance. The tram was empty.

"What was all that about?" Sam said. He had uncovered his eyes after adjusting to the brightness of the tram car.

"It's a very small community and people have many

questions," Mr. Kimble replied, taking a loud breath in and out.

"I don't know why people automatically think the boy is the special one," Fern said, rolling her eyes at Sam.

"Oh, like you would've rather been hugged by that weirdo? I took one for the team," Sam shot back.

"Both of you settle down now. People are just curious about you because they've never seen children inside New Tartarus," Mr. Bing said.

"Anybody that's here has gone through a rigorous screening process," Mr. Kimble added without any of the empathy of Mr. Bing. "Everyone has a job in a specific department, helping to serve the Alliance. Imagine children walking around the CIA's headquarters. People will continue to find your presence here strange. You'll have to get used to it." It was as if Mr. Kimble was trying to comfort the children but didn't know how.

The tram zipped along smoothly and silently. The twins sat next to each other on two cold white bucket seats. Fern clutched the cell phone Mr. Kimble had given her before she boarded the Atlas. Even if she had wanted to call her mother—even if she managed to forgive the Commander for sending her first on a truck ride that almost killed her and then to this concrete den of deceptions—there was no way she could. The phone had zero reception. Mr. Kimble must have known this when he'd given it to her.

Fern's initial anxiety about the trip had disappeared. In its place there was frustration—frustration that her strange reception was the beginning of a visit where she could only rely on other people for answers. She wasn't sure what Harry Rogers and the horde of watchful eyes wanted from her, but she knew it must be something enormous. The mere thought of what being an Unusual must entail made her sink down into her seat, paralyzed from the weight of unknown but mighty expectations resting on her slender shoulders. Fern wished she was just like Sam and Eddie— not the least bit otherworldly or unusual at all. The train continued to zoom along to the Alliance Offices. Fern and Sam had no idea what to expect when they arrived, but each felt a vague sense of dread for what lay ahead.

16

the integration initiative

The tram slowed down.

"Now approaching Alliance Offices. Please wait for doors to open completely before exiting the train. Thank you."

The doors opened. Sam and Fern were the last to disembark. The light was dimmer outside the train. The concrete efficiency of the tram hub station had been replaced by marble splendor. White marble pillars buttressed arches that outlined a blue dome. A large stone-carved archway opened to a well-lit courtyard, complete with a bubbling fountain and a marble statue of a bearded shirtless man. Above the arch on the other side of the courtyard there was a sign that read OFFICES, QUARTERS, LEGISLATURE HEADQUARTERS AHEAD.

A man in a tuxedo limped out of the doorway toward

the group. He had a cane in one hand and didn't appear to have another hand. His thin sleeve was pinned to his side. His mouth was full of long yellow teeth, and his stringy white hair was complemented by white stubble on his chin. He had a sagging face the color of wet sand. The crags beneath his cheeks and underneath his eyes made his face look like a skull. This, Fern thought to herself, was the oldest man she had ever seen.

He extended his cane in front of him and performed a small bow in front of Alistair Kimble and Joseph Bing.

"Good morning, gentlemen," he said. "And most honored guests. Chief Quagmire sent me to meet you. I am Chuffy Merced the third. Shall we proceed to his office?"

Mr. Bing looked at Chuffy and bowed ceremoniously.

"It's a pleasure to meet both of you," Chuffy said, smacking his lips together. "I've been hoping to meet you," he said, directing his watery eyes right at Fern.

"I've got some things to attend to," Mr. Bing said before turning to Sam and Fern. "But I'll be back to check in on you two. Let Mr. Kimble know if there's anything you need," he said. Having known the janitor for some time, Fern could detect concern in his voice. He was worried.

Chuffy limped ahead as Mr. Kimble, Sam, and Fern followed him down a long corridor. The ceilings were lined with crown molding, the walls were adorned with stern-faced portraits, and the floor was tiled with black and white marble. Unmarked doors broke up the stone walls on either side of the corridor every so often, but it seemed endless.

"Where do all these doors go?" Sam asked, never able to keep his curiosity at bay.

"Offices," Mr. Kimble replied. Chuffy quickened his pace. Fern fell behind and almost resorted to a trot. Finally she spotted a double door adorned with a bloodred flag at the end of the hallway. As the group got closer, Fern could make out a thick white ring in the middle.

"What country is that flag from?" Sam asked hurriedly, trying to keep pace with Mr. Kimble and Chuffy's forced march. For a man with a cane and one arm missing, Chuffy moved very quickly.

"It's not a country's flag," Mr. Kimble said. Chuffy stopped in front of the door. A large brass knocker protruded beneath the flag. Chuffy grunted as he lifted it.

"Well, hello, hello!" Kenneth Quagmire, nattily dressed in a dark cashmere sweater and brown pants, opened both doors. His warmth and hospitality was a stark contrast to the chilly demeanor of Mr. Kimble.

The office itself was warm and inviting. A brick fireplace housed a glowing orange fire. A large maple desk scattered with papers and pens sat in the corner and red oriental rugs covered almost the entire marble floor. A chandelier hung from the high ceiling and pictures in golden frames hung neatly on the walls. Two brass-studded red leather armchairs faced Quagmire's desk.

"Not exactly the Oval Office, but it gets the job done, right?"

Fern took a closer look around. Most of the pictures

and paintings were familiar. Every one had something to do with vampire lore, ranging from a famous sketch of Dracula to the front of a cereal box featuring Count Chocula. Sam and Fern began to scan all the pictures and paintings.

"Everyone always focuses on the walls. Pretty neat, huh?" Chief Quagmire said, admiring them himself. "The idea is to present a pictorial view of vampires and how they've been represented through the ages." The chief gazed down at Fern and offered her a warm smile.

"You'll notice that although the vampire legend lives on, not much has changed in the way we're depicted. Most of the time we are categorically beastly, frightening, unintelligent, brutish, full of ravenous desires, and with little to no civility. We live in cages, caves, and graves. You'll meet a nice vampire every now and again, like George Hamilton in *Love at First Bite* or the vampire with a heart of gold, but still, the vampires in these movies and stories can't seem to figure out a way to live without feeding off other people. They can't live in the light of day. I keep thinking some investigative reporter or historian will catch on."

"What do you mean?" Sam said, unimpressed by Chief Quagmire's stature.

"Well, Sam, vampires are very much still a part of popular culture. There are hundreds of portrayals of vampires a year," Chief Quagmire continued, thoughtfully, "and no one seems to have figured out the fact that if vampires are still around, and have been around for thousands of years, we would have evolved—we would have formed organized communities and our own form of government. Other-worldlies—the whole lot of us—are intelligent, thoughtful people. Thanks to many advancements made in the laboratory by the World Association for the Advancement of Vampiric Equipment, we now live full lives in the bright light of day. We've set up a democracy of our own. We have one of the most advanced communication networks in the world. And New Tartarus, if I do say so myself, is a facility any civilized country would be proud to call its own."

Chief Quagmire looked up and smiled, almost as if he had become self-conscious. "I didn't mean to bore you with my political speech. All of my talk is meaningless, of course. This lack of change is most likely because our people down at the Debunker Bunker are doing their jobs effectively. So no new information gets out."

"The Debunker Bunker?" Sam said, pulling his eyes away from an enlarged commemorative postage stamp featuring Bela Lugosi with fangs and a widow's peak. Fern noticed Mr. Kimble look askance at Chief Quagmire as he sat down in one of the red leather chairs and crossed his legs.

"Every once in a while there's an incident—whether it be due to a Rollen or a Blout—that provides evidence confirming our existence to the outside world. The Alliance tries to control these occurrences to make sure the legend of vampires does not grow any more radiant."

"How?" Sam asked.

"Anytime an Otherworldly, say, harms a Normal in a very vampiric way, it raises suspicion. If the suspicion becomes a measured threat, agents from the Bunker intervene. They go out in the field and do whatever it takes to make sure these things don't begin a ripple effect," Chief Quagmire said. He paced across the room and sat in the chair behind his desk. He put his arms on the top of his head and leaned back. "If you want to know the truth, it's much like what I did for Fern at Disneyland, pretending to be Don Camille. A little mind-managing here, a little mind-expunging there. Of course, it's a lot easier if the whole thing hasn't been shown on television," Chief Quagmire finished and smiled, winking at Fern. This made Fern uncomfortable; there was something too forced about the chief's manner.

"Is there still a district meeting today?" Alistair Kimble interjected.

"Yes," Chief Quagmire said, looking down at his wrist. "In fact, you'd better get going—you have your reputation for promptness to uphold."

"What is your plan for Sam and Fern?" Mr. Kimble said coldly. Fern wondered if she was the root of the tension between them.

"My plan?" Chief Quagmire said absently.

"Where will I be able to find them after I'm finished?" Mr. Kimble responded.

"Chuffy is going to show them around a bit and then

take them to the cafeteria. Does that meet with your approval, boss?" Chief Quagmire questioned sarcastically.

"I'm not trying to second-guess you, Kenneth, but I made a promise to their mother that I'd keep an eye on them."

"That is why we brought them down here—so they'd be out of danger," Chief Quagmire said, his boyish charm turning patronizing in the span of an instant. "What exactly do you think is going to happen to them? Quit worrying and go to your meeting. You have larger problems to contend with."

Alistair Kimble didn't bother shutting the large doors behind him as he left the room. Fern could tell he was upset.

"Chuffy, stop hanging around, you nosy old man, and leave me to chat with my two young friends for a few minutes."

"Yes, sir," Chuffy said, hobbling out of the room. The sound of the doors closing echoed through the long hall.

"Chuffy means well, but he's a little slow, if you know what I mean. I've taken him under my wing here, but he needs constant guidance. He's a bit of a problem case. Anyway," Chief Quagmire said, changing his tone, "take a seat, you two."

Sam thought he was trying hard to sound avuncular even though he was far too suave and well-groomed to fit into the uncle role. Sam and Fern climbed into the red chairs and felt small as their feet dangled in the air.

"I know this must be very difficult for you both . . . and your mother." Chief Quagmire oozed sympathy. "But we'll get this straightened out. You made the right decision by coming here."

Sam and Fern stared at Kenneth Quagmire without so much as blinking.

"You've probably got a zillion questions about New Tartarus, but once Chuffy takes you exploring a bit, you'll begin to see what we're all about down here." Chief Quagmire looked expectantly at the McAllister twins. "I do have a few questions for you both first, which will help us with all this Vlad business."

"All right," Fern said, looking at her brother. She was so grateful he had come along; his presence was one of the few things preventing her from bolting out the door.

"Some of the things I ask you might be rather basic, but answer them anyway, please." Chief Quagmire took a pair of reading glasses from his desk and perched them on his nose. They looked out of place on his handsome face. He held a clipboard and a pen in his hand.

"Do you have the ability to teleport?" Chief Quagmire said reading from his clipboard and making his voice very formal.

"Yes, Fern does. I've seen it," Sam said, deciding to answer on behalf of his sister, much to her relief.

"Can she control it?" Chief Quagmire said, rapid-fire.

"Kind of," Sam said. "She can if it's a place she's been a lot." Fern was waiting for Sam to talk about their work with *The Disappearance Directory*. He didn't.

"How many times has it happened?" Quagmire persisted.

"Three times," Sam said, shading the truth, once again. Normally, Fern would've looked at her brother with raised eyebrows, but she didn't want to give anything away.

"What about other special qualities that Fern possesses? Have you noticed anything else?"

"Yes, she can predict the weather and she's very sensitive to the sun," Sam said, choosing not to discuss her hearing capabilities or her talent for moving water. Fern knew her brother well enough to know these omissions were deliberate and purposeful. She took his lead: They would be truthful to a point, but would not be entirely forthcoming, with Kenneth Quagmire. Why not wait to tell him everything until they were sure he was on their side?

"What about hearing? Some Otherworldlies have exceptional hearing."

"I don't think so," Fern said, jumping in to the interrogation. "It's not any better than Sam's."

"It's worse," Sam said, smiling at Fern. "Though sometimes I don't hear things when I don't want to. Our mom calls it 'selective hearing.'"

"Anything else? Fern, would you care to add something else?" Chief Quagmire raised an eyebrow.

"I get stomachaches a lot. But I'm not sure that's a special quality," she said, knowing if she looked at Sam, she might break into a smile. Chief Quagmire didn't hesitate, even for a beat.

"Now, when Vlad came to talk to you, what did he say?"

"Do we really have to go through *this* again?" Sam said.

"It's fine," Fern said, not wanting to tip Chief Quagmire off to their omissions. "I don't mind. He found me in Anderson's Grove, which is in San Juan Capistrano. He said he'd come to tell me that he'd be back for me in a month. He explained to me that I didn't belong with Normals and that he wanted me to go with him when he returned."

"Do you want to join him? Did you want to join him at the time?" Chief Quagmire said, without revealing how significant the question actually was.

"No," Fern said, agitated. "Definitely not." She had no idea if she was telling the complete truth.

"Why are you asking something like that?" Sam said defensively.

"The reality of the situation is," Quagmire said, looking over the top of his glasses "that many people who think they'd never succumb to such things—to a dark life based on fear and wickedness—do submit in the end if nudged in the right way at the right time. We've lost many Rollens in exactly that way." Fern looked Kenneth Quagmire squarely in the eye. Was that what had happened to Fern's birth mother, Phoebe Merriam?

"And you're saying you think I'm going to do that?"

"As long as you're honest, Fern, we can help you avoid any such event." Fern wondered what honesty had to do with it. She was sure Chief Quagmire was trying to manipulate her; she just didn't know how exactly. Part of Fern thought she much preferred her face-to-face encounter with Vlad. At least she knew what to expect from him—he had come out and told her exactly what he wanted from her.

"How will I know if that's happening?"

"There are some very dark and disturbing aspects to vampires, to be sure, but there is a dark and disturbing side to most human beings."

"But what's the difference between a Blout and a Rollen, really?"

"Well, Blouts still believe that feeding off Normals is acceptable behavior."

"Why do they still do it?" Sam asked.

"Besides the fulfillment of a desire? Well, blood is extraordinarily useful to Otherworldlies. Say you're a Hermes or a Poseidon—the sucking of blood may increase your special talents by twofold. Blood also extends the life of an Otherworldly. Say you have an Otherworldly who is on the brink of death—his life can be extended by regular feedings. So you see, it's incredibly tempting for any Otherworldly. But at what cost? The sooner we can acknowledge the temptation and move past it, the better off we are. Many Otherworldlies share this view. I think it's why my integration initiative has been embraced by all Rollens."

"Your integration initiative?"

"It's a plan I developed, and the reason I believe I've gained so much respect within the Alliance."

"What is it?" Sam asked. Chief Quagmire jumped at the question.

"Given the right strategy, I believe humans and Otherworldlies can live side by side, without persecution." Chief Quagmire beamed. "It's what all of us here at the headquarters are working toward. We won't need a place like New Tartarus—we will no longer have to hide underground like animals."

"Why are you telling us all this?" Fern asked suspiciously.

"Because my hope, Fern, is that you'll be actively involved in all this. I think you'll be an instrumental force of change."

Fern put her head in her hands. The words swirled in her mind. *An instrumental force of change?* She hadn't even passed geometry yet. How could people possibly be expecting such things from her?

"Where does Vlad fit into all this? Is he opposed to the integration initiative?" Sam asked.

"Vlad is another matter entirely."

"He sucks blood, though, right?" Fern said, instinctively grabbing her neck.

"I've never seen it firsthand, but . . ."

"But he does?"

"He believes that Otherworldlies and Normals were never meant to live side by side. He is a Blout through and through."

"What's he planning, then?" Sam said.

"No one is sure," Quagmire said, putting his pen down on his desk. "But we're pretty certain it has something to do with Fern and the other ten Unusuals. Which is why you were both met with such curiosity at the tram hub."

How did Chief Quagmire know about that? Sam looked at Fern, who was wearing her fear on her face.

There was a knock at the door. Chuffy stuck his head into Quagmire's office.

"Excuse me, sir, but are you quite done with the children? I didn't know if a reasonable amount of time had passed."

"Why must you always insist on bothering me and questioning my authority? If I were done, Chuffy, I would have *called* for you. Sometimes I think that you're simply not worth the trouble and that I should send you back where you came from." Chief Quagmire rolled his eyes as Chuffy shuddered. "Because you're already here, I suppose you can start the tour." Chief Quagmire got up from his chair and pointed Sam and Fern toward the door. "They belong to you for the afternoon. Don't do anything foolish, Chuffy, or you know exactly where I must take you," he said threateningly, but with a smile still on his face.

"Anywhere but there, sir," Chuffy said, practically

trembling. "I will not diverge from the planned activities."

Fern looked at the ancient shadow of a man before her and was repulsed. She didn't want to belong to him for one second, let alone the whole afternoon. Silently, they followed Chuffy down the long corridor and toward the tram. She looked at Sam, appreciative once again that she wasn't all alone. Soon she would have reason to be even more grateful.

17

the heck

Fern let out an unintentional shriek on first spying the huge hairy being. She knew there was thick plate glass between herself and the creature, but that didn't stop her heart from jumping and her stomach from churning each time the thing moved slightly. Although the hairy giant was clearly sleeping, it still qualified as the scariest thing she'd laid eyes on since they'd arrived at the Preserve.

The Preserve, Chuffy had explained, was run by the Institute for the Study of Indigenous Creatures and included a huge cavernous area covered with all sorts of vegetation, closed in by plate-glass windows. Chuffy, it turned out, was a magnificent tour guide. For the first time since Fern and Sam had arrived at New Tartarus, they felt like they were not being talked down to. He eagerly told them about the newest expansions to the

Preserve, the rehabilitation wing, and the number of watts it took to imitate the bright light of day. He seemed to know every inch of the place, and it became easier for the twins to overlook his ghastly appearance.

The oddest part about the whole compound was that it looked like sunshine was radiating from the ceiling. Fern could not spot where the Preserve ended through all the flowering bushes, trees, and ivy. The ceiling was white and sloped upward at least thirty feet. It reminded Fern of the avian habitat at the San Diego Zoo, except that it was larger and had monsters instead of birds.

Next to Fern, Sam put his head to the glass so he could fully see into the Preserve. The monster Fern had spotted was sleeping under a banyan tree. Each time it took a breath, its whole body would rise up and then come crashing back down. Scales the color of midnight covered its whole body, culminating in a human-looking head with red hair.

"It must be twenty feet tall," Sam said, crouching by the edge of the slanted glass.

"Seventeen feet and ten inches, to be exact," Chuffy exclaimed, peering down at the slumbering creature.

"What in the world is it?"

"A giant," Chuffy said.

"A giant? Like a giant human?" Sam asked. Chuffy laughed at Sam. His face turned childlike as his skin stretched out when he smiled.

"No, no. Giants are not human." He chuckled.

"Where did he come from?"

"The East."

"What's his name?"

"He calls himself Lagog," Chuffy explained.

The pitter-patter of dress shoes came echoing down the hallway. A man in a white coat stopped in front of Chuffy and the children.

"Can I help you?"

"We're just having a gander at this magnificent creature," Chuffy said. "I'm in charge of their tour," he said, nodding his head in the direction of Sam and Fern. He put his shaky hand into his coat pocket, pulled out a pink slip of paper, and handed it to the man in the white coat, who grabbed it anxiously.

"How do you get all the plants to grow underground here?" Sam asked.

The man in the white coat ignored Sam. As soon as he laid eyes on the writing on the pink slip, his eyes bulged from his head.

"I hope the chief knows what he's doing," the man mumbled. "After what happened the last time, I'm beginning to wonder if he fully comprehends the danger here."

"What do you mean, doctor, sir?" Chuffy asked as worry spread across his face. "The children aren't in any danger, are they?"

He handed the slip of paper back to Chuffy and stared at the McAllisters. "Hmph. Good luck to you," he said, looking right at Fern before walking down the white tile hallway. "You'll need it."

"What did he mean by that?" Sam said to Chuffy and Fern.

Fern felt uneasy now, as if they were in danger they couldn't yet detect.

"Not to worry, children. The Preserve is one of the safest places in all of New Tartarus. The doctors get very cranky with visitors, I'm afraid," Chuffy said.

The glass was very thick. The monsters were being carefully looked after. She and Sam were *not* in danger, Fern repeated to herself.

The outer hallways of the Preserve that formed the barrier between the wildlife and the observers were completely sterile. Like a hospital without the clutter, every inch of the place smelled and looked like it had just been scrubbed with Lysol concentrate. The white tiled walls and floors gleamed.

"Giants are very rare," Chuffy explained, taking his coattails and flattening them with his one arm. "There are only a few left on the planet." He crouched down to Sam's level. Sam hadn't been able to take his eyes off the creature.

"In fact, we have giants to thank for all of New Tartarus," Chuffy said, trying to bond with Sam, giving him a warm look and revealing his yellow teeth.

"Really?" Sam said skeptically.

"Young miss and young sir, this whole place was a

former giant habitat. The first Tartarus was occupied many, many years ago by all types, including giants, who were banished from the Earth. Everyone in Tartarus was a reject. Like me, you might say," Chuffy said, laughing so hard the empty sleeve of his coat flapped up and down.

"You're a reject?" Fern asked.

"Some think so," Chuffy said. "Why, take a look at me!" he said. "I look half-dead." Chuffy smiled. Fern and Sam looked horrified. "Oh, don't worry children. I don't take it personally. When you're as old as I am, you're just happy to still be here.

"Anyhow, many Otherworldly underground places of occupation exist thanks to the power and strength of giants. You see, once aggressive hunting forced giants, much like the Cyclopes, underground centuries ago, they started building habitats like these across the globe. The one thing a giant can do better than anything is dig. New Tartarus was their most advanced and significant underground structure. It became a refuge for those who no longer had a place in the modern world."

"They were forced underground?"

"Yes, exactly. Normals feared the giants as a threat to their power," Chuffy said, bowing his head in thought for a moment. "Otherworldlies and giants have been allies for millennia. Look around! It's a marvel. Of course, it's been thoroughly modernized since then, as you've probably noticed."

"Why aren't giants still living here? I haven't seen any except this one."

"They've been on the brink of extinction for several hundred years now. It's all very sad," Chuffy said, furrowing his already wrinkled forehead to convey his sadness. "They are really quite peaceful creatures, unless upset, of course."

"Why's that one in the Preserve and not out here with us if giants are friendly and peaceful?" Sam asked, inching closer to the glass slope, mesmerized by the giant's huge mouth.

"Depression," Chuffy said casually, limping down the hallway. "They can be very difficult to handle at times. The institute specializes in creating underground habitats that treat depression and many other diseases that come from prolonged exposure to underground climes. It's one of the reasons that the Preserve was built." Chuffy laughed raucously again. "I sound very knowledgeable, don't I? I should after knocking around for a dozen centuries!"

Sam and Fern stole a flabbergasted look at each other. He didn't look a day older than five hundred.

"What else is in the Preserve?"

Chuffy gestured for them to follow him. They turned the corner once more. They were now closer to the back of the habitat. Here there were fewer trees and more plants and shrubs. This part of the habitat looked more like the chaparral of the hills of San Juan. Creatures roamed in the underbrush. Sam and Fern ran up and down the hallway looking for wildlife. Fern's fears deserted her. She got caught up in the majesty of seeing things that had only existed in stories.

"Fern! Look at this one!"

"That's a goblin, young sir."

The goblin was more wrinkled than Chuffy, with slimy green skin and eyes so large they left little room for his squished mouth and nose. He ran to the glass and let his greasy hands slide down it in front of Sam. Fern turned around from her window and screamed with impish delight.

"*You* come over here!" Fern shouted louder than was necessary. "A chimera! It's so small!"

Sam ran to Fern's side of the hallway. The scraggy thing was the size of a small cat, with the fluffy brown mane of a lion and a snakelike tail. It looked positively domesticated. It ran around a low bush, chasing its own scaly tail, as smoke poured from its nostrils.

"As with most creatures who dwell in the dark recesses of the globe, how the thing looks is the least of it," Chuffy said. "Put that there chimera in the right conditions and it becomes one of the most fearsome things you'll ever en-counter." Chuffy shuddered at the thought, bringing his shriveled hand to his face. "Of course, all these creatures you see here have something amiss. That's why they're here—so they can be properly monitored. This chimera is a young orphan with behavioral problems. And the goblin you saw, for instance, made its way out of an underground habitat and attacked a Normal. Not that I blame him," Chuffy said, chuckling.

"Hey now!" Sam said defensively.

"Young sir, I meant no offense, I truly did not," Chuffy said, running in front of Sam with a sad look on his face. "You do not represent those Normals I have come into contact with. I should not have generalized."

"It's fine," Sam said, though Fern could tell he was still a little bitter.

Down the hallway, something thundered toward them. Sam and Fern scurried to catch up with Chuffy, who had continued to walk down the hall after issuing his heartfelt apology. Both knew he wouldn't offer much in the way of protection from whatever it was that was causing such an extraordinary cacophony.

A beastly creature that looked much like Telemus, but was four times his size, turned the corner.

"Greetings!" The creature's voice sounded as if it had traveled through miles of gravel and dust in order to reach his mouth, which was not at all what Fern expected—Telemus's voice had been high and shrill. Then again, Telemus wasn't the size of three upright oxen. This creature's brown tufts of hair and large cloudy black eye made him look the part of the beast.

"Greetings, Telemor. I have with me two esteemed guests: Sam and Fern McAllister."

Telemor took his green-clawed foot and placed it behind him. Ceremoniously, he lowered his torso until it was parallel with the floor. Telemor bowed in front of the McAllister twins.

"Welcome, Fern and Sam. I will hold a fond hope that you enjoy your sojourn here." He unbent his body and stood upright once more. He began walking past the group, and each step he took caused a small reverberation.

"That, young sir and young lady, was the head caretaker of New Tartarus. His whole extended family has a hand in the day-to-day operations of this place."

"Telemus?"

"Yes, Telemus is Telemor's youngest. They don't make them in the mold of Telemor any longer. He is a holdover from the old guard."

"The old guard?" Fern asked, her mind swimming with a hundred questions.

"Those that came before Mister Kenneth. Not that I do not loyally serve Mister Kenneth. I will for all my days. You see, I do. Do not say otherwise." Chuffy paused before stammering, "I mean no disrespect to Mister Kenneth."

Though Fern had been repulsed by Chuffy originally, she was beginning to harbor a fondness for him. His time-riddled face and body aside, he seemed loyal and honest—two qualities in short supply in her current world.

"We know. Don't worry, Chuffy. What were things like before Mister Kenneth?" Fern said, realizing that Chuffy was the first person she'd met recently that she sort of trusted. He was the only person who didn't seem to *want* something from Fern.

"They were merely different." Chuffy's dried-out face almost appeared as if it would crack in half. Before long, he smiled sheepishly. "Don't pay too much mind to a foolish old man and his musings." Chuffy leaned his cane against the tile wall as he matted down his stringy white hair with his one good hand. They had reached the end of the hallway, which stopped right in front of a massive cave that was built in the side of the retaining wall of the Preserve. Piles of thick black hair were scattered around the outside of the cave, and a grimy pool of murky water lay in front of it. In this corner of the Preserve there was no vegetation—just dark, flat earth. The artificial sunlight was dimmed, almost as if this part of the Preserve had been long neglected.

"What in the world lives there?" Sam said as he snuck up to the glass.

"The hecatonchire, or heck," Chuffy marveled. "It has a hundred hands. It's the most fearsome creature the world has ever seen!"

Fern wondered if there was anything housed in the Preserve that was not fearsome. She crouched and twisted her head so she could view the top of the outermost part of the cave.

"Oh . . . my . . . ," she murmured. Vlad's Legion of Hundred-Handers! Was this beast somehow connected with all that?

A huge furry mass had attached itself to the edge of the

top of the cave. It slowly crept out into the light. Soon the hecatonchire had filled the entire entrance to the cave. It crawled along the edge of the cave—using a hundred brown woolly arms connected to woolly hands. They were everywhere. The sight of the thing made Fern sick to her stomach. It was roughly the size of a small trailer.

"What is it, Fern?" Sam said, crouching near his sister. His jaw dropped. "Whoa. What *is* that?" he asked, backing away. Fern made out the back of a round head amongst the fleecy web of arms and hands.

A dull wail began and soon turned into a deafening screech. The hairy mass jumped down from the top of the cave. With a motion that looked like a windmill of appendages, the wall of screaming fur quickly approached the children and Chuffy. Once it reached the pool of water, it stopped.

A hundred fists pounded the pool with furious anger. Water splashed high up in the air, dousing the plate glass in brown liquid. The dirty water obscured the onlookers' view of the creature.

The pounding soon stopped. The water stopped spewing forth like a fountain, and the spray lessened.

The heck had disappeared.

"Where'd it go?" Sam said, panicked.

"Probably back in the cave or something," Fern said, looking around behind her.

The screeching started up again, only this time it seemed much louder to Sam and Fern. The McAllister twins covered their ears in absolute pain and horror, unable to think, unable to do anything but hold their heads, paralyzed. Fern was looking up at the glass from her crouching position. There was no sign of the heck, but the sound grew louder and louder.

The sound of plaster hitting tile mingled with the terrible screech. Fern, Sam, and Chuffy turned around. The ceiling was falling down in front of them. Giant chunks of plaster and concrete crashed to the floor.

The three backed up against the glass. There was nowhere to go. Fern panicked and thought of teleporting once again. But once again, she knew she couldn't abandon Sam. Though she felt tremendously guilty for it, a small part of her wished she could relinquish the burden of protecting Sam.

Chuffy jumped in front of Sam and Fern, holding his cane out as if he would offer them all the protection they needed. Dozens of slender hairy arms slinked through the new hole in the ceiling. Terror filled Sam and Fern.

"Stay behind me," Chuffy ordered, his voice quivering as the arms reached the ground and inched toward him. He growled at the creature. Finally, the thing funneled its entire body out of the hole it had made. It rested in front of them, over ten feet high and ten feet wide, blocking the only path out of the Preserve and back to safety.

The thing was disgusting. It looked like a dozen couch-sized spiders piled on top of one another, squirming and writhing. It lay close to the floor like giant hairy spaghetti noodles, filling the entire hall. Sam and Fern cowered. Chuffy continued to stand guard bravely in front of them.

Fern peered over Chuffy's frail shoulder. A small round object lifted itself out of the mess of arms and hands. This was the heck's head. She shut her eyes immediately, bracing for the worst.

Sam continued to look on as two midnight eyes bulged out of a small globe in the middle of the web of arms. A mouth opened and let out a squawk that echoed off the glass wall. The sound had the force of a dozen small earthquakes all at once. The glass behind them cracked and then shattered into a thousand pieces around them. Fern looked at her brother, sure that they would both be ripped apart in a matter of seconds. The heck's army of arms crawled toward the children.

The heck snaked its head down until it was level with the Preserve's visitors. The creature began using its hands to pound against the tile of the hallway. Shards of glass jumped off the floor from the reverberation. Fern and Sam stood absolutely still. The heck advanced. It shrieked again and again. After a minute, there was little doubt: The animal was shrieking at Fern.

"Fern!" Sam yelled in Fern's ear, over the thundering noise. "I think it's looking at you."

Fern opened her eyes. The heck's head floated toward Fern like a balloon on a string. It snaked over Chuffy's shoulder until it was inches away. It got closer—so close, in fact, that Fern could feel its steamy breath on her face. She quivered, looking into its cloudy black eyes. *Go away,* she thought. *Please, go back to your cave and leave us.* The animal opened its mouth, revealing seven clawlike teeth. It hissed at Fern. Its mouth was open so wide, it could have swallowed Fern's head whole. *What a terrible way to go,* Fern thought, closing her eyes once more.

Slowly the head snaked away. The army of arms was on the move again.

The heck was climbing back into the ceiling!

"What in the world . . . ," Sam said, unable to contain his thoughts. He'd thought for sure they were all goners— that they were going to die in this miserable underground fortress. "Fern, you made it leave," he said in disbelief.

"I don't know *what* I did."

Chuffy turned around after the heck was safely out of sight. He got down on one knee and grabbed Fern's hand in his own.

"You, young lady! You tamed the heck! With your eyes! Not in a thousand years has that happened!" A few minutes ago, Fern would have wanted to take her hand away from Chuffy's immediately. But this frail white-whiskered man had stood between her and the ugliest and most unimaginable beast. He couldn't have saved her, but he would've died trying.

Tears formed in Chuffy's eyes. "Young lady, you have prolonged my unworthy life. It is a deed so great, I will not soon forget it."

"I didn't *do* anything," Fern said, helping Chuffy up. "I just stood here like both of you."

Footsteps echoed down the hallway. The doctor in the white coat they had met earlier ran toward them, along with four men just like him. They stopped short of the destruction on the floor of the hallway. It now looked as if a tornado had rolled through the end of the Preserve. Gathering around it, they all peered up at the large hole in the ceiling.

"What an utter mess," one of them said.

"What happened here?" one of them yelled to Chuffy.

"The heck. It escaped."

"Are any of you hurt?"

"No, sir," Chuffy responded.

"How is that possible?" one doctor said to the other softly, but loudly enough that Sam and Fern could hear. "No one survives in the path of an angry heck." He whistled to himself. The five men stared at Fern. She stared back.

"We need to get this patched up immediately or we'll have a hallway filled with crazed goblins and werewolves," one of the men said. "Someone must have left the hatch open. I bet it climbed right into the ventilation system, the clever thing."

"Why don't you get these children out of here?" the original white-coated man yelled to Chuffy.

"Yes, sir, of course." His voice trembled slightly.

Sam and Fern didn't even glance beyond the plate glass

at the Preserve as they followed Chuffy out. They would have been satisfied if they never laid eyes on another goblin or giant again. Fern felt lost, confronted by another part of herself she couldn't understand. Deep in thought, she fell behind Chuffy and Sam. It wasn't long before she realized she was behind the group. Fern quickened her steps, still wondering what, exactly, the heck had seen in her eyes that she herself couldn't see. Terrified as she walked along the tiled hallway, Fern hoped she could avoid looking in the direction of the glass wall and into the Preserve so as not to wake any of the other slumbering beasts.

18

the bait

"You're famous," Sam said, lying on his back with his hands under his head.

"Quit being an idiot," Fern said from the lower bunk.

"Everyone in the cafeteria was staring at you."

"They were staring at you, too. They probably heard about the heck attack."

"They weren't just staring at you. They were . . . admiring you. Like you were Santa Claus."

"What does that make *you* then?" Fern said.

"Rudolph, I guess."

"Oh, shut up, Sam," Fern said, unable to fully contain her laughter.

"Hey, do you think I could special order one of those detector things from the lab?" Sam said, referring to their afternoon visit to the World Association for the Advancement of Vampire Equipment (W.A.A.V.E) laboratory. "I'd love to know who at St. Gregory's is a vampire. I bet you a million bucks that Mooney is."

"Don't insult my kind," Fern shot back.

"Can you believe Mr. Kimble's run-in with that Millie woman?" Sam said.

"I know! She totally hated him. I bet he dumped her." Fern paused. "I can't imagine him touching anyone, let alone dating someone."

"Vampires need to be loved too, Fern," Sam said, bursting into laughter.

"You think you're sooo funny, Sam," Fern said, pretending to be upset but unable to stop herself from laughing right along with her brother.

Although their mood was jovial, the fear and uncertainty of their circumstances lurked less than an inch below the jokes. After the hilarity died down, Sam spoke up.

"Fern, do you think someone here wants to kill you?"

"What?"

"I mean someone at New Tartarus."

"I'm here because people *up there* want to kill me, Sam," Fern said, pointing to the ceiling.

"That man in the white coat said that someone 'left the hatch open.' You're telling me with all the technology and stuff they have here, someone did something like that by accident?" Sam said.

"They're trying to help me here," Fern said. She didn't

want to think about the possibility that no one in this whole mess was on her side—that maybe Vlad was more right than she wanted to admit.

The mood had changed from breezy to broody.

The starkness of their quarters didn't help matters. Chuffy had deposited them here at the end of their long day. Their makeshift bedroom was three doors down from the chief's office. It was a plain square room, with wood floors, bunk beds, and a sink. The sheets were overstarched and the place smelled like wet paint. Chuffy explained that since Kenneth Quagmire had become chief, there were actually very few places to lodge for the night at New Tartarus, namely because people were not encouraged to stay there for more than twenty-four hours. Otherworldlies, Chuffy went on, were meant to live aboveground just as Normals did. He then bade them good night, telling them they had provided him with a joyous day. Chuffy, Sam and Fern decided, was all right by them.

Sam shifted in the bed above Fern until he was able to grip the edge and hang his head upside down. His fine blond hair hung down like it had been victimized by static electricity.

"Hey there," Sam said, now looking at his sister.

"If you keep your head upside down like that, you're going to get a blood clot in your brain," Fern said.

"What do you think is going on with the chief and Mr. Kimble?" Sam said, his tone suddenly serious.

"Huh?" Fern said, yawning.

"This morning. Didn't you see it? They were acting like they hate each other," Sam said, his face turning red from the rush of blood.

"Maybe Mr. Kimble doesn't like taking orders from Chief Quagmire," Fern posited.

"Yeah, well, I don't like Chief Quagmire. He's a phony. Nobody's that nice."

"Eddie's that nice," Fern said.

"Eddie doesn't count. He's an alien," Sam said.

"At least he's not a vampire."

"Oh, you know what I mean. Eddie's just different. He's in the clouds most of the time. It's probably not a bad place to be."

Footsteps echoed in the hallway. Fern and Sam, both conditioned by the roving night presence of the Commander, quieted down instinctively. There was a knock on the door.

Sam jumped down from the top bunk. He opened the door.

Chuffy, wearing white satin pajamas and a long green nightcap that looked like a large sock, stood in the doorway.

"Young lady, young sir, may I come in?" Chuffy questioned meekly. In his pajamas and nightcap, he looked like he'd escaped from the Sunset Manor Retirement Home and had lost his way.

"Of course, Chuffy," Sam said, ushering him in and closing the door behind him.

Chuffy collapsed in the chair against the far wall of the room. Within seconds, he was sniveling and sniffing, blotting the tears flowing from his eyes with his satin sleeve.

"Chuffy?" Fern said, getting out of bed. "What's wrong?"

"I'm . . . I'm . . ." Chuffy breathed in deeply. His lip quivered violently. "I'm deeply sorry, young sir and young lady!" he cried out. "I had to bring you to the Preserve! But I failed both of you!"

"Don't say that, Chuffy," Fern said, having nothing but warm feelings for the old man. "You were a great tour guide, and you had no way of knowing that would happen."

Chuffy looked up, his eyes full of appreciation.

"You look so much like her," he said to Fern. "You are her spitting image."

"Who?" Fern asked.

"I do not believe . . . I do not believe Mr. Kenneth meant to injure you, but if I had known his plan, I never would have taken you there!" Chuffy said as sobs violently escaped between words. "He meant to test you. Please do not let anyone know that I have told you such things."

"Of course, Chuffy. You can trust us. Was Mr. Kenneth the one who let the heck escape?"

"I . . . would . . . never . . . hurt you. I . . . will not . . . let such a thing . . . happen again," Chuffy sputtered. "I . . . will . . . do . . . whatever I can . . . to . . . help."

"We know it's not your fault," Fern said, placing her

hand on his shoulder. "Chuffy, can I ask you a question?"

"Anything you wish, young lady."

"When Chief Quagmire threatened to 'send you back,' what did he mean?"

"The Reformatory," Chuffy said in a quiet voice. "It is the most awful place in existence. It is where deficient Otherworldlies are sent."

"Why are you so loyal to Mr. Kenneth? You could live somewhere else and not be at his mercy," Sam said. "You know that, right?"

"Mr. Kenneth saved me from my evil ways—from a depraved existence—and he rescued me from the Reformatory," Chuffy said. "I am nothing without . . . his help." Chuffy looked up and wiped his eyes once more. They glimmered in the fluorescent light. "But this time . . . he has gone too far." Anger replaced sorrow. "I will not rest until I have repaid you in some way." The room grew quiet.

Footsteps echoed in the hallway once more. Two voices accompanied the footsteps. Chuffy's eyes widened as he put his finger to his lips.

The voices grew louder.

"Who is it?" Sam whispered.

"It's Mr. Kimble and Chief Quagmire," Fern whispered back.

"What are they still doing here?" Chuffy said softly. "No one is to stay overnight."

"Can you hear what they're saying?" Sam whispered.

The voices grew distant as Fern honed in on them. A door slammed shut. The voices and footsteps were gone.

"I must go!" Chuffy said, getting up hurriedly. "If I am caught here, oh dear! It will be bad," he said. "Very, very, very bad for us all!" He shuffled toward the door and opened it. "Don't pay too much mind to a foolish old creature and his musings," he said as if he were a broken record.

"Good night, young sir and young lady."

As soon as he was gone, Sam jumped to Fern. "Focus, Fern. See if you can hear them!"

"I'll try," she said. "But I can usually only hear people who are talking about me."

Fern was in luck, for at that moment, Kenneth Quagmire and Alistair Kimble were doing exactly that.

Chief Quagmire, though capable of great charm and gregariousness, was speaking with a gruffness Fern had not heard before.

"If we wait, the problem becomes more serious," Quagmire said, his voice dripping with authority.

"We haven't used all our resources to explore other possibilities," Mr. Kimble said, his voice reaching new heights of volume.

"Listen to me, Alistair. Vlad is out there, and we're no closer to figuring out what his plan is than we've ever been."

"Our failing has nothing to do with Fern McAllister," Mr. Kimble insisted.

"It has *everything* to do with Fern McAllister. Right now she is our only link to Vlad and the Hundred-Handers," Quagmire said harshly. "We have reliable sources telling us that Vlad has someone from the Legion watching her. If she disappears for a week, it will raise suspicion that something is out of the ordinary."

"Even when you were *convinced* that she was another false case—that there was no way Phoebe Merriam produced an Unusual—you wanted her down here for safekeeping. Now you believe she is an Unusual and you want to release her?" Mr. Kimble said, his voice full of accusation.

"Things have changed," Quagmire said with a surly tone.

"Have they changed because you found out she can tame a hecatonchire?"

"I'm not sure what you're getting at," Quagmire said disdainfully.

"Must I spell it out for you? There's only one person who could have let that hecatonchire out of the Preserve: you."

"I'd be very careful about making wild accusations like that, Alistair," Chief Quagmire said. Fern heard two hands hit the table. "You must calm down."

"Fine," Mr. Kimble said. Fern could tell he was holding back anger.

"What happened today was unfortunate," the chief began. "I'll find those responsible for the security breach and have them held accountable. But, yes, some good did come of it. No one has been able to fake the ability to tame a heck. Fern's status as an Unusual is a certainty, we know that now. The fact of the matter is, she can't stay here any longer. She and the boy have been enough of a disturbance as it is. I can't imagine they're entirely happy themselves, being shoved down here with no place to go."

Mr. Kimble cleared his throat. "So you bring her down here in order to put her to the test and, miracle of all miracles, she passes. Now you no longer want to keep her down here? What's the alternative, Kenneth? We take her home and then just watch to see what happens?"

"We have no choice," Chief Quagmire said.

"We need more information. I'll go gather it myself if I have to, but if we release Fern now, we're putting her life in danger. I'm sure of it."

"The vigilantes in the area will be keeping a close eye on her," Chief Quagmire said, shifting back into his easy, charming persona. "When Vlad shows up, we'll be there and able to catch him off guard, ready to silence him once and for all."

"That's why you're releasing her? You're using Fern as *bait*?" Mr. Kimble seemed angry enough to overturn Chief Quagmire's desk.

"I would hardly call returning a little girl to her family using her as bait."

"You never intended to keep Fern at New Tartarus. You had to see for yourself if she was the real thing, and now that you have, you're sending her back. And you used *me* to do it. Kenneth, Fern represents one of our only hopes of stopping Vlad and the Hundred-Handers. You're making a terrible mistake. Your actions are unconscionable!"

Quagmire began cavalierly: "There is little that separates the actions of those whom we deem evil and good. It is the *cause* a person serves that history judges and the results that person produces. Bringing Fern here was a strategic move, but one that serves a greater cause. Do you know how long we've all been working to find the Unusuals? How many people have dedicated their lives to our pursuit of integration? Rollens are tired of living underground. Word of Fern's visit to New Tartarus—word that she's on our side—will spread!" Chief Quagmire's voice rose to an impassioned plea. "Fern McAllister represents hope of a better life to each and every Rollen!"

"Then why are we putting that hope in danger?"

"You're a valuable member of the Assembly, Alistair, but I'm afraid you've always lacked the political savvy to lead. Think for a moment: You and I both know Fern doesn't come from the best lineage. She may join the Blouts despite our best efforts. The Lins are investigating the existence of what we believe to be two more Unusuals, one on the East Coast and one in Europe. Both cases are very promising. Fern may be the first Unusual to be confirmed, but the sad truth of the matter is that we can afford to make one mistake."

"You're sick," Mr. Kimble said. Hearing the noise his

chair made as it slid backward, Fern could tell he was standing up now. "Vlad is going to show up and make you look like a fool!" The door of the office creaked as it swung open.

"Now, now," Quagmire said, his voice condescending, "don't become treasonous on me, Alistair. As chief of the Alliance, I must make the hard decisions. This is one of the hardest. You'd better hope we're not made to look like fools . . . if not for the Alliance's sake, for Fern's," Quagmire said agressively. "After all, it seems you've grown quite attached to the girl." With Quagmire's words still hanging in the air, Fern heard Kimble's footsteps as he stormed out of the office and down the hall.

19

The Homecoming

H e should be thrown in jail! I'll kill him if I have to!"

Sam's reaction to Fern's report on what she'd over-heard was pure rage. He paced around the room, unable to sleep as he thought of what he and Fern could do to stop Chief Quagmire.

In the morning, Chuffy came by to tell the twins they were to go to Chief Quagmire's office for details of their departure. Sam was set on confronting the man in charge of the Alliance. By the time they left for the chief's office, Fern had gotten Sam to promise that he wouldn't mention what they knew, convincing him that no good would come of it. They needed to get out of New Tartarus safely, and then they could think of what to do next. As they stepped over the threshold of the chief's office, Fern tried to calm herself. Though Sam had promised her he wouldn't, she knew there was a good chance her twin brother would confront the head of the Vampire Alliance anyway.

Fern, it turned out, had little to worry about. As soon as Sam sat down in Chief Quagmire's office, the anger drained from his entire body. His eyes were empty. His expression was blank. Chief Quagmire began to drone on about their departure, staring intently at Fern and then at Sam.

"You had a good time here, didn't you?" Chief Quagmire asked. His voice was so slick Fern thought it sounded slimy.

"Yes," Sam said flatly.

"There were no mishaps to speak of?" Chief Quagmire asked again.

"No," Sam said, speaking like a zombie might. Fern grew wide-eyed. Chief Quagmire had some sort of hold on Sam. He was not acting like himself.

"What about you, Fern? Did you have a good time?"

"Yes," Fern said with no emotion. She was trying her best to play along.

"There was no trouble during your stay here, I hope?"

"No," she said, managing not to tremble.

"What did you do while you were here, Sam?"

"I don't remember," he said, his eyes completely vacant.

"You had a tour of the laboratory and you ate at the cafeteria, didn't you?"

"Yes," Sam responded.

"Fern, can you tell me where New Tartarus is located?"

"I don't know."

"That's right," Chief Quagmire said, smiling widely.

Fern and Sam each answered a few more questions about the duration of their stay as Chief Quagmire fed them other small details. It wasn't long before Mr. Bing and Mr. Kimble were knocking on Kenneth Quagmire's office door, ready to take Sam and Fern back to the above-ground world.

This time, Fern knew what to expect when she strapped herself into the Atlas. Sam, however, was scaring Fern. He was acting as if he'd never laid eyes on the truck before. Fern tried to ask him questions, but he ignored her completely, as if he couldn't hear her at all. He marveled at the leather chairs, oriental rugs, and ornate mirrors. Mr. Kimble was silent and expressionless in his chair. Fern figured he must have realized that Sam was not himself.

"Mr. Kimble?" Fern said.

"Huh?" Mr. Kimble responded with a puzzled look.

"Sam's acting very strange. He doesn't seem to know who he is or where he is. I think Chief Quagmire did some sort of mind erase on him."

"Sam?" Mr. Kimble asked. His eyes were glassy, and he wore the same expression Sam did. Chief Quagmire must have gotten to him, too! He was as useless as Sam. Fern took a deep breath as the engine started, taking some solace in the fact that they were leaving New Tartarus for good.

They were rolling along the freeway in no time. Fern tried to switch on her view box, but it was no longer operational.

Sam remained groggy and out of it. She wanted to unload on him, to tell him everything and share the burden of truth, but he was useless right now. It wasn't long before he dozed off completely. She looked over at Mr. Kimble's chair. He'd fallen asleep too.

Fern grew restless and afraid. She wanted to reach Mr. Bing, but there was no way to get to him in the driver's seat from where she was.

The view box blinked on. FERN MCALLISTER: REPORT TO MOBILE GREENHOUSE scrolled across the screen in block letters. She immediately unbuckled her seat belt and wandered toward the front of the truck. Pulling the curtain aside, she stepped up into the mobile greenhouse. The bright light filtering in through the ceiling made Fern's eyes water. The humidity made it seem ten degrees hotter than in the main compartment. She scanned the images the wall of green shrubs displayed.

"Greetings, Fern McAllister!" Telemus said in his characteristic croak, sitting in his same chair, his eyes roving over all the images.

"Hi, Telemus," Fern said, inching toward the wall of Sagebrushes. She had her back to the bushes.

"Fern McAllister, why is it you look so worried?"

"Huh?" Fern said, taking a step back from the wall of vegetation.

"What is it that you want to know, Fern McAllister?"

"Um . . . ," Fern said, totally taken off guard. "I came because I saw the note on the view box. You paged me."

"Yes, but what is it you want to know?" Telemus persisted.

"I'm not sure I understand."

"You must want to know something."

Fern, not knowing what else to do, asked the first thing that came to mind. "Mr. Kimble and my brother Sam . . . why are they in some sort of trance?"

"They will be fine by the time we reach our destination, I assure you. I have never lied in my whole life. The procedure is a common one," Telemus said.

"The procedure?"

"I have something to give you," Telemus said, beginning a new conversational thread. Fern was utterly confused.

"Is that why you paged me?"

"Many of your kind—and I mean no offense to you, Fern McAllister—they only treat kindly those whom they think can help them most. This is often a mistake."

"I'm not sure I understand anything. . . ."

Telemus hopped down from his swivel chair. His squat furry body moved nimbly to the wall of Sagebrushes. He reached behind a plant, pulled out a loose branch, and held it out for Fern.

"You are to have this," Telemus said.

Fern took the branch. "Thank you, Telemus."

"It is not I who give it to you, Fern McAllister. A friend of yours requested that you have it."

"Who?"

"I cannot say. I have been instructed to tell you to keep your eye—excuse me, your *eyes*—on this. It keeps track of the place you first teleported to," Telemus said, pointing at the white-flowered branch.

"Okay," Fern said. *Pirate's Cove!* she thought.

"I have also been instructed to tell you that you are the spitting image of your mother. I have been instructed to tell you that she was a kind woman. I have been instructed to tell you to not believe all that people say about her. Finally, I have been instructed to tell you that another knows of her struggle and that in the end, she found herself on the right side."

"You knew my mother, Telemus?"

"No, I did not. Please do not make it known that the branch is in your possession until after you have departed from the Atlas. It should be set in soil as soon as possible and watered weekly." Telemus looked away from Fern and began scanning the Sagebrushes of Hyperion once more.

"Thank you, Telemus."

"Thank you for visiting, Fern McAllister. It is a lonely job watching the world. I appreciate your company, as it has brought about a brief diversion."

"You're welcome," Fern stammered, not knowing quite what to say.

"Please go back to your seat and buckle your belt for safety purposes."

Fern, grateful to the Cyclops, followed his orders and left the mobile greenhouse.

Who was responsible for giving her the branch?

You are the spitting image of your mother. Of course! Chuffy had said something like that to her during his late-night visit. He must have given Telemus the branch. Fern's jaw dropped. If she'd known that there had been less than a handful of instances of Cyclopes breaking protocol, even as a special favor for an old, crippled friend, her jaw might have dropped an inch further. Chuffy had used what little influence he had to help her. Just how he meant to help her, though, she had no idea.

As she made the way back to her seat, thoughts of Chief Quagmire's plan to use her as bait plagued her. The reality of her situation felt like a punch to the stomach. Fern was all alone—the only other people who knew her predicament had been brainwashed.

As soon as she got home, she would go to the grove and plant the branch. She would discern what it was Chuffy wanted her to know. She knew she must find out where Vlad was and what he wanted before he arrived back in San Juan Capistrano.

Fern returned to her seat, feeling only slightly calmer. Though she had little else, a one-eyed monster and a one-armed elderly man were on her side, and she trusted them completely.

Fern had spent the last twenty-four hours in an underground fortress, bearing witness to events beyond her imagination, and yet one thing brought her back to reality faster than anything else could: middle school.

No one could have blamed Fern for forgetting that there was life outside Otherworldlies, Vlad, New Tartarus, giants, hecks, and a centuries-old manservant named Chuffy. But it wasn't until she walked through St. Gregory's iron gate, with Sam and Lindsey by her side, that Fern realized the speculation about her appearance atop Splash Mountain had captivated her classmates during her brief absence. To Fern, her trip to Splash Mountain seemed like a very long time ago.

There were, of course, several theories floating around the palm-tree-lined quad. One suggested that once at Disneyland, Fern had bought a bushel of balloons and floated up to the crest of Splash Mountain. A simpleminded classmate named Stephen Bucks figured that she must have tied a rope to one of the sky buckets and rappelled down to the mountain, despite the fact that the sky buckets hadn't been operational for several years.

The most popular theory by far was that Fern had bribed whoever operated Splash Mountain in order to scale the heights in another of her sad ploys for attention. This theory's popularity was buttressed by the tireless efforts of Blythe Conrad and Lee Phillips, who sacrificed their recesses and lunches to spread the word. They seemed to follow Fern at every turn.

Fern tried to steady her step and her nerves as she made her way through St. Gregory's. That morning she'd worried incessantly about when Vlad might come back for her. This was completely different. Although there was no "aha" moment where everyone noticed her, pointing and staring as she walked past the cafeteria and across the blacktop to Mrs. Stonyfield's classroom, she could feel one pair of eyes on her, and then another and another. She didn't say a word to Lindsey or Sam. Lindsey broke off to go to her class, giving Fern a solemn look before she parted. Fern looked around her and locked eyes with a girl from the grade above. She could see revulsion in the girl's eyes. *Freak*. The girl's expression was more curious than cruel, but even after everything Fern had been through, it made Fern uneasy. Being weird wasn't the problem, Fern realized. It was the isolation being weird brought about. Though Fern had Sam by her side, she'd never felt more alone.

Fern experienced a wave of relief as she crossed the threshold of Mrs. Stonyfield's classroom. The room, normally abuzz during the two minutes before the tardy bell rang, fell silent as soon as Fern entered. Mrs. Stonyfield's stern gaze traced Fern's progress to the back of the room. Fern slid into her seat and sucked in a big breath. While class was in session, at least, she could disappear for a while. Though not literally, of course.

"Do you have a note for your absences?" Mrs. Stonyfield said when she reached Fern's name for roll call. She had somehow grown fatter since the last time Fern had seen her. Her lips jutted out like a pair of large pepperoni slices as she pursed them in Fern's direction. Fern made her way to the front of the classroom.

"I see," Mrs. Stonyfield said, reading the note that Mrs. McAllister had written an hour ago. "So you were sick, were you? Catch a cold camping at the top of some mountain somewhere, no doubt?"

Almost on cue, every student erupted with boisterous laughter, marking the first time Mrs. Stonyfield had successfully cracked a joke in the classroom setting. Fern reddened and retreated to her desk in the back row.

Mrs. Stonyfield strode to the front of the classroom and pulled a map of the world down over the chalkboard. She pointed to Mongolia and began gesturing at the territory above and below. The class had begun their unit on world history and were now studying Genghis Khan, who, Mrs. Stonyfield informed people, had the largest contiguous empire in history.

"In his day, Genghis Khan was known to all the people of the Mongol nation as a hero," Mrs. Stonyfield exclaimed, putting a picture of the goateed man up on the overhead projector. "Of course, he probably wasn't nearly as famous as our star of the evening news, Fern McAllister!"

Fern realized that hiding under her desk was not a

viable option, but she seriously considered it anyway. Her face was hot and it felt as if acid were crawling up her throat. She imagined all of the terrible things she could do to Mrs. Stonyfield if she really wanted to. If she had to deal with the terrible burden of having supernatural powers, why couldn't she at least enjoy them a little?

Much to Fern's dismay, everyone in the class burst out with squeals of delight once again—everyone except Sam, that is. Mrs. Stonyfield, encouraged by the idea that the class was on her side for once, mercilessly pressed on.

"In fact, before we get to Genghis Khan's conquests, perhaps we should ask the conqueror in our midst what it's like to have stood atop a theme park ride—to have conquered it once and for all!" Mrs. Stonyfield threw every bit of dramatic intonation she possessed behind her comment, raising her fist triumphantly. Some students turned around to look at Fern while they laughed. Fern concentrated on the pain in her abdomen as a means of dealing with her utter humiliation. It seemed as if thousands of tiny arrows were piercing the inside of her stomach.

To Fern's relief, Mrs. Stonyfield focused her energy on Genghis's war with Western Xia.

It wasn't until Mrs. Stonyfield sat back down at her desk and instructed the class to silently read a chapter from their world history textbook that Fern noticed the coffee cup to the teacher's left. She eyed it, thinking about how she might use it to her advantage.

In front of her the steam dissipated into nothing.

Fern could tell she had cooled down the hot beverage, delighting in the discovery of another facet of her powers. Every couple of minutes, Mrs. Stonyfield would grab the mug and bring it to her lips and slurp loudly into it. Fern waited patiently for Mrs. Stonyfield to slurp again.

She narrowed her eyes and fixed them on the cup. Mrs. Stonyfield picked up the cup and brought it close to her face.

A brown stream of liquid hit her squarely in the face, all at once.

"ACK!" Mrs. Stonyfield exclaimed as she leaped up from her seat, her face dripping with coffee. Coffee spilled onto the desk and down the front her ill-fitting blouse.

"Are you okay, Mrs. Stonyfield?" Gregory Skinner, always the brownnoser, said from his seat in the front row.

"I'm fine," Mrs. Stonyfield said gruffly. She grabbed a handful of Kleenex and patted her soggy face down. Because she was afraid of what she might look like with some of her makeup rubbed off (especially her lipstick), she kept the tissues pressed against her face. "Everyone is dithmissed ulay fow lunch," she mumbled through the wad of Kleenex.

Filled with an equal mixture of satisfaction and guilt, Fern flew out of her chair. Sam caught up with her on the blacktop.

"Why'd you do that?" he accused.

"Do what? With the coffee?"

"Are you kidding?"

"She made a fool out of me in front of the entire class!"

"The coffee could have seriously burned her."

"It was lukewarm. I cooled it down before I moved it onto her face."

"How do you know that?"

"I thought about it and I could just tell. I've learned to trust my instincts."

"Really, you cooled it down?"

"Yes, really," Fern said proudly.

"You know what? I don't care what you can do. I know I sound like Lindsey Lin here, but you can't go around doing things like that every time you're upset," Sam said. Fern had always been the shy one in the family, hesitant to criticize or say anything that might hurt someone.

"Says who?" Fern said defiantly. "You don't know what it's like, Sam, when you can't trust anyone and everyone thinks you're a freak."

"I know it's hard, but people are going to catch on if you keep it up."

"That's what the Debunker Bunker is there for," Fern said, intentionally making a reference that she knew Sam would not get. He'd forgotten everything about New Tartarus.

"Don't do that. You can't make references like that and then refuse to tell me what happened."

"What if you don't believe me again?" Fern said, bringing up what had already become a sore subject between the twins.

Last night, Fern had begun to tell Sam all that had happened at New Tartarus. When she launched into a description of the Preserve and the heck, Sam was beside himself. For the briefest moment, he didn't believe her. His own memory of the event was clear in his mind—a memory that Chief Quagmire had put there. Sam made the mistake of expressing his disbelief.

Because Sam was the one who always believed Fern, no matter what, the fact that he didn't, even for a second, crushed Fern. She shut him off completely. She could have ignored his doubting her and chalked it up to fatigue, but the truth was she was tired of explaining the things that had happened to her, to Sam or to anyone. If she explained only one more thing for the rest of her life, it would be one too many. Vlad didn't need any explanations, and for the second time, she wondered if she really did belong with the Blouts. Maybe they weren't as evil as the Rollens made them out to be. Vlad, at least, had not tried to kill her. Not yet, anyway.

"Fern, I'm sorry for saying I didn't believe you at first. But you don't understand. It's weird to not remember a whole day! When you started talking about goblins and giants, it just sounded so ridiculous, I thought you were playing a joke on me. But now I do!"

"No one believes me."

"I promise, I *believe* you, Fern. You can't do this alone.

You have to tell me what happened!"

"Nothing, really," Fern said, full of spite. "We played pin the fangs on the vampire and made some blood stew. Just your standard vampire stuff." She knew she was being overly sensitive, stupid even, but her status as an outcast had made her raw.

Fern caught sight of Blythe Conrad and Lee Phillips, who were making their way from Mrs. Stonyfield's classroom over to Sam and Fern. They both had determined looks on their faces. They were coming to torment her again.

It was too much for Fern to bear. Without another word to her brother, she ran up the steps and across the blacktop. Once she reached the library, she pushed open the doors to the Hall of Legends.

It was empty, just as she had hoped.

She ran to the end of the hallway, finally collapsing against the marble statue of Socrates. Holding her head in her hands, Fern began to cry. The sobs came easily to her.

"Fern?"

Fern looked up. Sam and Lindsey were standing in front of her, out of breath.

"Fern, what happened at New Tartarus?" Lindsey demanded.

"Nothing," she said, drying her tears.

"Please tell us, Fern," Sam said.

"Fern, Sam can't help the fact that he doesn't remem-

320

ber. Chief Quagmire performed a Mnemosyne Obliteration! I'm sure of it." Lindsey said.

"Huh?"

"Chief Quagmire erased Sam's memory. Which, by the way, is highly illegal without a permit," Lindsey said in a low voice.

"Why didn't he erase mine then?" Fern said.

"He probably thought he did. Chief Quagmire is known as one of the most powerful Mnemosynes in history. He can manipulate anyone's memory to reflect anything. I'll bet he's never had an Obliteration fail before." Lindsey lowered her voice suddenly. "If you played along with Sam, he would have no way of knowing that it didn't work."

"Oh," Fern said.

"Come on, Fern. You've got to stop moping around and start letting us help you."

"Kenneth Quagmire let a heck loose on us while we were visiting New Tartarus. He almost killed us," Fern said, almost under her breath.

"The chief?"

"Yes, the chief. And he told Mr. Kimble he was sending me back here to lure Vlad out of hiding so they could catch him. I'm the bait."

"I don't believe it!" Lindsey exclaimed.

"That figures," Fern said. She got up to leave.

"Wait a second. I didn't mean it like that, Fern," Lindsey said. "You need to stop being so sensitive. Of course I believe you—I just can't believe the chief would do something like that."

"Hold on," Fern said, now eye level with inscriptions on the opposite wall. She gasped.

"What is it?" Sam said, following behind his sister. Fern made her way to the opposite wall.

"That!" she said, pointing to one of the Greek inscriptions on the wall behind Aristotle.

Οὐδὲν ἄγαν

"That's it!" she said, pointing to it again. "'Nothing in excess,'" she said, reading the translation beneath the Greek letters. "That must be what it means!"

"What is she talking about, Sam?"

"The day I disappeared to Pirate's Cove! There was this strange hole and I climbed through it and there was an inscription just like that."

Lindsey's face turned the color of concrete. "Nothing in excess," she repeated. "Nothing in excess. Fern, are you *sure* you're not mixing up your Greek letters or something? I mean, you don't even speak Greek."

"I'm sure," Fern asserted. "I remember it clearly."

"What's wrong?" Sam said, noticing Lindsey's pale face.

"That's where the stone is," Lindsey said with emphasis.

"What stone?"

"The Omphalos," Lindsey responded. "The one that

prophesied the Unusuals and everything else."

"What? How do you know that?"

"Because that's the way the legend goes. The stone is said to be buried underneath the inscription 'Nothing in excess.' A long time ago, the stone's influence was used for all sorts of terrible things, one of them being the murder of giants. As a response, the giants took the stone and buried it far under the ground, with a warning carved in the ground above for all who crossed its path: 'Nothing in excess.' I think it's supposed to mean that too much power in anyone's hands is a bad thing."

"What's that got to do with us?" Sam said.

"I don't know, but the stone's probably the most coveted item in the world. People have been looking for it for hundreds of years, thousands even."

"And you're saying it's resting at Pirate's Cove?" Sam asked. "That all this time it's been there?"

"If Fern is remembering those letters correctly, then yes."

"What if Vlad wants the stone? He must know it's there! That's why he was there that day on the beach, isn't it?" Sam asked.

"I wonder why he didn't just get it while he was there," Lindsey said. "I wonder if he's waiting for something—something to occur." Fern wondered what role she played in his plan. "We need to start monitoring that place," Lindsey said, practically frenzied. "Can we get there? What about your brother, Fern? Can he drive us? I'm not sure how to make a Sagebrush of Hyperion pick up a certain place, but we've got to try." Lindsey was talking a mile a minute. "I can take part of the existing one and then we'll plant it."

"I don't understand. Why do we have to monitor Pirate's Cove?"

"In the wrong hands, the Omphalos can destroy entire countries. If Vlad gets to that rock before we do, the whole world's in trouble!" Lindsey said. "Vlad's already leagues ahead of the Alliance if he knows where it is."

Fern shook her head in disbelief. So that's why Telemus had given her the branch!

"You don't have to figure out how to track a place," Fern said proudly.

"What do you mean?" Lindsey asked, wide-eyed.

"I've already planted a Sagebrush that will show us the cove. It's eleven trees to the right of the Kimble Sagebrush in the grove."

"Are you serious?" Lindsey said.

"Yes. Telemus gave it to me."

"The Cyclops?"

"Yes."

"How in the world does he know where the rock is?"

"He doesn't. Chuffy must, though," Fern said.

"You were pretty busy while I was sleeping on the ride home, weren't you?" Sam marveled.

"You could say that," Fern said. It felt good to have her brother back.

If she had any chance against Vlad, she would need

Sam's and Lindsey's help. She sat down once more, this time resting her back against Aristotle's cold marble legs. Fern took a deep breath, pushed her explanation fatigue aside, and began from the beginning.

By the end of lunch, Fern, Sam, and Lindsey had devised a plan for monitoring Pirate's Cove. Sam and Fern would check the Sagebrush before and after school, and Lindsey, who had a much easier time sneaking out of her house with no Commander lurking around every corner, would check once after dinner. Lindsey tried to give Sam and Fern a quick tutorial on the Sagebrush, teaching them to rub it in just the right way in order to coax the image out of the plant. Neither Sam nor Fern, it turned out, could make any progress. They would have to rely on Lindsey to keep the image alive.

As they raced home from the grove, their heads were processing the new information. Fern let Sam keep pace with her, and by the time the twins reached the kitchen table, they were out of breath.

"How was school?" Mrs. McAllister asked casually.

"Fine," Sam said, refusing to look at Fern.

"Fern?" Mrs. McAllister followed up.

"Yeah, it was fine," Fern said.

"Well, was there any talk of Fern's adventure at Disneyland?"

"No," Fern jumped in. "Curtis Bumble dyed his hair green and had to go to the office. Everyone was talking about that." In actuality, the Curtis Bumble incident had occurred three weeks earlier, but Fern knew Sam wouldn't dare rat her out. The Commander looked skeptical, but let the matter drop.

"I've got to go upstairs and do my homework," Sam said, sliding the chair out and exiting the kitchen.

"Yeah, me too," Fern said, following Sam up the stairs.

Normally the Commander would have been thrilled by her twins' industrious study habits. But as Mrs. McAllister sat alone at the kitchen table, unrest took hold of her.

When Fern and Sam had returned home after one night at New Tartarus, Mrs. McAllister was so relieved, she thought she might faint on the spot. The entire day her children were gone had been torturous. Although she'd called Alistair Kimble's cell phone until her fingertips were numb, she never reached Fern or Sam. Just when she thought she could stand no more, her children had arrived on the doorstep. The truck, with Mr. Kimble in it, was pulling out of the driveway before the Commander answered the door. Mr. Kimble wanted to avoid finding out what Mrs. McAllister might say or do to the duplicitous man. Any desire to throttle Mr. Kimble at that moment was swallowed whole by the joy of having her children safely home.

She'd asked a multitude of questions about New Tartarus—what they had seen, where they had stayed, whom they had met. Fern had responded with terse and unemotional answers. Odder still, Sam seemed to have nothing to say about his stay besides a few uninteresting details.

Fern had recounted their morning, explaining that Mr. Kimble had driven them home because word had come from Chief Kenneth Quagmire himself that she was now out of immediate danger.

"Thank heavens for that man," the Commander had said, clapping her hands. The words had sickened Fern, but she could not bring herself to ruin her mother's happiness.

The Commander's elation was short-lived. The more questions she asked, the less firm Sam and Fern became on the details. The fact that Mr. Summers had come by again asking about Fern only heightened Mary Lou's unease.

Fern, once lively and lighthearted despite all her idiosyncrasies, was distant and strange now.

As Mrs. McAllister sat at the kitchen table, her concern was overwhelming. She and Fern hadn't really talked since before they all met that day in Kimble & Kimble's conference room. There had not been enough time. Though she had no idea what she was going to say, the Commander climbed upstairs and knocked on Fern's door.

"Fern," she said, poking her head in Fern's room. She saw Fern lying on her back on the bed with her hands over her eyes.

"Is everything all right?"

"Yes," Fern said, her voice shaky. Although Fern knew Sam was on her side, for better or worse, she was still unsure of her mother. Fern felt like the Commander had been angry at her ever since her first disappearance. Vlad's predictions weighed heavily on her mind. What if the Commander had begun to think she didn't have any real obligation to Fern? After all, Fern was not her real daughter.

"You don't seem like yourself," Mrs. McAllister said, coming in through the door. "What's wrong?"

Maybe, Fern thought, her mother didn't know who she really was. Fern might not ever know herself. After all, her perception of herself kept changing—first she was an outsider with no friends, then an Otherworldly with special powers, then a vampire and the daughter of a supposed Blout, and then finally an Unusual, whatever that was.

"Nothing," Fern said, turning toward the wall.

"Was it a bad day at school?"

"Yes," she admitted.

"Do you want to talk about it?"

"No." Talking about it, Fern knew, would mean talking about *all* of it.

"You sure?"

"Yes," Fern said, lying once again.

"I love you." Mrs. McAllister said, closing the door behind her.

What if I became a blood-sucking vampire? Would you still love me then? Fern put her hands to her face once more, plagued by the thought she might not be the only one lying.

20

the most famous rock of them all

Although the McAllisters were now inextricably linked to vampires, as the days passed, they were acting more and more like zombies.

Fern and Sam had become obsessed with checking the Sagebrush. Anytime they could get away, they'd go to Anderson's Grove and monitor Pirate's Cove. Lindsey made sure to keep the image alive so they could. They'd seen a couple engaged in an indecent act, two middle-aged men in a brawl, and a Brownie troop having a cookout, but no sign of Vlad (or dead birds). Upon careful inspection, the cave in question appeared to have no secret openings. Things were just as they should be. One week passed, then two, and then three. Fern's stomach began to hurt constantly again and her rail-thin frame grew frailer still. Sam often woke up with dark circles around his eyes.

Eddie, though gone a lot because of social and sporting obligations, noticed the grim undertone of the household. He kept an eye on the twins, but couldn't figure out why both were so distant.

But Mrs. McAllister worried most of all. She was disturbed by the mood of the household and felt powerless to bridge the growing distance between herself and her two youngest children.

Which is why she didn't hesitate when Mrs. Lin called to invite the whole McAllister family over for dinner. The way the Commander figured it, the invitation was part of some sort of vampire outreach program. The Lins would welcome the McAllisters to the club, though Fern was the only real member. While she was there, the Commander might be able to ask Mrs. Lin for some practical advice about raising a teenage vampire.

That evening, Mrs. McAllister was dressed in a red skirt and white silk blouse and wore her blond hair in loose curls around her shoulders. Fern and Sam both wore jeans, and as they piled out of the car, they looked the part of the Salt and Pepper Twins. Eddie wore a polo shirt and slacks and looked as clean cut as ever. Fern's stomach was acting up again, partly because she was sure that a white sedan had followed them from their house to the Lins. And because she, Sam, and Lindsey were all at dinner, no one would be monitoring Pirate's Cove from the grove. Though Fern tried not to think about it, it was almost a month to the day since Vlad had last visited.

Lindsey had braided her hair into two neat pigtails and was waiting on the screened-in porch for the guests to arrive. She came bounding across the lawn as soon as she caught sight of the McAllisters. San Juan Capistrano was alive with a warm breeze and the chirping of crickets.

"Welcome to Casa de Lin," she said, holding her arm out behind her as a means of presenting the house to her guests. "I hope you're really hungry—my mom cooked enough to feed forty people." She opened the screen and led them into the house. Mrs. McAllister's heels clomped on the wooden floors.

The Lin house was as pristine as it had been the last time the twins visited. Antique furniture and colorful rugs highlighted the living room. The dining room was awash with shiny maple and there were fresh flowers everywhere. If this was indicative of how vampire families lived, Mrs. McAllister thought, then they lived very well.

The smell of spices and meat wafted from the kitchen. Mrs. Lin, looking as young and sprightly as ever, careened out of the kitchen wearing a ruffled apron.

"Hello, McAllisters!"

Her large oval eyes flashed warmth, and the heat of the kitchen had flushed her cheeks in a very becoming way. "I'm May," she said. May Lin's face matched the pristine interior of her house; there was nary a cranny or wrinkle. Vampires certainly did age well.

"I'm Mary Lou," the Commander said in her most gracious tone.

"Hello again, Fern and Sam," Mrs. Lin said genially.

"You must be Eddie," she said, looking at the oldest McAllister sibling. "I've heard so much about you.

"Mike will be here any minute," May continued. "Dinner is ready now and it's no good cold, so you'd better head on in."

The McAllisters took a seat in the dining room. With its grandfather clock and maple table, the room was more Norman Rockwell than Bram Stoker. A lace runner and centerpiece of lilies divided the table down the middle.

Carrying two platters in each hand, Mrs. Lin returned to the table and unloaded a heaping plate of vegetables and noodles, a dish of meat and nuts slathered in brown sauce, one punch bowl of soup, and another with scallops and more vegetables.

Mr. Lin walked in through the doorway. He looked tired. "I hope you haven't been waiting too long," he said, loosening his tie and sitting down at the end of the table. "I got caught at work."

"Always at work," Mrs. Lin said, spreading her napkin on her lap. "You'd think he was married to the place."

"Maybe when they change the laws," he said dryly. The Lins were so natural with each other and their guests, it was easy to forget that they were prominent Otherworldlies in their own right.

Small talk persisted for the first few minutes of the meal. They spoke of Mrs. McAllister's real estate business, the rising cost of tuition at St. Gregory's, and how lackluster this year's Swallow's Day Parade had been. Once the ice had been broken so thoroughly that large chunks of it floated freely, Mrs. Lin began talking with a more serious tone.

"Lindsey, Fern, and Sam have become such good friends," Mrs. Lin began, spooning broccoli and scallops onto her plate, "we decided it was high time we all got together."

"May and I would be lying if we said we didn't have ulterior motives for inviting you over," Mr. Lin added, smiling at Fern.

"Yes, well," Mrs. McAllister said, "all of this has taken us by surprise. It's been an adjustment. This isn't the kind of thing you imagine can happen in real life."

"The Alliance must have extraordinary faith in you, Mary Lou, to let you in on all this and make you Fern's guardian," Mr. Lin said. "Eddie and Sam, too," he said, not altering his dignified tone.

"I'm going to say this as plainly as I can: What we've been hearing from the Alliance does not match up to what Lindsey has been telling us about Fern," Mrs. Lin said.

"Under normal circumstances, we'd never involve you in the inner politicking of the Alliance, but both May and I have started to question its actions of late. We decided, together, that we could not sit idly by and do nothing."

"What do you mean?"

"Lindsey disclosed all that had happened in the last couple months and we made a decision," Mrs. Lin said.

"The information we're about to discuss is highly

confidential. We hope that you'll respect our wish to keep what we talk about from leaving this house."

"Of course," Mrs. McAllister said, her eyes brimming with anticipation.

"There's a new memo circulating around the higher-ups in the Alliance detailing that claim number one-twenty-four has been officially dismissed," Mr. Lin said.

"I don't understand," Mrs. McAllister said.

"Children who exhibit signs that suggest they might be Unusual receive a claim number in order to protect their identities should they turn out to be an Unusual. No one is certain who the Unusuals are because they were hidden across the globe soon after the storms hit, in the event the storms were a fulfillment of the prophecy."

The Lins continued to disseminate information as if they were teaching a class to bright pupils.

"There have been over a hundred cases of people claiming to be Unusuals. Each claim is submitted to the Alliance's investigation bureau and each case is pursued," Mr. Lin said.

"Because we do work as claim investigators, we're privy to information before it's released officially," Mrs. Lin said, picking up where her husband left off.

"What are you saying? That Fern is lying about her special powers? She's never *claimed* to be part of this Extraordinary Eleven group."

"Unusual Eleven," Mrs. Lin corrected Mrs. McAllister.

"Whatever it's called. It's a label you people have

put on her. Her powers have been getting stronger, not weaker. Why would her claim be dismissed?" Mrs. McAllister said.

Fern saw headlights flash through the Lins' front window. She looked out the front windowpane for any trace of the white sedan.

"That's exactly what we were wondering, Mary Lou," Mrs. Lin said. "Who would want to make it look like Fern wasn't part of the Unusual Eleven? And why? We believe Fern is an Unusual. She must be. She presents the most convincing case we've ever investigated. We believe the memo is false."

"You've investigated me?" Fern asked.

"We have been involved in many such cases," Mr. Lin said dismissively.

Fern began to wonder exactly how many people were watching her at any given time. Between Mr. Bing, Mr. Summers, Vlad, and the Lins, she was probably being watched all the time.

"We wouldn't normally bring this up, because ultimately it does not matter who thinks Fern is part of the Unusual Eleven in the short term. That will take care of itself. But because tomorrow is April twenty-third, better known as St. George's Day, we thought we might keep an eye on Fern."

"St. George's Day?"

"St. George's Day is a dangerous day for Otherworldlies. And Normals, for that matter. People get carried away.

Now, there have also been reports that Vlad has been caught and is in custody. So we don't see any real threat, but Fern is an Unusual, which makes her a logical target of some sort of scheme. Since her claim was rejected, it doesn't look like the Alliance is going to be providing Fern with any extra protection. One of us would like to be at your house, just for tomorrow, in case there's any sign of trouble," Mr. Lin said.

"We'll walk the kids to school and pick them up. I've already talked to Mr. Bing and he'll be close by during school hours." Mrs. Lin paused, reading the worry on Mrs. McAllister's face. "It's really just a precaution," she said.

"I really appreciate you telling me all this," Mrs. McAllister said, still processing all this new information from the Lins. "But are you sure we shouldn't contact the chief or something? I don't quite understand this day, but if it's as dangerous as you say . . ."

"No, it's best if we pretend you McAllisters aren't privy to any of this information."

Lindsey, Fern, and Sam were growing impatient.

"Ma? Can I show Sam and Fern my room while you work out the details?"

"Take your plates to the kitchen first," Mrs. Lin said in a firm tone. Eddie asked to be excused to head to Kinsey Wood's house to study. Mrs. McAllister agreed. Sam, Lindsey, and Fern rushed through the swinging door with their plates.

When Fern had had only superficial knowledge of Lindsey as one of St. Gregory's most popular students, she had imagined her room filled with an impressive collection of memorabilia: edgy pop posters, avant-garde CDs, cork-boards full of adoring-friend photos. In fact, Lindsey's room was almost austere. The bed frame was dark wood and matched the wide dresser. There were no wall decorations, no stacks of anything anywhere, and not even one picture frame. The room looked slightly more hospitable than a jail cell.

Lindsey took a seat on her bed, careful not to mess the tidy order of the pillows. "Oh, yeah," she said, able to tell that Sam and Fern were shocked by the stark contrast between her personality and room. "I don't like clutter or bright colors. It's a vampire thing."

Fern surprised herself by laughing out loud.

"What's so funny?" Lindsey asked defensively.

"I don't know," Fern said, relaxing for the first time in several weeks. "I guess I kinda forgot that all the other vampires out there have weird habits too. You seem so normal at school."

"I've spent my whole life overcompensating, I guess," Lindsey said, trying to lessen her own embarrassment. She paused, then added, "I had no idea my parents were going to drop that kind of bomb. That's the first time I'd heard any of that. I'm sorry I didn't prepare you for it first."

"It's okay. You didn't know."

"Well then, you think Vlad's really been captured?"

"No."

"Do you think your parents are up to the job of protecting Fern?" Sam said, sitting Indian-style against the far wall of Lindsey's room.

"At this point, they're our only option," Lindsey said. "Besides, they have a huge network of friends. They can call for help in an instant."

"Do you really think Chief Quagmire doesn't have someone watching me now that I've been dismissed as an official claim or whatever?"

"Chief Quagmire needs you to catch Vlad. I'm sure someone's watching you. I don't know why he wanted to get rid of the 'official' cover, but he's up to something."

Sam and Fern looked fear-stricken. Lindsey focused on them.

"Seriously, we don't need to get too panicked. My parents don't know what we know—that Chief Quagmire is actually planning on using you to get to Vlad. That means if he hasn't been caught, the chief *will* have someone watching you. You'll have protection."

"I wonder who it is?"

"It could be someone at school," Lindsey said. "Like Mrs. Larkey. The Alliance has so many informants out there, my parents have started calling it the V.I.A."

"We have to be careful," Sam said, deep in thought.

"You're right," Lindsey said.

"Careful?" Fern asked, mystified. "Careful about what?"

"You know what I don't understand," Sam said. "Why was Vlad snooping around after the stone? What does he want with it? Why didn't he just grab it?"

The room was silent.

"OF COURSE!" Lindsey said, jumping off the bed. "He wants it for Cronus's Curse! That's why he didn't steal it—that would have drawn too much attention to him. He was waiting until he could actually use it!"

"What?" the twins both said at once.

"It's all part of the same legend about the Omphalos Oracle; every Otherworldly over the age of four knows it. Normals even have their own version of it. A long time ago this guy, Cronus, led a powerful group of Otherworldlies called the Titans. Everything was going along fine for him, but when he learned that one of his children would soon overthrow him, he totally freaked and decided he would kill all of his children to prevent this from happening. So he started eating them," Lindsey said.

"That's disgusting," Sam said, sticking his tongue out.

"Things were different. Trust me, it was less weird back then. Anyway, his wife, Rhea, decided to trick him into sparing one of the children—Zeus."

"I've heard of Zeus," Sam said.

"Everyone's heard of Zeus," Lindsey said, rolling her eyes. "Are you going to let me finish or what?" She continued, "They dressed a rock up in Zeus's clothes. Cronus swallowed it, thinking he had polished off all his children and had nothing to worry about anymore. That rock he swallowed was the Omphalos Oracle!"

"What happened to the stone after that?"

"He threw it up and the stone took on all these magical powers. That's where the stone came from!"

"That's ridiculous," Sam said.

"What happened to Zeus?" Fern asked, ignoring Sam.

"He went on to overthrow Cronus, just like the prophecy said. They called Zeus and all his friends the Olympians. There was a big war, the Titanomachy. Eventually the Olympians and Titans were forced underground by Normals."

"What are you trying to say? That Zeus was a *vampire*? That all those gods were vampires?"

"No, of course not. But they're ancestors of ours. It's why all our special capabilities are named the way they are."

"What does all that have to do with Fern and the rock?" Sam said, fussing nervously with his blond hair.

Lindsey's eyes lit up. "Well, Zeus overthrew his father, but not before Cronus had a chance to curse the Omphalos. Most people believe that if a person invokes Cronus on St. George's Day with the stone in hand, they can make any Otherworldly completely mortal."

"Mortal?" Sam questioned. "Isn't everyone mortal?"

"No, I mean that the person's powers are taken away," Lindsey said.

"Including mine," Fern said with straight face.

"So let me get this straight," Sam said, furrowing his

brow. "You're saying that Vlad is planning to come to San Juan Capistrano tomorrow, on St. George's Day, and collect the Omphalos from Pirate's Cove so he can use the curse on Fern."

"He wants the Omphalos more than he wants to kill Fern, I'll bet—but yes, that's what I would guess."

"Why would he want to kill me?"

"Because you're a threat."

"Wouldn't he have killed me already, then?"

"Maybe he couldn't before."

"I still don't understand what we think we're going to do about it," Fern said. Was Vlad really lying? "Why don't your parents protect the rock?"

"They don't know where it is! They don't know Vlad is after it!"

"Then maybe we should tell them," Fern said.

"We can't do that now. If Vlad doesn't show up, we'll all look like liars and fools," Lindsey said. "And word might get out about where the rock is. There's a reason it's been buried for so long."

Sam stood up and faced Lindsey. Clenching his fist, he took on a look of grave determination. "Well then, if he does show up, we've got to get that rock before he does!"

21

the swallow cemetery

Mrs. McAllister slept soundly knowing that for the first time in weeks someone else was looking out for her daughter. Mr. Lin was to arrive around midnight and act as sentinel from a post outside in his car until morning. Mrs. Lin would relieve her husband and walk the children to school. The Lins, Mrs. McAllister was certain, could be counted on. They wanted to help and, more important, they had been proactive about it.

When Mr. Lin arrived at a quarter to midnight, he had no idea that Fern and Sam had already snuck out the window, climbing down the jacaranda tree over an hour before his arrival. As Mr. Lin settled into his post, prepared for a long vigilant night, things outside the house were quiet.

Meanwhile, Lindsey, Sam, and Fern were weaving silently through the grove's rustling orange trees. Had the Commander or the Lins known that their children, far from being safe in their beds, were busy at work on a plot to save Fern from the hands of the most feared Blout on the planet, surely they would've been worried sick. Perhaps, though, they were fortunate in their ignorance.

The San Juan Capistrano night was warm and clear, its black construction paper sky full of white pinholes. Tonight, against the backdrop of the red-tiled train depot and white-walled mission, Capistrano felt like a drowsy small town.

Fern, Sam, and Lindsey arrived at the grove with two flashlights and three sweatshirts. They silently made their way to the easternmost corner. The grove was quiet and the only light came from the beams of their flashlights.

"AHHH!" Sam jumped up in the air and let go of his flashlight, which went flying into the trunk of a nearby tree.

"What in the world is the matter with you?" Fern said. "You scared me half to death!"

"Gimme your flashlight," Sam demanded.

"Huh?"

"Your flashlight. Give it to me."

"What's wrong?" Lindsey asked with apprehension in her voice.

Sam grabbed Fern's flashlight. He used the beam to trace his path back to where he had first jumped.

"There." The beam shone down on a small lump that

blended into the caked dirt of the grove.

"It's a swallow," Fern said quietly.

"It's a *dead* swallow," Sam said. He moved the beam of the flashlight to the orange tree a half foot away from the bird.

"I think it flew into that tree and died from the impact," Lindsey said.

"There's another one over here," Fern said, shining the beam low to the ground as she inspected it for more bird corpses.

Lindsey ran in the opposite direction with her flashlight. "Guys! There are two more over here!"

"Oh no," Sam said, his eyes wide with fright. He went over to Lindsey. "They're all over the place. But why would they fly into the trees?"

"Because Vlad is in town," Fern said. Her stomach lurched. Though she dreaded seeing Vlad again, in the back of her mind, she was curious. He might have more answers. He might not be all bad, and maybe he would tell her more about her real mother.

"Oh yeah," Lindsey said. "When Vlad transmorphs, birds in the area begin to act in all sorts of demented ways."

Sam gasped. "Oh man."

Fern closed her eyes and took a deep breath, all the while wishing for strength. Sam wondered when they would find time to bury and hold appropriate memorial services for all the dead swallows.

They walked gingerly through the grove, nearly tripping over several more swallows, all of which had seemingly died in the same bizarre manner. Once in front of the Sagebrush, the threesome settled in for what they all knew would be a long, tense night.

They had decided to take turns watching the Sagebrush. If Vlad did show up there, then they would call the Lins and have them notify the Alliance's network of vigilantes. They had already decided on a hiding place for Fern where nobody would find her. Even if he did manage to get the rock, Vlad wouldn't get very far with the cove surrounded.

Though the children watched the Sagebrush's images intently, there was no activity at the beach. The full moon lit the sand and cave with the brightness of a spotlight.

All three children were awash with nervous energy. The grove had taken on a positively spooky quality with the dead swallows and darkness surrounding them. Sam kept looking around, afraid that Vlad might appear in the grove at any moment.

"Are you scared?" Sam asked Lindsey.

"I wasn't before this place turned into a bird cemetery. It's pretty creepy," she said, looking around the ground for more dead swallows.

A horn blew twice in the distance. The last train was leaving the San Juan Capistrano depot for the night. That meant it was a few minutes to midnight—the official beginning of St. George's Day.

Fern, Sam, and Lindsey moved closer to the epicenter of the Sagebrush. They tensed instinctively, searching Pirate's Cove for something—anything—out of the ordinary.

"There!" Lindsey said, putting her finger so close to the white circle that she sent a ripple through the image.

"What?" Sam said.

"In the far corner of the beach. That man! It must be Vlad."

"Fern, is that him?" A tall, slender man in coattails strode across the beach toward the westernmost cave. The gold watch on his left wrist gleamed in the moonlight.

Fern took a breath. "Yes," she said. Sam and Lindsey pulled their faces closer to the image to get a better look. They'd never seen Vlad before.

"We've got to find Mr. Kimble. And tell my parents!" Lindsey said. "Let's check Kimble's Sagebrush and see if we can find out where he is. If he's at his office, Fern can teleport there!" Lindsey was nearly frantic. "Fern, stay here for a second and yell at us if Vlad makes any sudden moves."

Lindsey and Sam ran down the line of Sagebrushes. Fern hesitated a minute. Because Sam and Lindsey had run off with the two flashlights, the only light in her corner of the grove was the blue glow of the Sagebrush. Though Sam and Lindsey were still close, she could no longer see them. She could only make out the white burn of their flashlights. She studied Vlad intensely.

She jumped when she heard several loud thumps come from Lindsey and Sam's direction. She whipped her head around toward them. The light from their flashlights disappeared completely. What sounded like dozens of feet pounding dirt echoed through the grove. Fern tensed.

"Lindsey?" she said. "Sam?"

No answer. She raised her voice to a yell. "LINDSEY! SAM!"

Still no response. Where could they have gone? She ran across the row of trees. As she made the dash, her foot caught on a root. She fell hard to the ground. Her head landed right next to a small round object. She scooted closer to it.

"Ugh!"

Fern's face had landed two inches away from another dead bird. She jumped up, full of terror.

"Sam?!?" she repeated. Her heart was pounding now and her head was spinning. She knew there was no way that Sam or Lindsey would play such a cruel game of hide-and-seek on tonight of all nights. They were gone. But where?

Brushing the dirt off her knees, she looked at her hands. Her palms were bleeding, but she couldn't feel any pain. The only thing she could focus on was how terribly alone she was.

She walked, more carefully this time, toward the other Sagebrush. In the darkness, she counted off the right number of trees. Starting from the middle of the trunk, she made her way down to the base of the eleventh orange tree. She recognized the pointed leaves of the other Sagebrush of Hyperion. Lindsey had not awakened the plant, which was completely lifeless. Fern crouched next to the plant and rubbed it furiously. A few white flowers fell from the plant. She was destroying it. Taking a deep breath, she tried again, this time more gently.

"Please work," she said, hoping that if she found out where Alistair Kimble was, she might be able to ask him for help. Fern, thoroughly working over the plant, wasn't getting so much as a crackle out of it. Vlad was probably seconds away from getting the stone. His next task, of course, would be finding Fern.

Worse yet, her brother and Lindsey were missing.

She put her head between her knees and tried to think. She must. Getting up, she resisted the urge to kick the uncooperative Sagebrush and began running. She ran through the grove back toward the McAllister house. Her legs were tired, but her fear carried her swiftly home.

Once she was in sight of the McAllister house, she walked up the middle of the street, hoping Mr. Lin would catch sight of her. There were two cars parked on the street and both were empty. Fern panicked. Where was Mr. Lin? She was gasping for air, trying not to let the dread overwhelm her lungs. She ran to the jacaranda tree and climbed, wasting no time by leaping in the window from a branch. She ran down the hallway to Sam's bedroom. He wasn't there. She bounded into Eddie's room. It was empty too. With no other choice, she burst into the Commander's room. Her bed was unmade but empty.

"Mom?"

Again, no answer. Every one of the McAllisters was now unaccounted for. Fern fought back tears. She ran back to her bedroom. Sticking her head out into the night air, she looked up and down the street. The streets of San Juan were placid.

What if there was no one to protect her? What if this was the last she ever saw of her family? What if they were dead?

Fern closed her eyes, trying to calm the terror bubbling up inside her.

What if the entire thing was a big distraction to keep Fern away from monitoring Pirate's Cove? What if Vlad now had the rock? She'd left her post in the grove! No one was watching!

Dead tired but determined, Fern burst out the front door. She paused, out of breath. Whether it was force of habit or because she was so alarmed she couldn't think straight, she'd forgotten she could easily teleport back to the grove. She leaned against the tree, closed her eyes, and pictured the grove, now littered with dead swallows.

Once she was back at the grove, it didn't take Fern long to locate the Sagebrush, which was still glowing with blue light. She headed straight for it, without giving any thought to where she was stepping or what she was stepping on. She stopped in front of the image of Pirate's Cove, still bright and clear. There was now a fire glowing to the right of the cave. Fern focused on the image. A group of people circled the fire. As Fern drew closer, she could make out the circle more clearly. Every person was covered from head to toe with a brown cloak. They looked like friars except for the fact that each cloak had one black handprint on the back.

When Fern spotted Sam and Lindsey, tied together near the fire in the center of the circle, her knees buckled and she almost dropped to the ground. Their heads hung limp, their eyes were closed, and their ankles and hands were bound with rope. They sat back-to-back, and the only life on their faces were the shadows created by the dancing flames of the fire. She covered her own mouth to keep from crying out.

Fern leaned toward the Sagebrush, searching for Vlad. He stood on the outside of the circle, observing as the group closed in on Sam and Lindsey. He walked away from the group.

Instinctively, she zeroed in on one of the stones jutting out from the beach, realizing what she must do.

22

the curse for a day

Teleporting was now like clockwork for Fern.

She had no trouble transporting herself from Anderson's Grove to Pirate's Cove. In under two seconds she'd left the grove and was shivering as she kneeled in the cold sand. Under different circumstances, she might have marveled at her own skill.

Fern peered out from behind the large rock that stood between her and the roaring fire farther down the beach. Slowly moving around the rock to get a better view, Fern took several deep breaths and tried to quell the fire in her stomach. She closed her eyes, trying to gather courage.

"Fern," Vlad said in his deep voice, "come out from behind that rock." Fern's stomach sank. Vlad was now standing near the front of the cave. Her knees wobbled as she stood upright and took a step down the beach, toward the cave and Vlad.

"Do not be afraid," Vlad said. Fern saw his leather shoes first, then neatly creased pants, coattails with a dress shirt, red suspenders, gold watch, that unmistakable goatee, red lips, and white fangs. Vlad towered above her. He was soon an arm's length away. The fire glowed farther down the beach.

"What have you done to them?" Fern cried out.

"Calm down, Fern. Let me speak to you for one second. I brought them here because it was the only way I could ensure you would come. This is too important, but I will not hurt them. You have my word." Vlad's thick voice was full of sympathy.

"Let them go!" Fern screamed.

"Fern, do you not see that they will never be free as long as you are around? Even in the last few weeks, have they not been tormented because of your presence?" Images of Sam's terrified face staring up at the heck rushed through Fern's head. Vlad continued. "Have I lied to you yet?"

Fern thought for a moment. Vlad had scared her, certainly, but he had not lied. "No," she stammered, overcome.

"Your family is doomed if you stay with them. If you do not come with me now, there will be others after your family because of their association with you. They will never be safe! The others will not be as considerate as I have been."

Fern wore her agony on her face.

"The only way you can truly protect your brothers and the woman you call your mother is by leaving them! You must realize that!"

Distraught, she looked at her twin brother's peaceful face, and her heart wrenched. As the flames from the fire illuminated Sam's soft features, Fern became overwhelmed with love for her brother—Sam, who had been there every day of her life. Sam, who had stood by her.

"I . . . I can't . . . I can't leave," she pleaded, beginning to run toward her brother and friend.

"I would not take another step in that direction if you want them to live," Vlad said, turning malicious in an instant. "I will not hurt them, as I said, but I cannot promise the same for the Hundred-Handers. They get very angry when someone they do not know tries to approach them. Besides, they are very hungry," he continued. "You see, they have a habit of being quite vicious, though I try to restrain them."

Fern almost doubled over at the thought of the Hundred-Handers feasting on Sam and Lindsey.

"I don't understand! Sam and Lindsey can't help you. Please let them go!"

"Ah yes, Fern. But they can ensure that *you'll* help me. In case your mind has grown soft by living with these Normals and you do not see things as they truly are."

"The Alliance is coming," Fern said, defiantly. "They've been watching me. They'll capture you and you'll never get that rock."

"No one is watching you, Fern. They all believe you have teleported to the mission. And since the Legion happened upon your little friends among the orange trees before they had a chance to tell anyone *anything*," Vlad hissed, "no one is coming."

"No!" Fern cried out.

"Do not be foolish, Fern. This does not have to turn ugly," Vlad said. "You and I are the same. Quagmire and his wretched Alliance do not have your best interests at heart." Vlad flashed his fanged smile. "We have both been misunderstood all our lives. We arrived before the world was ready for us!" Vlad's eyes blazed.

The thought that Fern was responsible for bringing all this upon her family struck her like a knife to the heart. Maybe, she thought, she could appease Vlad without truly giving in to him. "Please just release them . . . and I'll do what you want. Release Lindsey and my brother," Fern pleaded.

"That boy over there," Vlad said, baring his fangs, "is *not* your brother. He is so far beneath you—so insignificant and pitiful when matched up against what you will become!"

Vlad put his hands behind his back and reined in his rage. He began to look pensive. "Was I not right, Fern? Your mother sent you away, did she not?"

"She did it to protect me," Fern said boldly.

"Are you certain she wasn't trying to protect herself?" Vlad paced up and down the beach thoughtfully. "Answer me this, Fern: Does she look at you the same way she used to before she found out you were a vampire?"

Fern willed her mind not to remember all the times she felt her mother looking at her with vacant eyes—like she was staring at a stranger.

"Of course she does not. Which leaves you with a choice. Are you going to put your life in the Alliance's hands? Why did they leave you all alone, then? Why is there no one here now to protect you? They want you dead because they know you are one of us!" Vlad said with a tone so vicious, it almost knocked Fern over. "Soon the McAllisters will feel the same way. Including that mangy being you call your brother!"

It couldn't be true, and Fern knew it, but her head was spinning. Nothing would be like it was.

"I want you to fulfill your promise, Fern. You have shown great promise already. You know why I am here, do you not?"

"You want to get the stone and use it against me." Fern's body was stiff with fear.

"Use it *against* you? Do you think I would have shown you exactly where it was that day on the beach if that was my plan? I am here to get the stone, yes. But I have no intention of using it against *you*. Fern, I am your only friend in this. Why can you not see that?" Vlad stroked his goatee with his index finger and thumb. "We are going to use the rock together, Fern. You and I."

Vlad turned his back to Fern and walked toward the

cave. Fern looked at her comatose brother and Lindsey. Sam had spent his entire life trying to protect Fern, but it was her turn now. She would do whatever she could to see that her brother made it out of this alive. Even if that meant abandoning him. With no other option, Fern followed Vlad into the cave.

Fern noticed strange yellow light coming from within the cave. When she got closer, she realized the hole she'd crawled through the last time she was here was open again, emitting a bright yellow light.

Once he was inside, Vlad pointed to the etched out letters.

MLM + PM

"Your mother used to come here often when she was your age," Vlad said. "Those are her initials."

Of course they were her mother's initials. Mary Lou McAllister. Fern no longer believed in coincidences.

"Who is PM? Is that my father?"

"PM *is* your mother. *Phoebe Merriam*," Vlad said. Fern took a step back, to consider.

"What?"

"We will have time for specifics later. Fern, if you help me, I will make sure that the Legion lets your friends go, unharmed. It is simple game of quid pro quo—a favor for a favor."

"How do I know that you won't hurt them anyway?"

"I have no interest in two people so insignificant."

"What do you want me to do?"

"The chamber through here," Vlad said, pointing at the glowing hole in the cave, "opens two days a year. The first day is the anniversary of the Titanomachy—the day you arrived on the beach. The second is St. George's Day, today."

"So?" Fern questioned, trying to draw the conversation out.

"The Omphalos Oracle rests under the chamber. I need you to help me retrieve it."

"Why can't you get it yourself?" Fern asked.

"Because it is buried under thousands of feet of bedrock."

"I don't understand."

"No one can reach it," he said, his fangs radiating from the glow of the hole. "It has been buried here for thousands of years."

"You need me to teleport there?"

"Yes," Vlad said. "Ironically, only an Unusual can get to the stone. When the giants buried it, they made sure of that. A few have tried to tunnel to it. Many people thought the Unusual Eleven were just a fairy tale and that the rock was lost forever. Then you arrived. That day you appeared on the beach, I knew the rock would be uncovered at last." Vlad's black eyes sparked, and he smiled, revealing his white fangs. "You will use the drawing inside the chamber to teleport there and retrieve the rock."

"I'll give you the rock if you wake them up and let them go."

"I had an inkling that you would make the right choice," Vlad said, smiling with his big red lips. He began walking once more to the cave. Fern followed dejectedly behind him.

"I will be waiting here for you," Vlad said as Fern began to crawl through the hole into the chamber. "If you do not reappear here in less than three minutes, your brother and friend will no longer be here. The Hundred-Handers look very hungry." He grinned mischievously.

Fern's terror was gnawing at the lining of her stomach. The light from the uncovered hole was so bright, Fern had to close her eyes and feel her way through the rough-hewn rock. The stones tore at her knees and already-bleeding palms as she scrabbled forward. Once she felt above her and felt nothing, she knew she'd cleared the hole. She opened her eyes.

The brightness was bursting from the words written on the center of the round floor.

Οὐδὲν ἄγαν

Beams of light emanated from each letter and made the chamber bright. Fern wasted no time. She limped, knees aching, to the opposite wall, focusing only on the drawing of the stone room that housed the rock. The image of the black rock in the center on the marble pedestal became all she could see. She tried to imagine the room, building a picture in her mind.

She opened her eyes.

Fern hadn't moved an inch. Vlad had asked her to do the impossible. She'd never been near this place; maybe she couldn't teleport somewhere she'd never been before!

She tried again. This time she kept her eyes open. She stared at the drawing of the rock. She stared and stared, keeping her eyes open so long, they filled with tears.

Then she thought of Sam and Lindsey.

"I have to do this," Fern said aloud.

Her eyes clamped shut. She felt her legs slip out from underneath her. Blackness took hold.

It was happening! Floating, Fern relaxed slightly for the first time while in the throes of teleporting, knowing that she would open her eyes and the Omphalos would be within reach.

The room that housed the Omphalos looked like the inside of a vault. The walls were stone and square, not curved like the chamber she had just left. Fern shivered; the room felt refrigerated.

The Omphalos was a sight to behold. Roughly the size of Fern's head, it rested in the center of the room on a small marble pillar. The stone was smooth like a skipping stone, shiny like patent leather, and emitting a dark blue light—the only light in the room. Fern wanted to feel the walls, to take the room in—a room that no one had been in for a thousand years. The air smelled ancient, like no one had breathed it since time first thrust the cliffs up from the sea. Calm enveloped her.

When she lifted the Omphalos off the marble pillar, it was heavy, like a basket of wet laundry, and it radiated warmth. She brought it close to her stomach, which warmed under the stone's presence. The pain from her knees and hands disappeared.

Part of her wanted to stay in this room and rest, even if it was for only a few seconds. She was so tired. Here, her skull tingled and her body felt light and relaxed. Her mind was clear. She hadn't felt this good since she and her family had visited Carlsbad Caverns. She sank to her knees and cradled the rock, feeling woozy. Fern was convinced she could stay here forever.

She stretched out on the hard floor.

When Fern rolled over, she felt *The Disappearance Directory* dig into her side. She removed it from her waistband. She turned the pages, still groggy. Sam's note stared back at her. Her mind snapped back into focus. She must get back. Sam's and Lindsey's lives depended on it!

Fern gripped the stone more tightly than ever. She flipped to Pirate's Cove in the *Directory*, closed her eyes, and imagined what lay waiting for her on the beach.

Pain shot up Fern's rib cage as she opened her eyes. She had landed on the Omphalos.

She rolled off the rock. The fire was blazing on the

western end of the beach.

"I see you made it back safely," Vlad said calmly as he stood over Fern. Fern, now lying in the sand, stared up at Vlad himself.

Fern rose to her feet. She clutched the stone, trying to earn herself more time to think. She began to stall.

"Can I ask you a question?"

"Of course," Vlad said, his mood light, his eyes bouncing from Fern's face to the stone.

"How did you know that we were in the grove tonight? How did you know that I would show up in the grove that first time?"

"I have been watching you—watching *out* for you, Fern—for a long time."

"But how did you know?"

"In the interest of full disclosure, Fern, I will tell you the truth. Your classmate, Lee Phillips, collected hair from your scalp. One of the Hundred-Handers has been monitoring you from a Sagebrush since that time."

"Lee . . . Lee's a *vampire? That's* why she attacked me in the bathroom?"

"No, she is not. She would have been much harder to persuade if she were a vampire. Humans can be bought for almost nothing. I paid her a few visits not too long ago once I heard there might be an Unusual in the area. Of course, I did not look as I do now. It did not take much to bribe her; she abhors you so deeply, I believe she would have done the task for nothing," Vlad said, almost laughing.

"That day Sam and I saw the swallow hanging from her house—you had been there!"

Fern thought of her brother and looked over at Sam and Lindsey, lifeless by the bonfire, encircled by the huddle of Hundred-Handers. Vlad sensed Fern's anxiety.

"Do you not understand? Humans will hurt one another at the drop of a hat. They are disloyal. Why would you want to ally yourself with them? They will only let you down, if they do not try to destroy you first."

"That's not true," Fern said, protesting.

"Fern, there is no delaying the inevitable. Yes or no: Will you join me?"

Fern stood up straight and clutched the Omphalos tightly. She looked over at the Hundred-Handers and was sickened by the prospect of them feeding on her brother and friend. She was sickened by the thought that she could ever follow in the footsteps of the Blouts, who fed off other people.

"I'd rather be dead than be like you," she said, closing her eyes, hoping to teleport to the first place her mind thought of. She knew her only chance of saving Lindsey and Sam was to keep the stone and use it as a bargaining chip with Vlad.

"That is the wrong decision!" Vlad screeched. He stared back at the rock.

Vlad spread his arms out, shrinking slightly before morphing into the large black condor. The bird flapped violently in front of her, and as it swooped down, its large talons scratched at her face. Fern dropped the Omphalos, crying out in pain. She held her hand over her brow, which now gushed with blood. The condor dove, snatching the rock up from the ground. It landed about ten feet away from Fern. As the condor's wings spread wide, Fern lay in the sand bleeding, almost fainting with shock, fear, and pain. She watched, helpless, as the bird transformed into the human version of Vlad once more.

Vlad held the rock in his hands as tenderly as if it were a newborn, wide-eyed.

"The will of Cronus be done," he said, then repeated, "The will of Cronus be done." His voice got louder as he uttered the phrase over and over.

Fern crawled painfully to her knees. The Omphalos Oracle turned from black to red as it seemed to radiate in Vlad's hands.

Fern lurched to her feet, feeling dizzy. She stumbled to the shore, immersing her hands in the tide. Frantic, she closed her eyes and began to move her hands above the foam. Clenching her teeth, she concentrated on the water and then on Vlad, who was now in a near trance, still chanting. Blood dripped down her forehead and into the swirling foam. The ocean water followed her hands as she whipped them toward Vlad. A stream of water lifted from the lapping waves, and shot up violently. The water hit him with force, drenching his fine silk suit.

Vlad opened his eyes, the rock still glowing in his hands, and threw his head back. He cackled, staring at Fern.

"Do you think you can drown me, you impetuous runt? Soon you will not have the strength to perform that pitiful trick. You will be even more powerless than you are now!" Fern set her eyes upon the Omphalos, which was now fiery orange. Instantly she felt as if something had clotheslined her. Her feet flew out from under her and she crashed into the surf, swallowing a mouthful of salt water as she landed. The tide rose over her, soaking her through. She couldn't get up. A wave crashed on top of her again, sucking her across the wet sand, farther into the sea.

Help, she thought. *Somebody please help me. Help. What can I do?*

Fern was in a fog of ocean and pain, so when she heard a voice clearly for the first time, she thought she must be imagining it. The Voice grew louder, then louder still.

He derives his power from his watch. Destroy it and he will no longer be protected.

Of course! The Commander had told Fern about the watch after her lengthy talk with Mr. Kimble. Fern couldn't tell if one voice was speaking or several, but it didn't matter just then. Someone had heard her.

Destroy his watch, the Voice repeated.

How? Fern thought back.

The ocean. The mightiness of Poseidon. Use it. Freeze it. Stay there. Use it. Freeze it. Stay there.

With all the strength left in her, Fern lifted her head out of the water and turned to Vlad. Her whole body was submerged, but she focused on Vlad's watch. She fought to stay afloat, and with one exhausted hand she brushed her wet hair from her eyes. She must concentrate. She began to think of any cold thing that came to mind. Ice cubes. Smoothies. Frozen peas. Snow. Glaciers.

A look of single-minded determination consumed Fern's face, as if she were arm wrestling a stronger foe and wouldn't give in. Her face reddened. She kicked to remain above water.

But something was happening on the beach. Crystals were forming on Vlad's clothes where he had been soaked by Fern's blast of seawater. Veins of ice ran down his jacket sleeves. Suddenly the face of Vlad's golden watch shattered. It had frozen solid.

"The Keeper!" Vlad screamed, stopping the chanting. "The count's watch! What have you done?" It was working.

Fern focused on his legs. Pain jolted through her skull, and she felt herself floating farther out to sea. But nothing would deter her. She could not let up. She continued to focus her gaze, though she was losing strength. She felt her legs go numb, then her arms.

Vlad's teeth began to chatter. Fern could see he was struggling to move. He fell over, his body stiff, and his face took on a blue hue. He still muttered Cronus's Curse with each breath, but the breaths came slower and slower.

The Hundred-Handers, torches in hand, surged toward

Vlad. After they reached him, they began tracing the outline of his body with their torches, trying to thaw him out.

One cloaked man spotted Fern.

"She's there! In the water!" A group began to charge toward her. Fern submerged her whole body. She felt herself gather strength as the current rippled over her.

Fern hoped she had one last stand in her.

She popped up out of the water once more. With all her remaining strength, she waved her hands frantically over the waters. The ocean swirled around her like a whirlpool. With one swift motion, she threw her arms out toward the Hundred-Handers, who were either running toward her or warming Vlad's body. A thirty-foot wall of water rose up from around her. With the force of a tidal wave, it crashed down on the beach. The wave slammed a handful of Hundred-Handers against the stony cliffs. Every torch was extinguished, and screams of agony filled the night air.

Fern spotted Vlad. He was pushed up against one of the cliffs and beginning to squirm again. She focused on him, trying to finish what she'd started, thinking of nothing but freezing him solid. She valiantly tried to keep her head above the rising water.

But soon she could no longer fight the excruciating pain. Fern looked and focused and focused and looked, until salt water covered her eyes and crept into the corners of her mouth. She felt nothing but the cold current of the ocean around her. She lost sight of Vlad. Her body had been bankrupted of energy. Physically unable to hold out any longer, Fern McAllister closed her eyes, finally giving in to the restless waters of the Pacific.

23

the first confirmed case

When Fern awoke in her own bed, wrapped in blankets and washed clean of all dirt, sand, seawater, and blood, she was shocked. Her head felt as if it might implode from the pain.

"You're awake!" Sam said. Sam had only left Fern's room for bathroom and food breaks, though Mr. Bing assured him that his sister would awaken in fine shape. Anxious for something to do while he waited for Fern to regain consciousness, he'd decided to put on Fern's Breakfast Sunglasses, which were resting on her nightstand. He was still wearing them now, though it was close to two in the morning. Byron, who had kept watch as loyally as Sam, jumped up from the foot of the bed and began furiously licking Fern's face.

"Sam?" Fern said weakly. She fondled Byron's ears.

"Sam? Are you okay? Eddie? How did we get home?" she asked groggily. "Ohhhhh," she said, trying to think clearly through the pain. "Where's the rock?" She shifted in her twin bed as everything came back to her. "Are you okay? Did we do it?"

"Whoa, Fern, one question at a time."

"Are you okay?" Fern asked again, scanning Sam's body for injuries.

"I'm fine. Everyone's fine. You're the one that everyone is worried about. You've been out for a day and a half."

"Are you wearing my sunglasses?" Fern said, trying to form a smile.

"Um, well, yeah," Sam said, laughing as if he'd been caught in an embarrassing act. "I'm wearing them because my future's so bright."

Fern let some frail laughter escape.

"I was bored, so I put them on," Sam said, taking them off. His eyes were puddles of sagging fatigue.

"Is Lindsey okay?" Fern asked weakly.

"She's good. Vlad just put us in a trance or something."

"What happened? I don't remember."

"I didn't wake up until there were a hundred people from the Alliance on the beach. From what I've been able to piece together, Mr. Kimble and a bunch of people from the Alliance showed up at Pirate's Cove right after you froze Vlad."

"I *froze* Vlad? It worked?"

"Yup," Sam said, reveling in the excitement. "I guess I

shouldn't have gotten so mad at you for messing around with Clownface's coffee, you know, since it probably saved my life. Mr. Kimble was saying that if you hadn't been in the ocean, you would have been a total goner. Because you're a Poseidon and everything, the ocean gave you strength. You were able to resist Cronus's Curse."

"I heard voices, Sam," Fern said.

"What do you mean?"

"I was crying for help and someone responded. I heard them in my head. They told me to use the ocean and that I should go after Vlad's watch."

"His watch?"

"Yeah," Fern said.

"What if it was another Unusual who was speaking to you? Maybe you can communicate with them."

"You and your theories." Fern looked at Sam doubtfully. "It could have been anybody," she said, playing it cool. She took comfort, however, from the fact that someone, somewhere, had heard her plea for help. "What happened when the Alliance arrived?"

"Those men that took us from the grove, the Hundred-Handers, must have looked a lot scarier than they actually were. As soon as the Alliance showed up, they ran! More like the Hundred Cowards."

"They ran?"

"When Mr. Kimble arrived with a whole army, they knew they were outnumbered. Did you know that the Alliance has a jail? The Reformatory—it's what Chuffy was talking about. Apparently it's really scary. I bet they were afraid of being thrown in there for life. And," Sam said excitedly, unable to stop talking, "Mr. Kimble would have been there sooner except there was an elaborate distraction plan. Vlad must have been planning all this for weeks! One of the Hundred-Handers, Vlad's right-hand man named Paole, is a very powerful Hermes and made everyone believe that you'd teleported to the mission. That's where the Lins and the vigilantes who had been watching you went. Get this—Mr. Summers was leading the team of Alliance Intelligence who was supposed to be protecting you. Some job he did," Sam said as an aside.

"I ran back to the house and no one was there."

"That must have freaked you out."

"You could say that," Fern said, not wanting to think about it. "Hey, what about the rock?"

"Huh?"

"The stone . . . where is the Omphalos . . . ? "Fern said, trying to sit up.

"Oh yeah! I haven't figured that one out yet. Everyone's saying that it was destroyed, but Lindsey swears that she woke up right when Mr. Kimble arrived. She says that he took it and handed it off to someone."

Sam saw the concern rush over his sister's face. "Don't worry, Fern. If it is with Mr. Kimble, it's in good hands. You know that he's the only one who turned out to be trustworthy in this whole thing? Well, him and Mr. Bing, of course."

The window to Fern's bedroom was propped open, letting in the cool Capistrano breeze. *Für Elise* began. It took Fern a second to recognize the noise as the doorbell.

"Someone's at the door?" Fern looked at her clock. "It's after midnight!"

"Hah!" Sam said, shaking his head. "Are you kidding? People started coming by last night, even in the middle of the night. No one's actually rung the doorbell though—all your visitors have kept a very low profile. People keep leaving notes and flowers on the back porch. We've had to empty the mailbox four times because people keep stuffing it full of Get Well Fern cards. All night long they were coming by. One woman drove in from Phoenix. You know the man who donated the St. Gregory's library? He stopped by and left a whole envelope of cash to 'thank you for your efforts.'"

"Why in the world—"

"Vampires are a bunch of gossips. The word that one of the Unusual Eleven lives here, for certain, in this very house, has spread like wildfire. They're calling you the Dracula Destroyer. I think it's a little spooky, to be honest."

"Are you serious?" Fern marveled at her reception.

"Dead serious," Sam responded. "You're officially famous—in this weird vampire way, but it still counts. The Commander's already talking about installing a security gate and surveillance cameras. You know she won't put up with unwanted visitors stopping by." Sam wasn't even coming up for air anymore. "You know, if you ask me, all this activity sure isn't helping the Rollens keep a low profile, the idiots.

"Mr. Summers stopped by around two and explained himself to Mom. Apparently the fire was a Blout attack. No offense, Fern, but I still don't want Mom dating him, since he's a vampire. It's too complicated, you know? Call me old-fashioned, but vampires should stick to dating other vampires." Sam stopped talking as he moved to the window and stuck his head out to see who was at the door.

"It's Chief Quagmire."

The Commander's stern voice drifted up to the window.

"I'm not shocked at the hour, Chief Quagmire. I'm shocked that you have the audacity to show up here after the spineless, immoral way you behaved!"

Chief Quagmire's voice was more muffled. He was responding to Mrs. McAllister, but neither twin could hear him.

"What's he saying, Fern?"

"I can't tell." Fern paused. She really couldn't tell. Her hearing was gone. Sam smiled at his sister.

"Oh, don't panic, Fern. Mr. Bing said you might have a temporary loss of your powers because you were so close to the Omphalos and Vlad nearly pulled the curse off."

"So this is what it's like to be normal," Fern said, feeling her face for dramatic effect.

"Oh, you'll never be normal, Freaky Fern. Not even

for a day." Sam smiled at his sister. "But we still like you anyway." When she smiled back, it pleased him. Mr. Bing hadn't lied. Fern was going to be okay.

The Commander's voice carried through the window again. "There's nothing in the world you can tell me that won't make me hate every fiber of your being for putting Fern in danger," Mrs. McAllister shouted at Chief Quagmire. "Fern's not joining your Alliance. She's got her own alliance right here in this house! Leave and never come back! You may not suck blood, but that doesn't mean you're not a parasite."

The door slammed.

Fern grimaced, wondering if the Commander had succeeded in waking every neighbor they had on La Limonar. According to Sam, half of them were vampires anyway, so it probably didn't much matter.

"So you told the Commander everything? Even what happened at New Tartarus?" Fern said to Sam as he moved away from the window and sat back in Fern's desk chair.

"You just heard her, didn't you? Would you've lied to her?"

"Why did Chief Quagmire say I was a false claim?"

"According to Lindsey's parents, he thought that Vlad would let his guard down if he heard that you were no longer being protected. He wasn't trying to get you killed; he thought he was outsmarting Vlad."

"I don't understand."

"He thought Vlad wouldn't fall for the trap unless he

made it known that you were no longer thought of as an Unusual. That's why he disseminated the false claim memo. The ridiculous thing is, because Vlad ended up getting caught, it makes it seem like his stupid plan worked."

A soft knocking at the door stopped Fern from answering her brother's question.

"Do I hear talking in here?" Mrs. McAllister, still stunning in her terry-cloth bathrobe, stuck her head in.

"Sam, I thought I told you to come get me as soon as Fern woke up," Mrs. McAllister said sternly, though she was unable to stop from smiling at the sight of her conscious daughter.

"Anyway . . . I'm beat," Sam said. He mouthed *Good luck* at his sister before heading out of the room and closing the door behind him.

Mrs. McAllister sat on the edge of Fern's bed, careful not to squish her daughter's feet. She was still flushed from her heated front lawn discussion with McAllister Enemy Number One, Chief Kenneth Quagmire. Her blue eyes were still capable of penetrating to Fern's very core, even as tired as they were.

"How are you feeling?" Mrs. McAllister said.

"I'm a little headachy," Fern said, "but okay." Fern began to grow nervous about what her mother might say to her. After all, Fern had kept so much from her.

"I have no idea how you must be feeling right now or even what to say," Mrs. McAllister said. This admission took Fern by surprise. Were adults supposed to admit such things? Fern continued to stare up at the ceiling. "Things have really hit the fan in the past few days, haven't they?"

"Yeah," Fern said, touching the Band-Aids that covered the scratches above her left eyebrow.

"I'm so relieved you're all right," the Commander said. Her voice was shaky. Fern could hardly believe it.

"You're not mad that I didn't tell you the truth about New Tartarus?"

Mrs. McAllister took a deep breath and regained the form in her voice once more.

"I'm disappointed, Fern. I'm disappointed because you must have been going through torture these past few weeks and you kept it from me. But then I realized something. I haven't been forthright with you either," she said, inching closer to Fern. "Ever since that day at Kimble & Kimble, in the conference room, I've wanted to talk to you, make sure you know how proud I am of you . . . how happy I am to be your mother . . . but I never knew exactly what to say, so I said nothing at all." Mrs. McAllister put her hands together and folded them in her lap. "I may be a 'commander,' but I sure lost touch with my troops."

Fern gaped.

"What?" the Commander said, smiling coyly. "You thought I didn't know about your little nickname?" She laughed and smiled all at once. "It's quite all right. There are worse things children call their mothers. But remember: I'm always listening."

Fern had never seen this side of her mother before, and

although she didn't know what to expect, she could feel the gap between them slowly start to fill. She remained motionless.

"Phoebe, your mother, and I—well, you don't know this, but we went to St. Gregory's together. I was an only child, and so was she. We spent all our time together. She was a lot like you, Fern. She looked a lot like you too. She even had all sorts of problems with her stomach. Phoebe was the best friend I ever had."

"I saw your initials at Pirate's Cove . . . with hers," Fern said, as a lump began to form in her throat, though she didn't know why.

"Is that still there? Phoebe and I would go there all the time. It's why I first started taking you there, actually. Phoebe loved that place more than anything. She was just like you."

"Really?"

"Yes. It was her idea to carve our initials into the cliff. She was always doing impulsive things like that. I guess you could call her a rebel. In fact, she caused the first ever Emergency Conference at St. Gregory's. I bet you didn't know that, did you?"

"What did she do?" Fern asked, enraptured.

"Well, a boy named Roger Webster had humiliated me. We were in eighth grade at the time, and he made up an awful rumor about me—something so awful, so terrible, I was in tears for weeks. Phoebe, being the fireplug she was, was not about to let that go on. One day she marched right up to him and demanded he take it back and tell everyone that it wasn't true. He didn't, of course.

"So the next day at recess, Phoebe cornered him in the boys' bathroom. Roger came running out, minutes later, covered in every vile substance you'd find in a bathroom, screaming and carrying on. Phoebe was spotless. It became a big deal; Phoebe's father was called in and she was nearly expelled—except for one thing: no one could figure out how she'd done it. How could she have gotten sewage all over Roger without getting any of it on herself? Of course, Roger claimed she had brought a bucket in with her, but no bucket was ever found anywhere near the bathroom. She never told me and I'd always wondered. The day Mr. Summers's house caught on fire, it all became clear to me."

"She was a Poseidon too?" Fern sat up on her bed, though it made her head ache even worse.

"Call it what you want, but she had your special talent for moving liquid. In this case, disgusting liquid," the Commander said, shaking her head with amusement.

"Vlad told me that Phoebe was a Blout."

"Well, maybe she was. After she moved up north, I can't be sure about what she was up to. Maybe she fell in with some bad people, Fern, and it's possible, for a while, that she was in a very dark place. But I never saw that side of her. She was an extraordinary person and an extraordinary friend. That's what counts."

Fern was unable to let go of the subject.

"So you don't know what happened to her?"

"No, I don't," Mrs. McAllister said.

"But what does that make me?"

"Even more extraordinary," the Commander said sympathetically.

"What if I become evil like Vlad?"

"You'll never be like him. People choose to be like that."

"What if all of a sudden I start sucking people's blood? Am I a Rollen or am I really a Blout?" Fern asked.

"You're a McAllister," the Commander said. She paused.

"Blouts, Rollens, Hermes, Poseidons, Otherworldlies—who knows what any of those words really mean, anyway? They're just words. You know what? Vampires are just as guilty as Normals. Everything has got to have a label attached to it. There are some things that can't be categorized."

Both the Commander and Fern let smiles creep across their faces. Fern had a thousand questions she still wanted to ask. Was her mother a true Blout? Why did she change? Why did she move up north? Fern realized that the questions she most wanted answered were the ones furthest out of reach.

After a long pause, the Commander continued. "I'm not going to pretend to know what it's like to be you, with the prophecy and your special talents and all this Unusual Otherworldly business. But you saved lives today. Special powers or not, you stood up to someone when you could have done otherwise and you did it all on your own with no help, using your own inner strength." Mrs. McAllister had an earnest look on her face as she turned to Fern and looked her daughter in the eye. "Fern, I'm so very proud of you. Each day that passes, I grow more and more thankful that Phoebe chose me. To be able to watch you grow up in front of my eyes, well, it's a privilege."

Fern's eyes pooled.

The Commander breathed a sigh of relief. She had finally said to Fern what she'd wanted to. Fern noticed the shoe box on her mother's lap for the first time. Mrs. McAllister picked up the shoe box.

"This shoe box has almost every letter Phoebe and I wrote to each other. Like I said, I lost touch with her near the end, but I want you to have it, Fern. I don't know how to make things right; I can only express how sorry I am for keeping your past from you." Mrs. McAllister held out the shoe box. Fern reached forward and took it, handling it gingerly, as if it were a ticking time bomb.

"You might be bored to tears. They're all about our daily lives, checking in and all that. But they're yours to keep."

"Thank you," Fern said.

"You must be exhausted."

"Not too much. I slept a whole day straight," Fern said.

"Sure, but I doubt saving the world from evil is easy

work." Mrs. McAllister let out puzzled laughter. "Now there's a sentence no mother has probably ever said to her daughter before." Mrs. McAllister got up and gave Fern a dry kiss on the forehead. "I guess they don't call you Unusual for nothing," she said with a half smile. "I hate to bring this up, but Headmaster Mooney called about scheduling your second Saturday school."

"Oh no," Fern said, realizing that she only had a month in which to complete both.

"I wouldn't worry about it. We had a talk and he'll give you an extension to serve it, but do try not to make him upset again. I don't know how long I can use scare tactics with him."

"Okay," Fern said, glad that her mother had talked to Headmaster Mooney. She may have recently found her own inner strength, but even her inner strength had its limits. Just weeks ago, Fern had served her first Saturday school and the word *Otherworldly* wasn't yet a part of her vocabulary. Fern marveled at how much had happened since then. Mrs. McAllister got up to leave.

"Mom?"

"Yes?"

"Thanks for the letters."

"Good night, Fern."

"Good night," Fern replied.

Mrs. McAllister closed the door behind her.

Fern opened the shoe box and took out the first letter, which was wrinkled and brittle to the touch. She folded it out in front of her. Her eyes stared at the first line: *Dear Phoebe*.

Her eyes drooped and her head felt heavy. She put the letter back in the shoe box and closed the lid.

Fern no longer wanted to be alone.

Creeping down the hall, avoiding the spots where the floor squeaked under the carpet, she slipped into Sam's room. He was already fast asleep, exhausted after spending a full day awake, waiting for Fern to regain consciousness. His noisy breathing was enough. Fern curled up on the floor at the foot of her brother's bed and closed her eyes. Byron, keeping watch as ever, told Fern "Good night" as he lay down next to her.

She would read the letters tomorrow.

Although Fern fell fast asleep, leaving behind the worries and troubles of the last few days, for many, the workday was just starting. Hiding in the shadows of the McAllister's large jacaranda tree, Mr. Joseph Bing, having transmorphed into a wild parrot once again, stood watch on a low hanging branch. He was tired, but he would stay there as long as necessary to make sure Fern was completely safe. Five blocks away, on the other side of Ortega Highway, May and Mike Lin sat at their kitchen table, hard at work drafting an internal memo entitled "The First Confirmed Case: Fern McAllister and the Unusual Eleven." The memo was to be disseminated to every member of the Alliance Assembly in the morning. A few miles away, in his office just around the corner from Mission San Juan Capistrano, Mr. Alistair Kimble pored over the detailed educational plans he was drawing up, running through every single potential danger Fern would face in the coming weeks, months, and years.

Meanwhile, in a makeshift crisis center down the road, Chief Kenneth Quagmire was calling to order an emergency meeting with members of the Assembly, who were deciding what kind of facility could possibly hope to contain someone as dangerous as Vlad, once he thawed out. Many people had grave concerns. After all, the Reformatory had never housed a criminal as powerful as Vlad. Despite the challenge, Chief Quagmire was basking in the positive publicity Vlad's capture had brought to his office. In fact, Kenneth Quagmire had never been more popular with his Rollen constituency.

At exactly the same time, fifty miles to the south and half a mile underground, Chuffy Merced III, first assistant to the chief of the Vampire Alliance, had just received the good news from Telemus. Smiling to himself, he hobbled over to the cupboard in his drab room and poured himself a dark red drink from his secret bottle, toasting the news that his friend Fern McAllister had saved the day after all.

'm fortunate to have been surrounded by remarkable people as I wrote *The Otherworldlies*. In particular, I would like to thank, first and foremost, John and Clare Kogler, the best cheerleaders a girl could ask for; Kristy Cole and Leigh Meredith for being huge nerds and reading draft after draft; Bradford Lyman for being an ideal sounding board; Marnie Podos for providing the soundtrack; Bob and Janice Wilhelm and Mike and Charlene Immell for their unwavering support; Lisa Hart for her skill with a camera; Fred Hargadon for his general incorrigibility; Sarah Sevier for stepping in; Clare Hutton, my tireless editor; and Anne Coxon, whom I could hear whispering in my ear while I wrote.